little black dress
· IT'S A GIRL THING ·

Dear Little Black Dress Reader,

Thanks for picking up this Little Black Dress book, one of the great new titles from our series of fun, page-turning romance novels. Lucky you — you're about to have a fantastic romantic read that we know you won't be able to put down!

Why don't you make your Little Black Dress experience even better by logging on to

www.littleblackdressbooks.com

where you can:

- Enter our **monthly competitions** to win **gorgeous** prizes
- Get **hot-off-the-press** news about our latest titles
- Read **exclusive** preview chapters both from your **favourite** authors and from brilliant new writing talent
- Buy **up-and-coming** book~~~~
- Sign up fo~~~~
  our **fortnig**~~~~

We love nothing ~~~~ an
addictive romance ~~~~ me you
into the Little Blac~~~~

With love from,

The *little black dress* team

Five interesting things about Julie Cohen:

1. In high school in the USA, my best friend and I used to spend our chemistry lessons writing novels about us having sex with rock stars.

2. Despite this lack of scholarly application, I graduated summa cum laude from Brown University. While I was there I wrote a daily comic strip about an Elvis impersonator and his pet squid.

3. I came to live in England because of the Beatles, and because I fell in love with a guitar-playing Englishman.

4. I have a postgraduate research degree in fairies in children's literature, which has very few practical applications.

5. The Englishman and I have recently had our first child, who will be English as well, I suppose.

Also by Julie Cohen

One Night Stand
Spirit Willing, Flesh Weak
Driving Him Wild
All Work and No Play . . .
Married in a Rush
Delicious
Being a Bad Girl
Featured Attraction

Honey Trap

Julie Cohen

little
black
dress

First published in 2008 by
LITTLE BLACK DRESS
An imprint of HEADLINE PUBLISHING GROUP

A LITTLE BLACK DRESS paperback

4

ISBN 978 0 7553 4137 5

Typeset in Transit511BT by Avon DataSet Ltd,
Bidford-on-Avon, Warwickshire

Printed and bound in Great Britain by
Clays Ltd, St Ives plc

Headline's policy is to use papers that are natural, renewable and
recyclable products and made from wood grown in sustainable forests.
The logging and manufacturing processes are expected to conform to
the environmental regulations of the country of origin.

HEADLINE PUBLISHING GROUP
An Hachette Livre UK Company
338 Euston Road
London NW1 3BH

www.littleblackdressbooks.com
www.headline.co.uk
www.hachettelivre.co.uk

For Dave, who rocks!

Acknowledgements

With thanks to Dave Smith, Slow River Slow, and all his rock 'n' roll friends for telling me about life on the road and backstage, and not laughing too much when I didn't know Hawkwind from a handsaw. Any errors are mine. And as always, thanks to Anna Lucia, Brigid Coady and Kathy Love, and to my agent Teresa Chris and my editor Cat Cobain.

Bar 42, Reading

Sophie Tennant had never seen her date in real life, but she knew he was brown-eyed, brown-haired, slightly built, and a scumbag.

Please, at least let him be tall. She stood inside the doorway of the bar, scanning the room. To her relief, he wasn't an early bird. She smoothed down her red dress and rubbed her lips together to make sure her red lipstick was still fresh, both actions unnecessary because she knew she was wrinkle-free and she'd put on the lipstick in her car five minutes ago, after adjusting the adhesive tape around her thigh and beneath her bra. Sophie went to the bar, ordered a tonic water with ice and a slice, and brought it to her preferred table in the corner, facing the door with the light behind her.

It was the third time this month she'd been in Bar 42 and she was beginning to wonder if the bar staff thought she was desperate, a hooker, or both. She didn't like to be noticed and would have preferred to go somewhere else this time, but Keith had suggested it in his text.

It was a good location, anyway: not too dark, not too light, and just busy enough. Sophie'd had bad experiences with noisy, crowded pubs before, hours of work down the drain because some idiot beside her was talking too loudly. And the less she thought about what had happened in the unlit car park of that country pub two years ago, the better.

No, Bar 42 was fine. She didn't want to risk Keith getting cold feet by seeming to be reluctant about anything he suggested. It had taken her long enough to set this up.

She checked her watch, although she knew it was two minutes past six. She caught herself jiggling her foot and stopped it. She put her hands palms-down on the table, her fingers curled slightly so that her bitten nails were hidden. She could do the dress, she could do the shoes and the makeup and the hair, but she drew the line at false nails. They were hell to get off.

When she looked up, he was coming through the door.

He stopped and surveyed the room, much as she had. Then he spotted her and made a beeline for her table. 'Sophie?'

'Yes.' She stood, and instead of shaking her hand he kissed her on the cheek.

He wasn't tall. Okay, he was taller than her, but she was five foot four in three-inch heels, so that wasn't difficult. She thought maybe five foot five, five six.

Why were so many of them short? She could do a thesis on this if she ever went to university. He was clean-shaven and smelled of the cologne that had the advertising campaign promising that hundreds of sexy women would fall at the feet of the man who wore it.

'You smell nice,' she said, and he looked pleased with himself. Sophie supposed that if Keith believed the crap she'd written to him online, he'd believe anything, even advertising.

'You're even more beautiful than your photo,' he said to her. 'Would you like a drink?'

'I'm fine, thanks.'

'I'll be right back, then, keep a seat warm for me.'

She watched him go up to the bar. He was wearing a pinstriped suit and a striped tie, both fashionable enough. His shoes were very glossy. He was probably considered rather a snappy dresser.

Keith returned with a glass of red wine for himself and sat in the chair nearest her. 'To the lady in red,' he said, raising his glass. She pretended to simper a bit and drank her tonic water.

'I'm glad you agreed to meet me,' she said.

'You asked so nicely.'

She laughed. 'Well, I didn't want to wait another day of texting and chatting online,' she said truthfully.

'Oh, but it's been such fun, hasn't it?'

'It certainly has.' It was the challenge that did it: how to be a little bit leading without taking the lead, a little bit suggestive without actually suggesting anything. She'd learned a lot since the first time she'd done this, particularly how to keep her distance whilst seeming to get close.

She fluttered her eyelashes and took a sip of her tonic water. The move looked good; she'd practised it in front of the mirror many times.

She saw him notice, but he didn't take it further. Instead he leaned back in his chair and asked her, 'So how was your day?'

She'd prepared for small talk, too. She had any number of anecdotes about office work from her time as a police file clerk that she could polish up and serve as if they were recent news. Leaving out the bits about the police, of course. She didn't plan to use many of them. She was getting paid by the hour, but this wasn't the kind of work she liked to dawdle over.

'How about you?' she asked after she'd finished her false tale about her day at the office. 'I actually don't think you ever told me what you do for a living?'

'Oh, I own my own travel agency.'

'Really? Oh, how exciting. Do you get to travel a lot?'

She sounded like a bimbo and this was getting her nowhere, because Keith immediately launched into a travelogue of his recent trip to Kuala Lumpur (or 'KL' as he called it) instead of flirting with her or, even better, suggesting they have sex.

'Oooh. And what was the food like?' she bimboed.

Keith's fiancée Catherine wasn't a bimbo. She was a nervous, intelligent woman, training to teach secondary-school French. Catherine, strictly, wasn't Sophie's client; she'd been hired by Catherine's father, Mr Piers Birkbeck, who even sitting down towered over his daughter in Sophie's small office.

'I don't trust him,' said Mr Birkbeck, and Catherine had shaken her head and twisted her thin hands.

'I think he's very friendly and very busy, that's all,' Catherine had said. 'Really, Daddy, there's nothing in it.'

'Nobody's going to take my daughter for a fool.'

'I love him, Daddy.'

Mr Birkbeck ignored his daughter's plaintive words and looked straight at Sophie. 'You get the dirt on Keith Martin, whichever way you can.'

Now, getting the dirt, Sophie hid a wave of contempt for Keith behind her interested smiles and nods. His fiancée trusted him, and this was how he repaid her.

'What about you?' Keith asked at the end of his

recitation of Malaysian menu items. 'Have you travelled much?'

'No, I've hardly left Reading. I'd love to travel, though.' Maybe he'd offer to whisk her away for a dirty weekend in Vietnam or wherever.

Mr Birkbeck had given Sophie a list of Keith's inconsistencies. They were the kind of things Sophie had heard dozens of times before. 'He says he's working late but then when Catherine rings he's not in the office. He spends hours on that damn computer of his at night and he protects everything with passwords. He locks his mobile phone in a desk drawer. What kind of man does that?'

'He's very private, Daddy, I told you. People like their privacy.'

Including you, Catherine, thought Sophie, feeling pity for this woman who was so obviously overwhelmed by both the men in her life. Sophie didn't particularly want to know Keith's dirty little secrets either.

'I want you to follow him and tell us what he's up to,' Mr Birkbeck said. 'What is your fee structure again?'

Dirty little secrets were her job. Sophie had followed Keith, and photographed him on several evenings entering and leaving the house of a female colleague. The blinds were drawn, so she couldn't get any pictures of what they'd been up to. It wasn't cast-iron proof, but several of Sophie's past clients had had success with confronting their partners with similar photos.

'He did say he was at the office that night,' Catherine had said, reluctantly, when she saw the photos. 'But all this proves is that he was lying, not that he was cheating. He could have been working at her house, after all.'

Working on getting his rocks off, was Sophie's own

private opinion. But all she'd said was, 'All right, I'll try another angle.'

Keith knew more about computers than Catherine did, but not more than Sophie. A trawl through his hard drive found the internet dating sites he'd been visiting, and revealed his username. Sophie printed off page after page of chat transcripts and presented them to Catherine.

Catherine read them right there in Sophie's office, with her father looming over her shoulder. At the end her cheeks were pink as she looked up from the paper and said, 'But he's not doing anything. He's just flirting in these places.'

'Three of the women gave him their mobile numbers.'

'But we don't have proof he ever rang them, let alone met up.' Catherine shook her head. 'I mean, it would be one thing if he were having cyber-sex or whatever it's called, but these conversations are pretty tame.'

Tame or not, if Sophie ever were to have a fiancé – which was looking more and more unlikely the more she got to know about men in general – she'd haul off and punch him if he spent hours online with strange women, no matter what he talked about.

'I'll look for something more definite,' she'd said, 'but it might mean I have to get involved.'

'You catch him,' said Mr Birkbeck grimly. 'Nobody hurts my little girl.'

Sophie used one of her online personalities and visited the sites until she recognised Keith's username. Luckily he'd approached her quickly. An hour or two of carefully constructed flirtation later, Sophie gave him her mobile number.

Catherine had gone through the transcripts. Her cheeks went even pinker, and Sophie knew that these meetings were drawn-out torture for her. Surely it would be easier for her if she just accepted that there was something dodgy going on without knowing the sordid details?

Mr Birkbeck read them with relish, grunting with contempt at intervals. Sophie wondered if his motivation was as straightforward as he'd said. There had been that man last year who'd been a voyeur and was getting his kicks out of the photos Sophie took of his wife and her lover. But then Mr Birkbeck handed the transcripts back to her and wiped his hands on his pinstriped suit, as if the paper had been covered in a fine film of grime.

'We're this close to nailing the bastard,' he said, and Sophie watched Catherine flinch. She was even thinner than when she'd first come into Sophie's office; her hair looked brittle.

Sophie spoke directly to her. 'Are you sure you want to take this any further, Miss Birkbeck? Maybe the fact that your fiancé hasn't been caught doing anything unforgivable yet means that you should forgive him and move on.'

Catherine raised her head and looked Sophie straight in the eyes. She was too thin to be pretty, but her eyes were clear hazel, bright and beautiful.

Her father answered for her.

'Nobody does that to my little girl,' he said. 'If he's cheating, I want you to get him good.'

Catherine stood up and left the room.

'I'll get him good,' Sophie said, watching her go.

Now, in Bar 42, wearing a digital video-recorder strapped to the inside of her thigh, and a scarlet dress she wouldn't be seen dead in during her normal life, Sophie nodded and chatted and made her tonic water last.

Sophie herself didn't need the proof. Even if she hadn't caught him at it yet, she knew that Keith Martin was a cheater. She'd seen enough of them in her time to recognise this particular type: the cologne, the shoes, the compliments, the lack of height. He was a short man making up for his shortness through his conquests.

'Would you like another drink?' Keith asked her.

'Oh, no, thank you, I'm fine.'

He stood. 'I insist. That one must be lukewarm by now, we've been talking so much. What is it, vodka or gin?'

Sophie glanced at her drink. The ice had all melted, so she couldn't protest that it wasn't lukewarm. 'I'll have vodka, thanks. And tonic.'

'I'll be right back, don't get lonely.' He winked at her and went to the bar.

Tall men didn't have so much to prove. They were impulsive in their sins. They didn't need to impress you. A flash of thigh, a bit of cleavage, lick your lips and Bob's your uncle, you've caught a tall man.

Short men, on the other hand, could take ages.

She stopped her fingers tapping on the table when Keith came back with their drinks. She gave him her best smile.

'So how has someone like you managed to stay single?' she asked, and then pretended to look worried. 'You are single, aren't you?'

'Free as a bird. I guess I never met the right woman. How about you? You must have loads of boyfriends.'

'Oh, you know, nothing serious. I guess I haven't met the right person either.'

Keith raised his glass. 'Here's to meeting the right person.'

She took the smallest sip she could and suppressed her grimace. Sophie wasn't much of a drinker even when she was off duty, and the vodka tasted terrible to her, even with the tonic to mask it.

Time to get a move on. She leaned forward on the table

in a pose she knew enhanced her cleavage. Slowly she rubbed her finger around and around the rim of her glass. She met his eyes, held his attention for a moment, and then dipped her gaze to his lap. When she raised her eyes to his again she could see that her carefully learned flirting techniques were having an impact. Keith's pupils had dilated, and he licked his lips. The camera probably only captured the lip-licking, which was too subtle to count as proof for Catherine.

'Tell me, Keith,' she said, making her voice husky and warm, 'what would you like to do with the right person?'

'Well,' he began hoarsely, and he had to clear his throat before he could speak properly.

She caught her lower lip between her teeth, leaned forward a little bit more, and widened her eyes. Amazing, really, how female sexual posturing required you to look like both a little girl and a slut.

'I would probably start by buying her a drink,' Keith said.

'And then?'

Keith's left thumb was rubbing against his index finger, slow caresses that matched her stroking of her glass.

I bet you have a really filthy mind, Sophie thought at him. *I bet you try to do all sorts of things you wouldn't dream of asking your fiancée, you bastard. That's why you spend so much time talking, trying to get inside your women's heads, so once you've got them, they're putty in your hands.*

'I'd find out what sort of person she was. Really get to know her. Inside and out.'

'And?'

Tell me. Tell me what you want to do to me so I can record it and get the hell out of here in time to watch CSI.

'And . . . well, this is a little embarrassing.'

'Oh, Keith, nothing you'd ever say would make me judge you, you know that.'

She leaned forward more, close enough to breathe in his cologne. Close enough, nearly, to touch. Certainly close enough so that the camera masquerading as a dress button would pick up his adulterous desires.

'I'd want her to know who I really was, too. No secrets between us. Only the pure truth.'

'Oh, Keith, I think that's sweet.'

You lying, cheating, mealy-mouthed, height-challenged, time-wasting scumbag.

He smirked. 'I suppose that deep down, I'm just a romantic at heart.'

Eine Kleine Nachtmusik beeped electronically out of Keith's suit jacket pocket. Keith retrieved his mobile phone, looked at the number, and smiled at her apologetically. 'I'm sorry, Sophie, I need to take this. Please excuse me.'

'Of course.'

He stood and went outside. Through the plate-glass window she could see him, standing with his back to her, answering his phone. It wasn't his fiancée; Catherine knew Keith was meeting with Sophie tonight. Most likely it was another of his fancy ladies, trading more conversation about being romantics at heart.

At this rate, she wasn't even going to make it home in time to catch the late movie. Sophie quickly dunked her hand in her drink, fished out the ice cubes, and put them in her plain tonic water. She shoved the mostly full vodka glass to the side of the table next to the empty glass from Keith's first drink. Lucky thing the bar staff were inefficient at clearing tables, or she would have had to 'mistakenly' spill the vodka and tonic on the floor. And with the chivalrous charade that Keith had going on, it was unlikely he'd let her go to the bar herself to buy a non-alcoholic drink.

He returned to the table, snapping his phone shut. 'Sorry about that,' he said, and then paused before sitting down. 'Would you like another?'

Even with the ice in it, her tonic water was only a quarter full. 'No, thank you,' Sophie said, 'I was just thirsty, I guess.'

'Nothing wrong with that.' He slid into his seat. 'We're here to have a good time and enjoy ourselves, after all.'

I'd enjoy myself much more if you got on with trying to have your good time. 'So we were talking about romance,' she said, smiling winningly.

'That we were. What do you think is the most important aspect of a romance?'

Sophie pretended to consider. 'Mutual attraction?'

'That's interesting. Me, I think it's trust. How can you love someone if you don't trust them? Love without trust can't be real love, can it?'

Sophie would have smirked at the irony, but she had a bimbo image to uphold. Still, she couldn't resist saying, 'Or you could say that people in love might trust someone who wasn't worthy of it.'

'Did you hear that thing on the radio the other night? About women who are hired to try to trap guys into making a pass at them so their wives can find out if they're cheaters? What's it called – sugar-baiting?'

Sophie shrugged, making sure to do it in a way that would make her breasts bob. 'I don't know, I didn't hear it, I'm sorry.'

'Now maybe I'm old-fashioned, but I think that's sneaky and dishonest.'

'Oh, I don't know,' Sophie said. 'I mean, the guy doesn't have to take the bait, does he? Nobody's forcing him.'

Keith grinned suddenly, and Sophie felt a measure of relief, because if this conversation went on for much longer she was going to be sorely tempted to bring up the little matter of his fiancée.

'You're right,' he said, 'nobody's being forced. Listen, I've got a great idea. There's a lovely little Italian not far from here. Would you like to go for a meal with me?'

Sophie mentally saw the evening stretching out and out, through Prosecco and antipasto, marinara sauce and red wine, with, if she was very lucky, Keith making a fumbled pass at her over the tiramisu.

Meanwhile, the adhesive tape holding the wires in place under her dress was beginning to itch, and if she was going to be more than two hours she was going to have to change the batteries on the video recorder. 'That sounds gorgeous,' she said, and stood. 'I just need to visit the ladies' before we go.'

She tried to put a spring and a sway in her step, as if she were irrepressibly joyful about an Italian meal with Keith Martin; instead, halfway across the room she stumbled in her three-inch heels and had to grab on to a chair for momentary support. The rest of the way to the loo she muttered under her breath about the stupid, impractical things that men found attractive.

Tape adjusted, battery changed (whoever said these recorders had quick-change batteries had never worn one of them inside a hold-up stocking), Sophie leaned on the sink and studied her reflection in the mirror. As always, for a moment she thought she was seeing someone else. The black eyeliner and mascara made her plain grey eyes appear smoky and seductive; the glossy red lipstick plumped out what she'd always thought of as a no-nonsense mouth.

This was a uniform, a tool of her trade, she told herself. Something she'd studied and practised for hours – no, years – to get right. Usually when she was in full get-up she didn't study any more than the makeup in the mirror to make sure she'd applied it correctly. That was all her subjects were going to see, anyway: the mask, the image she'd created for their benefit.

But she was in there, underneath. If she looked hard.

The door to the women's loos opened. Sophie, self-trained to notice everything, glanced over.

Keith was in the ladies'. He hadn't stuck his head through the door; he was standing right inside, watching her.

'Are you all right?' he asked. His voice sounded merely friendly and concerned, but the expression on his face had gone back to that pupil-dilated, lip-dampened desire.

Instinct told her not to move, but instead stay leaning on the sink, her hair falling over one shoulder. He'd only see the mask, only notice the act. A honey trap only worked if you became a blank screen on to which men projected their own wishes.

'Hi there,' she said.

Keith kept his eyes on her, and moved swiftly. With his foot he swept the chair that stood by the sinks underneath the door handle.

Bingo! He was the quickie-in-the-lavatory type. She needn't have changed the battery.

'You drank that drink really quickly,' Keith said, still all smooth concern. 'Are you feeling a little lightheaded?'

He wanted her to be lightheaded.

Again acting from instinct, she nodded, and then

gripped the sink harder, as if she were trying to keep from falling down.

He came up behind her. Sophie watched him in the mirror without turning her head.

He put his hands on her hips: lightly, but to Sophie it felt as if he were holding her to keep her from running away.

'You're a beautiful woman,' he said. 'I can see why you thought I'd be tempted. How do you feel? Your legs weak? Having trouble focusing your eyes?'

She nodded. He thought she'd drunk the drink he'd given her. So this was how the scumbag got his kicks.

He stroked upwards along her rib cage, and Sophie watched, picturing the camera capturing every single thing. If she could get him to admit drugging her drink, she'd have him and good.

'Wh-what's happening to me?' she wavered.

'Don't worry, love, you won't remember a thing in the morning.'

'My drink – did you spike my drink?'

His hands were like spiders, creeping over her, close to the wire taped to her skin. She could end this, but one more second – one more chance for him to say what he'd done and what he wanted—

His fingers touched the wire and he stopped.

Keith Martin's smile was wide and dangerous.

'I know who you are,' he said, murmuring in her ear so close she could feel his breath. 'I know my bastard future father-in-law hired you to catch me.'

Sophie's heart leapt, her body tensed, and in a split second she had corrected herself so that she lolled forward slightly.

'You think you're so smart, with your lines and your manipulation,' he said, and bit her ear lobe. One of his hands rapidly followed the wire down her body to her inner thigh. His fingers curled around the recorder and pulled at it through her dress as he pressed his erection against her from behind.

'You know, when I planned this, I thought I'd get rid of the camera, but now I don't think I want to. I want to watch afterwards. I want you to watch and see what you made me do.'

He pulled her skirt up. The mirror was too high for her to see her bare legs, and therefore the camera wouldn't catch it either. 'Don't,' she slurred, still pretending to be too drunk to resist, but knowing there would need to be evidence that she hadn't consented to sex if she wanted to get him for attempted rape as well as drink-spiking. 'Don't touch me. Why are you doing this?'

'Catherine and I would have been quite happy, you know.' He punctuated his words with a sharp nip on the skin of her neck. It took all her willpower not to flinch. 'She adores me. She wouldn't have cared about anything else, as long as she had me. It's her father that hatched all of this up. Her father and you.'

She heard the rasp of his zipper going down.

Evidence. Evidence. Think of what they needed to put him away. Wait until the last possible minute.

She clenched her teeth and gripped the sink tightly. She had the advantage here. He only saw the mask. One movement and she could take him out. Keep calm. Wait.

She felt hot skin on the back of her bare thigh.

'You bitch,' he muttered, his breath heavy with lust. 'You deserve this.'

He put both of his hands over hers and she was trapped, pinned between him and the sink, and panic exploded in her. Bracing her stiletto-heeled shoes on the tiled floor, she wrenched her right hand from under his, brought her right arm back behind her and drove her elbow into his stomach.

She whirled around. His expression was almost comically surprised, his body doubled over in pain, his hands clutching his middle, his trousers sliding down his legs.

'My mistake,' Sophie said, pulling down her dress. 'I thought you were only a scumbag.'

She gave him a right hook to the jaw and he collapsed on the floor.

She stood there, framing him in her button camera for her own personal satisfaction, and then she pulled the chair from the door and hurried out into the bar.

'Don't touch that drink,' she ordered the barman, about to clear her table, and dialled the police on her mobile.

Thames Valley Police Station, Reading

'If you'd just sign your statement here, Ms Tennant.'

PC Jane Stanley pushed the forms towards her and Sophie gnawed on a fingernail as she read over what had been written there. She nodded, and then signed.

'We have some leaflets for you,' said PC Stanley, handing over a sheaf. 'I'm sure you'll want to go home now, but someone will be in touch with you soon from Victim Support. When would be a good time to ring?'

Sophie shook her head and stood, leaving the leaflets on the table. 'I'm not a victim. I was doing my job.'

PC Stanley was good at keeping her expression neutral, but not so good that Sophie didn't notice her blinking slowly, as if she were keeping her own opinion forcibly to herself.

'What do you think the chances are for a successful prosecution?' Sophie asked.

'I couldn't say. I should think your videotape would be useful evidence.'

The policewoman escorted her down the corridor,

which to Sophie still felt familiar from years ago, when she'd worked in this building as a clerk. The uniforms, the notices on the walls, the smell of overworked computers and half-emptied mugs of tea and cardboard file folders and towers of paper: it was all the mechanism of justice. She'd considered joining the police at one time, and decided against it because she didn't like taking orders. She still liked the police station. In the end, this was where the baddies got put away.

And tonight she'd helped that happen. Hours in a comfortless room had leached away her adrenalin, but Sophie felt a quiet, tired triumph. She'd nailed a bastard – not merely a bastard, but a drink-spiking would-be rapist.

At a moment like this, Sophie felt as if she were actually doing something worthwhile, something that went beyond the sordid world of adultery and temptation.

'Sophie?'

PC Raj Criss, wearing a Day-Glo-yellow jacket, stopped dead beside her and looked her up and down. 'Sophie?' he said again.

'Raj,' she confirmed, nodding at him.

'Gosh, I didn't recognise you in—'

Sophie had registered PC Stanley's sudden interest that they knew each other. 'I need to be getting home,' she said. 'Have a good night.'

'Oh. Okay, you too.'

As they walked the short distance to the exit, PC Stanley asked, 'How do you know—'

'Thank you for your time,' Sophie said to her. 'I appreciate your professionalism.' She shook hands with the policewoman and pushed open the door that led to the waiting room.

She stopped dead when she saw Catherine Birkbeck.

She was thin and pale in a metal chair. For the first time in Sophie's experience, her father was not with her, and she looked different, somehow cut loose.

Catherine didn't appear to see Sophie; she was staring at the posters on the wall telling her to *Be Aware!* and *Be Alert!* No doubt cursing herself for the years when she had failed to be either. Sophie went to her.

'I'm sorry, Miss Birkbeck,' she said quietly. 'I had no idea he was going to do that.'

Catherine blinked. She lifted her head and slowly focused on Sophie's face. Then she scanned Sophie's body, the tight red dress, the killer heels. Back up to the spot where Keith Martin had bitten her on the neck.

Catherine's expression transformed from blank despair to mouth-curling, hard-eyed revulsion. As if Sophie shouldn't exist, as if she cheapened the very air around them.

'You really threw yourself into this, didn't you?' she said to Sophie.

'I know you're blaming me right now, and that's normal,' Sophie said. Experience told her that she was correct, but memory told her she had seen that expression before, on other people's faces, and her good feelings curdled. Of its own accord her hand went to her mouth and she chewed on a fingernail that was already bitten to the quick.

Her small gesture of uncertainty made Catherine's lips thin, her eyes narrow.

'Who else should I blame?' she asked. 'My father? He was only trying to protect me.'

'I would think that Keith would be pretty high up on the list.'

'He rang me to come here for him. He needs me. I love him.'

Sophie's mouth dropped open. 'You do know what he tried to do to me, don't you?'

Catherine stood up. 'Have you ever been in love? So in love that nothing else matters?'

'Miss Birkbeck – Catherine, he didn't love you. If he loved you, we wouldn't be here right now.'

Catherine scanned Sophie up and down again. 'Look at you,' she said, her voice contemptuous. 'You don't know anything about relationships. You only know about cheating and dressing up and playing games. One day I hope you find out what it's like. To love somebody and then have them taken away by a little . . .'

Her voice broke. Sophie was aware of other people in the waiting room, staring at them. Catherine swallowed, and then she recovered herself.

'Please send your invoice to my father,' she said, and turned away.

Sophie shut the door to her flat behind her and for a moment let herself sag back against it. Her keys dropped from her fingers and hit the hardwood floor with a thump.

Traffic noise filtered through the windows, even this late at night. In the distance she could hear a train. Orange bars of light from the streetlamp outside striped the blank wall opposite. The flat was never silent, the flat was never dark. Other people's noise and light filled the edges of it, like static. Normally she ignored it. It was what happened when you lived in an urban area. Sometimes it was even reassuring.

She kicked off her shoes and left them with her keys on the floor, and in the semi-darkness walked to the bathroom. In this modern flat it was a pure white cube which dazzled her when she turned on the overhead light. The only colour was a single row of toiletries on the side of the bath, and her reflection in the mirror.

Her makeup had come off in places. She looked like herself, smeared in paint and glitter. A weird collision of two worlds.

Sophie scrubbed her face clean. Her red dress was crumpled, especially around the hips where Keith Martin had pushed it up. She pulled it over her head and dropped it on the tiled floor. Her recording equipment was at the police station to be used as evidence, but there were still marks on her skin from the adhesive tape.

I want you to watch and see what you made me do.

All at once she saw another room lined with white tiles, another mirror reflecting two people. The nip of teeth on her neck, the touch of flesh behind her. Hands over her own, holding them down.

She quickly went into her bedroom and found clothes to cover herself. She pulled on plain white underwear, grey sweatpants and a white T-shirt. She combed the tousle out of her hair without looking in a mirror and snapped it into a neat ponytail by feel and experience.

Her mouth felt stale, from hours with nothing to drink but tonic water and police coffee. Oh, and that one sip of vodka and Rohypnol.

She should brush her teeth, but instead of going back into her bathroom she went to her cramped kitchen and poured herself a large glass of water from the tap. She drank it, then refilled it. It was cold and clear. She knew she'd only ingested a tiny amount of the drug and it was long gone from her system by now, but she drank more water anyway, trying to dilute the clogged, dirty feeling inside her.

When the intercom buzzed, she nearly dropped the glass on the floor.

No, he was in custody, and besides, he wouldn't know where she lived. Though Sophie knew at least six ways that he could find it out.

She went to the intercom and pressed the button. 'Hello?'

'Sophie, it's me.'

She closed her eyes for a moment and listened to the traffic outside, amplified through the intercom. 'Raj, it's nearly one in the morning.'

'Can I come up?'

'I thought you were on shift.'

'I got finished early. Please let me in.'

She sighed and hit the button. Raj knocked on her door so quickly he must have sprinted up both flights of steps. When she opened the door he was panting a bit.

'Are you all right?' he asked instantly. He was in civilian clothes, brown cords and a navy jacket.

She'd known Raj for years, from all the way back when she worked for the police and he was a new recruit. After she'd left to set up her own agency, every once in a while they'd meet up by chance in town and go for a coffee. He'd tell her about interesting recent arrests, share gossip about mutual acquaintances. Occasionally, when it didn't interfere with duty, he discussed leads on her cases. A member of the police on your side was invaluable for a private investigator and Sophie was always glad to see him. It was only five months ago that he'd started asking her out on dates.

He was the polar opposite of Keith Martin: responsible, honest, law-abiding, probably too sweet to be a policeman. From his nervousness when he'd asked her out, Sophie thought that he'd probably never two-timed a woman in his life. He was medium height, medium weight, and had brown eyes that were as soft as his mouth. He reached out his arms to her.

Theoretically, Raj would be the perfect antidote to Martin, a reassurance that not all men were scumbags. Some were decent and faithful and kind and volunteered at animal shelters on the weekend. Some could date a woman for several months and only make tentative suggestions that they might go further than kisses goodbye.

She stepped aside without touching him and let him into the flat. 'I take it you read my statement.'

'It was all I could do not to drag the guy outside and beat him to a pulp.'

The thought of Raj beating anyone, let alone a suspect in custody, was so implausible that Sophie smiled. 'That would be nearly as unethical as reading my statement in the first place.'

'Sophie, I needed to know what had happened to you. I didn't even recognise you in that . . .' He gestured to mean the whole thing, hair, makeup, shoes, dress. 'He didn't hurt you, did he?'

'He came out of it worse.' She remembered the glass of water in her hand. 'Do you want something to drink? A cup of tea?'

'No, I want . . .' He opened his arms again for her. He wanted to offer her comfort, protection, more of his soft kisses and a cuddle on the couch. Maybe he wanted to stay until morning.

'I'm fine, Raj,' she said firmly. 'I'll make you some tea.'

In the kitchen, filling the kettle, she wondered how quickly she could get rid of him, and then felt instantly guilty. Five minutes ago she'd been half wishing for company, and now she had it. And Raj's kisses were pleasant enough. They'd had some nice times; he meant well and she respected that. She didn't exactly have supporters queueing up outside her door. She should appreciate him. She did appreciate him.

It was only that over their last few dates she'd sensed that he wanted more, some kind of passion she didn't possess, some kind of caring she couldn't summon, and it made her feel drained and dry. She'd had too much demanded of her tonight already.

And none of this made her feel like a better person.

She heard him enter the kitchen behind her.

'It's late,' she said without turning around, pouring water into mugs. 'Let's have a cup of tea and then I want to get some sleep.'

'I could stay. It would make you feel safer.'

'Not tonight, Raj.'

She felt his eyes on her back, willing her to turn around, to look at him. To give him something of herself.

'Listen, I've spent all night being what someone else wanted me to be,' she said, stirring sugar into Raj's tea with more force than necessary. 'I just want to be alone, okay?'

'I know what you've been through tonight. You need to talk about it.'

'There's nothing to talk about. The subject was a villain, he tried to hurt me, I hurt him instead. It's over. Here's your tea.' She turned around and pushed the mug into his hands.

'Sophie, I've had training with victims of crime, and though that's not how you like to think about it, that's what you're going through. You need to open up. Not just about this, about everything. We've been seeing each other for months now, and you never—'

'Raj, if you came here to make me feel like a victim

because that's the way I'm supposed to feel, it's not going to work.' She walked past him into the living room, the wooden floor cold under her bare feet, and sat on her beige couch. As soon as she did, she wished she'd sat on the matching beige chair, because Raj came and sat beside her.

'I only want to help you,' he said softly. He put his hand on her knee, and without thinking, Sophie pulled away. She instantly regretted it when she saw the hurt on his face.

'I'm sorry, Raj,' she said. 'You're a good man. But I don't need help. I was only doing my job.'

'Your job is half the problem,' he said. 'You're all secretive and wary, all the time. And the honey-trapping is the worst of it. I didn't realise what it was like until I saw you at the station. I don't like you dressing up like that, putting yourself at risk. Something like this was going to happen sooner or later.'

She welcomed her anger. Anger meant someone else was wrong.

'Are you saying that I asked for what happened tonight?' she said. 'To have someone try to drug me and then rape me on camera?'

'That's not what I meant. I meant . . . Look, you know you're putting yourself in danger, going out there alone to meet people you don't know.'

'I'm in the same danger when I do surveillance. Or when I go down to the shops.'

'You should have back-up. We would never go out on an operation like that on our own.'

'I work alone.' She put down her mug on the coffee table. 'Full stop.'

'But you can't like it, can you?' His voice was pleading.

'*Like* it? Looking like a tart? Making inane

conversation? The scumbags drooling over me, thinking they'll have a fumble? The only decent thing about it is the pow—'

She stopped. She'd been about to say 'the power'.

'Is the money I get paid. It's my job,' she said firmly. 'Liking it or not has nothing to do with it.'

'I meant you can't like always being alone.'

Sophie stood. 'Look, I know what this is about. You want to come in here in your shining armour and rescue me from whatever and we can live happily ever after together, right? You get to restore justice to the universe and be a hero.'

Raj was slow to anger, trained in communication skills and non-aggressive confrontation. She knew she'd really achieved something when he put down his tea and stood facing her, his face carefully composed. 'That's not what I want. I want you to trust me, that's all.'

'No, you want me to need you. And I'm not going to, Raj. I'm sorry, but I'm never going to need you. So you should find someone else who will.' She went to the door and opened it.

'Not bothered about asking me for information, though, are you? Handy to have your own tame policeman to help you with your inquiries.'

She felt herself flushing all the way to the roots of her hair. Despite that, she stood firm, looking at him steadily, refusing to argue further.

'I tried with you, Sophie. I really did. One day you will need help, and there will be nobody there to give it to you, because you've pushed them all away.'

'I don't need to be rescued,' she said, and he walked past her out the door.

The flat still wasn't silent after he'd gone. Sophie

dumped out their undrunk tea, washed the mugs and went into the bathroom to take her shower.

The dress she'd discarded lay on the floor in a curve like a red smile. Full and crooked and tempting, the smile of a honey-trapper luring in her prey.

Sophie grabbed up the dress and tore at it. The silky material resisted her strength. Why couldn't she have bought something made in China, something cheap and easy to destroy?

She turned it over in her hands, looking for a seam where the dress would be weak, but then she stopped.

This was a dress. It was clothing she wore when she was doing her job. What had happened tonight wasn't the dress's fault. It was Keith Martin's fault because he was a scumbag. Pure and simple.

Sophie turned on the shower, and while the water warmed up she hung the dress carefully over a rail. She'd have it dry-cleaned in the morning. No sense in abandoning a useful piece of clothing just because of how she had felt while she was wearing it.

You bitch. You deserve this.

Sophie turned the water up hotter before she stepped into the shower. Her flannel was rough and she rubbed it over and over herself, trying to feel clean.

The Tennant Detective Agency, Reading

Four hours' sleep and four cups of coffee didn't do much for her head or her appearance, but taking the day off work would just be proving that Keith Martin had got the better of her. Sophie was at her desk bright and early, finishing off her case notes for the Catherine Birkbeck/Keith Martin file. She printed out hard copies of the notes, her photographs and her transcripts, backed the whole thing up on her laptop, and there were only two things left to do.

Please send your invoice to my father.

She chewed on her nails. Damn Keith Martin. She'd been all set for an open-and-shut case, a routine honey trap, and now she had to decide whether the hours in the police station were billable or not.

The second thing was to ring Raj. Raj was a decent man who didn't deserve a brush-off like the one she'd given him last night. She'd have to find the correct words to apologise for hurting him, and yet to make it clear that she didn't want to date him any more.

He'd say he wanted to help her. He'd say she needed to open up. She didn't want to hear any of it this morning.

She pushed the laptop aside and arranged the hard copies tidily into a file. Strictly speaking, she didn't need paper copies of her cases; everything was recorded digitally anyway. But when she'd started her business and hired this office she'd installed ranks of filing cabinets, and she liked the way they looked. She'd imagined them filled with records of mysteries solved, persons located, evidence gathered. All the good she'd do in people's lives would be filed away by type of case and then alphabetically by client name.

Seven years later, in reality, it wasn't quite like that. Of course, she had solved some mysteries, and the records were in those cabinets. She could pull them out if she wanted to and remind herself. But the truth was that one cabinet was fuller than all the rest, so full in fact that the case files had begun spilling out into the cabinets on either side: the cabinet marked 'I' for 'Infidelity Investigations'.

She pulled open the top drawer of the adjacent cabinet and revised her thought. The infidelity files hadn't begun to spill out into the other cabinets. They were already there. This drawer was full of them. Ditto the other four drawers. And the next filing cabinet, labelled 'Missing Persons', only had one recent file in it, that of Eleanor Connor, who'd been looking for the father of her unborn child after a one-night stand. He'd been found, though not by Sophie. There were eight other files, four of them dating back more than five years. The cases were all closed except for one, the oldest. Unlike the others, it was in a blue folder.

She touched the oldest file briefly with her thumb,

feeling the soft worn edges, and then she shut the cabinet. The replica Maltese Falcon perched on top of it as a joke wobbled slightly.

Nine missing persons cases in seven years, and one of them didn't really count as she'd never been hired to solve it. And missing persons, and mysteries like them, were what she'd gone into this business for. Not the burgeoning files full of betrayal.

She glanced at the cork board beside her desk. She used it to pin up information and notes while she was working on a case; she also kept a section of it to display thank-you notes from her clients. Originally she'd envisaged it as a display of success, a more visible version of the solved cases files. And she did have a few recent notes up there. There was one from sweet elderly Roberta Thomas, thanking her for finding the vandals who had made her afraid to leave her house. A note on glossy Breadman & Blandy letterhead thanked her for investigating corporate fraud. Near the corner was a photograph of the result of Eleanor Connor's one-night stand, a smiling baby girl named Emily.

But there weren't many notes. Wives didn't tend to thank you for confirming their worst suspicions. Especially when you'd confirmed their suspicions by attracting their husbands.

The door opened without a knock and Piers Birkbeck walked into the room, large in his pinstriped suit. 'Miss Tennant,' he said.

'Mr Birkbeck.' She stepped away from her cork board and, gesturing him to a seat, sat behind her desk. 'I take it you've heard from your daughter about what happened last night.'

He nodded curtly. 'I spoke with Catherine this

morning. I'm pleased to say that she won't be seeing Mr Martin any more.'

'If you'll forgive me for saying so, that wasn't the impression Miss Birkbeck gave me last night.'

'She won't be seeing him any more.' The words were spoken with finality.

Normally Sophie tried to draw a line under cases that she'd finished, though she didn't always succeed. In this instance, as she was going to have to give evidence against Martin in court, it was even more difficult. Somehow the Rohypnol and the attempted rape made her feel more personally involved. Funny, that.

'She believes she loves him, Mr Birkbeck, and Keith Martin is a master manipulator. I don't think it's going to be as easy—'

'I can handle my own daughter, Miss Tennant. I came by today to deliver a cheque in payment for your services in advance of your invoice.' He held out a folded rectangle of paper.

'It was certainly an unusual night at work,' Sophie said. She waited, but Mr Birkbeck only continued to hold out the cheque. His hazel eyes were smaller than his daughter's and his hands were large.

I'm sorry you were attacked, he didn't say. Nor did he say, *I do apologise for those hours in the police station and the fact that you had to break up with a man you've been seeing.* He most definitely didn't say, *Please pardon me for hiring you to perform services and actions that have led you to question the very bedrock upon which your career is based.*

In fact he offered no apology whatsoever.

Finally she said, 'I haven't prepared the invoice yet.'

'I believe you'll find this covers it adequately.' He tilted the cheque in his fingers, a prompt for her to take it. She did, and unfolded it, and for a moment she stared at the amount written on it, which was much more than what she'd have charged even if she'd billed full rate for all of her time in the police station and while she was breaking up with Raj.

'You succeeded far above my expectations,' Mr Birkbeck told her. 'With Keith Martin in jail, my daughter has no choice but to end her relationship with him. I congratulate you, Miss Tennant.'

She remembered how her client had touched the transcripts of online chat with Keith Martin as if they were filmed in grime. Even with the cheque held with only the tips of her fingers, she felt as if it were polluting her.

'It wasn't the outcome I had anticipated,' she said. 'I can hardly take credit for it.'

'I think you can, Miss Tennant.' Piers Birkbeck hefted his bulk out of her chair and walked to the door. 'I shall be recommending your services to my friends and acquaintances who require them. If I'm not mistaken, you can look forward to several lucrative contracts.'

'I didn't get into this business for the money,' she said.

'Of course not. But it's only what you deserve.'

He closed the door behind him.

The office wasn't silent. She could hear traffic and a train and Birkbeck's retreating footsteps.

'Why am I here?' she said aloud.

She didn't expect an answer. She was alone.

Carefully and thoroughly Sophie tore the cheque into strips, and then squares, and then confetti. She tipped the entire mess into the bin.

She unpinned the thank-you notes and the baby photograph from the cork board. Then she retrieved the

33

oldest of her missing persons cases from her filing cabinet, the person whom she had still not found.

She tucked the blue file and the notes and the photo underneath her arm, and went out the door. She locked it behind her.

The Broken Wheel, London
Eighteen Months Later

Dominick Steele propped his chin on both his hands
and stared at the Jack Daniel's in front of him. It was
a double measure in a half-pint glass, which was scratched
from the pub's glass-washer. The liquid glittered dully
golden, the colour of a hunting tiger's eyes.

There had been times when it would've been fifteen-
year-old single malt in front of him. Then again, there had
been times when it would've been a plastic litre bottle of
rotgut. Vintage champagne to supermarket cider, and on at
least one documented occasion a bottle of rubbing alcohol:
Dominick Steele was a man of wide tastes when it came to
booze.

It ain't what gets you there, it's where you go, he had
always said. Usually when he was cadging drinks off a fan
nearly as pissed as Dom wanted to be.

Mr Jack would start off this last journey just fine.

Dom watched the bourbon and breathed the air. The
bourbon didn't appear to be moving, but he remembered
from way back in his school chemistry lessons that if you

could smell something it was because a substance emitted molecules that travelled through the air and entered your nostrils. So even though he hadn't yet taken a sip, this Jack Daniel's was already in his body.

He'd made his decision by buying it; now all he had to do was have the guts to take the final step.

'Not too thirsty?' The bar was moderately crowded on a Sunday evening, and the bartender, collecting glasses, paused in front of Dom and the drink he hadn't touched for the past half an hour.

'I'm very thirsty,' Dom said, and he smiled at the barman.

He'd never been in this particular south London pub before, but he liked bartenders in general. A bartender had never caused any of the million and one things Dom had done over the years. All a bartender did was sell you what you asked for.

The bartender smiled back, but he also moved away quickly. Glancing at the mirror behind the bar, Dom could see why. His teeth were white and straight, and when he smiled, they gleamed like the grin of a skull.

He turned his attention back to the bourbon.

From a sound of rustling and a breath of perfume he knew that a woman had sat on the stool next to him. He felt her leaning on the bar.

'Hi,' she said.

Dom looked at her. She was probably about twenty years old, wearing tight jeans and a pink top and hoop earrings. She had nearly finished the Bacardi Breezer she held.

'It smells different in this pub,' he said. 'Why is that?'

The girl looked confused. 'I don't know, different how?'

He inhaled. Her perfume, the beery towels on the bar,

the leather of his jacket, the Jack Daniel's which surely had entered his bloodstream by now without him having to drink it. That was all.

'Nobody's smoking,' he said.

'Yeah.'

'Why not?'

'Because it's illegal to smoke in public. Has been for ages now. Where have you been?'

She had a Brummie lilt and her expression was incredulous and it made Dom laugh. The laughter felt so good that he turned his shoulder towards his drink, not ignoring Mr Jack, no, but giving him a little bit of down time, and faced the girl completely.

'I haven't been in a pub for quite a while,' he said.

'Where have you been, abroad or something?'

'Something like that. Would you like a drink?'

She showed him her Breezer. He caught the bartender's eye and ordered another.

'Are you that guy from Dirtysweet?' she asked. 'The singer?'

'No,' said Dom. 'I don't know who you're talking about.'

The bartender came with the girl's drink and she addressed him. 'Do you remember the singer from Dirty-sweet? What was his name? The really famous one?'

The bartender thought. 'Yeah, it was some Catholic name. Damian?'

'Dominick!' The girl snapped her fingers. 'Dominick Steele. Haven't you heard of him?' she asked Dom.

'Never.'

'They were really famous. Don't you think he looks like him?' she asked the bartender.

The bartender considered, obviously remember-ing Dom's Grim Reaper smile. As far as Dom could recall, that particular look had never featured in the publicity photos.

'Maybe a bit.'

'A lot.' The girl took a drink of her Bacardi and started peeling the label off the bottle. 'You could be a lookalike. I heard they pay a lot of money if you look like Paris Hilton or someone famous. You'd have to grow your hair.'

'To look like Paris Hilton? Yes, I would.' Dom tugged at his black locks.

The girl elbowed him. 'To look like Dominick Steele! What do you do, anyway?'

'I'm a carpet-fitter.'

'Oh. That's good. My uncle's a carpet-fitter. Do you have those funky trousers with the pads in the knees?'

'Sure.'

'My uncle's dead rich.'

'Lucky man.'

'Are you?'

'Am I lucky? I don't believe in luck. You make a right decision, or a wrong decision. You can't blame anything else.'

'No, I meant are you rich?'

Dom laughed again. The girl had peeled most of the label off her bottle and it was lying in curls on the bar. She was young, the same age as the groupies who used to slip under the fences and wait near the tour bus and offer up anything, anything for a few minutes touching fame.

'I used to be rich,' he said. 'Not any more, though. What do you do?'

'I'm a student. Studying hospitality management.'

'What's hospitality management?' Dom tried to remember if he'd ever talked so much with any of the girls outside the bus. In his head they were all a blur of glossy lips and knowing eyes, so he guessed he probably hadn't.

'Hotels, restaurants? I want to manage a club, you know, something upmarket? I used to have sort of a crush on Dominick Steele. I had a poster of him and everything.'

'I guess you'd know what he looked like,' Dom said.

'Yeah.' The girl looked at him more closely. 'I can tell you're not him now. You're tall like him but your eyes are different.' She took a long slug of her Bacardi. 'But you know I came over here because I thought you might be him.'

'Sorry to disappoint you. I do that pretty often, I'm afraid.' He noticed her drink was nearly gone. 'Want another?'

'Pineapple this time, please.' She waited while he ordered it. 'Whatever happened to Dominick Steele, anyway? Didn't he become some alkie or something? Or was it drugs?'

'I wouldn't know.'

Shreds of the new label joined the detritus on the bar. 'Imagine that. Having everything and just pissing it all down the toilet. Do you think it's the fame that makes people do stuff like that, or do you think it's something wrong with them?'

'I think it's something wrong with them,' Dom said firmly.

'Yeah. Famous people are so weird.'

'You're right.'

Oddly it was a relief to talk about himself in the third person with a stranger, as if his life were a story told by someone else, something out of his hands, about somebody he didn't look like any more. Like luck, it was an illusion he wished he could believe in.

The drink used to make him feel like that. Still would, when he picked up the glass. Any minute now.

'Don't you like music?' the girl asked. 'If you never heard of Dirtysweet?'

'I love music. I mostly listen to classical these days, though.'

The girl snorted. 'Boring.'

'I guess I'm pretty boring, now that you mention it.' His gaze travelled back to his glass of Jack Daniel's. Once he'd had a few of those, he'd start being entertaining.

It was waiting for him. He could already feel the burn, the kick, taste the sweet smokiness, the need for another even as he swallowed.

'Why don't you drink it?'

He realised he'd been staring for several minutes in silence. 'I'm going to,' he said, and he curled his hand around the glass. But he didn't lift it.

'The last time I had a shot of Jack Daniel's,' he said, 'I woke up in Las Vegas.'

'That sounds pretty cool.'

'It would have been, except I'd had the drink in Nottingham two days earlier.'

The girl laughed. 'You're funny. Are you single?'

Dom gave himself some credit: these days he actually looked at the finger where his wedding ring used to be and had the good sense to be regretful. Which was a lot more than he used to do back when he was married.

'I'm divorced,' he said.

'Okay,' she said. She was a nice kid, he thought. Friendly and fearless. She was tipsy by now, but aside from that she seemed to be talking to Dom because she wanted to, not because of who he was. Or rather, who he used to be. It was a change.

Unfortunately it was too little, too late.

Dom lifted the glass. It was oddly light for something

that was going to erase two years of sobriety.

After the first sip, the rest of the night would follow a predictable course. He'd have another, and another, and then several more. He'd go home with this girl, or if she disappeared, with a different girl.

The prospect held no appeal for him. It was just the way the story about Dominick Steele went.

He'd tried to start a new story, but there was no point if you didn't know who the main character was.

'Well,' he said. 'Here's to you.'

He brought the glass to his lips. Nearer, the sweet smell of Jack Daniel's was almost overwhelming. It smelt of not only tonight's future, but Dom's entire future.

In his pocket, his phone buzzed.

For a moment, he considered not answering it. *Not at home, not available, on a journey with Mr Jack. Call back later. Or don't. I won't care.*

But somewhere in the past two sober years Dominick had regained a bit of the curiosity that had forced him, back in the beginning, to play music to see what he could create, to write songs to see what he had to say. Not much of it, a small scarred corner of what used to be everything.

It was enough for him to pause with the glass still in his hand, retrieve his phone and thumb the answer key. 'Yeah.'

'Dominick, mate,' cried a cheerful voice from the receiver. 'It's Max. Max DeMilo.'

The surprise was nearly enough for Dom to put down his glass. Nearly.

'Max,' he said. 'Good to hear from you.'

'I wasn't sure you'd remember me,' Max said. 'Last time we met you were pissed. How you doing?'

Dom considered his booze. 'About the same. How are you?'

'Splendid, man, splendid. Planning a big comeback tour, you might've heard of it.'

'I've ... been staying away from the business.' He mouthed an apology to the girl, who nodded and kept peeling the label off her bottle.

'Sorry to hear it. Listen, then, this might be no good for you, but I've got a proposition. Normally, of course, I'd get Gina to ring your manager, but I heard you don't have a manager these days, so I'm using the old direct approach.'

'What's your proposition?'

'Well, as I said, I'm re-forming the Venusians, and Digby – you remember, the bass-player? – his missus has just had triplets, and she says if he goes on tour she'll make sure he'll never be able to father any more children, if you catch my drift. And then we asked Dave Finlay, but he's been drafted in to do some Monsters of Rock tour, and then we asked Dillon Druce, and, this is quite embarrassing, but he died last month. Heart attack, you know. All those rolled-up cigarettes.'

Dom had known Dillon; they'd gigged together in the early years. Dillon had always stationed his current fag under the G string on the headstock of his bass, and put a spare behind his ear. In those days he used to regularly set his hair on fire when he switched the smouldering fag and the spare one by mistake. It was a measure of how distant Dom had become from the music business that he'd heard no whisper of Dillon's death.

'I'm sorry to hear that.'

'You and me both, mate. Anyway, I'm calling to ask you: are you on the straight and narrow these days?'

Dominick looked at his hand, holding the glass.

'Hold on a second, Max,' he said. He put down the glass and said, 'Sorry, I need to take this,' to the girl. He walked out of the pub on to the street. Twenty to ten on a Sunday evening in April; the air was grey and orange and smelt of wet asphalt.

'Why do you ask, Max?' he said into the phone, above the hum of the traffic.

'Well, I won't lie to you, Dom. You're my last choice. But I heard you were off the booze. Are you?'

'You need a bass-player?'

'I need to stop ringing around everyone in my damn address book, that's what I need. We start rehearsals in a week and I've got new songs. I know you're used to being the big shot in your own band, but hell, I figured that didn't work out for you, maybe you want to try something new. Give it another shot.'

'I . . .' Dom was surprised to feel his throat constricting. He couldn't remember the last time he had been moved by somebody's kindness.

'And frankly,' Max continued, 'I need someone whose name starts with D because it's bad luck to change initials in a band. But I'll only have you if you're on the wagon. What do you say?'

Dominick flexed his left hand. Maybe his story wasn't as predictable as he'd thought.

'I haven't had a drink in two years,' he said. 'I'm dead sober. I'm also dead broke.'

'It sounds like we need each other, mate. Excellent. Listen, I've got a guest at the farm and we had to put a sick cria in my studio anyway, so we're going to Stoneguard in Wiltshire for rehearsals. A week from today. You up for it?'

'Yes,' Dominick said. He decided not to ask what a cria was.

Three minutes later his phone was back in his pocket

and he was sitting back down on his stool at the bar. The girl greeted him with a smile.

'Good news? You look happy.'

Was he? Was that enough to make him happy – an invitation to be a session musician for a tour with a band that was only slightly less washed-up than he was?

'I've been offered some work,' he told her. 'The funny thing is that if I'd been offered it five years ago, I would've laughed. I would've thought it was below me.'

'But now you're glad of it.'

He glanced at the Jack Daniel's, still untouched on the bar. It looked like any old glass with some liquid in the bottom of it.

'Yeah, I am,' he said. Happy was too much to ask. But he was glad.

He caught the bartender's eye. The girl had finished her bottle so he ordered her another and asked for a Coke for himself.

'I've got to go,' he told the girl, who looked disappointed.

'Oh,' she said. 'I – I mean I thought we . . .'

Dominick smiled. 'What's your name?'

'Tracy.'

He held out his hand and shook hers.

'Believe me, Tracy, you're better off without me.'

The drinks came. She shrugged and drank her Bacardi. 'You off to fit some carpet, then?'

'Yes,' he said. He picked up his Coke and drained it in one. God, he'd been thirsty.

Stoneguard, Wiltshire

The village of Stoneguard lay nestled in the gentle cleavage between two rounded hills. On top of the larger hill lay the Neolithic stone circle that gave the village its name and a great deal of its tourism income. From the main street of Stoneguard the circle appeared as a curve of crenulated grey teeth snarling over the town.

Sophie had been up there once, when she first came to Stoneguard to start up her business six months before. It had been a rainy, windy day, but the tourists in their anoraks trudged doggedly ankle-deep in mud, determined to have fun while looking at a bunch of rocks which had been hauled by nearly superhuman effort hundreds of miles from their quarry to the top of this hill in Wiltshire, God knew why.

There was only one phrase for it: bloody-mindedness.

After locking up her PI business in Reading, Sophie had chosen a course in the local college's prospectus, though her choice had been limited somewhat by the fact that despite running her own business for seven years, her only formal qualifications were nine GCSEs and a black belt in aikido.

She'd stuck out the course for a year, got her certificate, and researched Stoneguard thoroughly before investing her savings in purchasing clinic space on the high street. Stoneguard attracted not only tourists but residents who believed in the whole 'mystic energy' of the stones; the manor house outside town had been converted into a good-sized recording and rehearsal studio which serviced a variety of performers, some of them very well-known, and most of them with their own quirks and alternative lifestyles.

It was, according to Sophie's research, the perfect place to set up as an aromatherapist.

Because even if the dream had gone bad, Sophie Tennant had wanted to be a detective since she was a little girl reading Nancy Drew and Famous Five books from the library. And if she was going to turn her back on her private investigations to be an aromatherapist, by God she was going to be successful. Even though in her now-educated opinion, Sophie personally thought the idea of curing people with smelly oils was a load of bunk.

Bloody-mindedness. She had something, at least, in common with these tourists and these stones.

Six months later, the bloody-mindedness was waning. Sophie dribbled some more scented massage oil on to her palms and went back to rubbing it into Sally Hershey's shoulders.

'Aaaah, that feels so good.' Sally wriggled her body into the massage couch in ecstasy. 'I'm telling you, Sophie, every time I come here I feel about ten years younger.'

Which would be about eleven years old, as Sally was surely no older than twenty-one.

'It's the bergamot,' Sophie said. 'It's got invigorating qualities.' Allegedly. It seemed to Sophie that if bergamot was so brilliant at invigorating people, she herself should feel invigorated, since she breathed in the bloody stuff for at least six hours of every day.

Instead, she felt tired. She hadn't stopped feeling tired since she'd seen Catherine Birkbeck's face after her fiancé was arrested.

Faithlessness, betrayal, lust and greed: it would be a relief, Sophie had thought, to inhabit a world where everything could be cured by a few whiffs of a pleasant scent. Her fellow students on the aromatherapy course had been so optimistic, so dedicated to the power of flowers, and Sophie had done her best to be like them. She'd always had a talent for blending in; she'd received top marks and one of her instructors had told her confidentially that she was one of the most gifted aromatherapists he'd ever trained.

Sally sighed again in pleasure. 'I tell you what, Sophie, the only things that are better than this are chocolate and sex.'

Sophie stifled her own sigh, this one of irritation rather than pleasure. For five months Sally had been coming to her for a weekly massage, and from the very first appointment she had blurted out far, far too much information for Sophie's liking.

Sally lowered her voice. 'I've got this new bloke,' she murmured, 'and he is a firecracker. Can't keep his hands off me. And gifts? I've had a bracelet, earrings, more underwear than you can shake a stick at, and the boxed set of the last series of *Sex and the City*. Mind you, I told him I wanted that one, but the others he chose all by himself.'

'Mm.' Sophie wasn't very good at not listening. She'd trained herself as a listener for years: how to pick up what was unsaid as well as what was said, how to remember every bit of incriminating or useful evidence. She had to forcibly remind herself that she wasn't being paid to be nosy any more.

She'd changed her life and come here because she'd had enough of other people's problems, especially the incurable ones, which they all seemed to be. There really was such a thing as too much information. Sophie's head had been clogged with it.

And yet ... she was curious. That was her own particular incurable problem.

'Older man,' Sally was continuing. 'You know, the younger ones have better bodies, but the older ones, they know what to do with them. Plus, in the end I think they're so grateful to have someone fresh and new to sleep with, they'll dedicate hours to sex with you. You know what I mean?'

'Not particularly,' said Sophie. 'The last man who tried to have sex with me ended up with bruises and a criminal record.'

Sally laughed. 'Oh, you have such a sense of humour! So funny. Charlie is like that too, he just makes me laugh and laugh. He spoils me, he really does.'

Sophie couldn't help asking. 'Is he tall?'

'Oh! No, not particularly tall, but good-looking, so distinguished. You've probably seen him, Charlie Raymond? You know, the' – she lowered her voice to a thrilling whisper – 'undertaker?'

Yes, she knew Charlie Raymond. Stoneguard wasn't a big town and Sophie was good at names and faces. Her hands stilled on Sally's back. 'Isn't he married?'

'Oh, shh! I'm so naughty, aren't I? I'm trusting you not to tell anyone, it's between you and me. I'd die if his wife found out. He says he's going to leave her anyway, but I'm only in it for a bit of fun, do you know what I mean?'

'I know exactly what you mean,' said Sophie grimly, digging her fingers into Sally's back and twisting the skin.

'Ouch!' Sally yelped.

'All done,' Sophie said cheerfully, patting Sally's shoulders where the skin had gone bright pink.

Sally sat up and rubbed her back. 'Was that a new thing, that pinch at the end? It hurt.'

'A little extra pressure to let the oils really soak in.' Sophie was already at the sink, scrubbing and scrubbing her hands. She felt faintly sick, as if she'd uncovered something rotten. 'That's it till next week, anyway. Will you excuse me, Sally, I need to check who my next client is.'

She left Sally grimacing and reaching for her clothes and went down the hallway to the small reception area, gnawing on a short, clean fingernail. A woman sat in one of the three chairs, her hair straightened, her legs crossed demurely. Sophie bit her nail a little too close to the quick and drew in a sharp breath of pain, and then she drew in a longer breath when she saw who her next client was.

Barbara Raymond. Wife of Charlie Raymond, the undertaker.

Barbara stood when she saw Sophie enter the room. Sophie shook her hand while her brain was trying to catch up with the situation. 'Hello, Miss Tennant,' Barbara said, 'I'm so pleased to meet you at last. All my friends have told me how marvellous you are and I'm looking forward to treating myself.'

Her manners were impeccable, her smile was strained, her eyes held an expression that Sophie had seen too many times. Sophie had about three minutes before Sally was dressed and heading for this room.

'I'm sorry, Mrs Raymond,' Sophie said, 'but I've had to cancel—'

At that moment Sally came in behind her. Sophie didn't see her, but she could tell because Barbara Raymond's face transformed from that of a pleasant, but weary, woman to that of a she-devil from hell.

'You!' she snarled. She dropped Sophie's hand and Sophie tried, too late, to grab her as Barbara leapt forward and wrapped her manicured fingers around Sally's slender neck.

'Stop!' Sophie cried. She readied her hands to fell one of the women but hesitated, uncertain of which one to strike – the one who was attacking, or the one who deserved to be attacked. She had decided, reluctantly, that brawls in her waiting room were bad for business and therefore she should try to pull Barbara off Sally, when Sally broke free and flew at Sophie.

'You bitch!' she screamed, her nails going for Sophie's eyes. 'You told her!'

Sally obviously was used to catfights; Sophie had to move more quickly than she'd expected to capture Sally's wrist and twist her arm behind her back. 'It's your own—' she began before Barbara slapped Sally round the face and Sally squealed.

Barbara wound back her right hand for what looked like it was going to be a proper punch, and while Sophie did think that Sally deserved a punch and more, she was morally against holding someone down so that someone else could beat them up. She made to let Sally go but then Sally growled at her, 'I'll kill you, you bitch,' so she held on tight and shifted her weight back on to her left leg, ready to kick Barbara's feet out from underneath her when she delivered the punch.

Except it never landed. Barbara yelped and Sophie saw that her arms had been pinioned by a long-haired forty-something man wearing unfeasible amounts of leather.

'I'll hold her,' the man said to Sophie. 'Why don't you get rid of the other one.'

Sophie marched Sally to the door and tipped her out. Sally stumbled in her high heels on to the cobblestoned street.

'Your massage oils stink!' she hissed at Sophie, tossing back her hair. 'Last week Charlie asked me if I'd been bathing in bug spray!'

'You'll be cancelling your next appointment then?' said Sophie sweetly, and closed the door on her.

When she got back, Barbara was standing with her face in her hands, sobbing, and the man was patting her on the back. In addition to the leather jacket, leather trousers, leather boots and some sort of hand-knitted woollen scarf, he was wearing six or seven silver and turquoise rings on his fingers.

'There, there, love,' he was saying, 'revenge is better served cold, believe me. Leave it for now, and get her when she's not expecting it.'

Although Sophie felt bad for Barbara, she didn't have much experience in what to offer in these situations, except for a portfolio of compromising photographs.

'Would you like a cup of tea?' she asked.

Barbara shook her head. 'I th-thought that a massage would m-make me feel b-better about things,' she hiccuped.

Even if she had believed in the extraordinary healing power of scents, Sophie had seen far too many betrayed wives to believe that a dollop of jasmine was going to do much good.

'I think the best thing you can do is probably to go to a lawyer,' she said, 'but if you want to, we can reschedule the massage.'

'Have you got a back exit to this place?' the man asked.

Sophie nodded and guided Barbara behind the reception desk and down the corridor to the back door. The strange guy looked as if he were a refugee from an eighties rock band, but he was good back-up.

When she returned to reception, he was leaning one slim hip against the desk. 'Thanks,' she said to him. 'I could've handled that alone, but it was easier with you.'

'Hey, no problem. I love a good catfight. Can't remember the last time I got in the middle of a proper one. Wait, yes I can. I got clipped upside the head with a high-heeled shoe. Probably why I couldn't remember it right away.' He held out his beringed hand. 'Max DeMilo. Pleased to meet you.'

Max DeMilo. Now Sophie knew why he looked like a refugee from an eighties band: he was one. Max DeMilo and the Venusians' guitar-clanging rock music had been on the radio all the time when she was growing up. Now that she looked at him more closely, she could see some strands of grey in his long hair and the lines made by a lifetime of performing in his face, and thought he was closer to fifty than she'd thought.

Sophie had dealt with famous people, notably rock stars, before. She braced herself for an onslaught of ego.

'Hello,' she said, shaking his hand and deliberately keeping any recognition or surprise out of her expression.

'Anyway, I'm sorry to butt in on you. We're rehearsing at the studio, and I came in on the off chance that you could fit me in.' He touched his shoulder under his leather jacket and scarf. 'Those guitar solos aren't as easy on the old joints as they used to be.'

She considered. DeMilo seemed like a talker, rock stars weren't known for leading blameless lives, and she'd had enough sordidness for today.

'I'll only treat you if you swear you're not embezzling money, committing fraud, or cheating on your wife.'

Max laughed. It sounded like a cackle and he threw his head back to do it, with an unselfconscious whirl of hair.

'The only money I've got was earned through good honest rock 'n' roll, I'm the lousiest liar you ever met, and I'm not married. And I'm not cheating on my girlfriend, either. Too scared of her,' he added, and winked, and despite herself, Sophie smiled for the first time in what felt like ages.

'That was my next client who went crying out of here, so I've got a free slot now,' she said. She made an unnecessary note in her appointment book on the desk, and led him through into the treatment room.

On her course she had been advised that one should make a treatment room as warm and homely as possible. Her fellow aromatherapists-in-training had nodded knowingly, no doubt picturing their ideal decor. Sophie, whose flat had bare white walls and beige furniture, whose car was silver because it blended in and whose clothes were chosen according to the assignment of the moment, had had to guess what 'warm and homely' meant. She had chosen a shade of yellow paint named 'Sunshine', figuring that was about as warm as you could get, and put a photograph of a tulip on the wall.

'Nice,' said Max in a way that Sophie could tell was pure politeness. It was the usual reaction. Maybe she should add another photograph.

She took a quick medical history and then said, 'Go ahead and take off your jacket and shirt and lie on the couch. Have you had aromatherapy massage before?'

'Oh, I've tried most everything, mate, though I draw the line at the leeches.' Max shucked off his clothes above the waist and lay down. His torso was in good shape for a man his age, and scattered with tattoos. Sophie made sure her hands were warm and gently touched the shoulder he had indicated, feeling how tight his muscle was.

'Okay,' she said, turning to her oils, 'we'll try a mixture of rosemary, ginger and grapefruit, and see how we get on.'

Rosemary relaxed the muscles, ginger warmed them, and grapefruit balanced and promoted goodwill. Sophie blended the scents with sweet almond oil, poured a small amount on to her hands and massaged it into Max's shoulder, above a tattoo of an animal that looked like some sort of tall, spindly-legged sheep, or possibly a long-haired camel. Max closed his eyes, breathed deeply, and appeared to be falling asleep.

Sophie, on the other hand, was again proving her theory that these damn oils didn't work. With every second as she treated Max's shoulder she felt her own shoulders tensing up. Despite being the perfect place for an aromatherapy clinic, Stoneguard hadn't proved as lucrative as she'd hoped. When she'd first arrived she'd had a flurry of appointments, as the village indulged their curiosity about her. Some of those, like Sally, had settled into regular clients. But far more were one-offs, people with stress in their lives who wanted forty-five minutes of relaxation and, more often than not, confession. Once that was done, they didn't contact her again. It wasn't because she wasn't competent at aromatherapy – on the contrary, even the one-offs told her they felt markedly better when they walked out her door. When she ran into them in the streets of Stoneguard, they said they'd never felt so relaxed. They said they must ring her soon to book again. But they didn't.

Repeat customers should be the backbone of her business, and now Sophie was going to have to cross Sally Hershey off her list – no, Sally and Barbara too – and for what reason? Another scumbag man and a brainless woman who thought about nothing but their own pleasure.

'So what was the catfight about?' Max murmured without opening his eyes.

'I'm sorry, but patient confidentiality . . .'

'That's all right, I can guess. The blonde is shagging the brunette's old man. Story as old as time.'

There wasn't any use in denying it, and besides, Sophie felt as if she were going to explode.

'It never ends,' she said. 'I chose this job because I thought, hey, aromatherapy is nice, the people are bound to be nice, the work will be relaxing. Ha! You put most people on a couch and let them smell a little lavender and boom, five minutes later they're telling you their life story. That's the third affair I've heard about this month. The third!'

Sophie didn't want to hurt Max, so she took a moment to pour a few more drops of oil into her hands. His eyes were still closed. Habit and instinct told her to shut up, but the words burned in her gut like a bad meal and the temptation to talk was too much.

It was probably the way other people felt around her.

'I thought it was my old job,' she continued. 'I mean, it makes sense: if you ask for immorality, it will come to you. I got sick of it, so I left, fair enough. But who tells an aromatherapist these things? Last month someone confessed to me that her husband had embezzled a quarter of a million pounds from his firm. She was frantic. Then the next person who came in told me this story about how he'd stolen, piece by piece, four or five entire computers from the company he worked for, then put them together at home and sold them. He thought it was a big joke. What is *wrong* with people?'

Max didn't say anything, only lay there with his eyes still closed. She kept on massaging his shoulder.

'It's lust, and greed, and selfishness. Pure selfishness, more than anything. That's what really gets to me. I mean, everyone's lustful and greedy sometimes, right? But you don't have to do anything about it. You can think about the consequences, about other people first. Doesn't anybody do that any more?'

Max opened his eyes. From this position, with Sophie behind him working on his shoulder, they saw each other upside down. He looked at her, carefully, consideringly.

Something about his face, about the way he was thinking, awakened a tiny glimmer of hope within her that he might know some kind of an answer. He would have travelled the world as a musician, met a lot of people. He would have learned wisdom.

'You know,' he said at last. Sophie leaned forward. 'You are one uptight chick.'

She sighed, straightened up, and returned her attention to his shoulder. 'Yes. Yes, I am.'

'Life's a bitch,' he said. 'For example, I'm a singer.'

'I was aware of that,' she conceded.

'Well I'll tell you, you want to see greed and selfishness? Get a gold record overnight and you'll see quick who wants to use you for themselves. Pretty often there's some lust involved, too. But you have to find something to believe in and cling to it as hard as you can.

For me, it's rock 'n' roll. And the llamas, of course.'

'The llamas.'

'Beautiful animals. They're the most trusting creatures you can find. When I'm hanging out with a llama, I can relax. You know?'

Sophie wasn't quite sure when this conversation had taken a turn from ranting to surrealism, but she supposed she knew now what the hairy camel tattooed on Max's arm was meant to be.

'Yes,' she said.

'You don't,' Max said, 'but you will. Are you finished with my shoulder?'

'Oh. Yes, I am.'

He sat up and rubbed it. 'That feels great.' He rotated it and did a few practice lunging motions. 'More than great. Wow. My shoulder feels about nineteen years old.' He pulled on his shirt. 'Pity about the rest of me, eh?'

'Rosemary can really work wonders.' She began to scrub her hands.

'Yeah, it's the rosemary. Obviously.' Max put on his leather jacket and wrapped his scarf back around his neck. 'You've got a talent there. Healing hands.'

'So they say.' When she looked up from washing her hands, he was watching her with that thoughtful expression on his face. 'Well, I'm glad I could help you, anyway, Max. Will you come through to reception when you're ready?'

At the desk in the front room, she took his credit card to pay for the treatment. 'What was your old job?' Max asked.

'Hmm?' She looked up from printing the receipt at the unexpected question.

'You said you met a lot of immoral people in your old job. What were you?'

'Oh. A hairdresser.'

Max shook his head. 'Full of lust and greed, hairdressers. Bad business. Don't blame you for getting out of it.' He took one of her cards from the stack on the desk, read it, and stuck it in the pocket of his leather jacket. 'Keep cool,' he said, and smiled at her before he left.

Sophie watched him go. She wondered if his scarf was made out of llama hair. What a seriously odd man.

'But a nice one,' she said aloud. A straightforward and honest one, it seemed. The kind of person she'd thought she'd be meeting here in Stoneguard until she found out it was a hotbed of sin.

For now, she didn't have any more clients scheduled, so she could spend the rest of the afternoon working on her accounts. One perk about being an aromatherapist instead of a private detective: you didn't have clients ringing to gripe about the amount of a twenty-four-hour surveillance invoice.

Sophie pushed her hair back and settled down with her ledgers. She started out by chewing on the end of her pencil, but within minutes she was biting her fingernails.

Faithlessness, betrayal, lust and greed. And above all, selfishness. Why did she ask the questions? Wouldn't it be easier not to know?

Except for Sophie, not knowing was like not breathing. She had to prise up that rock to see the things crawling underneath. She had to pick at the scab, break the seal and let the bacteria in to infect the wound. She had to worry and worry and bite until . . .

She tasted blood and looked down at her fingers, surprised. She'd torn off her index nail to the quick. A drop of blood welled up from the bitten skin.

She hadn't done that for a while. How interesting.

*

The Stoneguard community had successfully lobbied against having chain stores and fast-food franchises on its main street. The only place to get a cup of coffee to go was Ma Gamble's Whole Foods Emporium, which lay directly between Sophie's flat and Sophie's clinic. As all of Stoneguard passed, at one point or another, through its doors, Sophie had also used Ma Gamble's as a place to observe her fellow residents.

Today, though, she just wanted a coffee.

'Black, no sugar,' called Ma Gamble from behind the counter as soon as Sophie walked into the shop. She poured coffee from a filter jug into a recycled paper takeaway cup, popped an eco-friendly lid on the top, and put it on the counter, ready for Sophie to collect.

'Thanks,' said Sophie. As always, she was tempted to give the coffee back and ask for something, anything else, even though she did in fact want a black coffee with no sugar.

Ma leaned forward on the counter, tucking strands of curly salt-and-pepper hair back underneath her South American embroidered cap. At first Sophie had assumed that the 'Ma' nickname was because the shop owner, with her comfortably plump body and tie-dyed clothing, saw herself as an earth mother figure in the Stoneguard community. She soon discovered that it was in fact short for 'Major', Doreen Gamble's former rank in the British Army.

'So, Sophie, have you had any more fist fights in your reception since last week?' Ma asked. Word travelled fast in Stoneguard.

'I seem to have avoided them,' Sophie said. She also seemed to have avoided having any customers whatsoever, violent or not. It was Monday morning and her schedule for the week was nearly blank.

She took a sip of her fair-trade, organic, single-estate coffee made with local spring water, and as always had to admit it was pretty damn good. It wasn't the coffee that bothered her. The coffee was a symptom of everything else in Stoneguard.

Reading was a large town, a proportion of whose population was transient because of the university and the high-tech industries based there. After ten years of living there, Sophie had people she knew, people she'd investigated, and strangers. If she wanted to be sociable, she could be. If she wanted to blend in and be unnoticed, she could do that too. But Stoneguard was a village, and Sophie was discovering that in a village, nobody blended in. Everyone knew your business and how you took your hot beverages.

'We've got a gathering of the Ley Line Preservation Society tonight,' Ma told her. 'Coming?'

Another thing about Stoneguard: everybody belonged to groups. There were church committees, Morris-dancing and bridge-playing clubs, book discussion groups, yoga classes, even something called Friends of the Earthworm. They all seemed to arrange their meetings here in the Emporium, under Ma Gamble's direction. Evidently her time in the army had given her extraordinary organisational skills along with a passion for ethical and non-mass-produced food.

'I'm not really a group person,' Sophie said for about the thousandth time. 'Thank you, though.' She handed over a twenty-pound note to pay for her coffee.

The musical chimes over the door sounded and Joseph Bilton, he of the piecemeal stolen computers, came in.

'Good morning, Joe, tea with two sugars,' Ma greeted him, putting Sophie's twenty pounds on the side of the till and spooning sugar into a takeaway cup.

'Hello, Ma,' Joseph greeted her cheerily, and then he spotted Sophie. His smile faded and he nodded at her.

Sophie tapped her foot. This would be a good time to escape, but she didn't have her change yet, and twenty-pound notes weren't going to be easy to come by if she didn't get some clients soon. A year's aromatherapy training instead of working, and purchase of the necessary equipment, had used up most of her savings. The down-payment on clinic space and a flat in Stoneguard had done for the profit she'd made selling her Reading flat and office.

Joseph intently studied a display of home-bottled organic beetroot as he waited for his tea to brew. Ma Gamble's off-tune whistling didn't quite fill the silence.

What the hell. Sophie was proud, but she needed customers. 'It should be about time for a follow-up on your last appointment, Joseph,' she said. 'Can I book you in for next week?'

'Ah, uh, well, not next week as such, sorry.'

'I can squeeze you in the week after next, if you like.'

Joseph's eyes darted to Ma as he clearly willed her to hurry up with his drink. 'Thanks, uh, Sophie, but I think I'll give it a miss just the same. You know, very busy these days.'

'Of course, you've got all those computer projects, haven't you, Joe?' Ma said, bringing over the cup of tea at last. 'He repaired my ancient Apple in about ten minutes last month,' she told Sophie. 'He had exactly the part I needed in that shed of his. A marvel.' She took Joe's money and ambled to the till.

'Oh, do you have lots of spare computer parts, Joseph?' Sophie asked innocently, and was rewarded by Joseph gulping his hot tea and wincing.

The door chimed again. Barbara Raymond stood in the entrance, her hair a frizzy cloud around her face.

'Morning, Barbara, skinny cappuccino with—'

Barbara's eyes met Sophie's and her face went bright red. She backed out the door and shut it.

'Cinnamon,' Ma finished. 'Huh. Well, here's your change, Sophie.'

Sophie shoved the notes and coins into her pocket, thanked Ma, and left. Barbara was on the other side of the street, hastily getting into her BMW. Sophie decided to spare her the embarrassment of waving to her.

She could figure out the cause of her empty appointment book, anyway: once they'd confessed their dirty little secrets, her clients were ashamed to return. That was certainly it with Joseph and Barbara.

It would be a rather touching display of conscience and human frailty, if it weren't depressing to both her spirits and her bank balance.

Sophie unlocked her clinic door, turned on the light and drew the curtains from the plate-glass window in the front. She checked her appointment book in case she'd somehow missed something, but she hadn't.

Her mobile rang. It was a number she didn't recognise, and for a moment her stomach clenched as it always did, as she wondered if she'd been found at last.

She thumbed the button and swallowed. 'Hello?'

'Sophie! That you? It's Max DeMilo, remember me?'

She was standing by her desk with her lungs empty of air. She inhaled and said, 'Yes, hello, Max, I remember you very well.'

'Listen, mate, this is short notice and my girlfriend's gonna kill me for asking, but I've re-formed my band and we go on the road on Wednesday, and we could do with someone like you on board. It's seven weeks to promote the new album, theatres around the country, a couple gigs in France, ending up here in Wiltshire for the festival.'

Sophie blinked. 'You're inviting me to come on tour with you? Why?'

'You and your healing hands, babe. All of us in the band are a little past our guitar solo ages, if you know what I mean. Well, most of us anyway. It would be useful to have someone who could iron out our kinks for us, get us chilled out before and after a show.'

'You . . . but you don't know me.'

'I know what you can do with those oils. I've felt like a new man since last week. And listen, you need a break anyway, right? An escape from the bitch-slapping? Back in the day, we used to travel with an astrologer, a tattoo artist and a drug-dealer; seems like this time we could stretch to an aromatherapist.'

She frowned, remembering what she knew about rock stars. Max seemed different, but you never knew. 'Why would your girlfriend kill you for asking me?'

'Oh, because she's my manager and she hates to see me spending money. But we've got the money, so why not spend it on something that we'll all enjoy? That's my philosophy, anyway. There are four of us in the band, so it's not too much work for you, and we've all done enough wild living and are through with it now, so you wouldn't have to worry about all that lust and greed stuff. At least I hope all of us are through with it,' he added, in a mutter.

'That's really kind of you to offer, Max. But I'm busy here, I can't just drop all my clients.'

All her clients, indeed.

'Sure, no problem, mate, I'll just have to take it easy with the guitar solos if you're not there to patch me up. But think about it, think about it.'

'I will,' she said.

'You've got a few days to decide, plenty of time, yeah? Here, write down my number.'

She did, though she wasn't sure why, then bade Max goodbye and sat back down at her desk, sipping her coffee. A break from lust and greed? Was that really possible?

Surely people were the same everywhere. How would it be any different on tour with a rock band than it was in Reading or in Stoneguard?

Glass shattered in an explosion beside her, and Sophie leapt up from her desk in time to see a brick land on her reception floor.

She jumped over pieces of the broken window, ripped the door open and flew out into the street, where she just caught a flash of blond hair rounding the corner.

'Was it Sally Hershey?' she asked a bystander, Gloria Wheeler, who last month had confessed to her during a head massage that she had once thrown eggs at a homosexual couple's house. Gloria rolled her eyes and shook her head in a disapproving way, which Sophie took as meaning 'yes'.

She went back inside and looked at the brick. Someone had scrawled BITCH on it in what appeared to be purple crayon.

She stretched out her arm and retrieved her phone without moving from where she stood. It had stored Max's number, so she didn't have to read it off the note.

'You know this tour thing?' she asked when he answered.

'Yeah.'

'Do people chuck bricks at you?'

'It's been a while, but as far as I can remember, not generally, no. Other things, sometimes. Knickers. Pints of beer. Stuff like that.'

She nudged broken glass with her foot into a pile. 'I'm in,' she said.

Outside the Apollo Theatre, London
Six Days Later

The bus was bright turquoise and silver and was probably big enough to be seen from outer space. Sophie dragged her suitcases and portable massage table to the pavement beside it and knocked on the bus door.

Ten minutes later, she was still knocking. She had to be in the right place; Max had told her to meet the crew bus here, outside the venue for their first show. And this was unmistakably a bus. She pressed her ear to the door and heard the faint sound of gunshots and yelling.

She pulled her massage table to the side of the bus, unfolded it, and climbed on top of it. This gave her just enough height to be able to see through the tinted window. Four men were slumped inside on a U-shaped couch, staring at a television set showing a war film. Two of them had beards and England football shirts, one of them wore glasses and all of them were wearing jeans.

She banged on the window and they all looked up. The tall, skinny one with the glasses frowned and gestured for her to go away.

'Max told me to come here!' she shouted. The tall, skinny one shook his head, got up, and disappeared from view down a corridor. From her left she heard the bus door open and saw the man stick his head outside.

'This is the crew bus, love. The band isn't here yet. Doors open at seven.' He made to shut the door again but Sophie jumped down from her table and ran to him.

'I'm supposed to meet the crew bus,' she said. 'I'm coming on tour with you.'

He frowned again. From behind him she could hear the shooting and shouting of the film. It was turned up very loud. 'You what?'

'I'm Max's aromatherapist. Sophie Tennant.'

One of the bearded guys stuck his head through the door. 'What's up?'

'You heard anything about an aromatherapist joining the tour?'

The bearded man squinted and thought. 'Oh yeah, Max mentioned something about it. Is that you, love?'

'Yes.'

'Well, why didn't you say, instead of banging on the bleeding window?' said the first guy, but he was smiling as he said it. He jumped down from the bus. 'I'm Dempsey, I do the monitors. Sorry about before, I thought you were a bloody fan. Let's get your stuff on board.' He went to her suitcases.

'Griffin,' said the bearded man. 'Sound engineer. Come in. You ever been on tour before?'

'No,' answered Sophie, climbing the stairs to board the bus. It smelled of carpeting and air-freshener and very slightly of socks.

'Well then, I'll show you around. Welcome to your home for the next seven weeks. Appreciate it now, while it's still clean. This is the front lounge, where you can sit if you want a bit of peace and quiet. Peace and quiet being relative terms, seeing as you're on a bus.' Griffin gestured to four blue and black upholstered seats around a plastic-topped table. 'Then there's the kitchen area. Mind you don't bump your head on the microwave.'

It was a galley kitchen, with a sink, refrigerator, kettle and a microwave that stuck out slightly at the exact height of Sophie's forehead.

'They always put microwaves there,' Griffin explained. 'I can't tell you how many bruises I've had.'

The kitchen counter, of granite-coloured plastic, was piled with tins of beer, bottles of wine, and four super-size bags of cheese and onion crisps. 'Do you cook your meals in here?' Sophie asked.

Dempsey, who'd come up behind them, laughed. 'If you're very unlucky, Owen might make you his special Pot Noodle. No, love, it's strictly eating out on tour. Mostly at motorway service areas. This area is purely for decoration.'

'Much like this one,' added Griffin, opening a black door near the bus entrance and showing Sophie a cramped loo. 'Rule number one of the tour bus: toilet is for liquids only. Save everything else for the service areas or the hotels.'

'We get hotels?'

'If we're not travelling overnight, yeah. And for days off. Love hotels.'

'Love hotels,' agreed Dempsey. 'Except when I have to share with Bob.'

'You guys have been on tour a lot, huh?'

'Griffin, Bob and I have been touring together for donkey's years. Owen's the new kid on the block; he's only been on the job five years or so. We all just finished up with Girls Aloud.'

'Owen reckons he picked up a pair of Nadine's tights when she wasn't looking,' said Griffin.

'Here we have the sleeping area,' Dempsey continued. Columns of bunks lined the narrow corridor, each curtained off in blue and black material that matched the chairs' upholstery. 'You can have any bunk that doesn't have a bag on it yet, though don't take this one.' He pointed to an empty upper bunk.

'Why?' Sophie asked, dreading a story about groupies and orgies.

'Bob sleeps below it, and he snores like a hippopotamus.'

'And here,' Griffin said, leading her into the back lounge, which was where she'd peered through the window, 'is where we all get to watch TV. Bob, Owen, this is Sophie the aromatherapist.'

'There's a bird on the bus?' said Owen in a thick Welsh accent, standing to shake Sophie's hand. He was wiry, with blond hair that stuck up everywhere, and in his twenties, which made him at least fifteen years younger than the rest of the crew. 'You'd better watch your jokes, Dempsey.'

'And you'd better keep your mitts off her clothes, Owen,' replied Dempsey. Owen flew across the lounge at him, knocking him to the carpet, and the two of them wrestled playfully on the floor.

'Bob,' said Bob, shaking Sophie's hand as well. 'Ignore this lot, they have no manners.'

'So that's it,' said Griffin, stepping over Owen and Dempsey. 'That's the bus, and that's us. Got any questions?'

She looked around at the four men and the bus. If she'd

come on this tour as a break, she might as well ask up front. They weren't likely to tell her, but she had enough experience to judge from their reactions.

'None of you have any dark secrets, do you?'

The four of them grinned at her. 'Yeah,' said Dempsey, pointing his thumb at Owen, 'he's Welsh.'

Owen grabbed a tube of Pringles and bashed Dempsey over the head with it. The crisps spilled out on to the floor. Dempsey ate one.

Sophie smiled. 'I'll choose a bunk and get settled in.'

The Apollo Theatre

Dominick spent the day of the Venusians' first gig at the bank, arguing with the bank manager about why they should accept his late mortgage payment, of money he'd begged as an advance on wages for the tour, instead of foreclosing on his flat. It was at times like these that he wished he did believe in luck, so he could curse his own bad dose of it.

Though he supposed he was lucky in a way, that he'd chosen Leonie if he had to get married. A more vindictive woman would've demanded alimony as well as the divorce settlement, and he'd be even broker than he was now. He couldn't credit his own judgement about anything to do with that marriage, so maybe that was luck after all.

He bolted out of the underground train, took the escalator three steps at a time, and ran all the way to the Apollo. Gina, Max's tour manager and girlfriend, was waiting outside, one hand on her slim hip and the other raising her expensive watch to look at it for what he was sure, from the grim expression on her face, was the hundredth time.

'Sound check in five minutes,' she told him. She

sniffed, and Dom knew she was checking his breath for alcohol.

'Great, I'm in plenty of time.'

Gina raised her eyebrows at him and walked into the theatre. Dominick left a little space after her and then followed.

He hadn't been here in years, but it had barely changed since his own days before he was doing stadium tours, or even since he used to come here as a punter, a hungry teenager soaking up all the music, any music, he could. In those days it had been an electric palace of wonder. Now it looked a little dingy. Though most likely it was his hopes that had changed.

'Dom.' Mad Dog, the drummer, greeted him from the side of the stage, where he was eating from a jar of peanut butter with a spoon. 'Glad you could make it. You save the old homestead?'

'Safe and sound, until the pay cheques run out.' He joined Mad Dog, who offered him a spoonful of peanut butter. Dom shook his head, though he appreciated the gesture. For the past two weeks of rehearsals the band had looked sheepish whenever they cracked open a beer, as if they feared that the temptation of being in a room with an open can of Stella would be too much for him.

'Gina's got a bug up her arse,' Mad Dog said, licking the spoon.

Personally, Dom felt that Gina looked the sort who got a bug up her arse fairly often, but he didn't say so. She hadn't been altogether happy about his appointment as bass-player, and it wasn't a good idea to fall out with the tour manager.

'What's the matter?'

'Looks like Max went and hired some sort of therapist

to come along on the tour. She loaded her stuff on the crew bus today and that was the first Gina knew of it.'

They weren't going to go through band psychoanalysis, were they? The inside of his head was tricky enough without someone else poking around in it. 'What type of therapist?' Dom asked warily.

Mad Dog shrugged. 'She cures people with smells.'

'You mean, people who smell bad?'

'That's what I asked, and they laughed at me,' Mad Dog said. 'No, apparently she cures whatever ails you by rubbing oils that smell like flowers into your skin. I met her and she explained it to me. She's in the bus parked out back, in case Max hurts his shoulder again.'

'Oh, an aromatherapist.' Dominick knew what an aromatherapist was. He'd spent enough afternoons on his couch watching television in order to avoid going to the pub, and when you ran out of football, sometimes you had to watch girl TV.

So, they were going to have some hippy woman on the tour, all flowing skirts and wispy hair and theories about crystals. No skin off Dominick's nose, as long as she kept her flower oils off his instrument.

He got up to inspect his bass. Well, more like to appreciate it: if not for this tour, Dominick would have spent this afternoon choosing whether to sell his '62 Höfner or to lose his home. He wasn't sure which one he would have kept.

Max and Pete, the lead guitarist, hadn't shown up yet, and Mad Dog was still eating peanut butter. Dom slung the strap of his bass over his head and began to play. Not a Venusians song, all of which he could play upside down while wearing handcuffs. Not a Dirtysweet song either, because he had no desire to be reminded of those years.

Something improvised, something for the sake of playing and losing himself for a few minutes in a way he'd nearly forgotten he could do.

Now that he had rediscovered it, he knew it was the most precious thing in existence.

The frets, the strings, the vibration of the instrument against his thighs and the split second of wonder before he knew which note he was going to play. He closed his eyes to enjoy it for a moment, and when he opened them a woman had walked into the room and was standing quietly at the back.

She wore jeans and a white shirt and flat shoes. She was slender and had straight light brown hair, pulled back into a neat ponytail. The plain hairstyle made her eyes look large, her cheekbones high, and her mouth slightly wide. She wore no jewellery and no makeup and stood as if she did not intend to be noticed, and Dominick had never seen her looking like this. His hand slipped on the fret and his next note was dissonant, off-key and unexpected enough for the woman to glance in his direction.

She immediately recognised him, too.

'Oh shit,' Dominick said.

'Damn,' said Sophie Tennant, the woman who had broken up his marriage.

He was tall, even taller up on the stage, and he didn't bother to take his guitar strap off his shoulder when he stormed down from the stage and across the club to where Sophie was standing, her heart pounding, her stomach sinking, barely able to breathe.

Dominick Steele was quick-moving, black-haired, and absolutely the last person in the world she wanted to see. Ever.

'What are you doing here?' he demanded, and his voice was just as she remembered it, dark and rich, singing and speaking.

'I'm . . .' she began, and her own voice was breathy and thin. Sophie swallowed, hating this sign of weakness, and began again.

'I was going to watch the sound check, but now I'm not.' She turned to walk away, but Dominick's hand grasped her wrist and stopped her.

A big hand. Sophie's heart thumped painfully.

'I wouldn't do that,' she said, drawing herself even straighter, looking straight into his brown eyes and ignoring the fact that her knees were trembling. 'You remember what happened the last time you touched me.'

That did it. He dropped her wrist and Sophie could breathe again. She still felt as if the room had been sucked of most of its oxygen, but at least her throat was unblocked, her lungs were working.

'Why are you here?' he asked her again. 'Did Leonie hire you? Why would she do that?'

'I haven't seen your wife since I gave her the evidence she needed to divorce you,' Sophie said. She was pleased to notice that her voice held a great deal of scorn.

'What is it then? The bank?'

Although he'd stopped touching her, he was still close to her, close enough so that his guitar nearly brushed against the front of her jeans. His hair was shorter and she could see the beginnings of lines around his eyes. He'd aged a little bit in the past five years. He'd also become much more paranoid, although she didn't detect any scent of alcohol.

'Sounds like you've got a whole list of enemies,' she said. 'Keep going, I'm enjoying hearing about them.'

'Hey, Dom, you've met my aromatherapist.'

Sophie, who normally knew whenever anyone entered a room, started at the unexpected sound of Max's voice. He was standing on the stage next to his shaven-headed guitarist, Pete, and a short man with wild silver hair who called himself Mad Dog, and who played the drums.

Dominick Steele, the famously sexy, the hopping mad, looked slowly from Sophie to Max and back to Sophie. 'The aromatherapist?'

'The smelly woman,' Mad Dog said helpfully. 'That's who I was talking about. You two know each other?'

'Don't tell me I've hired one of your ex-girlfriends,' Max said. 'What are the chances of that, huh?' He seemed to consider. 'Well, actually, I guess they're pretty good.'

'No,' Dominick said, and his voice was dripping with disgust. 'This one is definitely not my type.'

'That's not what it looked like last time we met.' Sophie smiled at him sweetly and saw anger leap in his eyes.

'Well, I'm dying to hear all about your reunion, but it's time for the sound check,' said Max.

Dominick's eyes narrowed as he looked down at Sophie. 'You'll explain this to me later,' he said to her, and then turned and stalked back on to the stage. She hadn't noticed what he was wearing before, but now she did: faded jeans that had doubtless been chosen to make him look like some sort of god.

She should stay and watch and unnerve him, in revenge for feeling so unnerved herself. But her palms were sweating and her knees were weak, so she left the theatre, walking as slowly as she could to prove she wasn't running away. Then she climbed on to the bus and collapsed on to her bunk, shaking.

Dominick Steele.

76

Damn.

Sophie gnawed at her thumbnail and stared unseeingly at the blue and black patterned curtain that separated her bunk from the rest of the bus.

Surprise and shock were making her feel this way. Though she'd tried not to think about him – as she tried not to think about any of the scumbags she helped to expose – she didn't live in a cave, and she'd heard that his career had collapsed a few years before. She'd felt . . . well, she'd felt nothing, because he deserved it.

Right?

Well, she'd certainly tried not to feel anything, and she'd mostly succeeded. And now here he was on this stupid tour, which she'd foolishly agreed to do, and they was obviously going to be in each other's pockets for nearly two months, and my God, she wasn't even in the same building as him and she still couldn't breathe properly.

It was surprise and shock. That was all there was to it, because everything that had happened five years ago was down to her own inexperience and a lot had changed since then. A lot.

She punched the pillow.

She heard the bus door open. 'Right, where are you?' Dominick's voice thundered through the bus.

She started and bumped her head on the top of the bunk. Dominick's hand pulled the curtain aside and he stood there glowering, probably the most dangerous man she had ever encountered. Even counting the ones with knives.

'Come with me.'

By preference she would have stood so as to give the impression of strength, but she was a woman, she could be strong while lying on her bunk if she had to. 'I'm surprised you're asking me on a date, since you told the rest of the band that I'm not your type.'

'You're about as far from my type as a spiny anteater, and I'm not asking you on a date, I'm telling you to get your skinny arse out of that bunk and somewhere the rest of the band won't see us talking with each other.'

'Surely, Mr Steele, you're not ashamed of what I caught you doing five years ago? As I recall, it was public knowledge nearly as soon as it happened.'

'Thanks to you,' he growled. 'Now are you getting up, or am I slinging you over my shoulder? Because believe me, I have no fears that I won't be able to control my lust around you these days.'

Sophie regarded him. From the look on his face, she had no doubt that if she refused, he would indeed sling her over his shoulder. And if that happened, she would be forced to hurt him.

Not that that would be a tragedy in itself, but it probably wouldn't be a good idea to use violence on her first day in her new job.

She stood up and brushed imaginary dust off her jeans. Without a word she went past him, down the aisle of the bus, and out on to the street.

He followed her and then walked alongside her, setting a rapid pace with his long legs, looking straight ahead and brooding. He'd been a hell of a lot more cheerful five years ago, though she figured he'd probably had more to be cheerful about then.

'It wasn't thanks to me,' she said.

He blinked as if she'd disturbed his reverie. 'What?'

'The tabloids. I didn't tell them about your marriage. I operate under a strict code of confidentiality.'

He gave a short bark of laughter. 'Oh, so it's okay to

manipulate people as long as you don't tell the press about it?'

'I really don't think you're the person to be on the moral high horse here.'

He snorted, and kept walking.

Sophie had expected him to steer her into the first pub they came across, but he walked straight past one, and then another. 'Here,' he said suddenly, and pushed open the door to a shop called More of a Good Thing.

'Why are we in here?' Sophie asked as he went past the displays of women's clothes to the sale rail at the back.

'Because this is one place where the rest of the band are guaranteed not to come in.'

Sophie selected a garment at random from the sale rail. It was a pink flowered dress roughly the size of a tent and it dragged on the floor even when she held it up.

'This shop stocks clothes for tall and plus-size women,' she pointed out. 'I am five foot one and weigh less than eight stone. If you were looking for a place where you and I would be inconspicuous, I don't think you've found it.'

'I don't care about inconspicuous. What I care about is why you're pretending to be an aromatherapist. Is it me you're after? Or is it Max? Because if it's Max, I will personally escort you and your magnifying glass off that tour bus and back to whatever hole you climbed out of. I owe Max everything and I'm not having you play some sleazy little game on him for your own profit.'

'For a serial adulterer, you have an unusual definition of the word "sleazy". And no, I'm not after Max.'

'It's me you're after, then. What were you thinking, that I wouldn't recognise you without your miniskirt?'

'Quite honestly, I never suspected that you looked any higher than my chest. But in any case, I'm not after you, either.'

'Pete? Mad Dog? Griffin the sound guy? Whoever it is, you're going to have to choose another way of getting at them, because I'm blowing your aromatherapy cover as soon as we get back to the bus.'

'I really am an aromatherapist.'

A tall, plus-size sales assistant approached them. 'May I help you?'

Sophie barely had time to shoot Dominick an I-told-you-so look before he'd grabbed the pink flowered dress she'd pulled out earlier from the rack and held it in front of his body.

'The length is good, but I think it'll be too big around the hips,' he said. 'What do you think?'

He was about six two; the dress came down to mid-calf on him. 'It'll be good with high heels,' the sales assistant said, looking at him critically, 'but I don't think it's your colour. You'd be better off going with something in a flaming red.'

'We'll keep on looking,' Dominick told the sales assistant, and she smiled and went off.

Dominick tossed the dress aside. 'What do you mean, you're really an aromatherapist?'

'I had a career change. I gave up the private detective business over a year ago. I got sick of dealing with scumbags on a regular basis.' She shrugged. 'Who could have predicted I'd end up touring the country with the king of them all?'

'I don't believe you.'

'Oh, believe me, I've seen a lot of scumbags, and you truly are the king.' Actually more like the prince, she amended inwardly, thinking of Keith Martin. But she wasn't going to say that.

He exhaled sharply in irritation. 'I mean I don't believe you've had a career change.'

'You can check my credentials if you like.'

'Aromatherapists have credentials?'

'I do. You can also talk with Max. He persuaded me to come along, not the other way round.' She plucked another dress from the rack, this one black with a plunging neckline, and held it out to him. 'Try this. I think it will make the most of your cleavage. I seem to remember you were a breast man. Or was it legs?' She pretended to think. 'I guess it was probably both.'

Dominick appeared to be angry, exasperated and confused all at the same time. It would almost be funny, if she weren't looking at the possibility of being trapped with him for the next seven weeks.

'So you're saying that all you're doing on this tour is giving the band aromatherapy massages.'

'All the band except for you,' she said. 'I have no desire to put my hands on you.'

'Likewise,' he muttered. He turned and walked towards the door. Sophie put the black dress back on the rail and followed him.

He was going back the way they had come, and again he said nothing. She couldn't help glancing at him. Whatever had happened with his career, he still had that face that got him anything he wanted. It was meant for brooding: dark eyes, darker brows, slanted cheekbones, strong jaw, midnight hair, shorter than it used to be but still glossily dishevelled.

Uh. Sophie, stop it.

'Where are you going?' he asked her suddenly.

'Back to the bus.'

'Why? Are you planning to stay on the tour?'

Good question.

Sophie hadn't had time to think about her future, what with trying to deal with the shock of seeing her first honey trap again. She'd needed all her wits to keep one step ahead of Dominick, when her body reacted to him by going into fight-or-flight mode.

But she couldn't go back to Stoneguard. She had no clients and a boarded-up window. Plus, now that she'd seen a little of it, she was curious about the life of a rock band on tour. And she liked Max.

And she'd be damned if she let Dominick Steele affect any of her actions.

'Of course I'm staying,' she said.

'I'm not leaving,' Dominick told her. 'This tour is my last chance to claw something good out of my life, and I'm not losing it just because you fancy oiling up musicians.'

'Fine.'

'Fine.'

'We'll just avoid each other.'

'And never talk about what happened.'

'I have no desire to be reminded.'

'I don't either.'

They reached the door of the bus. Something occurred to Sophie. 'You're not staying on this bus, are you?'

'Not any more.' Dominick opened the door and climbed aboard. Sophie didn't want to be in that enclosed space with him again, so she waited outside. A few minutes later he emerged with a duffel bag, which she recognised as the one that had been lying on the bunk on top of hers.

God. She'd nearly had Dominick Steele lying on top of her. The thought sent a hot shiver through her.

She'd had a lucky escape.

He walked by her without a word, and despite herself, she watched his long, loose-limbed stride, the proud way he held his head up. The walk of a star. The same way he'd walked in the music videos she'd seen every now and then, late night on television, when she was tired and not quick enough to change the channel. Not quick enough, or not strong enough.

Sophie wrapped her arms around herself and climbed up into the bus.

She was kidding herself. She hadn't escaped at all, not from the first moment she'd met him.

The Tennant Detective Agency
Five Years Earlier

'I know he's cheating,' said the beautiful redhead, twisting her wedding ring around and around on her finger. 'A new woman every night on tour, maybe two or three.'

Sophie nodded. She closed the blue missing persons file that she'd been looking at when Leonie Steele walked into her office.

'It's not so bad when he's on the road,' Leonie continued. 'I don't have to think about it so much. But when he's home, I keep checking for signs, looking for lipstick marks. I can't stand it any more.'

Sophie thought that Leonie Steele looked the part of a famous rock star's wife. Her hair was Pre-Raphaelite, her skin porcelain. She wore expensive, floating clothes that suited her tallness. Her makeup failed to conceal that her green eyes were red-rimmed from lack of sleep or from crying.

'Mrs Steele,' Sophie said gently, 'I specialise in missing persons. But I have done three or four infidelity cases, and

I know how difficult they can be for everyone involved. So forgive me, because before we go any further, I need to ask you a question and I need you to answer it as honestly as you can.' She paused for Leonie to nod. 'You may feel that you are owed the truth, but do you really need to know what your husband has been doing?'

Leonie Steele twisted her wedding ring around. It was platinum set with diamonds and rubies. Sophie recognised a nervous habit when she saw it. She thought this one was also symbolic.

'I need to know for sure,' Leonie said. 'None of his bandmates will tell me anything. It's like a boys' club, like some twisted code of honour. "Whatever happens on tour, stays on tour." I can't go on suspecting the worst. If I know, I can end our marriage.' Her voice cracked slightly at the last.

'Right.' Sophie glanced at the blue file she'd shut, and pushed it to one side. Then she pulled over a notebook and opened it. 'So. Do you suspect your husband of having a long-standing affair? Or is it more like—'

'More like every girl in sight,' Leonie finished grimly. 'They throw themselves at him. Groupies. He's never resisted a temptation in his life.'

'I see. So you're looking for evidence of a pattern of behaviour rather than any specific relationship.'

Leonie put her hands on Sophie's desk. Her ring finger was rubbed pink.

'Do you have any idea,' she said, 'what it's like to know that women – not any specific woman, I'm talking about *millions* of them – want to sleep with your husband?'

'I can't say that I do.'

Leonie had been full of nervous energy when she walked into Sophie's office; she'd flung the door open and entered in a whirl of floaty designer dress and brilliant hair. Now, all at once, she seemed smaller and weary.

'I've had enough of it,' she said. 'I want you to do whatever you can to catch him. I've believed in him for so long. I can't do it any more.'

Her face was pale against the almost hectic brightness of her hair. She twisted her ring.

Sophie ran her thumb along the blue edge of the file she'd shoved aside. The edge was soft, as if she'd done this many times. She asked herself the question she'd just asked Leonie Steele: did she really need to know?

She made a decision and pushed the file underneath a pile of envelopes, out of sight.

This case was safer.

'I'll do it,' Sophie said.

The girl in the white smock behind the makeup counter in House of Fraser was blonde and eighteen, with pink shimmery lips. She was staring into space and tapping her long nails on the glass countertop.

'I need some help,' Sophie told her.

The girl started, and then gave her a shimmery smile. 'Oh, okay, sure, yeah, what can I help you with?'

Sophie gestured to the array of cosmetics gleaming around them. 'Everything,' she said. 'I need to put on makeup and I don't know how to do it properly.'

'Oh, sure, cool,' said the girl. She pulled out a stool and Sophie sat on it. 'How do you mean, you don't know how to do it properly?'

'I bought a load of magazines and had a look at the photos. But every time I try putting makeup on myself I end up looking like a clown.'

'Okay, so is this for a special occasion?'

Dominick Steele wasn't on tour with his band, so every night for nearly three weeks now Sophie had followed him as he'd left his large gated home outside of Henley-on-Thames. Though he'd gone to a different boozer every night – the dodgier the better, it seemed – he spent his time drinking and talking, not chasing after women.

If Sophie was going to get any more from this case than a comprehensive knowledge of seedy bars and what a rock star looked like from a distance, she needed to take matters into her own hands.

'Yes, it is a special occasion,' she said.

The girl began selecting a range of colourful products from the displays around her. 'So what is your normal facial regime?'

'I wash it.'

'That's it?' The girl looked sceptical.

Of course she was sceptical. The makeup counter girl was one of the vast clique who had learned about being female from a sister, a mother, a bosom best friend. The makeup counter girl had experimented with eyeliner and lipstick at age nine, and she had sneaked blue eyeshadow out of her house under her parents' noses and put it on in the toilets at school at breaktime. The makeup counter girl thought that glittering and getting dressed up was every woman's birthright.

'I use mascara and some powder,' Sophie admitted.

'Oh, okay,' the makeup counter girl said, evidently relieved that Sophie was more or less from the same planet. 'You don't really need it anyway,' she added tactfully. 'You've got good skin and bone structure.'

'Thank you.'

'That said, though, a good skin-care regime and the proper products can enhance your features. So you say you've been looking at magazines; what sort of image are you going for?'

Sophie thought about it.

'Slut,' she said.

'Uh, pardon?'

'Sexy,' she amended. 'I want someone to think "sex" when they see me across a crowded room.' Or, more probably, across a smoky, dimly lit pub.

The makeup girl brightened. 'Sexy I can do.'

Sophie watched, asked questions and remembered techniques. She focused on each part of her face in the mirror as the girl worked on it with brushes and swabs, watching her eyes become ringed and smudged with black and blue. Her cheekbones were sculpted and hollowed and dusted with gold. The girl smoothed on lipstick from a tube of passion red.

Forty-five minutes later the girl sat back with a satisfied 'There.' Sophie closed her eyes, and then opened them again to look at her face as a whole, as a man or a stranger would.

'Wow,' she said.

Someone else looked back at her: a woman with eyes full of mystery, a mouth made for pleasure. *Look at me!* she seemed to say.

Sophie smiled and the woman in the mirror also smiled. It lit up her entire face.

'I can't believe that's really me.'

'It's like I said, the proper products can really enhance what you've already got.' The girl appraised her work. 'You look gorgeous.'

'I look like my mother,' Sophie said, without thinking. Then she shut her red mouth and bit her shiny lip.

The girl reached for pink lipstick and touched up her own mouth. 'Your mum must be hot stuff, then.'

Sophie stood up from the stool. The woman in the mirror stood up too. She was wearing the same clothes, but they seemed to cling a little more to her figure.

'I don't know why I said that. I certainly don't look mumsy,' Sophie said hurriedly.

What a ridiculous thing to say. The woman in the mirror was Sophie herself, learning about the new tools of her trade. Nothing more.

But she did look different. Exotic. Fascinating.

She experimented with pursing her lips, sucking in her cheeks, fluttering her long, thick eyelashes.

Look at me!

'Thank you so much,' she said to the girl. 'This is exactly what I need.'

Outside Henley-on-Thames That Night

Sophie huddled in her coat, her bare feet tucked beneath her on the car seat and a pair of binoculars held to her eyes. It was May, but it was chilly, and she'd been in this car watching the Steeles' house for an hour and a half now.

From her surveillance of the last three weeks, she'd learned that Dominick Steele was a creature of habit, but only to the extent that he went out drinking every night. Sometimes it was as early as half past four; sometimes it was more like midnight; sometimes he had friends or colleagues with him; sometimes he went alone. He didn't drive, which Sophie thought was at least a small point in his favour.

Tonight it would be just her luck if he didn't go out at all, and she would have to apply two tons of makeup and hair-styling product and squeeze herself into this skirt all over again tomorrow.

A taxi passed her car where it was parked in a layby a discreet distance from the Steele residence. It pulled up to the gate, which opened after a pause. From this distance and with the taxi headlights pointing in the wrong direction, Sophie couldn't make out the features of the man who emerged, but she didn't have to. She'd been watching him for long enough to recognise his lean figure and thick dark hair in silhouette, and besides, he even walked like a bloody rock star.

While he got into the cab, Sophie uncurled her legs, slipped on her strappy shoes, and started her car. When the cab began to move she was ready to follow it. She hummed as they wound through country lanes, feeling her pulse quicken. It didn't matter who the quarry was – fraudster, vandal, disappeared person, or a husband with roaming eyes and several platinum records – the chase itself always gave her a buzz. And of course this time she was trying out a whole new skill.

If it worked. Maybe she wasn't Steele's type. Maybe he was only after a drink tonight. Maybe he wasn't even a cheater after all – though her experience with these cases, while not extensive, told her that Leonie Steele was right. Women like her didn't go to the trouble of hiring a private detective unless all the signs were there. And of course Sophie had been watching Steele, how he acted and moved and drank. She thought the only reason she hadn't yet caught him was because he hadn't yet been offered sufficient temptation.

The taxi pulled up outside the Bull, a pub in one of the small surrounding villages. It was an appropriate enough name, she thought as she parked in the car park round the back of the pub. She took off her jacket, folded it on the passenger seat, and did a last check of the recording equipment concealed in her handbag. Then she used the mirror in the driver's-side sun visor to make sure she hadn't inadvertently smudged her makeup. For a moment she couldn't keep from staring at the face she saw there.

The car park was gravel and she tottered a bit in her heels. The outside air was cold on her bare legs and snaked up underneath her short skirt. She was grateful to get inside the pub.

Steele was already at the bar, talking to the barman. In the time that it had taken her to park, check everything, and walk inside, he had ordered and received a pint of Brakspear's bitter and a double measure of what Sophie knew from watching him was whisky. He was raising the whisky as she walked through the door, and though she'd clocked him right away, she didn't think he'd noticed her.

She went to the other end of the bar and ordered a Diet Coke from the barmaid, which she took to an empty table near the door, better to scope out the lie of the land. There was no point in approaching Steele at once; some drinking time would loosen him up, and besides, if she was lucky, he'd approach her himself.

She looked around the pub. It had the requisite low beams and horse brasses. There were two old men discussing a copy of the *Daily Mail* over their pints and two old women conspiring over gin and tonics. A clump of young men clustered around a quiz machine in the corner and another group of them sat around a table with several girls; three twentysomething women were playing pool and laughing. Maybe Steele would go for one of them, or maybe all three. That would save her a lot of work, and she could catch it on video.

But she had to admit that she sort of hoped that after all these weeks and all this effort, she'd catch him herself.

She tugged at the hem of her miniskirt, hoping for a little warmth, then remembered she was supposed to look like she wore these all the time, and folded her hands in her lap instead. She glanced at the women playing pool. Two of them were wearing short skirts, and one of them was also wearing a strappy sleeveless top, and they didn't look cold. In fact, the strappy-top one looked positively flushed.

Maybe it was something you got used to with practice, like standing very still so as not to be noticed, or finding the best-sheltered spot for surveillance. Maybe your skin got used to all the exposure, as if you had a whole-body callus.

If I do this again, I'm getting something comfortable to wear, she told herself. She fiddled with her Diet Coke and then remembered she wasn't supposed to be doing that either.

'Hi.'

For a wild moment she thought it was Steele talking to her, and she froze. But then she saw it was one of the young men from the quiz machine, standing by her table holding a half-empty pint of lager in his hand.

'Hi,' she said.

'I'm Mike. Are you alone here? Can I get you a drink?' His gaze travelled over her face and settled on her breasts.

'No thank you, I'm waiting for a friend,' she said.

'Come on, why not have a drink with me while you're waiting? Can't hurt, can it?'

Yes, as a matter of fact, it could screw up my entire operation.

'It's very nice of you, but no thanks.'

At the bar, Dominick Steele had knocked back his whisky and was well into his pint. Even if she hadn't been watching him professionally, he would have stood out. He was taller than nearly everyone else in the pub, his hair was longer, his clothes were better, and aside from that he had a confidence, nearly a swagger, that made him different. Fame could do a lot for a person, apparently.

The bloke who was talking to her followed her gaze. 'That's Dominick Steele from Dirtysweet,' he said. 'He comes in here all the time. I've got drunk with him before.'

Why would that be a point of pride, to get drunk with someone? Yet Mike was obviously trying to impress her. She should probably ask him some questions, to fill out the information she had. She dragged her gaze back to her companion, who took this as encouragement to keep on talking about the time he'd got wasted with a rock star.

She'd never been so close to Steele before; on previous nights she'd stayed as far away as she could while still keeping a clear line of sight for the camera. He took a sip of his beer, closing his eyes briefly as if savouring the liquid. He was a drinker and a sensualist, but then again she already knew that.

Sophie watched how Steele's arm leant on the bar, as if he owned the place. Imagine knowing when you walked into a room that every person's gaze would be immediately drawn to you, that they would talk about you, and be attracted to you. No wonder he looked so powerful. No wonder his wife was afraid.

Dominick Steele's leisurely survey of the pub wandered in her direction and Sophie fought instinct and training that both told her to look away before he caught her staring. Blatant and lingering eye contact was one of the first signs of sexual interest.

And then his eyes did meet hers and Sophie felt something very surprising.

A strange taste in her mouth, a stirring of the fine hairs

on the back of her neck, as all of that power concentrated, for a single moment, on her.

'Hello? Anybody home?' Someone touched her shoulder and Sophie blinked, breaking eye contact with Steele, and looked at the man next to her.

'I asked if you wanted that drink?' he said, and his own gaze was glued directly to her chest. She glanced down and saw that her nipples were erect and showing through her ridiculously flimsy top.

She had to get rid of this guy. Steele would never approach her if it looked as if she were attached already.

'I'm sorry,' she said to him, 'but I'm really not int—'

'You look thirsty.'

The voice was deep, rough-edged. Sophie hadn't listened to much of Dirtysweet's music but she knew the voice, again because it fitted the whole package of Dominick Steele. He stood next to her table, leaning against the horse-brass-studded wooden post, holding a full pint and a new whisky in one hand, and a glass of white wine in the other. She had felt his eyes on her while she was talking to the young man, but she hadn't felt him approach.

Now she felt him, all in a rush. The stirring, tasting feeling, like being too close to a strong electrical field.

He towered over the table and over the other man, and as she gaped at him, he smiled and put the glass of wine down in front of her. Then he took the chair across from her, the only vacant one at the table. Sophie nearly toppled out of her own chair.

She had to practise her observational skills more; she couldn't afford to be ambushed like that. Imagine if he'd had a gun. She'd be dead now.

'Hi,' she said, and then mentally kicked herself. Great

first chat-up line, Tennant. Not. Maybe she would do better against a guy with a gun after all.

'Dom!' cried the young man, as if he were greeting his best friend. 'How's it hanging?'

There, well, she could at least be proud she hadn't asked Dominick Steele how it was hanging. Still smiling, the rock star transferred his attention to the young man, who was lingering next to the table. Even seated, Steele dwarfed him, though more with presence than height.

'Very well,' he said. 'How about you, mate?'

From the 'mate', Sophie could tell that Steele couldn't remember this guy's name. She could also tell that he had enough charm to bluff it out and that this guy would never notice.

'Wicked. My band – you remember I was telling you about us – we've got a gig—'

'Great work,' Steele interrupted. 'Blow 'em away. Hey, you wanna give us a minute?' He indicated Sophie and himself with a casual wave of his hand.

'Oh. Oh yeah, of course.' The guy backed off, his smile wavering a bit. Usurped by the alpha male, with such finesse he wasn't sure how to protest it. Sophie watched him wander, bemused, towards the bar.

'Do you do that a lot?' she asked.

Steele shrugged. 'When it's necessary.' He extended his hand across the small table. 'I'm Dominick.'

She took it. Her hand seemed tiny in his broad palm. She wished she'd put on false nails or something.

'Sophie,' she said. She'd meant to let her hand linger in his, but she withdrew it, unsettled by the sensation.

She reached for her drink, encountered the wine, picked it up and took a sip to steady herself. Now that it was happening, she could admit to herself that she hadn't really expected Steele to be attracted to her. Though of course it was the makeup and the clothes he was attracted to.

'Why was it necessary to get rid of Mike, Dominick?'

Steele's gaze had flickered down to their joined hands when hers did, but other than that, he'd kept his eyes steady on her face. 'You're the most interesting person in the room, Sophie.'

'Why do you say that?'

'You're beautiful.'

Ah, flattery. The man had lots of practice at seduction. This was her cue to swoon at his feet.

She should turn it around, say something flattering about him, but she couldn't bring herself to do it. He had sycophants around him all the time; she didn't need to pretend to be adding to the adulation.

'Thanks,' she said instead, wincing at the thought of having to listen to this conversation later on the recording running in her handbag.

'No problem.' Dominick raised his whisky glass for a toast. 'Here's to you.'

She really should go back to her Diet Coke, but the wine was slightly in front of it and she couldn't think of how to discard the wine without putting him off. So she lifted her wine glass and clinked it on his whisky. 'Here's to you too,' she said and took a sip. Steele, as before, tossed the whisky back in one smooth move. Then he returned his gaze to her face.

'You're new here,' he said.

'Yes,' she replied, and then, thinking that although being a woman of mystery might be quite seductive, appearing to be a brainless idiot was not, added, 'I'm from Reading. I fancied coming somewhere different. Do you come here much?'

He shrugged. 'Sometimes. The barman's a nice guy.'

'What about Mike?'

'Let's talk about you. What's your middle name?'

She'd prepared fictional small talk about her filing job, about her social life, about being a Dirtysweet fan or not being a Dirtysweet fan, so she could be flexible and use whichever seemed appropriate at the time. But she hadn't made up a fictional middle name.

'Dean,' she replied, which was the truth, because she was on the back foot, dammit, and no other name sprang to mind.

He tilted his head. 'Sophie Dean,' he said, as if he were tasting the name. As if he were tasting her. It was all part of his game, but she shivered a little and tried to cover it up by taking another sip of wine.

'Why do you want to know?' she asked when she had swallowed.

'Everybody has a middle name, but nobody uses it. It's as if we each have a secret identity waiting to be pulled out. You look like you've got some secrets, maybe.'

'Not especially.'

The corner of his smile lifted, as if he didn't believe her. 'Mine is Angelo. I think my mother hoped I'd turn out to be a priest.' He took a long pull at his beer. 'Thank God that failed. Dean is unusual for a girl. Where'd it come from?'

'I don't know. It's on my birth certificate.' Okay, this conversation was not going as expected. She had to get away from middle names and on to the topic of sex.

Sophie leaned forward with her elbows on the table to deepen her cleavage. It also brought her closer to Steele, and she could smell him – warm aftershave, clean hair, and whisky.

'Why are you thanking God you're not a priest?' she asked. 'The celibacy?'

'All those vows to break. Imagine the guilt. And listening to other people's confessions would drive me crazy.'

'You're not interested in anyone but yourself?'

'I'm not interested in anyone else's sins. I'd rather be busy committing my own.'

He smiled at her, a flash of white teeth, and she felt herself wanting to smile back. She couldn't blame Leonie for falling for him.

In her mind she saw Leonie twisting her ring around her finger, the red mark it made.

Bastard.

'You're a real charmer,' she said.

'Only when I'm with someone I want to charm.'

'Does it get you into trouble, or get you out of it?'

'Both. I hope.'

Mostly in, she thought. Though he wouldn't know how much trouble until the night was over and he got the divorce papers.

She could feel sorry for him, if he didn't deserve it so much.

He drank down the rest of his pint, put the glass on the table, and then gestured to her wine, which she was surprised to notice was nearly gone. 'Fancy another?'

'Sure.' She shouldn't, but Steele was a drinker and he'd expect her to keep up. Fortunately he was drinking two drinks to her one.

She used the time while he went to the bar to breathe and go through strategies. Number one on the list was not to give away any more personal details. Number two was to make sure she had her handbag positioned correctly to film everything when he decided to make a pass at her. Number three was . . .

A glass of wine appeared in front of her and she felt, briefly, a strand of hair being stroked back from her face. Then Steele sat across from her again, both his pint and his short balanced in one hand.

He'd touched her. She seized the wine and took a drink, trying to dispel the feeling of that fleeting warm touch. The camera wouldn't have caught it, worse luck. With him sitting opposite she could only film him, not the both of them.

'Uh,' she said, 'do you mind if I move my chair over there with you? There's a draught here.'

He stood and helped her move around the table. 'I noticed you were shivering,' he said, his voice carrying the amusement of someone who knows he's caused the shiver himself.

'That's better.' She settled in the chair, crossing her legs so as to show more bare skin. Aside from the camera angle and being able to maximise the effect of her miniskirt, the other advantage to this arrangement was that he was beside her and so less likely to spend quite so much time staring directly into her face.

Of course the disadvantage was that she was closer to him. She could see how his trousers fitted his long legs, how his shirt lay over his lean stomach. The veins on the back of his hand as he casually held his drink.

For God's sake, Tennant, this is just a job.

'Well.' She held up her wine for another toast and he clinked his glass against it and downed his whisky. 'Tell me about your life, Dominick.'

And tell me about your wife.

He shrugged. 'I'm not working at the moment and I'm

going mad with boredom. I'm no good at rattling around inside the house.'

'You need your freedom?'

'I need something to keep me occupied.' He tapped his fingers on the table, as if he needed something to keep them occupied, too. 'I try to sit down and relax at home, but it only lasts about five minutes and then I'm walking around again, looking for something to do. I'm no good when I'm not working.'

'You love your work that much?'

'Yes. No. Yes, I do, but it's more than that. It's like if I stop, I might have to think too much, you know?'

'Yes, I do,' she said.

He caught the sincerity in her voice, a vehemence that had slipped out by itself, and leaned forward. 'You feel that way too? What's your job?'

'I'm – a file clerk.'

Steele smiled at her, quickly and fully and totally unrehearsed, and for a moment she felt not only that she liked him but that he liked her too, that they were in something together.

'What?' she said. 'You mean file clerks can't get obsessed with their jobs? I've got some very important files, I'll have you know.'

'I'm sure you do.' He took a drink, still smiling, and she wondered if he really did like her, or if this was only his act.

Hold on. Why was she thinking about this? She did not like men like Dominick Steele. She liked ordinary men, kind and decent and faithful men.

And in any case, he didn't know her. He knew the honey-trap girl, the image she'd created for her job. An image she had to concentrate on projecting, if she didn't want to mess up this case.

Dominick put his pint down on the table. 'You really are beautiful, Sophie Dean. I can't quite figure you out.'

She did an impression of laughing dismissively. 'You're trying to figure me out after meeting me five minutes ago? You move fast.'

'So they say.'

'I don't think you'll find much to figure out.'

'I think I will. Your clothes, for example. Are they new?'

'Yes, I went shopping yesterday. Do you like them?' This said with a little pout she'd practised earlier.

Steele looked down at her legs. 'I like them very much.' He took a swallow of his beer. 'You're not used to wearing them, though.'

She shouldn't drink any more wine. She did anyway. 'So what?'

'So the clothes, and the makeup, and the hair. You look like a little girl dressed up in her mother's things.'

Sophie gripped her glass hard.

'You really know how to compliment a girl, you know that?'

'It is a compliment. You've got all this sexiness, and then there's someone else inside. Someone who's not even sure that she's beautiful. It's very tempting.'

She should come up with a smart answer. She could only stare at him.

He stood and downed the rest of his pint. 'Drink up, Sophie Dean, we're getting out of here.'

'Where are we going?'

'Drink your drink and you'll find out.'

There was only half a glass left anyway. She drank it in three cool gulps and stood, picking up her handbag. 'I hope this is going to be good,' she said.

'Oh, I'm certain it will be.' He briefly glanced up and

down her body, and smiled, then he took her hand and threaded her through the pub.

It didn't seem as cold outside as it had before. Her hand was warm where it was surrounded by Steele's hand; her skin tingled. The two glasses of wine actually made it easier to walk in her high heels.

She'd drunk too much to drive home. She'd have to call a cab once she'd finished. And somehow, Steele had seen, however briefly, through her disguise.

But she didn't care. She felt exultant, excited, light on her feet. Tempting. Her plan had worked and she was about to land her prey. She wondered if he was planning to take her for a quickie in a back alley, or if he had a hotel room or even a flat he used for his illicit assignations.

They walked around a corner into a deserted street. The few buildings that lined it were barely lit by the sliver of moon. She thought it was probably too dark for her camera to pick up much, but she could still get the sound.

She glanced over at Steele. Outside, his hair appeared even darker, with a faint moon sheen on it that also cast his eyes into shadow, emphasised the angles of his face.

'What's it like to be famous?' she asked suddenly.

He glanced at her. 'Oh, you recognised me, huh?'

He didn't seem surprised, though she couldn't tell whether he was pleased. It was more as if he were acknowledging a normal part of his life, the way he expected it to be. The world was round, the moon waxed and waned, and people recognised Dominick Steele.

'Yes, I did,' she said. 'What's it like?'

'It's like normal life, only you have a lot more friends,' he replied. Yet another well-rehearsed line, like so many of the other ones he'd given her so far, though this one seemed particularly well rehearsed.

'Sounds great.'

'It is. All my dreams rolled into a big ball and come true at once.' He sounded bored. They turned into another street, this one equally deserted. 'What music do you listen to?'

He probably wanted his ego fed, but now that it came to it she couldn't bear to do it. 'Not yours, I'm afraid. I like more old-fashioned stuff.'

'The Beatles?'

'Frank Sinatra, Ella Fitzgerald, Louis Armstrong.'

'Ah, Satchmo.' He swung her hand and began to sing 'Mack the Knife'. His voice was a pitch-perfect growl and he didn't quite sing it the way Armstrong sang it, but a little slower, a little more deliberate.

He was a performer all right. Talented with it. He wanted to impress her and he wanted to seduce her and thank God she knew that his wife was sitting at home imagining what he was doing. The music echoed against the dark buildings and Steele pulled her closer to him and put his arm around her waist. His hand rested on her hip and Sophie thought about the way he'd acted as if he owned the pub, because now he was acting the same way with her.

The jaunty tune and the lyrics about murder. Sophie could feel each time Dominick inhaled, she could feel the lithe strength of his body against hers. The wine in her bloodstream mixed with the scent of whisky around Steele and the song had a relentlessness she'd never noticed before. Steele had seemed relatively sober, but now the way he concentrated on the lyrics, the loose-limbed way he walked, made her wonder.

They reached a bridge over the river. It was empty, with the water smooth nothingness beneath. '*Now that Sophie's back in town,'* sang Dominick, then seized her suddenly around the waist and swung her up on to the waist-height wall of the bridge so that she was sitting, held by his big hands at her waist, with her bare legs on either side of his body.

They were very close, this way. Her face was exactly even with his and her miniskirt had ridden up, and she was very aware that sitting like this, her crotch was also even with his. If he looked down he would see her underwear.

But he was looking into her face. He'd stopped smiling.

This is it, Sophie thought, and a thrill went through her body. She pushed her handbag a little to the side, aiming the lens at them.

'I think I've figured you out at last,' he said.

'Somehow I doubt it.'

'You came in the pub looking for me tonight, didn't you?'

Sophie's breath caught. *Oh, shit.*

'You came in looking for me,' he continued, 'because you want to fuck me.'

The lust that bolted through her body was so strong it was almost pain. *Cocksure, egotistical, cheating basta—*

Dominick Steele pressed the final inches closer and kissed her.

His mouth was hot, demanding, from nothing to everything in a split second. His tongue pushed inside her, he tasted of alcohol and dizziness, and Sophie felt it with every single cell of her body. Her brain switched off and she bunched her fingers in his hair, sighed deep in the back of her throat and into his mouth.

Dominick's hands were on her bare thighs, touching her as if he owned her, because he did own her, right that minute, and he pushed her legs apart, or maybe she spread them, and he leaned closer in so that she could feel the hard bulge of his erection through his jeans against the thin layer of her knickers. She moaned again, he devoured it, and he ran one hand up to the top of her thigh, his fingers brushing the inside of her leg, and the other up her ribcage towards her breast.

Sophie yanked her fingers out of Dominick's hair and clamped her hand down over his, right where it was, which was directly over the swell of her left breast. As if she were pressing him to her in passion, and not desperately trying to keep him from touching her nipple.

'Tell me what you want to do to me,' she whispered to him, her lips a breath away from his.

She felt him smile and felt the satisfaction thrumming through his body.

'I want to slip my fingers into these little knickers of yours and feel how wet you are,' he said, and Sophie could not breathe. His fingers were so close, and oh God she would be wet, you would have to be a stone not to be turned on by Dominick Steele, and he would feel her. She tightened her hand on his, harder on her breast, to distract him.

He chuckled, and it worked, because instead of invading her underwear he ran his thumb up the curve of her breast and squeezed her, and Sophie bit back another moan.

'I want to hear you scream when I touch you,' he murmured, 'and I want to hear it echo in the street and off the water.' He leaned forward and kissed her neck in a trail leading up to her ear. 'I want to stroke you up and down and in and out. I want to give you so much pleasure you don't care where we are.'

She tried not to picture it. She felt his left hand a

fraction of a thought away from her, searing the skin of her thigh.

Evidence. She should think of the evidence. She had his confession that he wanted to touch her and give her an orgasm, and dear Lord what an orgasm that would be, but she couldn't think about it right now because all she had to do to seal the deal was get him to describe how he wanted to have sex with her, get it all recorded and get the hell out of there before she let him do it.

'And then what?' she asked.

'And then I want to wrap your legs around me and fuck you until we both can't think.'

She had it. She'd won. Just one more thing, and she had a statement of intent to commit adultery, as clear as day.

'And are you going to do that?'

He nuzzled her ear, licked the hollow behind it, bit lightly on her lobe. Electricity sizzled down her spine. 'Do what?' he whispered, his breath hot and intoxicating.

'Fuck me?'

Even to her own ears it sounded like an invitation, not a question. Dominick straightened up enough to look her in the face, each eye an abyss, and in them she could see the act, wild and fast and oh the way he would feel plunging into her.

He kissed her again, which was not the answer she needed. A slow in and out of his tongue, a physical answer to her question, sensual and skilled.

Why did he have to be a scumbag?

Sophie pulled her lips from his with a gasp. 'Are you?' she demanded. 'Are you going to? Right here, right now?'

'Oh, yes.' He smiled the smile of a victorious man, a hunter who has captured his prey.

'Then will you just do one thing for me first?'

'What's that?'

'Will you take off my shoes?' Her voice was breathy, not completely by design, and his smile twisted up in one corner. He took his right hand from her breast and bent to unfasten her high-heeled sandals. He ran his thumbs over the arch of each of her feet, noted her small shiver, and then gave her her shoes when she held out her hand for them.

'Now what?' he asked her.

He looked so beautiful in the moonlight, with his lips moist from their kiss, with his hair dishevelled from her hands. Like a poet drunk with words, a libertine drunk with lust.

A rock star, plain drunk, and going down.

'I think all that's left for me to do is to inform you that this conversation has been recorded, and to thank you, on behalf of your wife Leonie, for the evidence she needs for a divorce.'

Her shoes in her hand, Sophie hopped off the wall and ran away as fast as she could.

Backstage at the Apollo Theatre
Present Day

'Thank you very much, good night!'

Max's exultant words rang in Dom's ears above the applause as he slipped his Höfner back on its stand and left the stage.

Backstage at the Apollo was so dingy that Dom's drummer Tick used to call it the Appalling, but Dom didn't care. He flung himself down on the ratty dressing room couch and grinned at the stained ceiling so hard he thought his face might split.

'Awesome show.' Max was only seconds behind him, along with Pete and Mad Dog. 'Awesome.'

The London kick-off show was theoretically one of the biggest of the tour, being as it was in London and marking the first public performance of the Venusians (or most of them) since 1991. The venue had been half-full, the PA had started feeding back during their penultimate song, they'd had to clear off the stage early to make way for the techno disco that took over the club until two a.m., and they were playing music that Dominick hadn't even listened to twenty years ago when it was popular.

'Yeah, it was awesome,' Dom agreed, still grinning his head off. Mad Dog, already rummaging through their rider, found a bottle of water and tossed it to Dom.

'Last time we played the Apollo, I jumped offstage and was carried all the way to the bar by a sea of people,' said Pete, grabbing a beer. 'Tonight I would've fallen on my arse!'

The band laughed, all of them high on the performance. 'We rocked!' Max said. 'It doesn't matter how big the audience was, we had an audience, people were listening. The Venusians are back!' He high-fived each of them in turn. 'And Dom, you fitted right in with us oldies.'

'It's the chemistry,' Dom said. 'I'd almost forgotten it. What you feel like when you're up on stage making music, any music.'

'Nothing like it.' Max cracked open a beer. 'That's what it's all about, mate, I'm glad you got it back.'

The door opened and Gina the manager bustled in. 'Why didn't anybody tell me there was an England game on tonight?' she demanded. 'We should have sold this place out.'

'Bob and Griffin were wearing England shirts and arguing with Owen about it all day,' Pete said.

Max grabbed her and planted a huge kiss on her lips. 'It doesn't matter, babe, it was a great show.' Dom watched as she smiled back at him and her whole demeanour relaxed. Good. He'd wondered why someone as laid-back as Max was with someone as uptight as Gina, but clearly it worked for them. She kissed him back, took a bottle of water from the rider, and excused herself to make some more phone calls.

'Speaking of great shows,' Pete said, midway through

his beer already, 'you remember Wembley back in eighty-seven?'

The Venusians launched enthusiastically into reminiscences, and Dom lay back on the couch and kept grinning at the ceiling.

He'd played Wembley several times himself, and had his own Wembley memories – or rather he would have had them if he hadn't killed them off. For example, the last time he'd performed there he knew he'd brought a bottle of vodka on stage, and he knew the crowd had been a sea of adoration. He didn't remember what he'd sung. Only blurred faces, watching him, cheering him, almost worshipping him.

Was it the drink that had killed it for him, or was it because the crowd had become more important than the music?

He finished the first bottle of water and reached for another. God, he felt great. For so many years music had been tied up with alcohol, even from the beginning, trying to convince the barman he was of age when he went to pubs to hear bands. He'd written his songs with an instrument in one hand and a drink in the other. Success brought you fame, and fame brought you more drinks, and then when his life had turned to shit and the music wouldn't come, he drank to get it back, and then he drank because he couldn't get it back. And then when he stopped drinking he'd thought the music had gone too.

But it hadn't. He'd remembered.

Alcohol made you forget yourself, but music made you remember. Even when he was playing someone else's music, in someone else's band, the rhythm of his heart had been his own. He'd been more himself, more alive, than he'd been in years.

Except, of course, for those fifteen minutes in the ladies' clothing shop with Sophie Tennant. When her eyes had sparked, her face had flushed, and she'd accused him of being everything he really was.

Or everything he used to be. He wasn't quite sure. Did the fact that he wasn't married any more and hadn't had sex for two years stop him from being a serial adulterer? Was he a non-practising adulterer, like he was a non-drinking alcoholic?

He wouldn't particularly have thought so before. While staying away from booze was pretty much the hardest thing he'd ever done in his life, and it didn't look like getting much easier, resisting women had been easy.

Except, again, for those fifteen minutes in the ladies' clothing shop with Sophie Tennant. When she'd thrown out yet another smart, contemptuous line and he'd realised that he was feeling at least as much desire as anger.

'Hey, smelly woman,' he heard Mad Dog say. Dom glanced over from studying the ceiling and saw Sophie standing in the doorway. She had her hair smoothed back into a ponytail, she wore a white smock over her jeans, and she held a small valise in her hand and a bunch of rolled towels under her arm.

'Hey, Mad Dog,' she said. 'Is it safe to come in or are you doing band bonding things?'

'Bonding,' said Max, 'but you're safe. My shoulder is killing me. Ain't as young as I used to be.' He winked at Sophie, and Dom saw her smile at him. It looked like a genuine smile; there was warmth in her face. But then again, she was a good actress.

She didn't so much as flicker her eyes in his direction. She went to the corner and unfolded a contraption Dominick hadn't noticed before and which turned out to be a portable massage table. 'Lie down and take off your shirt,' she said to Max.

'How I love hearing that sentence,' said Max. He shrugged off his leather jacket and began to unbutton his shirt. Sophie unfastened her valise and took out several dark glass bottles.

The rest of the band were watching her with interest. 'So what's that, some sort of magic potion?' asked Mad Dog.

Sophie poured an inch or so of straw-coloured liquid into a small plastic bottle and then began opening the dark bottles.

'It's rosemary and ginger and grapefruit, mixed in carrier oil,' she said, shaking a few drops of each into the plastic bottle. 'It acts as a muscle relaxant and soother, and the grapefruit gives an emotional lift.'

'And you sniff it?'

'I'll massage this into Max's sore shoulder, but he'll breathe in the aroma too, and that helps make it work.' She poured a small amount of oil into her hands and rubbed them together with brisk competence. Max relaxed on the couch and she stood behind him and began to smooth and then to knead the muscles of his shoulder.

'It works a treat, mate,' Max said, his head to one side. 'You should try it. In fact, it's a condition of the tour. I want everyone in my general vicinity to be chilled out.'

'That's what I'm here for,' said Sophie. 'I'll talk with each of you tomorrow and see what sort of blend of oils would be best for your individual needs.'

'And to think all these years I've made do with chip fat,' Pete said, laughing, and got himself another beer.

Dominick watched Sophie's hands working on Max. They were small. He remembered they were strong.

They'd tugged in his hair, held his hand to her breast. Now they circled, kneaded.

Dammit, he was getting a hard-on.

Dominick sat up on the couch and reached for a third bottle of water. This was a bad move because it made Pete notice him.

'So, Sophie, tell us about how you know our bass-player here,' he said.

Pete was one of those chummy blokes who liked a drink, the type of person Dom used to spend a lot of time with. He was hugely excited about the tour and liked to reminisce about the old days. That was why Dom had initially chosen to sleep on the crew bus, so as not to intrude on the original Venusians.

Sophie's hands didn't stop their practised movements on Max's shoulder. 'I don't know him,' she said. 'We had a brief acquaintance some time ago, which I had nearly forgotten.'

'Looked like more than that from the greeting you gave each other.'

'Dominick has that effect on women,' Max said. 'I think I used to have that touch, way back when. Did I, Mad Dog, or am I remembering it wrong?'

'You still got it,' Mad Dog said, and he drummed on the chair back with his fingers. 'Your Gina is a top bird.'

'Don't I know it,' Max said. 'Did I tell you lot how I met her? I was in Tesco trying to find a couple of coconuts, and . . .'

He had safely (and, Dom suspected, deliberately) steered the conversation away from his and Sophie's past. And Sophie was carrying on as if Pete had never mentioned anything. Except for the faint flush high on her cheekbones.

Dom looked away from her and back at the ceiling. One of the water stains resembled an eagle, or maybe it was a vulture. He still wasn't one hundred per cent sure Sophie had told him the truth. She did appear to have some aromatherapy knowledge, but surely anybody could pick that up from reading a book or two. And he'd forgotten a lot of things about his past, but hindsight and subsequent events meant he remembered that night five years ago, and what a good actress she'd been.

She'd come across as flustered, half tough and half naïve. She'd flirted and acted distant at the same time, winding him right round her little finger. He'd been convinced she was wildly attracted to him, right up until the moment she'd told him she'd been hired by his wife.

His eyes wandered back towards her. She was looking down at her work, her dark eyelashes like fans on her cheeks. The parting on the top of her head was pale and somehow innocent.

Yeah. About as innocent as he was. Dominick drew in a deep breath, smelled beer, and reached for Pete's acoustic guitar.

'Do you mind?' he asked Pete, who shook his head.

'You can play all you want,' he said, 'if you tell me how you know Sophie.'

Sophie glanced up from her work, then quickly back down as if she were pretending not to have heard the question. A good actress wouldn't have glanced, would she?

So what was it? Was she acting but lousy at it? Or was it all part of the package he was meant to buy, something to make her seem more human and more attractive? The way it had worked five years ago?

'You want to know how I know Sophie,' Dom repeated.

'Yeah, that was quite a greeting you gave her.'

He supposed it was. Flying off the stage and confronting her.

He could tell the truth now, and spare himself a lot of hassle later. He didn't think the band members would be too hot on knowing that there was a potential snooper in their midst. He didn't know of any skeletons in their closets, but that didn't mean there weren't any.

All he had to do was say, 'She's a private detective who split up me and my wife,' and she'd be off the tour. Peace and quiet. And no unexpected hard-ons just from looking at her hands.

Dominick held Pete's acoustic guitar. He strummed a few chords to get the feel of it and then he noticed that the air didn't smell of beer any more. It smelt spicy, earthy, refreshing. He glanced over and saw that Sophie was putting more oil on her hands.

She hadn't broken up his marriage with Leonie. He'd done that all himself.

'I thought she was someone else,' Dom told Pete, and he started to play.

The MacHeath Theatre, Edinburgh

'I'm with the band.'

Okay, those were officially the coolest words Sophie had ever spoken. So cool they made up for the sleepless overnight bus trip from London to Edinburgh, for the greasy motorway service area sandwiches that were exactly as dire as Dempsey had promised, for the fact that even off the bus, whenever she went into an enclosed room such as her hotel bathroom she felt as if the walls were still moving.

The bouncer at the door of the theatre nodded and waved her through to a special entrance guarded by a red velvet rope.

Now this was rock 'n' roll.

The woman at the door here checked Sophie's name against a clipboarded list and said, 'The guest bar is up the stairs and to your right.' She handed Sophie a sticker to put on herself, which served as a backstage pass, and gestured her through.

So guests of the band got a special bar separate from the

mere mortals who'd paid for a ticket? Sophie smiled at herself on the way up the stairs. This even made up for Bob's snoring.

She hadn't been able to appreciate the London gig, unsettled as she was by Dominick Steele's presence. She'd stayed on the bus arranging her essential oils and rolling and re-rolling towels while the band were playing, and only gone backstage once everything was over. But this time, her gear had been taken to the dressing room beforehand and she hadn't seen Dominick all day. Tonight, she was determined to soak up the atmosphere and learn what this tour was really about.

The guest bar was so crowded and tiny there was no space to move, and swathed in purple velvet that Sophie imagined was hell to get free of dust. She shouldered her way through the room, found a blessedly free patch of bar to lean against, and ordered a ginger ale. While the barmaid was pouring it she looked around the room as best she could.

Well. There was definitely an eighties revival going on in this room, at least. Sophie spotted vertical stripes, neon colours, big hair and at least one pair of leg-warmers, though this particular pair were worn on the woman's arms. About half the people in the room looked young enough to be wearing some of this stuff for the first time; the other half looked as if they'd been digging through their lofts. Some overenthusiastic soul even had a FRANKIE SAY RELAX T-shirt on.

She wondered who they all were. She recognised the couple down the bar from her as a famous Scottish brother-and-sister singing duo. The man who was talking with the Frankie girl was a soap opera actor. One or two other people looked familiar, which probably meant they were also very famous, since Sophie wasn't up to date on the UK entertainment scene, except for maybe *The Bill*. She'd got the impression that last night's London show hadn't quite gone as expected, and she suspected that Gina had been working overtime trying to get influential people here for this one.

But most people in here weren't famous. There were bound to be journalists, record company people, friends of the band and crew. Most likely there were also some friends of friends, blaggers and chancers.

She turned back to the bar to pay for her drink and felt a shifting in the crowd behind her. A male arm, wearing a dark blue long-sleeved shirt, appeared on the bar beside hers. The wrist was corded, scattered with fine dark hairs, and the hand was big and had plasters on two of the fingers.

She didn't need to see his face. Sophie tried to sidestep so she wouldn't be close enough to touch Dominick Steele, but the room was too closely packed.

'They messed up the rider and only had beer backstage,' he said. She could feel the vibration of his voice. Even though she wasn't looking at him, she knew he was speaking to her.

'Six bottles of water and a pint of Coke, please,' he said to the barmaid. His hand strummed lightly on the bartop.

She shouldn't speak to him. Certainly shouldn't give in to her curiosity about why he was at the bar ordering water and Coca-Cola.

'You're not drinking?' she asked. *Damn.*

'Seven hundred and forty-six days,' he replied.

'A fancy rehab place?'

'No. Just quit.'

'Ninety per cent of alcoholics have a relapse within four years.'

'Thanks for reminding me.'

'No problem.'

She had her ginger ale; there was no reason she shouldn't move off. The air around him was charged.

'Thank you,' she said.

She felt him looking at her.

'What for?'

'Because you didn't have to lie to Pete about thinking I was someone else. I know you're aware you could get me fired if you wanted to.'

She risked a glance at him. Max and Pete wore rock 'n' roll clothes: lots of leather and scarves and jewellery and such. Mad Dog wore jeans with holes and a collection of band T-shirts. Dominick had on indigo jeans, black boots, and a plain blue long-sleeved shirt. It was almost as if he'd chosen his clothes so as to blend into the background. Though of course Dominick Steele could never blend into the background.

'I didn't lie,' he said. 'I did think you were someone else. That's how you run those honey traps, isn't it?'

'Ran them. I don't do them any more.'

'So you keep saying.'

His drinks arrived and he paid for them, which Sophie thought was odd, because surely the band were given free drinks by the management? He got his change, but he didn't move.

'Why didn't you expose me?' she asked. It was one of the things, aside from the noisy bus and Bob's snoring, that had kept her from sleeping.

'Obviously because I'm crazy,' he said.

'Why really?'

'Do I need to worry about having my answer recorded?'

'No.'

He drank about a third of his pint of Coke in two deep swallows and then he glanced down at her. The eye contact made her stomach leap in the way she was beginning to find familiar.

'I don't know,' he said. 'I don't trust you. A few years ago I would've got you sacked right away.' He took another drink of his Coke. 'Maybe being sober has developed my masochistic side.'

'Dominick?'

He turned around and, for some reason, so did Sophie, just in time for a bright light to flash in their faces.

Dominick had swept his bottles of water off the bar and was pushing through the crowd away towards the exit even before Sophie had realised that someone had taken their photograph. A woman dressed in a neon-green *Flashdance*-style sweatshirt lowered her camera and smiled at Sophie.

'Never knew Dominick Steele to be camera shy,' she said, and then held out her hand. 'Nancy Chute.'

'Sophie Tennant,' Sophie said.

'Good to see the booze hasn't ruined his looks yet,' said Nancy. She leant on the bar beside Sophie, surrounding her with a cloud of Nina Ricci perfume. 'Or maybe it makes him even better. There's something so attractive about a man who's about to go off the rails at any minute, don't you think?'

'No,' said Sophie.

'You two were very cosy, though,' Nancy said. 'How do you know him?'

'I'm the band's aromatherapist.'

'Never! They have an aromatherapist on tour with them? That's too cute.' Nancy giggled in a way Sophie was sure was meant to be girlish and endearing. She tucked a curl of blond hair behind her ear. 'So Dominick Steele is definitely in the Venusians, then? I couldn't believe it when I heard it.'

'He is.' Sophie took in Nancy: blond hair, high heels, and boob job. 'How do you know Dominick?'

Nancy giggled again, this time a little breathless, as if hinting at past wild sexual liaisons. She looked like Dominick's type, so Sophie wouldn't be surprised. 'Oh, I work for *Hot! Hot!* magazine. I used to interview him back in the day.'

A journalist. Shit.

Sophie put her half-finished ginger ale on the bar. 'Must go. Nice to meet you, Nancy.'

She moved off, kicking herself for telling Nancy her name. Journalists were the only people who were nosier than private detectives.

The ghost of the flash was still floating in his vision when Dom pushed open the dressing room door. Mad Dog was sitting backwards in his chair, drumming with his hands on the back. Pete was standing in the middle of the room, while Max sprawled out on the couch, a tin of lager in one hand and his other arm around the shoulders of Gina.

'. . . and *Hot! Hot!* magazine,' Gina was saying. 'It's important to involve the fans you've already got, but I think we need to reach out to a younger market too.'

'Exactly,' said Pete. 'Exactly.' His head, freshly shaved for last night's gig, gleamed. 'We need to make the Venusians bigger than we've ever been before. Last night's show—'

'Your guitar solo on "Snakehips" was astounding, mate,' Max told him.

'Thanks, but I think we need to talk about why our big

London kick-off show was only half full. We sold out the Apollo three nights in a row back in eighty-six.'

'We've sold out here in Edinburgh,' Gina said.

'Yeah, but London—'

'London was great,' Max said firmly. 'We've never sounded better.'

Dom tossed a bottle of water to Mad Dog, who caught it without breaking his rhythm. Dom could feel Pete's dissatisfaction like a low buzz from an amp. It thrummed on his skin and between his ears, unaccustomed and yet familiar, as if he'd taken off protective headphones and could hear again what had been there all the time.

'All I'm saying is we should think about how to bring the punters in,' Pete said. 'Like the old days, give them a show to remember. Remember "Exploding Star" and that shower of sparks during the guitar solo? The crowds used to go wild.'

Max shook his head. 'It's all about the music this time, Pete. We don't want any *Spinal Tap* moments.'

Pete's face flushed at the reference. 'This isn't remotely like *Spinal Tap*. Except for the part about the girlfriend manager . . .'

Max sat up at that, keeping his arm around Gina. 'Oi, Pete, Gina is as much a part of this tour as you are.'

'And how many tours has she run?'

'I'm here, boys,' Gina said, detaching herself from Max and standing up. 'Pete, I apologise for the London show, but that's behind us now. Like Max says, the music is fantastic. The reviews are going to get you a whole new audience.'

'Gina is working her arse off for this band.' For the first time, Max's voice was raised slightly above his habitual laid-back drawl.

Dom remembered this atmosphere. Tick and Carver, cancelled gigs, smashed chairs, contracts lost and defaulted. His mouth was dry and the water in his hands wouldn't be any use to him. He headed for the dressing room refrigerator and opened it. To put the water in.

'I think we need more than Gina's arse,' Pete said, and Dom didn't have to look around to feel the tension escalate one hundred degrees.

'What did you say?' Max said.

Mad Dog's drumming stopped.

Dom stared into the refrigerator. Rows of lager stared back at him.

He thought he'd killed a lot of memories, but this one was still alive: four years ago in Berlin, smarting from a divorce that had dragged him through the dirt and left a hole in his bank balance, about to cancel the rest of his tour because all he wanted to do was crawl into a cave with a bottle. Tick and Carver had confronted him about song-writing credits on the next album and he'd flown off the handle.

He remembered the taste of whisky and bile and the smack his fist had made when it hit Carver's jaw. A bite more of whisky hadn't dulled the pain in his hand or the sting of being alone.

Dom touched a can of beer, just with one finger. It was cold, like ice sliding down a parched man's throat.

'Giant Squid,' said Mad Dog from the corner.

'What about . . .' Pete began, his voice angry, but then he trailed off. 'Oh.'

'Yeah,' said Max. 'Remember Bray?'

Dom put the water bottles in the refrigerator next to the beer, but he didn't close the door. He watched a bead of condensation trickle down the outside of one of the beers.

'What do squids have to do with this?' asked Gina.

'Not squids, Giant Squid,' Dom told her, without turning around. 'They played psychedelic rock back in the seventies. They were used to big arena tours, but when they got back together in the nineties they were playing clubs. One of their pyrotechnics set the stage alight. Killed a dozen people.'

'Including Bray,' Max said. 'He was a brilliant guitarist. We're not having special effects.'

Dom heard Pete walk out, and the dressing room door slam. Out of the corner of his eye he saw Mad Dog get up from his chair, as if to follow.

'Leave him,' Max said. 'He'll be all right. He always is. Just wants the glory days.'

The glory days. Yeah. Blood on Carver's face and disgust on Tick's.

Ninety per cent of alcoholics have a relapse within four years, he heard Sophie saying inside his head. He shut the refrigerator door and turned around.

'I thought this was all happy reunions,' he said.

'It is,' said Max. He was still on the couch, looking like he always did, though Gina's face had two red patches on her cheeks. 'I know Pete like a brother. He's just getting a little carried away. He's cool.'

'Well, you've got ten minutes until you go on,' said Gina, 'so I hope he is cool.'

Dom picked up Pete's acoustic and constructed an elaborate weaving of chords, trying to forget what he knew too well, that it was never only all about the music.

Down near the front of the stage it was crowded, though the back of the theatre was merely dotted with people. Since the music was so loud that you could hear it perfectly

well everywhere, Sophie assumed that the audience was
drawn towards the front in order to see the band better, or
maybe they'd been pulled there by that power all famous
people seemed to have.

She'd been pulled herself. Her intention had been to
stand unnoticed at the back, listen to the music so she
could talk to Max about it, and observe the atmosphere.
But when the band came on stage, little by little she'd
stepped forward and pressed through, until she was here,
guitars wailing and drums thundering in her head, bass
line thumping in her chest like a second heart.

Max wore leather and his llama-wool scarf, his hair flying
around his face as he sang. He was born to be at the mic,
winking at the crowd, working it. The stage lights gleamed
off Pete's shaven head, his muscular arms, and his black
electric guitar. Mad Dog was a bundle of pure stick-flailing
energy and noise. The three of them watched each other for
cues and met each other's eyes during choruses. Even from
down here Sophie could see the camaraderie, the band-ness.

And Dominick Steele stood slightly back in his dark
clothing. He watched his hands on the bass guitar; he
barely looked up to sing. He appeared to be in a world of
his own, yet as far as Sophie could tell, he was following
the music without a fault. At the end of a song Max would
beam at the applause, Pete would flourish his guitar, and
Mad Dog would wave his sticks in a pattern understood
only to him. Dominick turned his back to the audience to
check the levels on his amp and make minute adjustments
to his instrument, both with a manner of utter concentration. As if the crowd didn't exist and he were playing for
himself alone.

'That was from the new album, *Playing the Field*,' said
Max into the mic, 'which is out next—'

'Dominick Steele!' screamed two, or maybe three, female voices from the crowd to Sophie's right. His dark head, still facing away, inclined slightly, but he didn't turn around until the next song started and he could, once again, concentrate on the music.

Sophie remembered Dirtysweet videos – always artily shot, rough-edged, dramatic, with Dominick Steele in the centre. She remembered him with the entire pub in his thrall, how he'd dismissed a fan and swept her up into his charm, despite herself. He'd stood out, always alone, always powerful.

He was still alone, he still had power, but something had changed. She watched his long, sleek bass guitar, his long, sleek legs, his narrow hips and how his hands flew.

It was no good. She was going to have to learn more about him.

The Palace Hotel, Leeds
Two Days Later

The crew bus pulled up in front of the hotel at 6.31 a.m. and Sophie was the first out. After three nights on the bus she wanted a bed that didn't rattle, a toilet that didn't vibrate, air that didn't increasingly smell of several males living in an enclosed space. Most of all she wanted an internet connection and privacy for telephone calls.

The lobby was choked with houseplants that had sprouted out of control. Gina was waiting next to a twining twelve-foot philodendron. She had a stack of newspapers and magazines under her arm, and either she'd managed to survive a six-hour bus journey without incurring a single wrinkle to her clothes or the band bus had been here long enough for her to change. Sophie hadn't spoken much with Gina; the tour manager made it clear that (a) she thought an aromatherapist was a waste of time and money, but that (b) whatever Max wanted, he got. (Gina tended to speak in lists like this.)

However, they were the only two women on the tour and so far they had at least shared half a smile and a nod in the various ladies' rooms. That suited Sophie fine. She didn't need a confidante and she was used to being alone.

Now, Gina approached her and gave her the key card to her room and a magazine. 'Thought you'd like to see this,' she said. 'They worked fast.' She pointed to a page with a folded-down corner.

It was *Hot! Hot!* magazine, a glossy of celebrity gossip that Sophie had only ever picked up in a dentist's waiting room. The turned-down page was the 'Spotted!' section, with snapped photos of celebrities and reprinted text messages reporting sightings. Right in the centre was Nancy Chute's picture of Dominick and Sophie standing together at the guest bar at the Edinburgh show.

They'd been close. Really close, a hair's breadth away from touching, their heads inclined towards each other. From the photograph, it looked as if they were a couple. Seeing it again, Sophie felt the warmth and the electricity. It was as private as a surveillance photo. She read the caption underneath.

Dirty, or Sweet? Wild child Dominick Steele's hooked up with eighties where-are-they-now band Max DeMilo and the Venusians for their comeback tour. He's also, evidently, hooked up with tour aromatherapist Sofia Tenant. Leave some of the sweet stuff for us, Sofia! Or would we rather have the dirty . . .?

'Nice,' Sophie commented. Though it wasn't. In the photo, her hair was neatly tied back, her jeans and black top understated. But her eyes glittered. They gave away how excited she'd been. 'How many people read this magazine?'

'Easily half a million.'

Half a million people having their morning coffee and seeing her standing starry-eyed next to Dominick Steele.

Including, possibly, Leonie Steele, who would conclude right away that the private detective she'd hired to end her marriage had decided to snap up Dominick herself.

Good thing she wasn't a private investigator any more, because if she were, she'd be looking at her career going straight down the toilet.

'Damn.'

'Any publicity's good publicity,' Gina said.

To distract herself, Sophie read the titles of the newspapers underneath Gina's arm: a music paper, a London paper and a Scottish paper, all with pages folded down. 'Is this something you're going to be saying a lot today?'

For the first time, she saw Gina's real smile, though it was only a small wry one. 'Something like that.'

'Good luck.'

Gina shrugged her narrow shoulders. 'It's impossible to get rock bands up before noon, so I've got some time to put the best slant on things. Anyway, it's the name check that matters. You could use this one in your own advertising.'

'Yes, it would be very useful if I decided to change my name to Sofia.' She frowned. She'd snapped thousands of photos like this, and worse than this. In the grand scheme of things, the picture wasn't that incriminating. So why did it feel so intrusive?

'You should wear more makeup, but you're very pretty, even next to the pretty boy,' Gina told her. 'Don't worry about it.'

'I don't like having my photograph taken.'

'Then you'd better stay off his arm,' Gina said. 'I have a feeling he's going to get a whole lot more column inches before this is over.' She took back the magazine and left.

Sophie got into the lift with Griffin, Dempsey, Owen

and Bob, who were arguing over who was going to have which room.

'You're lucky you're a woman,' Dempsey told her.

'Yeah,' Owen said in his Welsh lilt, 'it means you never have to share a room with a snoring lampey.'

Bob punched Owen. 'It's not that bad.'

'It is,' the three of them said at once.

'I can make you a salve to rub on your upper lip that might help you,' Sophie told Bob.

'Nah, I like torturing these ingrates,' said Bob. The lift door opened at the second floor and the crew tumbled out, shoving each other good-naturedly and calling, 'Catch you later, bus bird!' Sophie waved at them and continued to the third floor and her room.

In the bathroom mirror, she tried to replicate the expression she'd had on her face in *Hot! Hot!* magazine. All she could come up with was a sort of goofy goggle. Gina had said she was pretty. Her eyes had sparkled, her mouth had looked almost lush. She'd looked like someone she recognised, but who was not the person she was used to.

She shook her head, hard.

In the shower, she felt the illusion of the walls moving around her. 'Bus legs,' Dempsey had called it. By the time she'd used up most of the little hotel toiletries, everything felt steadier and she was beginning to plan her morning. She dried herself off and got dressed in a T-shirt and loose trousers.

Aside from the explosion of houseplants in the lobby, the hotel was notable only for bland cleanliness, but it did have wi-fi. She sat cross-legged on the bed and logged on with her mobile phone nearby, ready for nine o'clock and the start of the normal world's business day. Then she began to work.

Sophie wasn't sure which was more difficult: trying to find information about someone who was nearly impossible to find, or trying to sort out the good information from all the trash in circulation about somebody famous. A Google search for 'Dominick Steele' yielded over ten million results. The first two websites gave her the public facts about his life: born in Islington, the child of ice-cream-parlour owners; attended the local comprehensive; formed his first band, Stainless, at age eighteen and signed to an independent label; broke up a year later and recruited a whole new set of musicians for his new band, Dirtysweet; two years of hard touring, marriage to Leonie, and then a year later the big hit, 'Sweet Nothings'.

And then the explosion had come. A triple platinum album, a Brit award for best newcomer, one world tour after another, television, radio, video, everywhere. The music was dark and complicated, catchy like a virus, commercially and critically successful. People mentioned Radiohead and the Doors. Steele was the lead singer, main songwriter, and played bass, and guitar and keyboards as well.

From the official online biography Sophie couldn't quite read between the lines to see where it all started to go wrong. Her own experience told her it was when Dominick and Leonie had broken up, five years ago; the Wikipedia article, which could've been written by anybody, said that 'Steele's substance abuse led to rifts within the band, especially when he cancelled a European tour without warning'.

Dirtysweet broke up, members Tick Gupta and James Carver suing for songwriting credits, the record company suing for contract violation. Steele released one single with the independent label that had signed him as a teenager. It sank without a trace.

And then, about twenty-eight months ago, Dominick Steele dropped out of the news. In fact, the last official item about him was a short piece in *Mojo* magazine where he listed his five most influential artists. There was nothing personal about himself.

She did a quick calculation. That was four months before Dominick had told her he'd stopped drinking. Four months unaccounted for – most likely longer than that, because the interview could have been a file piece. And then the sober days.

She searched further, beyond the mainstream sites. Most of the websites were badly spelled fan pages that contained utter garbage that hadn't been updated in at least a year but which nevertheless contained photographs that made Sophie involuntarily pause. For an hour and a half she clicked through, trying to glean facts and instead seeing Dominick singing, Dominick brooding, Dominick laughing, holding a drink, looping his arms around his band members, standing alone in a studio, taking off his shirt.

Jesus. Taking off his shirt.

Right. The best way to do this was to pretend that Dominick Steele was just an everyday citizen and do all the routine checks, and at least she'd have some confirmed information to tally the gossip against. She'd erased all the bookmarks from her laptop when she'd quit the detective business, but she had the main sites by heart anyway. She pulled up the first of them, used the room phone to ring for room service breakfast, and then reached for her mobile.

She was on hold with Maureen from the credit check agency when someone knocked on her door. Mobile in one hand, pen and pad in the other, she opened the door with her knee and let it swing open.

It wasn't room service. Dominick Steele walked straight past her into her room.

'Hold on, you can't . . .' she began, and then the woman at the credit agency came back on the line.

'Okay, Sophie, are you ready for this, because it's a long one? First we've got—'

'Just a second, Maureen,' Sophie said and followed Dominick. 'You can't just come in here,' she told him.

'I did,' he said, sitting on the bed next to her laptop. 'Hey, why do you have my postcode entered into this website?'

'I've got to go, Maureen,' Sophie said. She turned off her phone and reached for the laptop to turn that off too, but Dominick had already hit the mouse button and uncovered the window beneath the property check website.

He stared at the photo of himself with his shirt off.

Sophie snatched the laptop away from him. 'Get out of my room,' she ordered.

Dominick crossed his arms on his chest and swung his legs up on to her bed. He leaned back on the headboard in a pose that said clearly that he didn't intend to budge.

'Talk me through this,' he said. 'When you do a background check, do you always try to get topless photos of your subjects?'

'This is none of your business.' She shut off the laptop.

'I think it is. Especially since you told me your private detective days were over.'

'Those days are over, though I'll warn you that I'm still proficient in the martial arts.'

'And yet you're clearly checking up on me, which means you lied to me and you're still a private dick.'

'I'm not lying. Get out of here before I have to hurt you.'

'Who are you working for? I haven't got any money left, so you might as well tell them to call it off.'

'I'm working for Max. As an aromatherapist.' She wondered whether if she pulled the bedspread out from underneath him, he would slide on to the floor.

'You're really going to make me work for this, aren't you?' He crossed his legs at the ankles.

'You can work all you want, but you're not going to come up with anything. I'm not investigating you.'

'So why is your laptop full of my personal information?'

'I don't have any information that's not in the public domain.'

'But you've still been spending the morning collecting it. Why?'

She picked up her room phone. 'Thirty seconds, or I call hotel security and you get in the newspapers for refusing to leave a woman's room.'

'After all the reading you've been doing, you'll know that's not going to damage my reputation a whole lot.'

She began to dial.

'Of course your name would be in the papers as well,' he said.

Sophie poised her finger over the 'call' button, hoping he wouldn't call her bluff.

He swung his feet to the floor. 'Sophie, I don't like people snooping around behind my back, and I think you've done enough damage already. Tell me what the hell you're doing looking for more dirt on me.'

'I'm not looking for dirt on you.'

'Right. So what am I supposed to believe, that you're Googling me because you have the hots for me?'

She was unable to keep her cheeks from flushing.

His eyebrows shot up. 'Hold on. You *do* have the hots for me?'

'Tell you what,' she said. 'Let's find out. Why don't you make a pass at me, and we'll see how long it takes before I kick you in the crotch.'

Dominick smiled. He stretched his legs out on the bed again, with the air of a cat who has discovered a large and intriguing bowl of cream.

'That could be fun,' he said, 'but that's not why I came to your room.'

'Why did you come to my room?'

'I need your professional services.' He held up his hands, and for the first time Sophie noticed that every fingertip on his right hand, and two on his left, were wrapped in a plaster, some of them ragged and bloody. 'I mean as an alternative health practitioner, not as a nosy parker.'

'I already told you, I won't treat you.'

'Treating me is in the job description, isn't it? I am in the band.' He suppressed a smile, badly. 'Or is it because you don't trust yourself to touch me because you fancy me so much?'

'Was it all the platinum records that gave you this huge ego, or were you born with it?'

Dominick threw his head back and laughed and Sophie did her best not to notice the column of his throat, the dark stubble where he hadn't shaved yet this morning.

'Come on, Ms Sam Spade,' he said, still smiling broadly, 'help me out with the fingers. I'll take off my shirt if that's what you're after.' He reached for his shirt buttons with his bandaged hands.

'No,' Sophie said quickly. She went to the door, opened it, and held it open. 'Are you going, or do I have to stop being nice?'

'The thing is, Sophie, I'm thinking about what happens when I can't play bass tonight and Max finds out that you refused to treat me. He'll ask why, because all Max wants is for everyone on this tour to get on with each other. Which story should I tell him: that you're so attracted to me that you're afraid to touch me, or that you were too busy checking up on my private life?'

Sophie clenched her teeth. Dominick watched her.

She closed the door. 'All right,' she said. 'Let's see your bloody hands.'

He held them up without moving from his reclining position on the bed.

'I meant, take the plasters off.'

Dominick peeled away the plasters. She saw him wincing once or twice. Then he held up his hands again.

She had to bend over the bed to see them clearly, and she drew in a quick breath of sympathy despite herself. His fingertips were grooved, scored with blisters, some of which had burst and were bleeding and weeping.

'What on earth have you been doing to yourself?'

'Playing guitar.'

'You got these wounds from a musical instrument?'

'I haven't played for a while. And I've been doing it nonstop for the past few days, onstage and off. Eventually they'll form calluses again.'

'If they don't get infected first from being constantly reopened. Have you been going on stage with your fingers like this?'

'Well, I did try playing right-handed for a while yesterday. But then this happened.' He showed her the newer blisters on his left hand. 'Back in the day, I used to just pour vodka over the blisters and keep going. Killed the germs and the pain. Or maybe that was the vodka I poured down my throat. Anyway, that's not an option for me right now, and I hate doctors. So I'm all yours.'

Sophie shook her head. 'Okay. First we need to give them a good wash. Bathroom.'

Considering he'd been so difficult to shift from her bed before, he followed her to the bathroom sink with remarkable docility. She ran lukewarm water and opened up a new tiny bar of soap for him.

He winced again when the water hit his hands. For a moment, she watched him trying to manipulate the sliver of soap with his ravaged fingertips, and then she took pity on him.

'Here.' She held his left hand in both of hers and gently massaged soap over the blisters, then rinsed them off. His right hand was more difficult, because there were more blisters, and skin was hanging off in places. She took her time, finger by finger.

'You're good at this,' he said, so close that she nearly started.

'I used to skin a lot of knees on surveillance.'

'Your own?'

'Usually.' She finished and turned off the water. 'You'd better let these air-dry.'

He went back to the bed and sat on the edge of it, his hands held up in the air before him. Sophie opened her valise of aromatherapy oils and selected two phials.

'What are you doing?' Dominick asked. She was pleased to notice he sounded slightly less cocky. The washing must have hurt.

'Tea tree and lavender are natural antiseptics, and you can apply them neat.' She mixed them together in a small dark bottle.

'Are they going to make me smell like a girl?'

'You're welcome to question my advice, but if you do, I'd prefer you go and bleed elsewhere.' She got out cotton balls, gauze and surgical tape.

'I'll take my chances.'

She sat down beside him. 'Give me your hand.' She rested it palm-up on her lap and began to carefully dab the oil mixture on his wounds.

'Doesn't smell bad. A little bit like an old lady.'

'Yes, I'd say you're running a risk of people mistaking you for a female pensioner.'

She kept her attention on his fingertips. Not on how his forearm rested on her thigh. Not on the faint feather of his breath on the side of her face.

'I'm a dickhead,' he said.

That broke her concentration. She looked up at him.

'What?'

'That background check you're doing. It pretty much boils down to one thing. Dickhead.'

She blinked at him, his hand still in hers, cotton ball poised at one of his fingertips.

'You seem surprised,' he said. 'I guess you liked me more than I thought.'

'I'm not surprised about the dickhead part; it's more that you're admitting it.'

'Oh, believe me, I've done very little for the past two years but admit it. You have a lot of time to think when your only occupation is watching your bank balance disappear. Ouch.'

Listening and watching him, she'd let the cotton ball catch on the loose skin on his index finger. 'Sorry,' she said, and turned her attention back to the task at hand.

'What did you think of my wife when you met her?' he asked.

She cast her mind back to Leonie Steele: green eyes, perfect skin, and despair. 'She twisted her wedding ring around her finger as if she couldn't bear to let it go,' she said. 'She loved you. She was also sure I was going to find you cheating.'

'Let me tell you something you won't find in your background check. Leonie and I met in school. She wanted to be a classical flautist. She even played a few times with my first band, Stainless, but I didn't like how it sounded. So she used to drive the car with all the gear to our gigs.'

Sophie heard and felt him take a breath. She concentrated on treating his wounds.

'She was there all the time, right from the beginning,' Dominick said. 'And she loved me from the beginning, too. I was the first person she ever slept with, and the only one right up until the day of our divorce. I believe that, because she's the most loyal person I have ever known.'

'And you repaid her by cheating on her.'

'I've wondered about that. I thought maybe it was my way of pushing her away, of forcing her to end our marriage because it wasn't working. But I think that's making me seem better than I was. I thought maybe it was the drink, but I can't blame that either. Really, I cheated on her because I could. Because I wanted to and it was easy. Because I'm a dickhead.'

One of his blisters was still bleeding, and it spotted the cotton with red. She took a fresh ball and anointed it with oil, all the time careful not to look at his face because she wasn't quite sure whether she could handle Dominick Steele being honest and open, even if it was about being a dickhead.

But she couldn't be careful enough to damp down her curiosity. 'Why did you marry her?'

'I wanted to give her something, I guess. The flute wasn't working out for her and I was always on the road. After "Sweet Nothings" I had the money to pay for the wedding she'd always dreamed about.'

'But you were cheating on her even then.'

'Before we were married, yes. I stayed faithful for a while after we got married, though.'

'Months, or weeks?'

'I'd like to think it was months or maybe even a year, but I don't remember, to be honest. I've got whole chunks of my life that are little more than a blur. Probably just as well.'

Sophie put down the cotton and picked up the gauze. She began winding it around his fingers, securing it with tape. She was interested to observe that she was trying her best not to make him uncomfortable, to handle his wounds gingerly, and although she felt as if she were shaking with anger, her hands were steady.

'I think it's a despicable thing to do,' she said quietly. 'If you've made a promise to someone to be loyal, you should do everything in your power to keep it.'

'I shouldn't have married Leonie in the first place. But that wasn't her fault, it was mine. And it was my fault that I hurt her. That doesn't mean that you were right to manipulate me into hurting her one more time, though.'

'I was doing my job. The rest of it was your choice.' She finished winding gauze around the last of his fingers and patted the tape into place. Then, finally, she met his eyes.

He looked sad. Still impossibly good-looking, still upright and haughty as if he owned the world. But his skin was pale, his eyes were tired.

She was not going to feel sympathy for him. He didn't deserve it.

'Anything else your background check didn't turn up?' he asked.

'Any kids?'

He shook his head.

'Are you sure? You spread your seed far and wide, from the sounds of it.'

'I'm sure.'

'I couldn't account for four months before you say you stopped drinking,' she added. 'What happened then?'

He stood up so suddenly that she nearly lost balance and toppled off the bed.

'I don't want to talk about that. Do I have to put this smelly stuff on my hands again?'

She held up the phial. 'You should reapply it three or four times a day until you've healed. Definitely after you've played this evening. Or I can do it for you if it's too difficult.'

'I'll do it.' He took the phial. 'Thanks.'

And then he was gone, the door closing firmly behind him, leaving only the scent of old ladies and a little pile of cotton stained with blood.

Still the Palace Hotel, Leeds

Dom went from Sophie's room down to the lobby on a search for coffee, Coke, anything to calm this thirst, though preferably something containing caffeine. He'd had no sleep on the bus, and played Pete's acoustic all the way from Glasgow to Leeds. Once at the hotel he'd tried lying down, but his hands were throbbing and for some reason the fact that Sophie Tennant was in the same hotel had felt like an itch in his brain.

He'd wanted to see her. He wasn't quite sure why. Especially as he'd spent a good deal of the nights before in Edinburgh and Glasgow seeing her: in the guest bar, at the front of the theatre during the gigs. She'd stood out from the crowd in a way that drew his eyes to her, even when he was negotiating a crowd or playing music.

She was different. In a noisy crowd she was quiet, observant, not part of it. She was small and slender and yet strong, and she bit her nails when she thought nobody was watching.

And for some inexplicable reason he'd just spilled out his guts to her. As many as he could spill, anyway.

The lobby had so many houseplants he was surprised

there weren't any monkeys swinging off them. He went to the registration desk, at the far end of the jungle. 'Morning,' he said. 'Can you tell me where I can get a cup of coffee?'

The receptionist pointed through a leaf-festooned archway to the left. 'Our restaurant is through there, Mr Steele.'

He thanked her and followed her finger. So why *had* he spilled out his guts to Sophie? She'd already judged him – more or less correctly. And he didn't care what she thought of him anyway. He didn't care what anyone thought these days.

Max was in the restaurant, at a big round table with Gina, Pete and Mad Dog. It looked as if Mad Dog had eaten his breakfast (or maybe several), but the others had nearly full plates of eggs and bacon in front of them.

There were also copies of several newspapers and magazines on the table. Dom knew the drill. He switched direction and tried to step behind an umbrella plant before they could notice him. If he was lucky, he could catch the eye of a waiter and order coffee to go.

He wasn't lucky. 'Don't go bush on us now, Dom,' Max said and then cackled with his usual laughter.

Dom emerged from the plant and approached the table. 'Reviews?' he asked, unnecessarily.

Pete grunted. Mad Dog piled butter on to a slice of toast. Gina pushed the papers towards him.

'No, I'm fine,' he told her. 'I don't read reviews.'

'Read these,' Pete said. Dom looked at Max and Max shrugged.

He ignored the *Hot! Hot!* magazine and opened the *Melody Express* review of their London show, a couple of paragraphs at the bottom of the gigs page.

About as pointless as a pair of leg warmers . . . nearly

Remember the eighties? Remember hours with crimpers and neon makeup and shoulder pads and when you wanted to annoy your mother you put on a cassette of a hair rock band, like Max DeMilo and the Venusians?

No, I tried to forget it too. Max DeMilo wants us to remember. His gig is a ninety-minute concert of tunes that have dated nearly as much as the band themselves. 'Infamous' is a nice walk through nostalgia, but most of the tracks off the band's new album *Playing the Field* follow exactly the same path. To give the band credit, they prance around the stage as if they're still twentysomething glam rockers, but as for the music, you might as well sit at home and listen to your old cassette.

The only interesting development is the presence of former Dirtysweet frontman Dominick Steele on bass. What is the most self-destructive genius of the past decade doing with a washed-up retro band? And more importantly, what happened to his leather trousers?

Dom snorted and tossed the paper down.

'The *Times* and the *Scotsman* are better,' Gina said.

Max waved his hand. '*Melody Express* never liked us, they said we sold out when we released "Infamous". We were too successful, more like. Anyway, did you dig where they compared us to twentysomething glam rockers?'

'All publicity is good publicity,' Gina said.

Dom looked around for a waiter. 'Coffee, please,' he

mouthed at one who was lurking near a very big aspidistra.

'I thought it was a good photo of the smelly woman,' Mad Dog said through a mouthful of toast.

A quick chain of logic led Dom to pick up the *Hot! Hot!* magazine. In the picture Sophie looked half-shocked, half-knowing, and beautiful.

'You did well out of it,' Pete said to him. 'They mention you in the *Times* and the *Scotsman*, too. By the way, what *is* a self-destructive genius doing with a washed-up retro band?'

His tone was ostensibly friendly, but Dom had heard that subtle bite of sarcasm before. He opened his mouth and wondered how to answer in a way that wouldn't antagonise Pete and would reassure him that Dom had no intention of stealing any of the limelight from the original Venusians. Unfortunately he had very little experience in acting in a way that didn't antagonise people.

'I'm more interested in where your leather trousers are,' Max said before he could answer. 'A good pair of leather trousers is like your best mate; once you've got them worn in, you gotta hold on to them.'

'I think my ex-wife sold them on eBay,' Dom said.

'Coffee, Mr Steele?'

The waiter stood beside him with a pot and a cup. 'Thanks, mate. See you guys later,' Dom said, taking the coffee and escaping back towards his room.

And he'd stay in his room for the rest of the day, until they had to go to the venue for sound check. He'd watch mindless TV, drink coffee, dab this old-lady-smelling shit on his hands, and try not to think about any of his other wounds.

Liverpool
Six Days Later

Liverpool was rainy. Sophie hopped off the Magical Mystery Tour bus at Albert Dock and checked her watch; she had half an hour to get to the George Harrison Memorial Theatre if she was going to be in time to take a look at Max's shoulder before he went on stage.

She pulled her jacket up over her head and looked around for a cab. Not spotting anything besides the big turquoise and yellow bus she'd just disembarked from, she decided that if she hurried, she could just about make it on foot.

She'd never been to Liverpool before – hence the bus tour, since she figured she might as well learn about music while she was working for a band – but she knew that her sense of direction was good enough to get her to the general area of the theatre, and she could find her way from there. She crossed the bustling road that separated the docks from the city proper. She saw several cabs here, but she'd made up her mind to walk, and she ducked down another street in the correct direction.

Although she'd spent the afternoon with a bunch of Japanese tourists visiting Beatles locations, the song that floated through her head was another sixties tune: 'Ferry 'Cross the Mersey', by Gerry and the Pacemakers. It suited the lights of boats on the grey river, the red and grey and cream buildings, the shimmer reflected off the rain. Melancholy and sweet.

Sophie had no memories to relate the music to, but the feeling, the yearning in her chest was almost like nostalgia for something she'd never had.

Though to be fair, it wasn't Liverpool that gave her that feeling; she'd felt it since Saturday morning in the hotel room with Dominick. As if the regret she'd heard in his voice had stirred something in her. Wet, shiny Liverpool was like a grainy photograph with faint figures of musical ghosts. The city only echoed and intensified the feeling.

In her head, Gerry and the Pacemakers sang about people not caring what your name was, because you belonged anyway.

She shoved her hands into the pockets of her coat. She didn't feel bad for Dominick. He'd had a chance to be a good person and instead he'd chosen to be faithless and hurtful. If he regretted it now, that was only as it should be.

No, the reason she was feeling a little melancholy wasn't because on Saturday she'd seen a glimpse that if Dominick had made different choices, he could have been a person she liked. Sophie wasn't someone who ignored reality for daydreams.

It was probably just Liverpool after all.

She reached a corner and without having to think about it turned right. She was in two minds about watching the Venusians' gig tonight. On the one hand, the gigs were pretty fun. She particularly liked seeing Max on stage. He jumped around, wiggling his hips and tossing his head and generally looking like a cross between Mick Jagger and Stephen Tyler from Aerosmith with something extra, purely charming Max, added in. The man didn't have a single iota of self-consciousness. She liked watching Pete plying his guitar and the grey-haired whirlwind that was Mad Dog, too. And the crew, who were all insults on the bus, worked smoothly together. Every part, band and crew and music, meshed together to create something whole.

She also felt, rightly or wrongly, that part of her job as a member of the tour was to support the band when they performed. She hadn't been able to resist reading the reviews, and she felt the band deserved her loyalty even more because the press was giving them a bit of a roasting.

The music wasn't her type of thing, but it wasn't bad. There was a tune and everything, though it was pretty loud. When Max and Pete and Mad Dog got going, they had an enjoyment in what they were doing that infected the crowd, even if the songs did sound similar.

Although she'd noticed that the new songs heavily featured lyrics about gambolling in the fields. She wasn't quite sure what was up with that.

On the other hand, there was Dominick. Because when she watched the band, she was really watching him. It happened every night.

Then again, what was she going to do if she didn't go to the gig? Sit in her hotel room trying to resist looking at more pictures of Dominick on the internet? Wondering what had happened during those missing four months that he refused to talk about?

The next corner brought her to within sight of the theatre. The band's tour bus was parked in front of it. She slowed her pace, wanting to make up her mind before she saw the band. If she decided not to go, she'd need a good excuse. Maybe she could say she had a cold, or she had to research a new oil combination, or—

In front of her, a parked car roared into life. The headlights glared into her eyes and the car leapt forward, engine revving and tyres squealing, directly at Sophie.

'Hey!' she yelled to warn the driver in the split second before she realised that the driver meant to hit her. She flung herself sideways, on to the pavement, slipped in a puddle and fell against the wall of the building. Her shoulder screamed with pain but she scrambled to her feet and pressed herself against the wall as the car mounted the pavement and rushed at her.

It missed her by inches. She felt the heat of its exhaust and breathed petrol fumes. She pushed off from the wall and ran after the car, a silver Honda SUV. Its rear number plate had been removed.

'What the hell are you doing?' she screamed at it, and it stopped with a jolt of brakes. Instinct told her to stop too; the driver could be anyone, could have any sort of weapon in addition to the car. Bloody-mindedness told her to keep running after it.

Then the car's white reverse lights came on, and it sped, full-throttle, backwards at her.

Forget bloody-mindedness. Sophie turned and ran, as fast as she could, for the cover of the parked cars in front of the theatre, the roar of the SUV's engine in her ears. She jumped on to the boot of a Ford Ka and climbed over the windscreen, fingers slipping, trainers sliding on the wet surface. The SUV struck the Ka full force and she was flung off, tumbling on to the pavement and landing on her back with a woof of air from her lungs.

She heard the SUV moving, gathering space and

momentum for another strike. All she saw were spots of light. She forced herself to her feet, her head swimming, and ran, hoping she wasn't putting herself in the path of the car.

Sophie struck something hard and warm: a wall . . . no, a man, whose arms went around her and held her so tight she couldn't move. It was the driver, the person who was trying to kill her. She tried to suck in air for a scream and pushed, as hard as she could, against his chest.

'What's going on?' he said, and her head swam in one more dizzy circle before she realised the man who was holding her was Dominick.

'Somebody . . .' She craned her neck and saw the SUV speeding down the narrow road. It skidded around a corner and out of sight.

She struggled against him, but his arms didn't budge. 'Let me go, I have to find out who it was!'

'You're planning on catching a speeding car on foot?'

Good point. 'I might be able to find a witness.'

'Hold on. You're soaking wet and gasping for breath. Are you all right?'

'Fine. Let me go!'

'Not until I know you're okay. Your shirt is torn. What happened?' One of his arms held her close to his chest, but his other hand travelled gently over her back.

'It's not the time for you to go all manly, I need to— Ow!' She flinched away from his hand touching her shoulder.

'You're hurt and you're not going anywhere, especially as you're never going to catch that car. What was it, a drunk driver? Did he nick you on his way by?'

'He tried to do more than nick me.' She dragged in a deep breath, smelling tea tree, lavender and Dominick Steele. Breathing hurt her back and her shoulder and her head. 'I think he was trying to kill me.'

'Then you're definitely not going after that car. What if they're around the corner waiting for you?'

'But the witnesses . . .'

'After we make sure you're all right, I'll go with you to look for them.'

He was as bloody-minded as she was. She gave up.

'Bastard tried to run me down,' she said, 'and then when he missed he backed up and tried again. Smashed into that Ford.'

She felt his head turning to check out the Ka, and he sucked in a breath. 'Shit. They weren't joking.'

'No. You can let me go now, I won't run.'

He loosened his arms around her and she stepped away from him, only realising how much he'd been supporting her now that he wasn't.

She swayed and he caught her and gathered her up to him again. 'Right, we're going on to the bus,' he said, and steered her there, half-carrying her up the steps.

He was very tall. She gripped on to his shoulder to keep her balance and felt the sinew and muscle under her hand. He got her on to the bus and up the few steps to the front lounge, where she sank on to an upholstered L-shaped bench seat. Dominick bent down, took her feet, and swung them up to rest on the seat so she was half-reclining.

'Where are you hurt?' he asked.

'I hit the wall with my shoulder.' She felt it with her hand: it was sore, but not dislocated. Bruised was all. 'And when the SUV hit the Ka it tossed me on my back on the pavement.' She touched the back of her head and winced.

Dominick moved so he was sitting on the other arm of the L, behind her. He lifted her ponytail, made a sound of frustration and gently pulled the elastic out of her hair so it was loose. Then he parted it and she could feel him examining her scalp. The sensation of his eyes and his bandaged fingertips on her made her shiver.

'You've got a little cut and a big lump,' he said. 'Let's see your back.'

'No need.'

'You saw me topless, Sophie. It's only fair.'

'Oh for God's sake.' She pulled up the back of her shirt with her good arm. *Good thing I'm wearing a decent bra*, she thought, and then frowned at herself.

'You've got some scrapes. Hold on a second.'

He got up, switched on the kettle in the little kitchen area, and disappeared towards the back of the bus. Sophie pulled her knees to her chest, rested her head on them, and tried to slow down her heart rate. When she closed her eyes all she could see was the SUV stopping and then deliberately reversing towards her.

She opened her eyes and looked around the bus. The band bus had a slightly different layout from the crew one, but it was just as cramped and was upholstered in the same blue and black. If someone put up some chintz curtains and started a jigsaw puzzle on the table, it would look like the interior of a caravan.

The main difference from Sophie's bus was that someone had pinned up a *Smash Hits* magazine centrefold from the eighties, featuring Max, over the tiny sink. Eighties Max had a black marker moustache, devil horns, and fangs drawn on him. It also smelled different: instead of smelling mostly of socks, it smelled of Max's massage oil, with a little bit of sock thrown in.

She heard Dominick coming back to her. 'Where are the rest of the band?' she asked before she could see him. It seemed important to know this before she pulled up her shirt again.

Also because it would be useful to know where they were in case the person trying to kill her came back and tried to get on the bus. She bit her fingernail and tasted mud.

'They're out at a pub having a quick pint before the show.' He slid back on to the seat behind her.

'Why aren't you with them?'

'Besides the obvious?'

'You don't have to drink just because you're in a pub. I don't usually.' She risked a glance backwards at him. He was wearing his indigo jeans and a navy blue shirt, which had a large dark wet patch on the front of it. For the first time she realised her own clothes were soaked, especially down her back. She shivered.

Dominick handed her a blanket, which she recognised as coming from one of the bunks. 'They like to reminisce,' he said, 'and I think they need to bond.'

'Didn't like the reviews, huh?'

'Reviews aren't worth reading.'

'Especially when they're more interested in the bass-player than the original band?'

'This might sting.'

She felt a wet, warm cloth on the back of her head, and it did sting. She gritted her teeth.

'And this might make you smell like an old lady.'

She heard a phial being unscrewed and smelt tea tree and lavender. 'I made that for your hands.'

'Yeah, that's how I know it works.' She felt him dabbing it on her scalp.

'That stings, too.'

'You know, it's true what they say about revenge being sweet. Pull up your shirt again.'

She'd done it once; she figured she might as well do it

again. 'Revenge for me hurting your hands, or revenge for me honey-trapping you?'

'It depends how much this stings, I guess.' He began dabbing it on. 'Anyway, I feel better about the honey-trapping now that I know you really do want to have sex with me.'

'I don't— Ow!'

'See, that's what happens to liars. Take it from someone with a lot of experience. So who wanted to kill you?'

'I didn't recognise the car. Its number plates were removed, too.'

'Did you see anyone behind the wheel?'

'Too dark, and the headlights were on bright.'

He applied the oil to her back. She had to give him credit: he was a scumbag who was making far too much of the concept that she might fancy him a tiny little bit, but at least he wasn't trying it on. His touches were the minimum required to sanitise her wounds.

And they were enough to make her want to squirm.

'All done,' he said, and she pulled her top down. Because it was wet and because of his hands, she'd actually been warmer with it up around her neck. She flipped the blanket over her shoulders.

Dominick got up and found a mug in the little cupboard. 'Who would want to kill you?' he asked, dropping a tea bag and two spoonfuls of sugar into it.

Typical man, not even asking her if she wanted a cup of tea so she could have the satisfaction of telling him no.

'I don't know,' she said.

'There are that many, huh?'

'Nobody's ever tried before.' She considered. 'Well, not out of nowhere. I've been attacked, but that was usually in the heat of the moment.'

Dominick shook his head. 'You just bring sweetness and light everywhere you go, don't you?' He brought the cup of tea over to the bench and put it down in front of her on the table.

'I don't want a cup of tea,' she said.

'You've had a shock and you should have one. Come on, you're testing my first-aid abilities to their limit. Don't make me feel unappreciated.'

Why did he have to have that blinding smile? Sophie took a sip and grimaced. 'I don't like sweet tea.'

'It's what you have for shock. Drink up.'

'I'm not shocked, I'm angry.' But she drank the tea anyway and it did make her feel better.

Dominick was shaking his head at her again. 'It's incredible. You have no fear at all.'

Oh no, there you're wrong, she opened her mouth to say, but then she closed it again.

'Stop being nice to me,' she said instead. 'I don't buy it.'

He stood up. 'Okay, don't. Fine with me. Are we going to look for witnesses, or what?'

The bus door hissed open and Max's head poked through.

'Dominick Steele, Gina says to get your arse into that theatre right now or she's going to have your balls for a handbag, and I don't fancy the chances of mine getting through intact, either.'

'Shit, is it . . .' Dominick checked the clock on the microwave. 'Right, we don't have time to look for witnesses; the gig was supposed to start ten minutes ago. Anybody who was there is probably long gone anyway. Come on.'

'Witnesses?' Max asked. 'What have you two been up to?'

Sophie stood and brushed down her damp clothes. 'It

was nothing,' she said to Max, and then to Dominick, 'I'll look by myself.'

'No you won't. You're coming into the theatre with us and staying there where we can see you. And before you say anything, I'm not being kind, I'm protecting myself from feeling guilty if you get yourself killed. I've got enough on my conscience.'

'Get yourself killed?' Max stepped into the bus, hugely interested.

'If someone's out to get me, they're just as likely to go into the theatre after me as to lurk out in the streets.'

'And if they tried to run you down, they probably didn't want to be seen. I don't think they're going to try anything in a room full of witnesses.'

Sophie crossed her arms. 'Who's the professional here?'

'According to you, neither of us any more. Come on, I've got to go on stage. And before you try anything, yes, I will carry you if I need to.'

'Do the two of you know that you sound just like a TV show?' Max asked.

Sophie looked from Dominick to Max, her jaw set.

'Look,' Dominick conceded, 'it isn't very rock 'n' roll to suggest it, but I'll risk my balls to delay the show for ten more minutes while you call the police.'

'I don't need to—' Sophie began, and then she saw the blue flashing lights through the window of the bus. 'Well, that solves that,' she said to Dominick. 'Go on stage before Gina gets a very ugly handbag.'

15

The George Harrison Memorial Theatre, Liverpool

Sophie shook hands with the policeman. 'We'll be in touch,' he told her as he got into his patrol car.

She went back to the crew bus to change her clothes. She didn't expect the police to come up with much, as there wasn't much to go on. Rummaging in her valise, she found some muscle-healing eucalyptus globulus and breathed deeply, but her shoulder still protested when she lifted off her shirt and pulled on another, so she swallowed two ibuprofen from her secret stash. She tucked a packet into her jacket pocket in case.

The police were a little like aromatherapy, she thought as she slipped on a pair of flats and made her way to the box office to collect her Access All Areas pass. They seemed to work well enough for most people but not particularly for her. Because they were tied up with paperwork, constrained by too little time and too much crime, she'd found that they couldn't usually discover specific information as quickly as she could as an independent private investigator. She and Raj used to talk about it quite a bit. Back when they used to talk.

Then again, the police didn't have to spend a good proportion of their Friday nights dressed up like a tart trying to get men to snog them. They got to try to solve real mysteries, the sort of thing Sophie had hoped would come her way when she'd set up as an investigator in the first place.

And now she had a real mystery, though not precisely in the way she'd have chosen. For the dozenth time she tried to remember any details of the driver of the SUV – height, build, anything – but all she could picture were the glaring headlights and the growling engine. Perhaps the windows had been tinted, though she couldn't swear to that, either.

Navigating the corridor to the backstage area, she shook her head, and when that sent pain shooting through it, she swallowed another ibuprofen without water. Some witness she was. She'd trained herself for years, and when it mattered she hadn't noticed a single thing.

The steady rhythm of Dominick's bass guitar pounded through the walls, overlaid by the more complicated rhythm of acoustic guitar and drums. From here, the higher notes and finer details were muffled out by the building. She didn't know all the songs well enough yet to identify this one, from only the lower notes, but she did notice another beat, a quieter one out of time with the others.

When she rounded the corner she saw it was Gina, standing in the corridor banging on the wall with her fists.

Sophie stopped at the same time that Gina became aware of her presence and dropped her hands. The manager straightened up quickly.

'Sorry,' she said in the way that Sophie had noticed people often did when they were caught doing something embarrassing but for which they had no need to apologise. She tidied her already tidy hair and smoothed her ironed designer blouse.

'No, I'm sorry for interrupting,' replied Sophie. 'Are you all right?'

'Fine. Just letting out stress. Are you on your way backstage?'

Sophie nodded. They walked together for a moment as Sophie wondered whether Gina was the type who needed to be asked what was the matter, of if she was the type who talked better if she wasn't asked.

About forty seconds of silence told her the answer. 'You've read the reviews?' Gina asked her, stopping.

Sophie nodded again, relieved that it wasn't about Gina and Max. She liked Max and didn't want to know anything sordid about his life. His random stories didn't count.

'The reviews are shit,' Gina continued, 'utter shit, and I should have done better. I didn't know the London show was the same night as an England game when I booked it, and I made up for it in Edinburgh a bit, but then we'd lost momentum and we haven't gained it back. Pete says I don't know music and he's right. I mean, what in the world is a spinal tap?'

'Do you mean the surgical procedure or the film?'

'I have no idea. And Max is the kind of person who takes anyone on; he always feels he can help no matter whether it's good business or not. I mean, no offence to you, but look at how you came on board on a whim, and you're the least of our worries.'

She means Dominick, Sophie thought, and her stomach twisted in that way it did when she was hearing something unwanted. Though of course this wasn't a surprise, and she wasn't sure why it was unwanted.

Gina sighed. 'This tour is so important. I need it to go well because my other main client, a professional psych— I mean, performer, has had a shift in career. And Max has sunk huge amounts of his own money into this.'

Whoops. And he probably didn't need his aroma-therapist narrowly escaping death in front of the theatre where he was performing. Sophie had better solve this case, quick.

'It will be fine,' she told Gina.

'I don't even know why I'm telling you this,' Gina said. 'I'm not the type to spill my secrets to strangers.' She tidied her clothes and hair again, and Sophie could see she was even more embarrassed. 'Please don't talk about our conversation.'

'Don't worry,' said Sophie, 'I'm very good at keeping secrets.'

Dominick stepped up to the mic for the final chorus and sang in harmony:

'Eyes of fire, in the grass so deep
Roll up your woolly head and go to sleep.'

What the hell was this song about anyway? Dominick wasn't one to read into lyrics – he'd had enough people trying to dissect his own and coming up with all sorts of psychological rubbish – but he'd been singing Max's new songs for a few weeks now and he was really starting to wonder about some of them.

'Eyes of Fire' was almost like a lullaby (except of course for the screaming guitars). Dom watched Max as he finished off the song: he was hanging on to the mic stand, singing his heart out, his eyes closed with the hint of a tear coming out of one of them. It was personal all right.

And yet his girlfriend was Gina, she of the designer

suits, the perfect hair, the flawless posture. Someone further from woolly-headed he could not possibly imagine. Though you had to make allowances for love, he supposed.

And none of this speculation was distracting him one bit from the fact that Sophie hadn't turned up in the theatre yet.

The song ended, the audience applauded, and Dom visually swept the theatre once again. It was a lot more crowded than their previous shows, but Sophie wasn't there.

There were three songs left in this set and Dominick wasn't going to get off the stage to look for Sophie, because that would be career suicide, once again. She was stubborn and she'd probably gone off to find witnesses and if she ran into the person who was trying to kill her that was her own damn fault. He owed her nothing except for a bit of healing salve, which he'd given back to her anyway. He certainly didn't owe her for making a humiliating tape of him trying to get her to have sex with him five years ago.

He gritted his teeth. Why couldn't she do what she was told?

'One, two, three, four,' Max counted, and they launched into the next song, 'Baby, You're Hot.' At least Dom didn't have to wonder what this song was about.

She'd trembled in his arms, running away from death. And hell, he'd stormed off stage mid-gig for much worse reasons; why break the habit of a lifetime just because this was his last chance?

Dominick shrugged his guitar strap off his shoulder. Out of the corner of his eye he saw Max turn around from the mic to see why he'd stopped playing, but before either of them could take a step, Gina and Sophie had appeared in the wings by the side of the stage.

Sophie was wearing different clothes and carrying her valise; obviously the infuriating woman had gone to change and get her stuff before she'd bothered to come to the theatre and let him know that she was still alive. Knowing her, she'd probably taken her time to prove a point.

Dom reshouldered his guitar and picked up the beat. He shrugged and smiled at Max, who'd continued singing uninterrupted about the hot chick in the high heels and miniskirt. A verse that always brought one picture to Dominick's mind: Sophie Tennant, hot little honey-trapper, in her temptation-short skirt and bare legs, five years ago.

He glanced over at her again. She wore black trousers and flat shoes, but her legs were probably the same underneath. Smooth and firm and strong around his hips.

And the hard-on he was getting beneath his bass guitar was not caused merely by relief that she was still alive.

He concentrated on the bass line. Two and a half songs until the set ended, and he could haul her sexy little annoying body somewhere he could have a good yell at her for making him crazy with worry.

It would be the night Max decided to do two encores rather than one, ending the set with a speeded-up, rocked-out version of George Harrison's 'My Sweet Lord' that the band had played with on the bus the night before. The applause was louder than it had ever been so far, and the rest of the band came off stage flushed with success and pleasure.

Dom came off angry. 'Where the hell were you?' he demanded of Sophie as soon as he reached her.

Predictably, she lifted her chin and gave him a scornful look.

'I liked the Beatles song,' Gina told Max, kissing him.

'It's not a Beatles song, it's off George Harrison's first solo album,' Pete said.

'Why'd you take so long getting here?' Dom asked Sophie again.

Pete, walking by them, raised an eyebrow. Dom saw Sophie notice it and then turn back to Max, deliberately ignoring him.

'How's the shoulder?'

'Aching,' Max said cheerfully, 'and I think I've convinced Mad Dog to give your healing powers a try, too. He's got a touch of RSI from rocking too hard.'

Mad Dog rubbed his wrist. 'Gettin' old,' he said ruefully.

Gettin' frustrated, Dominick thought, picturing another hour sitting in the dressing room waiting for Sophie to be done with work. He took a moment to salute the photograph of George Harrison that was posted in a prominent spot between the stage and the dressing room. Then he heaved a deep breath for patience, borrowed Pete's acoustic again, and stationed himself on the couch to wait it out.

Pete sat beside him. 'What did she do to piss you off?' he asked in a quiet voice, nodding his head towards where Sophie was setting up her gear.

'I was worried about Mad Dog's RSI,' Dom said. 'Thought the man needed help as soon as possible.'

Mad Dog had set up a selection of mugs and plastic glasses on a table and was testing each of them for sound with a drumstick. He listened carefully to the tone of a Mickey Mouse mug, shook his head, and poured some of his lager into it before tapping it again.

'Yeah, I can see what you mean,' said Pete.

Dom smiled at him, glad that some of the tension he'd felt before seemed to have leached away. Pete leaned closer.

'Dempsey the monitor guy fancies her like crazy,' he said. 'He's trying to get up the guts to ask her out. I said I thought there was something going on between the two of you, though.'

Dom could practically sense Sophie's ears perking up. How did she do that – know when someone was whispering about her? And how did he know she knew?

'I've had my fingers burned with women way too many times, mate,' he said.

'Yeah, but this one can heal them up again.' Pete indicated Dom's bandaged fingers.

'I love the action on this guitar,' Dom said, picking out a wandering tune in D minor. 'I've got a sixty-two Gibson Hummingbird in storage but it doesn't feel anything like this. What have you done to it?'

That was the ticket. Pete launched into a discussion of fret fileage which was nearly interesting enough to keep Dominick from watching every single little thing that Sophie did with her hands and the way her body moved stiffly when she bent down to get another phial of oil.

Until Max started to ask questions, in his usual subtle way.

'So who's out to kill you, Soph?'

Mad Dog stopped tapping, Pete stopped talking mid-debate about the difference between a Gibson and a Martin acoustic, and even Gina stopped punching buttons on her palm organiser.

Sophie kept on using a circular motion on Max's shoulder. 'Oh, I think we were overreacting earlier, Max.'

'Hey, having somebody out to kill you isn't anything to

be ashamed of,' Max said. 'Did I ever tell you about this stalker I had back in eighty-eight? She used to write me letters, all about this fantasy life she was leading where she and I were engaged to be married to each other. Never met her in my life; the woman was mad as a fish brush. Anyway, I wrote her back, sent her a signed photo, and told her I was sorry but we weren't really engaged, and the next thing I know I'm walking to the tour bus and there's this crazy little woman waving a kitchen knife at me. Got me, too. Eight stitches.' He pointed to his left forearm and a well-healed white scar. 'Turned out she tried the same thing on Simon Le Bon, but she didn't end up stabbing him. Trust me to get the world's only unfaithful stalker.'

'Who's trying to kill you?' Pete asked Sophie.

'Nobody. I nearly got in the way of a drunk bloke having a car accident,' Sophie said. She glanced over at Dom and he could see it clear as day in her eyes: *Don't tell them.*

He frowned at her, and then looked at Max, Pete and Mad Dog meaningfully. If someone was trying to kill her, that could possibly endanger the band, too. She tightened her lips and shook her head the slightest bit.

Dom tightened his fingers on the neck of the guitar and his chord turned sour.

'Oh my God,' Gina said. 'Did they hit you?'

'No,' Sophie said, shaking her head more vigorously. 'Not even close.'

She winced, obviously in pain from the lump on the back of her head, and probably her shoulder, too. But she turned and pretended to be paying attention to her oils.

'Come on, Mad Dog,' she said, 'Juniper, black pepper and eucalyptus for your wrists. Muscle-healing and relaxation.'

'Wicked, a sneezy drunk koala bear,' said Mad Dog, and

presented his wrists to her. The aroma that filled the room was a cross between a nasal inhalant and a shot of clear gin. It smelled vaguely familiar, which shouldn't be surprising given the lengths to which Dom had gone to get drunk in the past.

He could see that every movement hurt Sophie. It was equally clear that she was trying to hide her own discomfort while she concentrated on alleviating that of others.

'You should have heard Soph and Dom in the bus after it happened,' Max said. 'Sounded just like an episode of *The Bill*. And cops all over the place outside; did you lot hear about that?'

'That's why you were late?' Gina asked Dom.

'They take drunk drivers very seriously in Liverpool,' Sophie said quickly.

'Don't I know it,' Max said. 'You remember that taxi-driver, Mad Dog? The one who reeked of Special Brew and who drove us straight into that brick wall? We saw a few coppers that night. Though come to think of it, I think that was in Blackpool.'

'Swindon,' said Mad Dog.

'For two people who have nothing going on with each other, you and Sophie seem to be spending a lot of time together,' said Pete to Dom. 'Should I tell Dempsey not to bother?'

'Dempsey can bother all he likes,' said Dominick. And Pete was full of shit; he'd seen Dempsey with Sophie and the monitor guy didn't seem the slightest bit interested.

He went back to playing the acoustic and studiously avoided looking or listening in Sophie's direction until Mad Dog said, 'Wow, that's better. Ta, Soph. Anybody fancy a quick pint before we shove off to Manchester?'

'Come on, Dom, the OJ's on me,' said Max.

'Thanks, but I think Sophie needs to work her magic on these fingers for a few minutes first,' Dom said, wiggling his remaining bandages. 'Go on ahead, I'll meet you.'

'Owe you one too, Soph, for my shoulder,' said Max, slipping his arm around Gina, and the rest of them left the dressing room.

Dominick waited until he was sure they were well out of hearing range before he stood up and put the acoustic aside. It was a tidy instrument; he didn't want to be tempted to take out his anger on it.

'I don't like this at all,' he said. 'It's one thing not to mention your past, but this is something that could be dangerous.'

Sophie straightened up. 'It's not dangerous.'

'Bull. Look at you, you're in pain.'

She crossed her arms on her chest and lifted her chin. She only came up to about his neck but she had the stance of a warrior. 'I'm fine.'

'I treated your injuries with my own hands, Sophie.'

'I've had worse.'

The woman was impossible. 'Have it your way. I'm also talking about the band. They deserve to know if a mental killer is after you, because sooner or later they're going to be affected by it.'

'No, they're not.'

He exhaled sharply. 'I know what Max is like. His stalker story was meant to make you feel better about your life being at risk, because that's the sort of kind, generous and fundamentally foolish person that he is. But I'm not as kind as Max. I don't mind getting you fired from your job if it means that the band get to stay alive.'

'Go right ahead and tell them, then. But we both know

what Max is like, and he's not the type to kick someone out on the street when they've had their life threatened.'

Dammit, she was right. Max was more likely to do something like hire a down-on-his-luck bodyguard for Sophie and keep her on the tour.

'Telling them will only freak them out, Dominick,' Sophie continued. 'And they've got enough on their plate as it is. I'll find out who's after me, and it will all be over, nothing to worry about. Now, do you really need your fingers seen to?'

'No, I don't.'

She turned away from him and finished packing away her equipment.

'There's one thing that I don't understand,' she said as she worked. 'I know why *I'm* angry; someone tried to kill me. But beyond the fact that you were there right after it happened, it doesn't have anything to do with you. Why are *you* angry?'

'Because . . .' he began, and then she turned around again and faced him, her grey eyes inquisitive and steady, and the answer that he'd been about to give derailed itself and a whole different answer took its place.

'Because I haven't been remotely attracted to a woman since I gave up drinking, and that's the way I like it, so why am I attracted to you?'

Her eyes widened. But he'd started now and he couldn't stop.

'I was drunk when I first met you,' he said. 'Not very drunk, but drunk enough, and picking up women was what I did. You shouldn't be different to anybody else I've ever met. And yet it's five years later and I don't want to be that person I used to be, and I still want you anyway. I crave you like a drink.'

She opened her mouth, that soft, pink, stubborn mouth, as if she were going to answer, but he saw the breath catch in her throat.

Knowing that he'd caught her speechless made him want her even more.

'Why is that, Sophie Dean? What is it about you? Or is it me, proving I can never change?'

'I . . . don't know,' she said, and her voice was so damn unsure, the turned-on act that wasn't an act at all.

'I need to know,' he told her, and he closed the distance between them and brought his mouth down on hers.

Five years ago, on a deserted bridge on the Thames, in the moonlight, with the echoes of a Louis Armstrong song in their heads. He couldn't have believed he would remember it so perfectly but he did, because she tasted exactly the same. Her lips were soft and slightly cool and he heard the hint of a startled moan in her throat.

She'd slap him now.

But she didn't. She opened her mouth for him, not much, but enough to be an invitation, and he touched the inside of her top lip with his tongue. Warm in there. His body hardened instantly. When she met his tongue with her own he felt a steel bolt of desire so strong it hurt and he gasped out a ragged groan.

The sound of his own voice in his ears made him realise he was holding Sophie, one hand around her waist, the other tight on her bruised back. He raised his head, and the flush on her cheeks, the desire in her eyes, even the pain, made him want to sink right back into her again.

Instead he let her go, and God, being without her was like reaching for a shot of whisky and finding out that it was cold weak tea.

'That's the answer,' he said. His voice was rough. 'I haven't changed at all.'

He left the dressing room. Then of course had to turn around and come back when he remembered he'd left Pete's guitar, but by then Sophie was gone too.

16

Somewhere by the Side of a Road in Wales

'What do you mean, he got away?'

One of Sophie's fists tightened on her mobile and the other banged on the shiny, dusty top of the crew bus, where she was sitting because that was the only place she could get a bit of reception. Even so, her connection was bad, and Raj Criss sounded much farther away than Reading.

'Martin didn't show up for his meeting with his probation officer,' Raj said, 'and when we went round to see him, he'd done a runner. The landlady says she hasn't seen him for nearly a week. It's probably nothing, but I thought you should know.'

Sophie stared at the seemingly endless array of trees and blue mountains around her and thought about Keith Martin, short man, drink-spiker and would-be rapist. 'Thank you, Raj.'

'I expected you to tell me to stop the overprotective male chauvinist pig act.'

He said it lightly, but Sophie bit her lip. Had it really

been over a year since their last conversation? 'No, I really appreciate it. Any idea of where he's gone?'

'No, but apparently he's still got his charm with the ladies. His girlfriend disappeared with him. We've had her dad in here demanding we find her.'

'Catherine Birkbeck?'

'Chantal Smith. She works in Glamour Nails in Friar Street.'

'Right.' Sophie typed the name into her laptop, perched beside her on the roof. 'Um, listen, Raj. I really meant to call you, but . . .' She stopped. 'Well, actually I don't have any excuse. I should have called you.'

'You were under a lot of stress.'

Sophie half smiled at that typical kindness. 'You should be yelling at me.'

'The chemistry wasn't there. I was angry at the time. I'm not now.' He drew a breath. 'Are you enjoying the rock 'n' roll lifestyle?'

'How do you . . .'

'Jane is a *Hot! Hot!* addict.'

And Sophie knew one reason why Raj wasn't angry any more. 'Ah.'

'You do realise that the tour schedule is advertised all over the place? Anyone who wants to find you knows exactly where you are.'

'It had crossed my mind,' she said. Actually, it had lodged firmly in the centre of her mind. But Raj didn't need to know about the killer SUV. He'd moved on.

'Just be careful, that's all. If you don't mind me saying.'

'I don't mind you saying it at all. Bye, Raj.'

After scanning the trees and mountains again, she

leaned to look over the side of the bus. Lucky, the driver, stood several metres away smoking a cigarette. He spotted her and ambled over.

'Done with your call?' he asked.

'I've got one or two more to make.'

'Want a cup of tea?'

'I'm all right, thanks.'

He smiled a broken-toothed smile at her. 'Nice of you to stick around here instead of pissing off with the rest of the crew.'

'No problem.'

'Do you think the guys were angry?'

Sophie thought back to the moment she and the rest of the crew had awoken to a horrible grinding engine noise, a hiss, and then a complete cessation of movement. They'd all stumbled out of their bunks to discover two things: that the bus's engine had packed in, and that because Lucky had decided it would be quicker to take his own route through Wales to Swansea rather than following the band bus down the motorway, they were now stranded on the side of a B road surrounded by mountains with unpronounceable names.

Or at least more unpronounceable than the names the crew were calling Lucky, which tended to be of two blunt Anglo-Saxon syllables.

As soon as the sun rose, Bob, Dempsey, Owen and Griffin had flagged down a lorry and asked the driver to take them to the nearest town with a café and a pub. They'd gone off still grumbling, Owen in Welsh.

'I'm sure they'll get over it,' Sophie told Lucky. She'd chosen to remain with the bus until a mechanic or a new bus arrived, though not to keep Lucky company.

'Well, I'm glad you stayed anyway.' Lucky grinned

again. 'I wouldn't want to think that Max's crew all hated me. I owe Max for this job.'

Here was another lame duck taken on by Max.

'Thank you,' she said. 'I'd better get on with my phone calls.'

He nodded and wandered off again, lighting another cigarette.

Of course, here on the top of the bus she was pretty much a target for anybody with any sort of projectile weapon. It was still preferable to being in the same city with Dominick Steele.

Sophie Dean, he'd called her. He'd remembered that conversation they'd had, five years ago, when she'd been lying and he'd been drunk.

The name had been even more intimate than their kiss.

She rubbed her lips together to banish the feeling of his mouth on hers, and looked up another phone number on her laptop.

Her call was picked up on the second ring. 'Piers Birkbeck.'

'Mr Birkbeck, this is Sophie Tennant. I don't know if you—'

'The private detective who saved my Catherine from marrying that Martin man, yes. What can I do for you, Miss Tennant?'

'Actually I was wondering if I would be able to speak with your daughter, Mr Birkbeck.'

'May I ask why?'

'I wanted to ask her if she's had any contact with Keith Martin.'

'She hasn't. Why would she be in contact with that criminal?'

'Good point, sir. I'd like to talk with her, though, to

find out if Martin has tried to get in touch with her.'

Birkbeck paused, and then he gave Sophie a telephone number. 'You won't be able to reach her on it, though, because she's on holiday.'

'Anywhere nice?'

'Yes. Now, if you'll excuse me, Miss Tennant, I need to get back to work. Goodbye.' He hung up, and Sophie felt, again, like the hired help. But at least she had Catherine's number.

She tried it and got the answering machine. 'Miss Birkbeck, it's Sophie Tennant, I wonder if you can give me a ring as soon as you get this. It's rather urgent.' Midway through leaving her number, she saw a movement in the bushes about three hundred metres from the bus.

She finished reciting the number, and then ended the call without taking her mobile from her face. 'Oh yes,' she said, turning her head so that she could watch the bushes without seeming to, 'I'm on tour with a rock band. You might have heard of them: Max DeMilo and the Venusians? You're right, that is pretty cool.'

She pretended to listen. The movement had stopped, the leaves on the bush only trembling at the ends. She kept talking, watching hard, not really thinking about her words.

'No, no, I don't know about that. I mean, he says he hasn't been attracted to a woman since he stopped drinking, and that's the biggest load of rubbish I've ever heard. The man thinks he's God's gift, he even kisses like a . . .'

Whatever, or whoever, was in the bushes was moving towards the bus. The movements were hesitant, as if the person were trying to sneak.

'An angel,' she said, her voice lower so she could listen for any tell-tale noises of a cocking gun, but keeping talking so she could maintain the charade of not paying attention, heart rate up, senses heightened, 'and I couldn't help kissing him back. God, talk about chemistry, it's like a nuclear reaction, but what if he's . . .'

The bushes suddenly began to tremble violently and Sophie tensed, ready to duck or to jump off the top of the bus, needing to see who it was. Her phone dropped and clattered on the metal roof.

A deer stepped out of the woods. It directed its soft gaze at Sophie, stock-still, staring, and then Lucky's voice cried, 'Hey, look, a deer!'

It turned on its splinter-thin legs and bounded back into the forest.

'Drat.' Sophie sank down on the roof, staring at the place where the deer had disappeared.

And thinking about what she had been about to say in her pretend phone conversation with herself, when her heart had sped up, her palms become slick with fear.

What if he's telling the truth and I really am the only one?

Sophie lay down on the bus and stared up at the blue sky above her, studded with clouds.

This was crazy. Someone was out to kill her, and all she could think about was Dominick.

She hadn't had a whole lot of kisses lately, maybe that was why. She couldn't count the clumsy attempted snogs during her honey-trap ventures. When you were an investigator you seemed to spend a disproportionate amount of time with dodgy geezers and shifty cheaters. It wasn't exactly a dating pool. Raj was the last person she'd kissed properly. And then since she'd quit, she'd been working too hard training to be an aromatherapist, moving to Stoneguard, starting up her own business, to even look twice at men.

But surely there had to be somebody else who kissed like Dominick Steele. She'd had boyfriends. She'd had sex. Not recently, granted. Not recently at all. In fact . . .

She frowned at the sky. Had she really not had sex since before honey-trapping Dominick Steele? For *five years*?

Right. This was ridiculous. Sophie rolled over on to her front and retrieved her phone. She had more people to call; for example, she should try to find out if Sally Hershey had left Stoneguard recently and what kind of car she drove. Chucking a brick through a window wasn't as drastic as trying to run somebody down, but Sophie had met dangerous bimbos before. Bunny Lawless, for instance, whom she'd done a security check on for a client, before discovering that she had a reputation for slashing the face of anybody who looked at her (current) man. Hit and run wasn't her MO either, but Sophie made a note to see what she'd been up to anyway. Oh, and Vic Viger, who'd attacked her in that car park three years ago for daring to point a camera in his direction.

Come to think about it, she should check out Leonie Steele, too. That *Hot! Hot!* photograph was a pretty good excuse for attempted murder.

Here was another legacy of her job. Sniffing out dirty little secrets didn't get you boyfriends, and it didn't make you friends, either. It got you lists of enemies and it got you kissed by the one man you shouldn't have anything to do with.

She banged her forehead against the top of the bus and groaned. Then she heard an engine approaching and looked up: in the distance, a big shiny blue and silver tour bus, the exact twin of the one she was lying on.

'Hey, Sophie!' Lucky came running up. 'It's the new bus! We should be in Swansea in an hour! Did you see that deer?'

Swansea, and Dominick Steele. Salvation had never looked quite so much like trouble.

17

Various Places Along the M4

Surprisingly, however, Dominick was very easy to avoid. She saw him only from a distance in the hotel in Swansea, and in Cardiff, and Bristol, and Bath, and Swindon. The only time she saw him properly was on stage and after the shows, when she worked on Max's shoulder and Mad Dog's wrist and occasionally Pete's headaches, and Dominick sat in a corner of the dressing room and devoted his entire attention to playing his guitar. They were strange melodies, intricate and unfamiliar, moving from a major key to minor and back again. Sophie had the strong impression that they were following the contours of Dominick's thoughts.

Not that she would know what was in his head. Or that she wanted to know.

She watched all the shows from the wings, because this also gave her the opportunity to scan the crowds for any sign of someone who might have tried to kill her. The crowds were getting bigger, which she noticed made Gina a bit happier, but she also noticed that there was a definite chorus of people yelling for Dominick each night. In Bristol, someone called 'Play "Sweet Nothings"!'

Dominick's head, usually bent to his bass, snapped up for a moment, and then he turned away and fiddled with his amp. His expression had been unreadable, but Sophie didn't think it was pleased.

Max, of course, took it in his stride. 'Play nothing? I hope you didn't pay much for your ticket, mate,' he said, and launched into 'Infamous', the Venusians' biggest hit.

Sophie set her equipment up in the dressing room while the gig finished up and was there already when Dominick, Pete and Mad Dog came in, without Max.

'Good show,' she said to them. Dominick looked at her and then away again. Pete went to the rider and poured himself a drink. The only one to smile at her was Mad Dog.

Dominick went straight to the armchair in the corner and sat down with his guitar.

'What was going on with your fan club out there, mate?' Pete said.

'Not my choice,' said Dominick, and began to play. His song was odder than usual, syncopated and dissonant.

'Ready for your koala juice, Mad Dog?' Sophie asked, and Mad Dog took a chair next to her.

'Lay it on me, smelly woman.'

She began to work. The eucalyptus and black pepper were meant to be stimulating and she'd added lemon to enhance the effect. It should be refreshing and uplifting.

She glanced round the room, which was silent except for the guitar. Pete was staring at Dominick, barely concealing a glower. Dominick frowned and bent his head so that his black hair hid his eyes. Without Max, there was no cheerful chatter, nothing to cover up and defuse the tension.

Mad Dog began to tap his feet to the tune Dominick was playing, apparently having no trouble following the irregular rhythm. Dominick hit a jagged note, rushed through a riff and then slowed and played it again, and Mad Dog laughed.

'Beautiful,' he told Dominick.

'Tricky,' said Pete. 'And what were you doing during "Eyes of Fire"? That's a straightforward bass line, man, it's not any of this fancy shit you were adding. You talk with Max about changing the songs?'

Sophie added a little more lemon oil.

Dominick paused in his playing. 'I didn't mean to add anything fancy,' he said. 'I must have lost track.' He plucked a simple single line, then bent back over the guitar and added a counterpoint.

Mad Dog was right about the tune; it was nothing like a pop song but dramatic and beautiful and strange, like a tragedy acted out on stage.

Not uplifting, but then again, neither were these oils, apparently.

'There's no room for egos in this band,' Pete said.

'I couldn't agree more,' Dominick replied, and even without looking Sophie could feel Pete bridling.

'What do you mean by—'

'Hey, gang, got good news.' Max appeared at the door, his arm around Gina. 'You know our day off a week Sunday?'

'I have a feeling this *isn't* good news,' muttered Pete.

'You're going to love it. Dino, my nephew, is getting married in Bethnal Green and he wants us to play at his reception! How cool is that?'

Sophie glanced at Gina, whose face said exactly how cool it was. She appeared to be resigned, however. Love made you do some weird things.

'You want us to play a wedding reception,' Pete said incredulously.

'My nephew wants us to play *his* wedding reception.

Hey, it'll be good crack. We're all invited to the party, we'll have a great time, us DeMilos really know how to throw a bash. And then we'll pick up a couple of guitars, play a tune or two. I bet we could put together a far-out version of 'Unchained Melody'. A rock 'n' roll wedding! What could be better?'

'A day off?' Pete suggested.

'I like weddings,' said Mad Dog.

'How about you, Dominick, you up for a little wedding music?'

'I'll do anything you want, you know that, Max,' said Dominick, picking out the first measure of 'Here Comes the Bride'.

'Pete?' Max sprawled on the arm of Pete's chair and rubbed the top of his shiny head. Sophie had seen pictures of the band in the eighties, when Pete had a vast mane of blond hair. She thought he probably shaved his head now to cover up the fact that he was balding. 'Come on, mate, when have I ever steered you wrong?'

'You mean besides the time you let me get off with that royal bird without knowing it?'

'Hey, I thought the paparazzi were snapping all over because we were famous, like, not because your little fancy girl was a second cousin to the Queen or whatever. Anyway, it was your fault for trying to walk on the posh side. What do you say about Dino's wedding, mate?'

Pete shrugged, and Max punched the air. 'It's gonna be great!' he yelled. 'Hey, you're invited too, Soph, I want you to meet the family.'

'Oh, thank you, but I was going to—'

'No excuses, you're coming, and I want you to wear a frock. And hey,' Max turned to Gina, 'we'll get to dance, babe. Slow dance, cheek to cheek.'

Gina looked a bit happier. 'And then the next day, on the Monday before the Nottingham show,' she told the rest of the band, 'we've got an interview with *Groovin'* magazine.'

Both Pete and Mad Dog nodded and 'mm'ed in approval, so Sophie took it that *Groovin'* was a magazine which met their exacting rock 'n' roll standards.

'I like "Unchained Melody",' Sophie said, and earned a glance from Dominick before he went back to his playing, improvising on Mendelssohn's wedding march.

'You know that koala juice really makes me feel bouncy,' Mad Dog told her.

18

The City of Fashion and Romance

'Phreeow!' Mad Dog soared his hand through the air, holding a piece of cheese as if it were an aeroplane. A bun waited in his other hand, in two halves like an open mouth. 'Zooommm . . . zooommmmmm . . . snap! Yum!' The bun-mouth caught the cheese and Mad Dog ate the entire thing in one bite.

'You sorta wonder what mealtimes are like in the Mad Dog household,' Griffin said to Sophie.

'I think we know already,' she answered.

The dining room of a Paris hotel looked much like the dining room of an English hotel, except the sugar came in little wrapped-up cubes and instead of toast racks and eggs with beans there were baskets of warm croissants and a selection of cheeses and fruit.

Sophie couldn't speak for the rest of Paris because she hadn't seen any of it properly. They'd come over on the buses on the Eurostar overnight, in a closed-in carriage, then driven to the hotel in the semi-darkness. Even peering as hard as she could out the windows, she couldn't see much. When they'd reached the hotel, everyone had tumbled stiff-limbed and yawning from the buses and straight inside to find something to eat. In the end, the promise of something other than crushed cheese and onion crisps had lured Sophie inside too, at least until it got light. Now she was trying her best to focus on the food and the cultural differences, rather than on Dominick's mouth as he ate.

Max popped a grape in his mouth and leaned back in his chair. 'So, you lot, we've got eight hours until the sound check. What are you going to do in this exciting city?'

'Sleep.'

'Sleep.'

'Sleep.'

Bob peered suspiciously into his cup. 'Can't get a decent cuppa in France.'

'Soph?'

The Eiffel Tower, Montmartre, the Louvre, the Champs-Elysées. All of it, all of Paris in one big gulp, all the drama and glamour and strangeness.

Everyone else had been here a thousand times, of course. Nothing special.

'Oh, I might wander around a bit,' she said.

'You and Gina should wander around together,' Max suggested. 'Go shopping. That's what birds do in Paris, isn't it?'

Gina raised a perfect eyebrow. 'There are one or two boutiques I wouldn't mind checking out. Sophie?'

'Uh, sure. That sounds good.' She could always duck out and go up the Eiffel Tower after an hour or so. Gina, being possibly even less into girlie bonding than Sophie was, wouldn't mind.

Thirty minutes later, she was walking down a street lined with flowers, passing a shop window full of elaborate pastries, smelling coffee and cigarettes from a café and roasting chicken on a rotisserie, trying not to gawp and failing.

'You haven't been here before?' Gina asked.

'I haven't travelled much.' Before this tour, her professional sightseeing had tended to be in back alleys and lurking in bushes.

'Every woman should have at least one item of clothing from Paris. Here.' Gina pushed open a glass door with brass art nouveau handles and they walked into perfumed stillness. The floor was marble, the walls were mirrored and the clothing hung from padded silk hangers. There was only one of everything, which gave the room the feeling of an elegant, spacious personal wardrobe.

The groomed woman at the shining counter greeted them quietly in French and went back to her work ticking things off a list. Her high heels clicking, Gina crossed the room, to where the skirts hung like reverent offerings.

There was one mannequin, standing on its own on the left side of the room in a pose that, though plastic, was somehow quintessentially French. It wore a dress of emerald-green satin, with a low-cut square neckline and a skirt that hugged its hips and legs. Sophie wandered over to it. She touched the hem. For a moment she saw herself in a darkened room, watching her prey, light gleaming off the satin.

'You've got a good eye,' Gina said near her shoulder, and Sophie jumped. 'That would look fantastic on you.'

'Oh, I – no, I was just looking. I wouldn't have any place to wear it.' *Not any more.*

'There's Dino's wedding next week.' Gina ran her fingers over the satin in a businesslike way. 'The colour would bring out your eyes. And the cut is so sexy.'

She imagined the caress of skin-warmed satin and the smell of sandalwood. 'It's beautiful. But it's really not me.'

Gina took a scarf from a nearby shelf and draped it around her own neck, watching herself in the mirror. 'Before this,' she said, 'I was on tour with a stage psychic. It was my first tour, actually, and it went horribly wrong when she was exposed as a fraud. She would observe people and deduce things about them from their appearance.'

'What did she deduce about you?' Sophie asked. The scarf matched Gina's auburn hair, and even casually draped, it hung in perfect folds.

'Appearances are important.' Gina made imaginary adjustments to the scarf. 'You show people what you want to allow them to see. You wouldn't guess, would you, that I grew up in a council flat and my father sells veg from a market stall in Lambeth?'

'No, I wouldn't.'

Gina replaced the scarf and selected a belt. 'I use clothes as a disguise. The fake psychic saw that about me. So did Max. You do it, too.'

Sophie laughed, though here in a mirrored wardrobe, it was self-consciously. She gestured to her black trousers, white top, grey cardigan. 'I'm hardly wearing anything deceiving.'

'Aren't you?' Briefly, Gina held a pink top up against herself and then against Sophie. 'It's one of the things I love about Max. Nothing about him is an act. He does everything he does because he loves to do it. He even wears leather to muck out the llama stalls.'

'I know you weren't thrilled about it, but I'm grateful to him for inviting me on the tour,' Sophie said.

'One way or another, Max has rescued everyone on this tour,' Gina said. 'Including me, and, I'm suspecting, you too. As far as I'm concerned, he deserves all the aromatherapy he wants.'

They had made a small circle and were back at the emerald dress. They both gazed at it.

'You should buy it,' Gina said.

'I couldn't.'

'That's what credit cards are for.'

'I'm not talking about the money.'

For a moment, for the first time this morning, Gina caught her eye. She pursed her lips slightly and nodded.

'Let's go to the Eiffel Tower,' she said.

Stoneguard, Wiltshire

She did, however, need suitable clothes for Dino DeMilo's wedding, so on the Friday, back in England before the Oxford gig, she took a train to Wiltshire and walked from Stoneguard station. She passed her clinic on the way to her flat, and saw that the window was still boarded up. Someone had spray-painted BITCH across it in pink.

She flinched. For a few days, escaping England, she'd forgotten her list of enemies. They had, apparently, not forgotten her. She scanned the street, but for once, the people of Stoneguard seemed to be absorbed in their own business. She saw Gloria Wheeler, egg-thrower, going into the Whole Foods Emporium. Nobody seemed to have noticed Sophie.

Just the way she liked it.

Sophie checked her front door carefully before she unlocked it. As far as she could tell, it was untouched, which was somewhat surprising. If someone really was out to harm her, it seemed as if they'd have started with her home, and as it was a first-floor flat, the front door was the most obvious way to get in.

The flat felt deserted when she stepped in, with post scattered inside the door, but she went round to every room and checked the windows just in case, opening the living room cupboard, pulling back the shower curtain in the bathroom. The air smelt stale.

Nobody had been here. And standing in her living room, Sophie realised it felt more empty than unoccupied. The unadorned white walls, the plain beige sofa and uncluttered side table seemed bare in a way she'd never taken notice of before, when compared with the cheerful, noisy chaos of the tour bus and all the dressing rooms backstage.

Maybe she'd have to scatter some magazines and DVDs around, and maybe some half-drunk cups of tea and men's dirty socks.

She smiled and went to her bedroom, where she opened her wardrobe. Her clothes, hung up neatly, fell into two groups: on the left were her normal clothes in white and shades of black, brown, grey and blue, and on the right was a bright jumble of silks and sequins.

When she was looking in this wardrobe every day, she didn't notice the honey-trap clothes. She just reached straight for what she needed without giving them a glance. It must be because she'd been away that she couldn't help looking at them now. She could smell traces of perfume on them.

It was as if a vivid shadow of herself was hidden here, tucked away because she wasn't useful any more. A vivid and seductive shadow.

Sophie reached to the left and pulled out her best black dress. It was knee-length, quietly cut, but fitted her well, and it would do for the wedding. She got out a pair of black heels and went to her dresser to find a plain fine silver chain and bracelet.

Something in the mirror caught her attention.

She stopped. The mirror faced the two windows in her bedroom, both of which looked out on to Stoneguard High Street below, and the stone circle in the distance. Without turning around, she studied the reflection. She stood still and watchful in the foreground; in the background, she saw nothing out of the ordinary. The angle was wrong to see anything in detail outside, but she might have noticed a movement.

And though the flat had felt empty before, now she felt as if she were being watched.

Sophie casually stepped towards her wardrobe, as if she'd forgotten to take something out of it, and as soon as she was out of the direct line of the windows she flattened herself against the wall next to one of them. Carefully, slowly, she peered sideways out through the pane.

She saw him right away. He was wearing black, sunglasses over his eyes though the day was overcast, leaning against the wall of the building society opposite as if he just happened to be waiting for someone. He had his hands in the pockets of his leather jacket and he looked as if he owned the place.

What the hell was Dominick Steele doing in Stoneguard?

She watched him for a few minutes. He was here to watch her all right. He kept on glancing up at her window.

A smile touched her lips in spite of herself. He was rubbish at surveillance. The first lesson was to be unobtrusive, to dress quietly, to do something that would make you blend in. He'd worn black, but the sunglasses, instead of obscuring his face, drew attention to it. Not only because it was a cloudy day, but because they emphasised his high cheekbones and the strength of his jaw. And in any case, Dominick Steele was not the type of person who blended in.

Not bothering to hide her actions any more, Sophie went back to her wardrobe and took down a garment bag. Her black dress, for example: that was the sort of thing you should wear when doing surveillance. It was occasion-appropriate enough to be invisible, stylish in a classical way that wasn't going to draw anybody's attention for either admiration or contempt. Likewise her shoes were slim and elegant, but not high enough to restrict movement.

She paused halfway through zipping up her garment bag.

Was she really wearing a surveillance dress to a wedding?

That wasn't very rock 'n' roll.

She opened her wardrobe and reached into the right-hand side. The soft materials brushed against her bare arm as she found red stilettos and a floaty scarlet scarf. She stuffed the shoes and scarf in the garment bag, added some silk underwear because she'd know that she was wearing it even though nobody else would, and zipped the whole thing up before she had time to think twice.

When she glanced out of the window again, Dominick was still there. On second thoughts, she put on a pair of wellies and tossed her flats in her bag. Then she locked her door behind her and went down the stairs to the street.

Dominick turned away and pretended to be reading the poster in the building society window as she stepped outside. Suppressing a smile, she walked past as if she hadn't noticed him, and at the end of the block turned left.

The street petered out quickly, narrowing into a path that squeezed between two hedgerows and climbed

Stoneguard Hill. It had been raining; the mud squelched around her wellies as she made her way towards the top. A moment when she pretended to drop something and pick it up showed her that Dominick was following her, trying his best to stay concealed behind a bend in the hedgerow and with mud on his black shoes. He was still wearing his sunglasses.

The stone circle was deserted when she got there. She pushed her hair back and breathed in deeply: earth and grass and stone. As she exhaled, the sun came out from behind a cloud. In bright light, the stones appeared twice as tall because of their shadows.

Imagine having so much faith you'd haul a huge rock up a hill.

Before she left the circle on the other side, she glanced back on the pretext of adjusting the garment bag's strap on her shoulder. Dominick was at the edge of the circle, the sun gleaming off his hair and his sunglasses. He looked good enough to be shooting a bloody music video. She considered turning around and asking him what he thought he was doing, but she caught a glimpse of another person behind him, in an anorak and carrying binoculars, and decided she'd rather save that confrontation for when they didn't have an audience.

Besides, she was quite enjoying this.

She headed down the path opposite the one she'd come up on. This one was a little tricky, so she had to watch her footing in her loose wellies and didn't get the chance to check behind her until she'd reached the bottom. There he was, a little closer than he'd been before, and she could see mud on one knee of his jeans. She pushed through a gap in another hedgerow, and emerged near the station, having taken a more circuitous and vertical route than necessary.

The train to Oxford was, luckily, just pulling in, so she hurried to the platform and got into the first standard-class carriage. She watched from the window as Dominick ducked into first class, which made her smile. If he didn't want to walk past her, he'd have to pay extra to stay in the first-class carriage.

A successful trip to Stoneguard all round. She settled into her seat and dialled information on her phone for the number of a glazier. Engrossed in her conversation, she didn't notice the person with binoculars who'd been at the stone circle walk past her window and board the train further down.

St Alonso's Church Hall, Bethnal Green

'H̲ey, smelly woman, you look nice.'

It was between sets, and the DJ had taken over the music for a while. Mad Dog had dressed up his uniform of jeans and a T-shirt with a turquoise silk tie knotted around his neck. Holding two glasses of champagne, he sat down beside Sophie at her table and gave her one.

'Thanks, Mad Dog,' she said. 'You look nice too. I like the colour of your tie.'

'Goes with my shirt,' he replied, indicating the picture of a Native American on the front of it. He lifted up his glass. 'Cheers.'

It was her second glass of champagne, and she'd planned to take it easy, but she clinked glasses with Mad Dog and drank anyway. 'It's a good wedding,' she said.

Mad Dog looked around the church hall, festooned with streamers and balloons. Folding chairs and tables covered with paper cloths stood around an impromptu stage and dance floor in the middle of the hall. As it was the wedding of the nephew of a rock star, Sophie had expected something much more grand. But the hall was bubbling over with laughter and conversation, most of it in strong East End accents, children ran giggling between the tables, and, of course, the drink was flowing.

'They're a good family,' said Mad Dog. 'Max and me were at school together. I used to call his mum "auntie".'

She'd met Mrs DeMilo earlier. She was a short, elderly woman with permed white hair and a flowered dress, who seemed like millions of other elderly women until she opened her mouth and laughed, and then Max DeMilo's cackle came out. She'd hugged Mad Dog (whom she called 'Billy') and Pete, and greeted Gina warmly, though it was clear she was meeting Max's girlfriend for the first time. She'd been just as nice to Sophie herself.

'I really don't belong here,' Sophie said now, taking another sip of champagne.

'Max always told me everyone belonged everywhere,' Mad Dog said. 'I didn't, though. It was better at his house.'

Sophie sent him a sharp glance, and she saw it: not quite sadness, but wistfulness, a yearning. It was the expression of a person who had also had an unhappy childhood.

'I'd have liked somewhere like that,' she said, and she saw she was right, because Mad Dog just nodded as if he knew exactly what she was admitting to.

'Dance?' he asked, standing up.

The music was a Bon Jovi power ballad. 'Sure.'

Gina and Max were already out on the floor. Max held her close to his chest and sang softly in her ear; Gina had a small and secret smile. There was another thing, along with happy families, that Sophie didn't know about.

'My wife Sherry says I can't dance for toffee,' Mad Dog

said, and in a very few moments Sophie found out that Mad Dog's wife was right.

'What does your wife think about you being on tour again?' she asked, trying to keep her pointy-toed shoes out from underneath Mad Dog's trainers.

'She takes the kids to see her sisters when I'm away,' he said. 'She likes it. I miss her, though. Look at Pete.'

Pete was sitting at a table by himself by the side of the dance floor. He had a half-full pint of beer in front of him and three empty glasses beside him.

'His wife left him three weeks before Max got the band back together,' Mad Dog said. 'I think he expected more hot chicks on this tour. Do me a favour and dance with him after me?'

'Of course,' Sophie said, 'though I don't think I'll make up for the hot chicks.'

'You're hot,' Mad Dog told her. 'I'd do you if I weren't married, and . . .' He glanced across the room, and Sophie didn't have to follow his gaze because she knew what was there: Dominick, sitting with a young man who Sophie thought was a relative of the bride. He'd been sitting there for the past half an hour. Not that Sophie was keeping track; it was just her Dominick Steele sixth sense at work.

'And what?' Sophie asked sweetly, prepared to deny any rumours or assumptions.

'And nothing, that's all, if I weren't married, and also old enough to be your dad,' finished Mad Dog, and kicked her in the left ankle. 'Whoops, sorry.'

'No problem,' she said. 'I enjoy a dangerous life.'

The next song was Elvis crooning about love. Sophie had another quick swig of champagne before leaving Mad Dog, and approached Pete.

'Mad Dog says you're a fantastic dancer,' she said to him.

It took a moment before he could focus on her, and then he smiled. 'That's because the man has no rhythm when he can't hit something,' he said, standing up and offering her his hand, and Sophie could smell the beer on his breath. She finished her glass of champagne in order to steel herself for more shoe-crunching and a bit of drunken lurching around.

Elvis was singing about not being able to help believing. Pete took one of her hands, put his other on her waist, and spun her around so quickly that she was back in his arms and swaying in time with the music before she even knew what was happening.

'Hold on,' she gasped, 'you can dance.'

'I took lessons,' he said, leading her backwards in a complicated pattern of steps Sophie would never have been able to produce on her own. 'That's not very rock 'n' roll, is it?'

'I think it is definitely rock 'n' roll,' she said, and was rewarded with a dip and a twirl that made her laugh out loud.

By the time the song was done she was breathless. Pete snagged them glasses of champagne from a passing tray and Sophie was thirsty enough to drink half of hers at a gulp. 'I don't think I've ever danced like that before. You're amazing.'

'I've got three talents,' Pete said. 'Guitar, ballroom dancing, and making love.' He smiled at her.

Oh, damn.

'Those are all useful talents,' she said carefully.

'Especially the last one.' He trailed one of his callused fingers along the side of her jaw, and then down her neck to the hollow of her throat. 'You should try it some time.'

'I have, several times. I enjoyed it.' She leaned back, but his finger stayed on her clavicle.

'It's especially enjoyable with me.' Pete closed the distance between them, angling his head so his lips were aimed at hers.

She sidestepped him. 'I'm sorry, Pete, I'm not on this tour for the lovemaking,' she said. 'Much as I appreciate the offer. And I loved the dance. You're right about being talented.'

Mad Dog appeared at her elbow. 'Hey, Fred Astaire, you owe me a beer.'

'I don't owe you any damn beer; you owe *me* a beer,' Pete said. His face was flushed red.

'I'll arm-wrestle you for it,' said Mad Dog, and plunked down beside him.

'Right, I'm getting out of here before I have to watch you undo all the good work I've done with your wrist,' Sophie said, and hastened away.

Walking in her stilettos wasn't easy at the best of times, and now the champagne and dancing had turned her legs to jelly. She waited until she was a decent distance from Mad Dog and Pete before she leaned against a wall to regain her equilibrium.

'And I wanted to know another thing. You know the third song on your second album, "False Memory"? I was wondering about a line in the chorus, what it meant when you said . . .'

She looked around. Her flight from Pete had brought her directly behind where Dominick was sitting. She couldn't see his face, but she could see the bride's relative: he was in his early twenties, thin, with spots on his face, a prominent Adam's apple, and a hairstyle that required lots of styling product. There was a zealous light in his eyes. And he had started to sing.

She sniggered. Dominick Steele, cornered by a persistent fan. Served him right for all the times he'd taken for granted the adoration of others. She remembered that enthusiastic man in the pub five years ago, who'd been desperate to be the friend of a rock star. Dominick had brushed him away as if he'd been a bit of lint on his sleeve.

'I don't like reading into lyrics,' Dominick said, and Sophie stopped mid-snigger. He didn't sound famous, or arrogant, or alpha male.

He sounded miserable.

'Not even your own lyrics, man?'

'Especially not my own lyrics. Listen, can I get you a drink?' He pushed back his chair and made to stand up, but the bride's relative grabbed his arm before he could rise.

'It's just that I have this theory about that song, and I want you to tell me if I'm right, because it sounds to me as if "False Memory" is all about your wife . . .'

Sophie didn't need to see Dominick's face to know that he had stiffened.

She pushed off the wall and tottered over to Dominick's table. Putting one hand on his shoulder, she said, 'Hey there, Dominick, sorry to interrupt you, but didn't you promise me a dance?'

When he turned to her, she knew she must be tipsy, because he actually looked glad to see her.

She had an Audrey Hepburn black dress and Jane Russell red shoes. She'd kept her hair loose and had on lipstick. Dom didn't think he'd ever seen anyone so beautiful, and not just because she was rescuing him.

'That's right,' he said, and rose and took her hand. 'Sorry, mate,' he said to Ian, the bride's cousin, who appeared none too pleased at being interrupted mid-theory.

'Don't worry about thanking me,' Sophie said as they left Ian's table and headed towards the dance floor, 'and try not to step on my toes, they're still throbbing from Mad Dog's dancing.'

'I don't dance when I'm sober, which means I don't dance at all. It ruins my moody image.' He tried to steer her towards the fire exit, where wedding guests were clumped having a cigarette, but she planted her heels.

'Nope, I saved you, you have to do what I want. And I want to dance.' She tugged on his hand.

'How much have you had to drink?'

'I haven't drunk anything. Come on.'

As far as Dom could see, she was tipsy as hell, could barely keep steady in her shoes. 'You're a lousy liar when you've had a few,' he told her, and followed her along to the dance floor.

It was Billy Idol's 'White Wedding', and Dom refused to dance like somebody's dad trying to be cool. He put his hand on Sophie's slender waist and took her hand in his and moved as slowly as he could get away with.

'I'm surprised you needed saving,' she said to him.

'I didn't know Ian was a fan until I'd already started talking to him.' And he'd started talking to Ian after the ceremony, just to talk to anyone, because he'd been unable to get the bride's expression out of his head.

So hopeful, so happy. So much like his own bride's had been all those years ago. 'I'm not eager to talk about my past,' he said.

'I meant that I'm surprised you didn't brush him off.'

'You've got a great impression of me, haven't you?'

She shrugged. The movement sent a delicate note of scent up from her slender shoulders and neck. She felt light in his arms despite her tipsiness. He'd seen her dancing with Pete, like two halves of one rhythm. He tightened his hand on her waist.

'Let's talk about something else,' he said.

'Let's. Tell me, how did you enjoy the Stoneguard circle?'

Dom stopped dancing. Sophie looked up at him with a devilish glint in those grey eyes.

'You little minx,' he said.

'You need some lessons in surveillance. I'd volunteer, but I'm out of the business these days.'

He shook his head. 'You ruined a perfectly good pair of shoes.'

'And made you pay for a first-class rail ticket. I hope it was worth it. Why were you following me, anyway?'

'Although it seems strange right at this moment, I was trying to make sure you didn't get killed. Going off on your own seems like a stupid thing to do when you've got someone after you.'

'I can look after myself.' She was grinning.

'So I see.' He started dancing again, if you could call swaying to Billy Idol dancing. 'Have the police caught whoever tried to run you down yet?'

He'd been jumpy as hell since Liverpool, wondering. And of course he couldn't stick close to her after that kiss, but he'd tried to keep an eye out for her as much as he could. He decided he didn't want to know if she'd noticed him watching her all of the other times. He thought he'd got away with it in Paris at least; she'd been absorbed in the sights there, more like a child than a hard-boiled detective.

'I've got some leads, but I can't get in touch with any of them. I did find out that the SUV was stolen in Liverpool, though.'

'Does that help you with anything?'

'No.'

The song changed to the Carpenters, 'We've Only Just Begun.'

They'd played this song at his wedding. He remembered the taste of single malt and he remembered dancing to the song with Leonie and he remembered listening to the lyrics about promises and the future. At that moment he had wanted so badly to make it possible.

He'd forgotten that wanting until this moment.

'I hate the bloody Carpenters,' he said.

'You'd better hope that Max doesn't want to do a cover version for your second set,' Sophie said, and kept dancing with him. This song was slower, and it meant she was a tiny bit closer. Her red scarf hung down from her neck and brushed against the back of his hand resting on her waist.

'I hate bloody weddings in general,' he said.

'Two out of five marriages in the UK end in divorce,' she told him. 'So look on the bright side: these two might split up and they can be as miserable as both of us are.'

'Both of us?'

She'd clearly blundered, because she flushed. 'You, I meant.'

He wasn't giving up an advantage that easily. 'Why do you hate cheaters so much? Do you have a personal axe to grind?'

'I just saw a lot of them in my job,' she said, but she didn't meet his eyes. 'Sometimes it felt as if there weren't any decent people left out there.'

'So you've never had someone do the dirty on you yourself?'

'I wouldn't let them.' Her voice was like steel.

'I bet you wouldn't,' he said.

'And I didn't mean that about splitting up. I want this couple to make it. They seem nice and they probably deserve it, and I wouldn't wish anything but the best for Max's family. It would be nice to believe in one marriage, at least.'

'It would,' he said quietly. The Carpenters sang about finding a place to grow. Sophie and Dominick danced together for a moment in silence. He wasn't holding her as closely as he had when he'd kissed her. But that kiss had been a battle, and this ...

Well, this was a dance.

'Is it hard not to have a drink at something like this?' she asked him.

'It's hard all the time, but right now it's not so bad.'

She studied his face. Over the years he'd had a lot of people look at him, but Sophie had a way of her own. It was as if she were trying to read him, and then look underneath and read him again.

'Why did you drink?' she asked.

'You're a nosy one, aren't you?'

'It's a prerequisite for being a private detective.'

'Which you're not any more.'

'I'm still nosy.' She grimaced slightly. 'Too nosy. So tell me, why did you drink?'

'I didn't have a traumatic past, if that's what you're angling for. I grew up in a normal family in a normal way. Didn't get bullied, didn't get kicked out of school, no tragedies. My parents still love me. In fact they're two of the few people from my past who still speak to me. I just drank. That's the person I am. No real reason.'

'There's always a reason. Why?'

The DJ interrupted them with his overamplified voice. 'Now this song is a special request from the bride, so let's have her up here to dance with her brand-new husband, Mr and Mrs Dino DeMilo!'

The music changed to a bubblegum-awful pop ballad Dom knew for certain hadn't been played at his own wedding, because the girl singer wouldn't have been out of nappies yet. Dino and his wife Kylie came on to the dance floor, holding hands, and all the dancing couples moved towards the sides to give them the centre to themselves. Kylie, in white satin and pearls, was about two inches taller than Dino. They smiled at each other, a private and a public smile all mixed together. The bridesmaids in pink lace pelted them with pink confetti. It stuck in their hair, on their clothes, in their eyelashes. Dino and Kylie laughed and kissed each other.

They didn't have regrets already. They believed in what they'd done.

Max and Gina danced by, and Max tapped Dom on the shoulder. 'This is the last song, mate, and then we're on again. Do you know "Chapel of Love"?'

'I think I can fake it,' he said, and Max moved off.

'So why?' Sophie asked.

'Why am I faking "Chapel of Love"? I know the tune but not the bass line.'

'Why are you an alcoholic?'

She wasn't going to give up. He looked up at the bunting-strewn ceiling, sighed, and thought about it. Because to tell the truth, for the past two years he'd been far too busy thinking about how not to drink to think about why he did it in the first place.

'I always wanted to play music,' he said. 'But not just

play music; I wanted to be a star. I wanted everyone to listen to it. I wanted people to know me.'

He looked down at her; she was watching him steadily. For the moment, all her tipsiness was gone. She was listening hard, the sort of audience he'd wanted all those years ago when he was only a kid with a guitar and a headful of lyrics, but of course he hadn't wanted only one person to hear him. Otherwise, he'd have stayed with Leonie.

'I wanted it all, the entire world,' he said. 'And then it happened. I got famous and I was a star, and the weird thing was that I was exactly the same person. Everything had changed, and I hadn't.'

Sophie nodded. 'You stay the same inside. Even with another job or another place. I know.'

'I drank so I could fake it. And then I got to need it.' He shook his head; if he was going to be honest here, and it seemed he was, he should use the right vocabulary. 'No, not "need". "Need" means I wanted it, that it was a positive feeling, and it wasn't. The reason I drank wasn't because I needed it, but because life without drinking was the most terrifying thing I could imagine.'

'Is it as terrifying as you thought it would be?'

He thought about sitting in that pub in south London, him and his malevolent friend Mr Jack.

'Some days are worse than others,' he said. 'I need to get on stage in a minute; have I satisfied your curiosity yet?'

Sophie tilted her head to one side, a motion that made her hair fall over her shoulder and over one eye. Dom wanted to stroke it back, but that could be even more disastrous than this pop song, because he'd want to touch her cheek then, and then her neck. The hollow beneath her ear, brightened by the small gleam of her silver earring. And then it was only a short trip to her mouth again.

He raised his hand from her hip to do it anyway.

'What happened in those missing four months?' she asked him.

He dropped his hand. For a minute there he'd forgotten why she was asking all her questions. For thirty seconds of it he'd almost believed that she cared.

Did he still want to be listened to so badly?

'You're the detective; you find out,' he said. 'Excuse me, I've got to go on stage and fake it for a while.'

21

A Hotel in Bethnal Green

One in the morning, and Dominick had just found pink confetti in his hair. He combed his fingers through it, listening to the phone ring on the other end of the line.

She was awake; she always was, until three or four in the morning. She'd be listening to music, reading books, chatting with friends, even hoovering. A night owl, like he used to be.

'Hiya.'

Leonie's voice was breathless, young-sounding, happy.

'It's me,' he said.

'Oh.'

In the silence following he heard a Vivaldi flute concerto in the background, in a major key, like her greeting.

'I've just had an argument with directory services over your number,' he said. 'They said there was no Leonie Nickson in Cambridgeshire. I didn't know you still used Leonie Steele.'

He could hear her inhale. 'What do you want, Dominick?'

Another piece of confetti fluttered to the bedspread beside him. It was a little flake of optimism and hope.

'It occurs to me that I never said I was sorry. I put you through a lot, Leonie. You didn't deserve it.'

The concerto tripped along, into the third movement, allegro. She was probably wearing jeans and an old, oversized jumper. He had a very strong memory of her playing her own flute along with this concerto, late at night. She'd had an expression of fierce concentration. He could remember the expression better than the exact lines of her face.

'Is that all?' she asked.

He considered asking her who she'd been expecting to call, when she'd answered with such happiness in her voice.

'A friend of mine was wondering where my leather trousers got to,' he said instead.

'I don't know,' she said, and he knew that she was lying. He smiled.

'Listen, Dominick, I'm expecting a call, so . . .'

'All right. Take care, Leonie.'

Three more bits of confetti swirled to the ground as he hung up the phone. He gathered them up and put them in the bin.

Champagne was not a good idea, champagne and high heels even less so. Sophie sat on the side of the hotel room bathtub, soaking her feet in cold water and massaging her throbbing temples.

What had she been thinking? Dancing? With Dominick? For three songs, at least, in full view of everyone she worked with? That was going to fuel rumours about their relationship, past and present.

And then asking him all those things about his drinking, his personal life, things she really didn't want to know because they widened her picture of him, made her see the contradictions and complexities so she couldn't label him in her brain any more. He'd been a 'scumbag', he'd been a 'rock star', he'd been an 'arrogant twat' and a million other less flattering things, but now he was a person who succumbed to weaknesses and had fears and then struggled with them.

Also, a person who'd slammed a shutter in her face as soon as she'd thought she was beginning to understand.

She dried off her aching feet and limped to the bedroom, where she swallowed a couple of ibuprofen with a glass of water.

And what made it worse was she couldn't get that annoying pop song out of her head, the one that had been playing when he'd looked as if he were going to kiss her again.

She should be feeling cynical. She'd seen the messy results of weddings too many times. Instead she felt almost protective of the couple getting married, she felt sorry for Pete whose marriage was over, and she felt guilty about the part she'd played in messing up marriages herself. All of it mixed up with the sour after-effects of champagne.

A bit of work would put her back into perspective; she'd emailed Raj to ask if he had any more news about Keith Martin, and the Liverpool police had said that they would have more information about the stolen car. She opened up her laptop and logged on to the wi-fi network.

There was only one email in her inbox, from <undisclosed>. Spam. She clicked on it to delete it, and then froze when she saw the text come up in the preview window.

YOUR FAMOUS BOYFRIEND WON'T HELP YOU. YOU'LL PAY FOR WHAT YOU DID TO ME YOU BITCH.

The Public Library, Bethnal Green

'It could have been any of these,' the librarian said, gesturing at the bank of computers. 'Or we have twelve more upstairs. Why did you want to know?'

Sophie rested her hand on a terminal. She'd traced the email she'd received this morning to a webmail account set up at the IP address of the Bethnal Green public library at 4.26 p.m. yesterday. It was about half a mile from St Alonso's church hall and Dino DeMilo's wedding, and less than five hundred metres from her hotel.

'It's to do with a potential crime,' she told him. 'Were you working yesterday at half past four?'

'Yes. It's a busy time, though, Sunday afternoons. We only began opening quite recently.'

'And anybody can use the computers?'

'We require that each person give the number of their library card.'

'And if they don't have one?'

'Then we require identification.'

'And you keep records of this?'

'Of course.'

Sophie smiled at the librarian, who had more hair in his

eyebrows than on his head. 'I wonder if I could take a look at those records for yesterday afternoon?'

The librarian's forehead creased. 'What did you say you were? A detective?'

'A private investigator, yes.'

His forehead contracted even more, and his cheeks went up to meet it, so that his eyes were barely visible. 'I'm not authorised to give you that information.'

Sophie restrained herself from sighing in frustration. 'Mr Johnston, I'm not going to misuse this information. All I want to do is check some names.'

'May I see your credentials?'

Of course she didn't have anything except for lavender-coloured business cards that said 'Aromatherapist'.

'Mr Johnston, I can assure you—'

'I'm sorry,' he said, his eyebrows firmly stuck in place low over his eyes. 'I can't give that information to anyone but the police with a warrant.'

She nodded, slowly.

'How about this. Did you see this man?' She showed him a photograph of Keith Martin. It was from one of the social websites where she'd chatted with him when she'd been preparing to honey-trap him. The thought that he was still registered on the website made her feel sick.

'He's short, about five six,' she added.

The librarian, to his credit, did look at the printout carefully, but then he shook his head. 'I can't say I remember him, but that doesn't mean much.'

'How about either of these?' She showed him a photo of Keith Martin's new girlfriend, Chantal Smith, that she'd pulled off her MySpace page, and one of Sally Hershey from the website of the estate agency where she worked.

'Not that I know of. I'm not really good with faces,' he added apologetically.

'Was there anybody else working with you yesterday?'

'Not at that time. I'd sent Phyllis home sick.'

Sophie closed her eyes briefly for patience, and started again.

'Surely you have regular visitors to the library who might have been here at that time? Are any of them here now so I can show them these photographs?'

He looked around the room. 'Not right now, I'm afraid. But you're welcome to stay here and ask questions of the patrons, as this is so important.'

She checked her watch: it was nearly ten o'clock in the morning. There were only two hours until the tour buses left Bethnal Green to travel up to Nottingham so the band could do a sound check and then their interview with *Groovin'* magazine before their gig. Max had already said he wanted her to be there to infuse the room with 'chilled-out scent for a good vibe'.

'Thank you,' she said to the librarian. 'I appreciate it. Do you mind if I use this terminal for a little while?'

'Certainly, it's open to all members of the public, as long as you show me some identification,' he said. Sophie showed him her driver's licence; he made a note of it, and then wandered away.

Sophie sat down and put her fingers on the keyboard. This could be the keyboard the person had used, writing a capital-letter shout. The same hands had been wrapped around the steering wheel of a murderous SUV. Their owner had followed her, to Liverpool and Bethnal Green at least, and who knew where else. Possibly everywhere.

And the only tool she had to catch them was old-fashioned snooping.

She found the webmail site easily. She'd discovered the username and password used to set up the account. Both of them were 'Sophie Tennant'.

Typing her own name twice into the login boxes, she felt a sliver of a chill.

The inbox held an automatically generated welcome message. The only message in the 'sent' file was the one she'd received yesterday. She read it again, touching the keys that might have generated it.

She heard, as she had all the night before, hot breath and whispered words in her ear. *You bitch. You deserve this.*

She blinked, hard, and focused on solving the mystery.

The language of the email was similar to Keith Martin's. But the language of threats was pretty universal. Sally Hershey liked to use 'bitch' too, apparently sometimes in pink spray paint. It wasn't an uncommon word to use against a woman.

There was nothing particular to indicate that the email had been written by the same person who had tried to run her down, but she thought they were connected. They were both cowards' attacks. Which meant that the person was frightened of confrontation, perhaps because they didn't want to be caught, or perhaps because, in some way, they were scared of Sophie. Maybe she could use that, somehow, to draw them out.

The bit about the famous boyfriend was interesting. It implied a measure of jealousy. If it was from a woman, it could mean someone who'd lost her lover, possibly because Sophie had caught him being unfaithful or doing something else – she knew of at least two marriages that had broken up because she had found out the husband was embezzling money. Or it could be a woman she'd caught cheating, through surveillance. If it was from a man, it hinted at someone who'd been attracted to her, who harboured bitterness about Sophie's sexuality in general because it had led to his getting caught.

It did tend to point to the infidelity cases she'd been involved with. Her gut feeling was that it pointed to the honey traps. But as those had comprised an increasing proportion of her business for the last few years, that wasn't a huge lot of help.

In other words, it could be anyone, even someone she wouldn't necessarily recognise. Even someone in this library right now. She felt an itching between her shoulder blades and on her neck, and she realised she was sitting with her back to the room. Quickly she stood up, logged off while standing, and got down to business.

The next two hours were a fruitless round of querying the library's patrons. She interviewed twenty or thirty people, only two of whom had been in the library the day before, and none of whom recognised the photos.

What she really needed to do was to interview people around the same time as the email had been sent; then she'd get the regular late-afternoon visitors. But that meant letting Max down, so at ten minutes to noon she left the library and walked back to the hotel to meet the tour bus.

Her stomach was jumpy from coffee and no breakfast, and her eyes ached from no sleep. She hated letting leads slip away. The person she was looking for was so close. Maybe even here, on the street in Bethnal Green, right now.

Watching her.

Sophie paused and looked in a shop window, surveying the street behind her in the reflection. The back of her neck felt bare and vulnerable but she saw nobody suspicious. She saw in her reflection that she was biting her nails.

She took her hand from her mouth and kept walking, worrying one bitten-edge nail with another.

After popping her head into the lobby to wave at Gina and let her know she was here, she went to the crew bus and climbed on. The bus was safe enough, and the journey to Nottingham would be a long one; maybe she could get some sleep.

Except when she got to her bunk, Dominick was sitting on it.

'Where have you been?' he demanded.

'At the library, improving my mind. Can I have my bunk back?'

'You look terrible.'

'Thank you.' He wasn't moving, and she considered climbing up to the top bunk so she could lie down, but all of her stuff was up there and she was far too tired. She sank down on to the bunk beside him. There wasn't room for two people to sit, especially when one was a tall alpha male leaning against the top end of the bunk with his legs stretched the length of it, so she had to perch on the edge.

'Why are you here?' she asked him.

'You'd disappeared and I wanted to make sure you weren't dead. What's the matter?'

'Nothing.'

'You look mad as hell.'

'Well, there is someone in my bunk.'

'You also look pale. Did someone come after you again?'

He clearly wasn't going away until he got some answers from her. 'I didn't sleep much last night. I was checking out a lead this morning.'

'A lead on what?'

'Is there any chance of you getting off my bunk so I can lie down?'

He raised his eyebrows and didn't move.

'I got a threatening email,' she admitted. 'It was sent from Bethnal Green public library. I've been checking it out.'

It hardly seemed possible, but Dominick seemed to get bigger and closer to her. 'What was it? You went there alone? Are you crazy?'

'It didn't say anything useful.' After being practically tossed aside after a kiss and a dance, she was damned if she was going to feed his ego by telling him about the 'famous boyfriend' part. 'Just that I would pay for some unspecified thing that I've done. And I'm perfectly capable of walking down a street to a library without being followed.'

Well, that's what she would have said not long ago, anyway.

Dominick sat up straight. His head brushed the top of the bunk and she wondered vaguely how someone so tall coped with sleeping in such a confined space.

'Right, that's it,' he said. 'I'm getting my stuff and moving to this bus.'

Oh, no. She could cope with Bob's snoring, she could cope with Griffin's socks, she could cope with the late-night loud arguments about who was better, AC/DC or Black Sabbath, she could even cope with Dempsey's predilection for leaving cheese and onion crisps wherever she happened to want to sit down, but she could not cope with sharing a motor vehicle, however big, with a man who kissed like a force of nature.

Especially because all she wanted to do right now was to curl up in his lap and ask him to hug her.

She blinked. Her eyes burned. This was not good. Really not good.

'Why aren't you arguing with me?' he asked.

'Because I spent the whole night tracing a threatening email and listening for someone trying to break into my hotel room,' she said, 'and the whole morning looking for someone who wants to hurt and frighten me. And because I'm meant to be an investigator and I can't track this person down. And because I'm tired.'

Dominick leaned forward, put his arms around her, and pulled her back against him in a hug.

He was warm and big and solid. She knew she shouldn't, but she closed her eyes and relaxed into him, her head on his chest, her hip against his, her hands resting on his arms. She felt him breathing and breathed him in.

When was the last time she'd leaned on someone else?

'I rang Leonie last night,' Dominick said. She felt his voice as a vibration against her ear and as soft, warm breath in her hair. 'I said I was sorry. She doesn't forgive me.'

Sophie nodded, because she didn't know what she could say to that.

'I don't blame her,' he said. 'But it got me thinking. I wish you'd forgive me.'

That surprised her so much she lifted her head and looked into his face, into his dark eyes. He meant what he said, though she couldn't think why.

'You haven't done anything to me,' she said, though that was wrong. And she knew he knew it was wrong, because he'd felt her kissing him back a few days ago, and right now she was in his arms.

With a rumble, the bus started up. Sophie exercised all her will and sat up, detached from Dominick.

'I'll go get my things,' he said, and swung out of the bunk.

23

The Victoria Theatre, Nottingham

TONIGHT: LEATHERED
SUPPORT: LIMOUZINE, KAT SKRATCH
DOORS 8.00

The band and crew stood staring at the poster in the lobby.

'Maybe it's an old poster,' Dempsey the monitor man said.

'It's a mistake,' Gina said firmly.

Dominick didn't have a good feeling about this. He envied Sophie, still asleep on the tour bus.

A fortysomething man in a T-shirt drifted in. 'Hey, can I help you?'

Gina hurried over and engaged in a frenzied conversation with him. Dom saw the man shake his head.

'Great, yet another fuck-up,' muttered Pete. He kicked the side of the box-office booth with his heavy boot.

'It's nothing, mate, Gina will sort it out,' Max told him. 'Hey, you remember playing here that time when Mad Dog got hit by a plastic pint glass?'

'Still got the scar,' Mad Dog said, rubbing his forehead.

The diversionary tactic wasn't working, though; Pete was in a foul mood, hung-over from the wedding, and from the smell of him he'd had some hair of the dog on the bus journey from Bethnal Green to Nottingham.

'Why'd you ride in the crew bus?' Pete asked Dom now. 'Sick of us already?'

'Fancied a change, that's all.'

'Fancied the aromatherapist, more like.' There was nothing to the words, but the tone of them was so insinuating and dirty that Dominick turned to Pete sharply.

'If you like her yourself, ask her out. You don't have to keep sniping at me about it.'

He regretted saying it right away. 'Sorry, mate,' he said, and put his hand on Pete's shoulder.

Pete shrugged it off and turned away. 'No worries, she's all yours.'

Gina rushed back to them. Her normally composed face was flushed and her eyes were wide.

'I don't understand how this could have happened,' she said.

Max instantly had his arms around her. 'What's going on, babe?'

'He said we're not scheduled.' She stepped out of Max's embrace and pulled out her BlackBerry, typing frantically at the keys. 'There, look, that's my itinerary. Nottingham, Victoria. I rang yesterday and confirmed.'

'He's got to be wrong, I'll talk to him.' Max ambled over to the man, waving a greeting. He was joined by two other people from the theatre's staff, all of whom were shaking their heads.

Something niggled at the back of Dom's brain. 'You definitely rang the Victoria Theatre?'

'I rang the number I've got here for the Victoria, yes,

what other number would I ring?' There was an edge to Gina's voice. Great, he couldn't open his mouth at all this afternoon without pissing someone off. Just as well Sophie was asleep, or he'd have started another war with her by now.

'It's just that—'

Mad Dog slapped his hand on his forehead, where he'd been showing off his scar before. 'The Victoria,' he said.

Dempsey and Owen the guitar tech had both twigged, and they were shaking their heads. 'Shit, the Victoria,' Owen said.

'What are you all talking about?'

Dempsey, Owen, Mad Dog, and Dominick all looked at each other. Finally Dom decided he'd risk the explosion.

'The Victoria is a pub on the other side of Nottingham,' he told her. 'It puts on gigs sometimes.' Years ago he'd done an acoustic show there, on a toilet tour with his first band.

'You've gone and booked us a gig in a boozer?' Pete's face was nearly purple as he turned to Gina.

'Well, they seem pretty adamant for some reason,' Max called from halfway across the room, on his way back, 'but I'm sure we can sort it out. It's probably some clerical error, and anyway, we've signed a contract so it's their . . .' He reached them and saw everybody's faces. 'What's up?' he asked.

'Go on, darling, tell him,' Pete said to Gina.

But Gina was punching a number into her mobile phone. She turned and walked a few steps away while she listened to it ring. Everybody stared at her back, except for Dominick, who needed air. He went out through the theatre's double doors and stood near the crew bus, breathing deep despite the odour of the driver Lucky's rolled-up cigarette. Dominick had made him promise not to go any further than directly outside the bus while Sophie was on it.

'What's going on, mate?' Lucky asked him.

'You don't want to know.'

Ten minutes later everyone trooped out of the theatre. Their faces told Dominick everything.

The Victoria pub was on a narrow street. Dom watched the walls of the building slide past the window, listening to the wing mirrors scrape against brick. Unfortunately Lucky made it through and Dom had to get out again and take a look at the pub.

It was even smaller than he remembered. The lounge was stuffed with battered wooden furniture and stained flock wallpaper. The stage was at the end, and featured one mic stand and an upright piano.

The Venusians, their tour manager and their crew took up most of the available space in the pub just standing there. The rest of the space was filled by two old men drinking, one on either side of the pub.

TONIGHT: MAD MAX AND THE VENUSIANS, said the posters.

'I can't fit our equipment on this,' said Owen.

'What the hell were you thinking?' Pete yelled at Gina. 'We're going to have to cancel the gig.' From the redness of his face and the paleness of Gina's, Dom could see this was a discussion that had been going on for most of the ride over here, too.

'Pete, calm it down, don't talk to her like that,' said Max, and Pete rounded on him.

'You're right, I don't blame her, I blame you. What the hell were *you* thinking, getting your girlfriend to manage this tour? In case you haven't noticed, this isn't the first time she's messed up, and this is our last shot.'

Last shot. Dominick smelled whisky and stale beer towels. He put both of his hands on the bar, leant on it and felt the familiar sensation of rounded wood.

'I think it's sort of funny,' said Mad Dog, and Dominick, who was looking down at the floor so he wouldn't look at the bottles and optics, felt the crash as Pete slammed his fist into the bar.

'I'll show you fucking funny! This tour is a bunch of misfits and muppets! We used to have it all, and now we have to deal with this crap! And this . . . bit of skirt you call a tour manager—'

'I am a tour manager,' Gina said, enunciating every word. 'I'm *your* tour manager. I'm sorry this has happened, but we'll make the best of it.'

'How are we going to make the best of this fuck-up? If you—'

'Pete, think before you say any more, mate,' said Max, very quietly.

'Leave her alone, Pete,' Dominick said to the floor. 'She made a mistake. We've all made them.'

'You more than most, right, Steele?'

Dominick straightened up and met Pete's eyes. 'Right,' he said, his fists clenched, his throat dry.

'You want to make another mistake right now?'

'We're not falling out over this,' Max said firmly. 'We're a band and we stick together. No questions. We make music and that's all that matters.' He patted Dominick on the back. 'It's all about the music, right, Dom?'

'Right,' said Dom again.

'You wanted some time off anyway, yeah, Pete?' Max said. 'You go cool off, mate, have a lie-down, chill out, and we'll all be laughing later.'

Pete looked from Dominick to Max. Max was holding

Gina's hand and he had his other hand on Dominick's shoulder.

'Whatever,' Pete said, and he turned around and left the pub.

24

The Palladium Hotel, Nottingham

'Eerie, and quiet like you wouldn't believe. So I dragged all the instruments out there, got manure all over the drum kit, and there I was. A lunar eclipse and me making music. I was all by myself so I had to play the keyboard with a stick, and then I dropped it, but I liked the sound so I forgot about everything else and grabbed the stick and laid into the ground, whacking it as hard as I could.' Max threw back his head and laughed. 'Glad I don't have any neighbours. Anyway, that's how the album got its name. *Playing the Field*. 'Cause I was.'

Janna, the *Groovin'* journalist, was in her early twenties, with pierced eyebrows, nose and lip, and an elaborate tattoo of a Chinese dragon down one of her arms. Despite her unconventional appearance she clearly had no idea how to respond to one of Max's random stories.

'Wow,' she said, nodding.

'Yeah, that's exactly how I felt,' said Max.

Sophie adjusted the oil mix in one of the diffusers. She had six of them scattered throughout the conference room, each one with a concentrated blend of lavender and five other complementary oils. From the expression Gina had

had on her face when she'd informed Sophie that the interview was going to take place in the hotel, and not in the Victoria Theatre as planned, Sophie had thought that heavy calming artillery was probably necessary.

Theoretically, everyone in this room should feel as if they had been hit by a tranquillity bomb.

Toc toc WHAP, a-toc toc WHAP.

Mad Dog was tapping on the back of his chair with his hands, and to a different rhythm on the floor with his feet. He'd been doing it since he'd sat down twenty minutes ago. The sound seemed to go straight to the back of Sophie's head and lodge there like an itch. Gina didn't like it any better; though she sat next to Max with his arm around her shoulders, and her grooming was perfect as usual, her eyes were puffy and she was biting her lipsticked lip. Every time Mad Dog stomped his foot she winced slightly.

'Do you have any Venusians records?' Pete asked Janna. He was sitting in an armchair, sipping from a can of lager, wearing leather trousers and a white open-necked shirt. His head appeared to have been freshly shaved. He gave Janna a smile calculated to charm.

'It was all a bit before my time,' Janna said.

Pete's smile wavered. He took another drink of lager.

'But I am like a ginormous Dirtysweet fan,' she said. 'Dominick, how did you join up with the Venusians?'

To the reporter, Dominick most likely seemed completely at ease. The reporter hadn't had years of training on how to disappear in a room and observe. She hadn't been on tour with Dominick, either.

He sat, like the other band members, in one of the chintz armchairs dragged into this room at the last minute by Gina and two hotel employees in an effort to make the atmosphere relaxed and comfortable. He wore jeans and a loose dark shirt, the same thing he'd worn this morning when he'd hugged Sophie. Even across the room, even next to a very strong scent-diffuser, Sophie could remember the smell of him as he'd held her.

Dominick nodded and smiled. Small lines around his eyes, a tiny tension in his hands as they lay on his thighs, betrayed his real mood to Sophie.

But his voice was easy. 'Max called me and asked me,' he said. 'They needed a bass-player, and I needed a job. It was one of the best things that could have happened to me.'

'Why?' No half-hearted confusion for Janna now; she was sharp, fully engaged, leaning forward in her chair, focused on Dominick.

'It gave me back the music,' Dominick said. 'I hadn't played in years. Now I am. I'll be grateful to Max for the rest of my life.'

He exchanged a smile with Max. 'Hey, it's you, man, you're the music,' Max said. 'No need to thank me.'

WHAP tic-toc WHAP. WHAP tic-toc WHAP.

The change in the rhythm drew Sophie's eyes to Mad Dog, and then to follow the drummer's eyes to Pete. The guitarist was watching Max and Dominick with an expression of pure fury on his face.

'So is this a comeback?' Janna asked, and Pete rapidly rearranged his features to pleasant confidence.

'You bet your little—' he began, but Janna interrupted him.

'I mean, after Dirtysweet broke up, there were like all these rumours that you were saying that you'd jacked it all in, that you were never going to make another album. And now here you are, playing in someone else's band.

What's next for Dominick Steele? Are you writing music again?'

'I don't ... No. Not really.' Dominick ran his hand through his hair. 'Anyway, I think we should talk about *Playing the Field*, which is a great album.'

'I had a blast writing it,' said Max. 'I don't know if you know that I've been up in Yorkshire for the past ten years? I've got my own little llama farm up there. Have you spent much time with llamas?'

'Uh, no,' said Janna.

'You should. Wonderful animals, so gentle and endearing and playful. You can learn a lot about life by watching a llama.'

'Okay.' Janna rubbed her forehead, where Sophie suspected a headache was brewing. Maybe these essential oils were a little strong.

'Llamas,' she said. 'That's very interesting. Uh, what have the rest of you been up to for the past twenty years?' The conversation's redirection into surrealism had evidently reminded Janna that she was meant to be interviewing the entire band.

'Five kids,' said Mad Dog, still drumming. *A-tic-a-tic-a-tic-a-tic-a TOC, a-tic-a-tic-a-tic-a-tic-a TOC TOC TOC.*

'I'm working on a solo album,' Pete said.

'That's very interesting. How about you, Dominick? Dirtysweet officially broke up like two and a half years ago, what have you been doing?'

WHUMP. WHUMP. A-toc-toc WHUMP.

'Nothing that I think would interest your readers,' Dominick answered.

'What do you think about Carver and Tick's new band?'

He looked surprised. 'I haven't heard them.'

Janna raised her eyebrows. 'You're kidding? I was at

their gig at Brixton Academy last month. It was like spectacular, though I don't think Tick quite does it as a frontman. It's a total change of sound, obviously, without you writing, and then they're missing that charisma, and it's not as dark as your later stuff.'

Dominick was rubbing the fingers of his left hand against his thumb, hard enough so that their tips were white.

'Well,' he said. 'Good for them.'

Pete put down his can with a bang. 'I thought you were, like, here to interview us about the tour?' he said, mimicking Janna's twentysomething lilt.

'Uh, sure. How do you all find it being on tour again? Is it like different from how it was in the eighties?'

'It certainly is,' Pete began. 'For one thing, back in the eighties, we never had to cancel a gi—'

Gina sat upright, and Max broke in. 'Yeah, they've changed all the windows in the hotels.'

'The windows?' Janna asked, puzzled once more. Pete sat back in his chair and glowered.

'They're unbreakable. You try to toss a television through one of those, it just bounces back on you. Man, you should see the bruises on my shins.' He slapped his leg and laughed again.

'Oh, okay,' said Janna. 'I get it. So listen, Dom, you've never gone on record about Dirtysweet's break-up, and I wondered if you—'

Dominick stood up so quickly that his armchair scraped back about six inches on the floor.

'I think that if I'm distracting you from talking about the Venusians, I'd better go.' He strode out of the room. The door slammed behind him, in the silence left by Mad Dog's sudden lack of drumming.

'Well, that'll be a good headline,' said Pete. He cracked open another can of lager.

Max caught Sophie's eye and nodded in the direction of the door. She put down her phial of oil and followed Dominick.

He hadn't gone far; he was in the corridor, leaning with his forehead against the wall, his hands braced above his head as if he were holding himself upright by an effort. He seemed to be staring straight at the wall, but when she touched him on the shoulder he spoke to her.

'I need you to help me with something, Sophie.'

'All right.'

He lifted his head and looked at her. During the interview he'd appeared normal, with only slight signs of stress. Now his face was chalk-white and drawn, a ghost of its normal self.

'Talk to me,' he said. 'Argue with me. Do something.'

She had plenty to argue with him about, she was sure, but right at that moment she couldn't think of a single thing.

'You're not as hot as all that with your shirt off,' she said.

She thought he was probably beyond smiling, but at that there was a small flicker in his eyes. 'You're lying,' he said. 'That's not going to do it. Try again.'

'You also look lousy in drag.'

'That, I can believe.' He took her hand. His palm was clammy and his fingers cold. 'Walk with me. Keep talking.'

'I don't know what to talk about.' They walked down the corridor, Dominick striding so quickly that Sophie had to trot to keep up.

'Anything. Tell me why you became a private detective.'

They were practically to the lobby now. 'I was good at watching,' Sophie said. 'And I wanted to know everything.'

'Why?'

'I didn't want to be noticed.'

'Why not?'

'It's very off-putting to be constantly asked "why" and "why not".'

'Now you know how I felt. Why didn't you want to be noticed?'

They were halfway across the lobby now, and Sophie noticed what she hadn't before: that the hotel bar lay between where they were and the lifts. Dominick's hand tightened on hers when he saw where she was looking.

'It was easier if I blended in,' she said. 'You want to fit in in foster homes. You stay quiet so they'll keep you there. And you learn what you can so you know what's going to happen to you.'

'You grew up in foster homes?' Fast, fast, striding past the bar. Sophie smelt the beer, heard conversation and glasses clinking.

'My mother gave me up when I was a baby. I stayed with my aunt until I was ten. Then I went into foster homes.'

'Your father?'

'I don't know, there was no name on my birth certificate. Tennant was my mother's name.'

Past the bar now, three more long strides, four, and they were at the lifts. Dominick punched the button, the door slid open, and he pulled Sophie in with him and hit a floor number.

The door shut behind them. Dominick leaned back against the side of the lift and closed his eyes.

'Thank you,' he said. There was sweat on his forehead and on his upper lip.

'Are you all right?'

'Thirsty.'

'What was it, Pete or the interviewer? Or the gig?'

'Everything.' He wiped his face with one of his sleeves. 'I have one way of dealing with stress, and we just walked past it.'

'Sounds like you need to work on some alternate strategies.'

'Thank you for letting me know.'

The door slid open again. 'Is this your floor?' Sophie asked.

He checked. 'Yes. Yours?'

'I'm one floor up. If I go to my own room, are you going to go right back downstairs to the bar?'

'I think it's probably even money right now.'

'Come on then.'

He led her to the last room on the corridor. When he dug in his pocket for his key card, Sophie noticed his hand was shaking.

'Here,' she said, taking the card. She slotted it in and opened the door.

His room was exactly like hers – bland and in all aspects rectangular – except his bag was on the bed and there were two two-litre bottles of water on the bedside table. One was empty, the other half-full.

Dom prowled around the room as if it were a cage. 'I need something to do with my hands,' he said.

'Where's your guitar?' Sophie asked.

'It's not mine, it's Pete's. I didn't want to ask to borrow it, not after I nearly lumped him this afternoon. Here.' He dug suddenly into his bag and pulled out a pack of dog-eared cards, held together by a twisted elastic band. He tossed them to Sophie. 'What do you play?' he asked.

'Gin?' It was out before she thought. 'Whoops, sorry.'

'Funny. Very funny.' He ran a hand through his hair.

'Why did you nearly lump Pete?'

'He was out of order. I've never hit anyone while I was sober. I don't want to. I don't think I want to sit with you on the bed, either. You're only slightly less tempting to me than a pint right now.'

Dominick was in such a state, she'd hardly registered that they were alone in a hotel room together. With his words, her body caught up with the situation and lust wrenched through her belly.

'You don't look like you feel very sexy,' she said.

On the other hand, he looked sexy. Even shaking, in the grip of a craving. He paced like a predator, his fevered movements graceful.

'It's oblivion,' he said. 'Drink would work, sex would work. Anything to get out of my head.'

'Well, that's very flattering.'

'I think it should be, considering that you're dressed like a lab technician.'

He pulled the table out from where it stood near the window. There was an armchair next to it already, and he hauled the desk chair over to it and sat down. 'Let's play gin,' he said. 'You'd better deal.'

'I like to dress professionally,' Sophie said, but she took off her white smock before she sat down. She was wearing a tailored white shirt underneath.

'Yeah, I remember you dressing professionally. Miniskirt and high heels. Deal the cards.'

She shuffled efficiently and dealt them each ten cards, and put the deck down in the middle of the table, turning a single card over to form the discard pile. 'If I'd known you got turned on by white smocks, I'd have saved myself the discomfort. Miniskirts are cold.'

'You didn't feel cold.' He abruptly shook his head. 'We can't talk about this. So you became a private detective because you wanted to track down your parents?'

She raised her eyebrows as she fanned her cards. 'Gosh, I never knew you were an amateur psychologist as well as a rock star.'

'I would have thought the mystery would be irresistible to you.'

'Unfortunately, there's no real mystery there. My mother was having an affair with a married man; he didn't want me and so neither did she. So I was stuck with my aunt. Or according to her, she was stuck with me.'

'It doesn't sound as if it was a happy time.'

'Aunt Laura wasn't fond of my mother. Called her a tramp.' Sophie arranged her cards into sets and runs, not looking at Dominick, trying not to think about why she was telling him this, except of course to provide a distraction. 'Are we going to play?'

Dominick hadn't sorted out his cards; they were in a messy pile in front of him. He picked up a card from the top of the pile and threw it down again without looking at it.

'I think I might win this game,' she said.

'I think you will. Is that why you have such a low opinion of people who have affairs? Because of what your mother did?'

She sighed, picking through her cards to decide which one to throw away. 'I think it has a lot to do with my recent history, too. I've seen a lot of people get hurt. Women think they want to know the truth when they come to see me, but it's always a blow when I confirm their worst suspicions. I used to spend a lot of time trying to convince them they were better off not hiring me.'

'But they did hire you.'

'I think I had one wife who decided against it.'

Dominick picked up the card she'd laid down. 'I bet you investigated the husband anyway.'

'He was having it off with the au pair whenever the wife took the children to dance class.'

He actually smiled. Sophie felt as if she'd given him a gift.

'Why do you need to know everything?' he asked.

She had to discard: either a two when she had the four and five, or a jack she had a pair of. Both cards she'd like to keep. But eventually you had to give something away.

'It's a compulsion,' she said. 'I can't help asking. I think that once I know, I'll feel better. But most of the time I don't.'

'Looks like we have something in common,' Dominick said, playing his card. 'Your curiosity, my booze.'

'You said that your drinking wasn't because of your childhood, though. If you live in a foster home you're always uncertain – I was in mine, anyway. They were good people, but I wasn't part of the family. Whenever there was a conversation behind closed doors, I was sure I was going to be sent away. Eventually, I was.'

'So you thought that if you'd only known, you could've stopped it.'

'It's not as simple as that, but it's connected. Knowing gives you power. It gives you control. In theory, anyway.' She took another card, slotted it in, and discarded. 'I've got gin,' she said, laying down her hand.

Dominick nodded and threw down his own cards. 'Deal again,' he said.

She scraped them all together, shuffled, and dealt. This time he did take a quick look at his hand before he played. He leaned back in his chair, tipping the seat back, and reached over to grab the half-full two-litre bottle of water from his bedside table. The action emphasised the long lines of his body, his casual strength. He unscrewed the top and drank straight from the bottle. Sophie watched his throat working with each swallow. In her imagination she felt the touch of dark stubble on his chin and neck, under her hand. On her own face.

He finished a long gulp and wiped his mouth with the back of his hand. 'Oh – did you want some?' he asked, holding out the bottle for her. There were only a couple of inches of water at the bottom.

If she put the bottle to her lips, she'd taste him. 'No thanks,' she said. She played her cards quickly and said, 'It's your turn.'

He finished off the water and then took his turn. For some time they played in silence, Sophie trying not to watch Dominick and Dominick picking up and laying down cards with apparently little thought.

Sophie glanced at her watch, but she understood that these games weren't going to be measured by time or by hands or by points; they were measured by breaths taken, heartbeats achieved. She was used to being patient and still and watching, though she wasn't sure if sitting in a hotel room playing cards with an overwhelmingly sexy man was preferable to crouching in a wet bush pointing a video camera at a second-storey window.

She had enough points to knock and lay down, but instead she let the game stretch out until she had gin. Dominick reacted with a shrug and a nod, and again he pushed the cards towards her.

Midway through their third game, he spoke again.

'Knowing doesn't always give you control. You must have found out a lot of things that you'd rather not know.'

'Yes, I did,' she said. 'That's why I quit. It got to be that I couldn't look at anyone without thinking about their dirty little secrets. It's not an easy way to live.'

'And you never tried to find your mother,' he said.

What was it, about this room, this game of cards, this hour, that meant she could say things aloud that she'd never said before? Was it because Dominick needed her?

'I have a file. It's in my bag in my hotel room. A missing persons file. It's got my birth certificate and a postcard from Brighton. And a snapshot of my mother from 1980.' She breathed in deeply, and out. 'They're the only three things I have of my mother. I could probably find her from them.'

'But you haven't looked.'

She shook her head. She expected him to ask why, but he didn't. And there were so many tangled-up reasons, she wasn't sure she'd be able to give him one if he did ask.

She glanced at Dominick, who actually checked his cards before finding one to discard. Some colour had come back into his face, and his hands seemed steadier.

Or maybe he knew already, without asking, what it was like to have parts of your life where you were afraid to go.

'So now indulge my addiction to knowledge,' she said to him. 'Was it the question about Dirtysweet that pushed you over the edge, or was it the journalist's overuse of the word "like"?'

'It wasn't a good breakup,' he said. 'I didn't behave well. I don't like to think about it. I don't even listen to the radio in case one of our songs comes on.'

'You'll have to think about it sometime or other,' she said, knowing she was talking to herself as well.

'Not if I can help it. And not in front of the press.'

She drew, and got the ace she needed. One more card, either a five or a ten, and she'd have gin. She felt bad thrashing him at cards when she had a big advantage, but not bad enough to keep from doing it.

'Oh well, at least the interview wasn't a total waste of time,' she said.

'Why's that?' Dominick picked up the four she'd discarded.

'I know now why Max's new songs are about gambolling in fields, et cetera. He wrote them all about his llamas.'

Dominick stopped in the middle of tucking his four into his hand. He stared at her. She stared back.

They both erupted into laughter at the same time.

'Oh my God,' Dominick gasped, 'you're right. Woolly heads. He wrote the album about his animals.'

He put his head down on his arms on the table. Sophie watched his glossy dark hair shake as he laughed.

When he raised his head, his eyes were more alive than they'd been. The stress lines were still there, but not as deep.

'Thank you,' he said.

'No problem. I like beating you at cards.'

'Those four months?' he said to her. 'The four months you couldn't trace? I saw a doctor, I don't know why. Maybe someone took me there. I don't remember. I do remember what he said to me, though. He said I'd already done serious damage to my liver, and if I kept on drinking, sooner rather than later I was going to die.

'So I went out and I got drunk. And that's what I did for

four months, though I didn't know how long it was at the time. I drank whatever I could get my hands on and as much of it as I could before I passed out, and then when I woke up I started all over again. Before that I usually drank with other people, but this time I think I mostly did it alone. It wasn't quite suicide, but it was the same thing underneath.'

'And after four months?' Sophie asked quietly.

'I woke up one day and stopped. Maybe it was something about the light that day. I realised I was by myself and the reason I was by myself was because I didn't want anybody to see what I'd become. And I knew that meant that I didn't want to die. But I wasn't sure I wanted to be alive, either.'

She looked at the man she had thought was a rock god, arrogant and untouchable.

She thought she'd had enough of dirty little secrets. But this secret was neither dirty nor little. It was part of Dominick Steele and what made him human.

'Thank you for telling me,' she said.

'You're welcome. I owed you one.' He smiled at her, a small smile that dented his cheek, and she smiled back. Then he looked down at his cards.

'Oh,' he said, 'and gin.'

25

Still the Palladium Hotel, Nottingham

'You bastard,' Sophie said. 'I thought you weren't paying attention.'

Dominick rumpled his hair with one hand, looking pleased with himself. 'We could make it best out of five. But I need a shower first.' He stretched in his chair and his stomach rumbled. 'And I'm hungry,' he added, evidently surprised.

'I'll order room service while you take a shower,' Sophie offered.

'Great. Get a couple more of those big bottles of water. Or even better, Coke. I won't be long.'

He went into the bathroom, and Sophie heard the water start. He would put his hand under the shower spray to check its temperature. She bet he liked it hot. Then he'd pull his shirt off over his head. His hair would be pushed further into disarray by the collar. He'd unbutton his jeans and kick them off his legs. Hook his thumb in his underwear and . . .

She got up and searched for the room service menu. It was poor distraction, but she needed it.

After ordering some sandwiches and chips and a

two-litre bottle each of Coke and mineral water, she sat at the table and shuffled the cards. Solitaire was an even poorer diversion, though, with Dominick Steele naked in the next room and his baggage right here on the bed.

Just a quick look. Just to find out what kind of underwear he wore. Because she was never going to find out otherwise, and right now it seemed like a really important question. How else was she going to torture herself with images of him getting undressed?

She went to the bed and unzipped the bag. It was made out of a black waterproof canvas material, with several pockets on the outside. His clothes were folded neatly, shirts on top, trousers on bottom. People used to living out of a suitcase packed methodically. Beside his clothes lay a battered paperback autobiography of Ray Davies of the Kinks, and a nearly equally battered iPod. His underwear was in a side pocket.

Boxers. Mostly black and dark blue, some of them cotton, some of them silk. She should have known.

A muffled noise came from the bathroom and Sophie froze, her hand gripping silk. It continued, getting louder, and she realised that Dominick was singing. She couldn't make out any of the words, and it wasn't a song she recognised, but his voice was rich and tuneful.

He was definitely feeling better. She smoothed down the underwear to its original state and quickly, systematically went through the other pockets. A notebook, mostly empty but with a jumble of letters that might be a chord progression, and a few words in sprawling black handwriting: *night rocket fire, juniper, innocent parting, calluses, confetti*. A collection of thin triangular plastic objects in a variety of colours that Sophie had to examine for several moments before she figured out that they were guitar picks. A mobile phone, turned off; a folded postcard of Edinburgh; a letter from a building society dated 25 April informing Mr D. A. Steele of the imminent repossession of his flat due to mortgage arrears. A passport with a moody photograph, due to expire next year.

It wasn't anything she hadn't known or couldn't have guessed. As she rezipped the bag, she felt a certain relief.

When the bathroom door opened she was halfway through a very unabsorbing game of solitaire. She glanced up from her cards and bit her lip to keep her mouth from falling open.

Dominick was wearing nothing but a towel around his waist. A damp towel. The hotel towels were big, but flimsy, and this one clung to his narrow hips and his legs and bulged out slightly at his crotch. It was white enough to make his skin look darker.

His hair was wet. He hadn't shaved. The scattering of hair on his chest and the line of it down his stomach was black and damp. Even from several feet away she could smell the freshness of his skin.

'Forgot to take my clothes in,' he said. He didn't meet her eyes, but went to the bed and unzipped his bag.

At any other time, Sophie would have thought first. But she couldn't detach, analyse, observe. Not with Dominick Steele, the Dominick Steele she was beginning to know, in a towel.

She stood up and went to his side. She put both of her hands on his chest, her fingertips just below his collarbone, her palms just above his nipples. His skin was warm and damp.

'Sophie,' he said, and she could feel his voice vibrate underneath his ribs and muscle. A drop of water fell from his hair and landed on her right hand, the one his heart was beating beneath.

'It's not a good idea,' he said, but he didn't step away. Instead he was watching her, his eyes going from her face to her hands to the opening at the top of her shirt.

'Why?'

'Because I haven't had sex in two years, not since I gave up drink. They're connected.'

'I'm not sure about that.' She leaned forward slightly so that her face was nearer to his chest, and breathed him in. 'I'm not drunk.'

'You're not an alcoholic and a serial adulterer.'

She didn't move her hands, but ran her thumbs back and forth along his skin, just to feel the crisp rasp of hair, the contour of ribs and sternum.

'Seems to me like you're stone-cold sober, divorced, and haven't had sex for two years,' she said.

'It's another way of escaping from real life.'

This time she did move her hands. She slid one up to his shoulder and rested it on the side of his neck, where his pulse beat hard and fast. The other she let fall to his hip above the towel and she used it to pull herself closer.

The towel was really flimsy. She could feel his erection through it and through her own clothes, pressing into her belly.

'I think this is real life, Dominick,' she said, and stood on her tiptoes and kissed him.

They'd kissed twice before and both times it had been Dominick who'd started it. Once because of the rules of the honey trap, and once because he was trying to prove something.

Sophie didn't have anything to prove. She wanted to feel his mouth on hers, pure and simple.

His mouth was generous and warm and he didn't kiss her back, but he didn't pull away, either. She pressed her lips to his for a long moment and then she eased back down off her toes and looked up into his face.

High-cheekboned, dark-eyed, rough with beard growth and strain. He had the face of a god fallen to earth. She raised herself up and kissed him again. This time she let her tongue touch the smooth, wet inside of his lip and tasted minty toothpaste and him. She heard and felt his breath hitch in his throat.

His tongue touched hers and she explored him. This wasn't a passionate, carnal kiss like the ones they'd had, but every inch as sexy. A kiss where she led and persuaded him. A kiss unlike anything she'd ever done.

She pulled back gently, but kept the kiss going by putting her hand on his face. Her fingers traced his cheek, the arch of his eyebrow and the line of his nose. Dominick closed his eyes, and she touched the fan of his eyelashes. When she ran her finger over his lip, he opened his eyes again. His pupils were wide. Beyond the slight touch of his tongue, he'd done nothing to her.

'I wanted you five years ago,' she told him. 'I would've preferred not to. I ran away so fast because I was afraid that I'd turn off the video recorder and let you do what you said you were going to.'

At that, he acted. He dipped his head and kissed her. Still gentle and slow and exploratory. But his hands on her waist told a different story. They wrapped around her and held on tight.

This was what it felt like to be fully in the moment, not observing. Sophie curved her body into Dominick's and ran her hands over his skin: smooth back, firm waist, strong arms.

Someone rapped at the door. Dominick raised his head

to look at her in enquiry, as if the knock had been an expression of her having second thoughts.

'Room service,' she told him. 'It can wait.'

She released him to unbutton her shirt and push it off. Then she reached behind her and unhooked her bra. She sat on the bed, then lay back and held out her arms to him.

'Thanks, leave it outside the door,' he called, then he joined her. He wrapped her in his arms and the feeling of her bare breasts against his chest, his entire body laid out along hers, was so shockingly pleasurable that Sophie couldn't move for a moment, could only experience.

He kissed the side of her face, the lobe of her ear. 'I don't have any condoms,' he told her.

'Me neither. I'm on the pill.' She believed that every woman who didn't want a baby, sexually active or not, should be on the pill.

'I was always careful when I was married to Leonie.' He removed the elastic band from her hair and ran his fingers through the loosened strands, gently as if he were smoothing out tangles. 'But afterwards I don't remember everything I did. I'm not going to put you at risk.'

Dominick was taking responsibility for her. Like that first hug he'd given her, it made her want to melt into him and resist him all at the same time.

'It's my risk,' she said. 'My decision.'

He shook his head and gave her half a smile. Then he began to kiss down her neck to her breasts. His rough chin and his soft mouth were two separate caresses.

Forget it. She wasn't going to argue. Just as long as he kept on doing what . . .

He licked one of her nipples and she gasped loudly enough to startle herself. This time he gave her a full-fledged smile, looking up at her from underneath his hair like a naughty boy, and then he bent his attention to her again.

Rap rap rap-rap rap.

Sophie put her hand on Dominick's head to keep him right where he was and shouted at the door, 'We're busy, please leave the tray outside!'

He chuckled against her. Then he got back to work, caressing and exploring her, nipping at her breast with his teeth and then smoothing it with his tongue. His hands were dark against her pale skin.

'How is this?' he asked her. His breath cooled where he had licked, bringing up shivers.

'It's . . . all right.'

'If it's only all right, I'd better try harder.'

Trying harder was so exquisite that she closed her eyes and groaned.

When she opened them he was propped up on his arms above her, smiling down and looking at her face and her chest, which was rosy from his touch.

'You're beautiful,' he told her.

His hair was beginning to dry and it fell in dark spikes around his face.

'I lied when I said you weren't all that hot with your shirt off,' she said.

'Told you so.'

'You're probably used to people telling you you're sexy,' she said.

'Not you.'

'Now that I've said it, can I see you without the towel?'

'I don't think you've actually told me yet.'

She put her hands on his shoulders and, with her legs as leverage, flipped the two of them over so that she was above him. His eyes widened in surprise.

'Surely,' she said, 'you don't need me to build up your ego for you.'

'Sophie, half the time I'm not even sure who I am any more. If you're going to build up my ego, you're going to have to do it from the ground upwards.'

He meant it. Her own eyes widened.

'Speaking of from the ground upwards,' he said, and while she was off guard, he flipped them over again.

'Hey,' she protested, but he was unfastening her trousers and peeling them down her legs and then running his fingertips over her ankles.

'I remembered your feet are ridiculously small,' he said, holding one of them in the palm of his hand. Held by him she seemed delicate, almost precious. It was another illusion she was tempted to slip into. Like her miniskirts and her red dress in the right-hand side of the wardrobe at home, it was an image that could get her into trouble.

She'd thought this was going to be so much easier, a mindless, passionate slaking of their hunger. A stripping-off of clothes, not of defences.

But of course he didn't know what he was doing to her. He was revealing himself, and the insecurities that she'd never suspected. But she'd only told him that he was sexy, that she'd craved his body. Not that she also craved his closeness, his compliments and his attention.

He kissed the back of her knee. The inside of her thigh. She reached for the knotted towel at his waist, but he stopped her with a hand on her wrist. 'Not yet,' he said.

'I want to see you.'

He raised an eyebrow. 'You've got to build me up from the ground, remember? It's been some time since I've been with a woman. I want to make sure I know how all the parts work.'

'All the parts?'

'Every single one.' He planted a kiss on her belly, above the band of her knickers, and then another on the rise of her pubis. She could feel his breath through the material.

She closed her eyes, better to feel the long, thrilling moments while he explored her without removing her underwear. But when he slipped his hand inside to touch her, when he guided the scrap of cotton down her legs and off her feet, she had to see. It was too much of a fantasy come true not to watch.

His face was level with her sex, his thumb lazily stroking her. He was grinning. 'You're very turned on,' he said, sounding ridiculously pleased.

'It's been a while.'

'You too, huh? Is that the only reason?'

She swallowed. 'Five years ago, you said you were going to make me scream.'

'I was a cocky sod, wasn't I? I'll do my best.'

He lowered his head to her and licked her. She screamed right away.

He looked up and raised his eyebrows again. She heard the echo of her cry in her ears and felt herself blushing furiously, though to be honest she was surprised she had any spare blood for her face.

When he smiled at her, though, she couldn't help smiling back. She even smiled when he began to lick her again.

Unhurried and gentle, as if he were going to take all night if he needed to. Sophie tried to count the stages of pleasure, from 'wow that's nice' to 'oh my God my head's about to explode'. But he brought her to each stage so gradually, so sweetly, that by the time she was close to orgasm she'd forgotten that she hadn't always felt this way, and when she came she couldn't count anything, not breaths, not heartbeats, nothing except for maybe the syllables of his name.

Then he did it again, this time with his hand as well as his mouth, his fingers moving inside her with a rhythm she hadn't ever felt before. A third time, and she was weak.

When he raised himself to lie beside her and kissed her lightly with lips that tasted of herself, she was far, far too pleased with him to think about ego-building or holding herself back.

'Dominick,' she sighed happily, and wound her arms around his neck and plied him with grateful kisses.

'Sophie Dean,' he agreed, and held her. She wondered if it were possible to get used to being in his arms and feeling his skin and his breath.

And then she remembered she hadn't seen him naked yet.

She practically leapt to her knees and grabbed the front of his towel. 'This is gone,' she said and tugged it off and flung it on to the floor.

Then she just sat and stared for a while.

Eventually he raised himself on to his elbows. 'Soph?'

She blinked and realised that she was chewing the nail of her index finger.

There was so much she wanted to know about him. What pleased him, what every bit of him felt like under her hands and her mouth and inside her. How it felt to watch him walk around naked on a Sunday morning, whether he smiled the first thing when he woke up. The taste of his sweat. The smell of the back of his neck where his hair curled under. What he dreamt about when he was asleep.

She could only have this. Sophie laid her hand on his penis. He was hard and hot and heavy and he groaned at the touch.

'I thought you rock stars stuffed marrows down your trousers,' she said.

'Never much liked marrow.'

'You're right, this is much nicer. Tell me what you do like,' she said, curling her fingers around him and stroking up experimentally.

'I like that.'

'And this?'

He threw his head back. 'Oh, Christ.'

She took that as a yes, and tried a new movement: light friction, quick feathers, and then slowing.

'You're a massage therapist,' he said. 'I'm in heaven.'

So was she. Dominick Steele both literally and metaphorically in her hands, and she'd wanted this for five years, since she'd first met him.

She took her time and observed the effect of each caress. How his scent grew stronger, how his breath quickened, how his face twisted with pleasure, how he grew hotter and more urgent in her hands. His voice, when he cried out in orgasm, was even more beautiful than when he sang.

And none of that really prepared her for how she felt when he took her into his arms and kissed her and wrapped his body around her, her head on his chest.

It was far too much like needing him.

'You were right, Sophie Dean,' he whispered drowsily. 'This is real life.' He kissed her forehead and his breath stirred her hair.

Far too real.

She curled into him, held on to him and moulded into his warm and heavy limbs. Closed her eyes, let herself drift into sleep, safe and tender.

Morning-After Land

When Dom woke up, he had no idea what time it was, but he did know two things. One, he was ravenously hungry, because his stomach was growling like a lion in heat. And two, he had definitely rejoined the land of the sexually active, because he had a hard-on the dimensions of a . . . well, of a Dominick in heat.

Sophie slept in his arms. She was curled on her side, facing away from him. Her cheek was pillowed on one of her hands and her lips were slightly open. The sweet curve of her backside pressed against his crotch, and was doubtless responsible for his arousal.

That, and the soft sound of her breathing. And the taste of her lingering on his lips. And the memory of her hands on him and that knowing smile along with uncertain eyes.

He wound a strand of her brown hair round his finger, and then let it drop.

Imagine if he'd had sex with her five years ago, when he'd been ready to have her right there on the bridge. She'd wanted to. If it hadn't been for her job, maybe they would have. He'd have slipped on a condom (he'd had them in the inside pocket of his jacket — he always had them), an action he could perform in those days with one practised hand. And then he'd have cupped her bottom in his hands and lifted her on to him.

It would have been good. More than good. From the first moment, he'd been attracted to her innocence, sexiness, vulnerability and strength mixed together – all the things she couldn't hide even when she was acting. He remembered her warm skin on the cool night, and now of course he knew how warm and slick and tight she was and what she sounded like when she came. It would have taken all of about five thrilling minutes.

And it would have been over. He would've gone back to the pub, drunk until closing, persuaded the barman to sell him a bottle of something, whisky preferably, but it didn't much matter, and he'd have gone home and with any luck passed out before he had an argument with Leonie.

And he wouldn't be here with Sophie right now.

She sighed in her sleep and shifted even closer to him. Her foot touched his. His cock grew, impossibly, harder and he wrapped his arm tighter around her waist.

He wanted her much, much more than he had five years ago. He wanted her more than he had last night, and that was saying something. He closed his eyes and indulged in a very detailed fantasy of what he would do with Sophie right now if he happened to have a condom. It would take much longer than five minutes.

Did room service deliver condoms? He thought he recalled doing that sometime in the past, but he'd been in much more upmarket hotels back then. It seemed like a lifetime ago, or maybe something that had happened to a different person.

He hadn't been a different person, though. His hair had grown and been cut, his skin cells had shed and renewed, he had different clothes, but aside from that – and quite probably the chemical composition of his blood – he was exactly the same person he'd been back then.

And the reason he and Sophie hadn't had sex five years ago wasn't because of her job. It was because of who he'd been.

Dominick gently let Sophie go and sat up in bed beside her. She sighed again and curled more tightly up into herself.

There was no question about it. Sophie had put her hands on his chest and two years of celibacy had gone straight out the window. He hadn't even fought it that hard. And now he was in bed next to a naked woman and he wanted to have sex with her.

Maybe he'd broken the dam and this meant that he was doomed to shag every willing female within a ten-mile radius.

He swung his legs out of bed and found a clean pair of boxers in his bag. As his erection hadn't noticeably subsided, getting them on was a bit of a struggle. He pulled a shirt on too, though that didn't conceal a whole lot. His litre bottles of water were standing empty next to the remains of Sophie's game of solitaire. He had picked one up and was on his way to the bathroom to fill it from the tap when he remembered Sophie had ordered room service, which had come when they were in bed together. So he went to the door and opened it, first checking the time on his phone. If anybody happened to be outside his door at 7.28 a.m., they'd just have to deal with the sight of him and his newly rediscovered sexuality.

But when he saw what was outside his door, he stopped thinking about his tented shirt.

'Holy shit,' he said.

There wasn't much edible left on the room service tray. From the pulp that was ground into the carpet, he guessed that Sophie had ordered something involving bread and possibly lettuce, and he thought he might be able to identify a chip. Half a dozen screwed-up, emptied packets of ketchup lay in a twisted heap on the floor. Mostly it looked as if their meal had been attacked by a blender. Or a sledgehammer. Or, more probably, a really, really pissed-off person.

His feet were bare, so rather than stepping on to the crockery-sharded carpet, he leaned out and looked down the corridor in case whoever had done this was still around to be seen. There was nobody in sight and the hotel was completely quiet.

'Damn,' said a voice beside him.

Sophie was wrapped in the towel she'd peeled off him earlier, and her hair was rumpled. Otherwise she looked absolutely alert and one hundred per cent sharp. She stepped past him, her bare foot unerringly finding the one crockery-free patch of carpet, and hurried down the corridor. Before he could go after her, she had checked both directions, the lift and the stairs, and was on her way back.

'Guess we're not getting anything to eat,' he said to her. 'I was starving, too. If I didn't know better, I'd think someone had it in for me.'

'It's not you they have it in for,' she said grimly, and he followed her gaze to look, for the first time, at the other side of his door.

BITCH. YOU'LL BE SORRY.

The words crawled up the door, written jaggedly in red. For a moment Dominick thought it was blood, until he remembered the crumpled ketchup packets on the floor.

'Fucking hell,' he said.

'You're not kidding.' Sophie picked her way through the debris and examined the writing. She scrutinised each letter and even took a sniff before she shook her head.

'I think they were wearing gloves,' she said, pointing to the O in 'SORRY', where the ketchup had run out and the finger trail was smooth and featureless. 'But a proper fingerprinting might pick up something.'

Seeing Sophie next to that scrawled hate, he had an impulse to pick her up, whisk her into his room, and shut and lock the door behind them. Since he knew that if he did he'd be risking a kick in the shins, he refrained.

'Do you think it's related to the person who tried to run you down?' he asked.

'It's the same language as the email I received, though it's not exactly imaginative. I think it's safe to assume it's not a coincidence. It's not my room, though.' Her brow creased with thought.

'If they were watching you, they would have seen us go in together.'

She nodded and kept staring at the door. 'They could have done it any time. There was that second knock on the door. They could have been out there then, while we weren't listening.' Without volition her left hand went to her mouth and she nibbled at the nail of her index finger.

The gesture was vulnerable, the mouth was sexy. And if he was thinking about sex in the middle of what was evidently a death threat, the dam of his celibacy had indeed broken.

He noticed that there was a plastic two-litre bottle of Coke more or less intact on its side by the wall, and he picked it up and started to take off the cap.

Sophie's hand landed over his. 'Don't drink it,' she said.

The order was crisp and definite and her hand was holding his tightly. 'Do you think I've destroyed fingerprints?' he asked.

'Just don't drink it.' She took the bottle from him with her other hand and put it back down on the floor. He noticed she didn't handle it with particular care for someone who was trying to preserve fingerprints.

'I think we should ring the police,' he said to her. 'Hotels are used to rock bands trashing their rooms, but this is serious.'

He could see she was thinking about it, and he expected an argument, but to his surprise she nodded her head. 'I'll ring them,' she said. 'Don't touch anything.'

She went back into the room, leaving him with the ketchup carnage. He surveyed it for any more clues, but he was obviously no good at this sort of thing. Sophie had shown him where to step, though, so if he wanted to vault over the mess and dart downstairs to the nearest men's loo, he could probably purchase himself some condoms.

Then again, he could hear Sophie agreeing on the phone that she would wait for the police, and saying yes, she'd get in touch with the hotel duty manager as well.

And dammit, how could he possibly think about leaving her alone even for a second after being threatened?

He went back into the room, filled his water bottle from the tap after all, then sat on the bed and watched Sophie talk to the duty manager and put on her discarded clothes at the same time. Watching her put on her bra one-handed was interesting, but in general he'd prefer it if the clothes were going in the other direction. And she was in danger. She could turn to him and ask him to hold her and keep her safe.

There didn't seem to be much chance of that, though. Her shirt and trousers were wrinkled from their hours on the floor, and her hair was still uncharacteristically mussed. Otherwise there was no sign in her manner that they'd just spent hours sharing orgasms and then sleeping in each other's arms.

She put down the phone and turned to him. 'Well,' she said, 'at least that saved us from awkward post-coital conversation.'

'Don't worry,' he told her. 'We're going to have plenty of post-coital moments. We can catch up.'

'The police said they had a car in the neighbourhood and should be here soon, and the duty manager said he'd come right away.'

He took the hint and pulled on some jeans. He patted the bed beside him as an invitation for her to sit down, but she went to the mirror and began smoothing her hair instead.

'I think we should probably keep what happened between us to ourselves,' she said to her reflection.

'Well, the police and duty manager are going to suspect we haven't been playing cards all night.'

'I meant from the band.' She pulled an elastic band from her pocket and wrapped it around her ponytail, taking more time than she needed.

'Are you sorry you got naked with me?' he asked her.

A quick flush touched her cheeks and she caught his eye in the mirror. 'I . . . no.' She focused on her hair again. 'I just think it isn't anybody else's business.'

'We're all living in each other's pockets. It'll come out sooner or later that we're sleeping together.'

She avoided his eyes and blushed even harder. Knowing her, she hated that blush as much as he liked it.

'I don't think we should necessarily assume that we'll sleep together again.'

'Are you insane?' he said. 'This was all your idea, remember?'

'Yes, but now we've done it, we can get back to normal.'

Dominick shook his head. 'No, we haven't done it. And I've got a lot of plans for us to do it. In many different ways.'

'Like you said, we're all living in each other's pockets, so—'

'Hello, duty manager,' called a voice from outside, and Sophie went straight to the door to answer it.

'We're not through with this awkward conversation,' Dominick told her.

'Do you mind if I have a word with you in private, PC Simmons?'

The policeman nodded, and he and Sophie went out into the corridor, leaving Dominick and the duty manager with the other constable, who was double-checking statements. They skirted the mess and went to the end of the corridor, next to a sealed aluminium window.

'I think I know who might have done this,' she told him. 'He skipped probation over two weeks ago, and he'd been convicted of assault on me.'

PC Simmons, who looked about eighteen and had been more than a little bored at being called out essentially for graffiti, perked up a bit.

'If you contact the Thames Valley Police, they'll be able to give you information on Keith Martin,' she added.

'I'll see if we can get a scene-of-crime officer here,' he said, fingering his radio.

'That would be great. I'm eager to have him caught.'

Though not particularly by PC Simmons. 'Martin is a known drink-spiker; it might be worth your while to have the SOCO test the bottles of Coke and water outside the door as well as look for prints.'

PC Simmons fingered his radio some more, though he showed no signs of using it. Sophie went back to the room, put her signature next to Dominick's on the statements, and bade the police and the duty manager goodbye. The duty manager looked a bit twitchy at having to leave the mess out in the hallway, but once PC Simmons mentioned a fingerprinting kit, there wasn't any choice. The manager went off after the police, chewing on his lip.

Sophie's best plan was to go back to her own room and call Raj to tip him off, but Dominick stretched and looked at his watch.

'If we're lucky we'll get down to breakfast before Mad Dog eats all the cereal again,' he said.

'I've got to get back to my room,' she said.

'No you don't.' He took her white smock from the back of a chair, folded it tightly and tucked it under his arm. 'We're going to breakfast.'

Her stomach was rumbling, but she ignored it. 'Dominick, I'm a mess. I need to—'

'You need to do nothing when there's a possibility that there's someone in this hotel who might want to hurt you. And you're not a mess, and we're both hungry, and besides, we haven't finished our conversation about us having lots and lots more sex yet.'

Damn him. 'I really need . . .'

He stepped forward and pressed a kiss on her neck, below her ear. His hair brushed her face and she shivered with wanting him.

'Save the arguing for the next time we need to play cards,' he said.

'Have it your way,' she said, and went out of the room, past the room service carnage, and towards the lifts, with him beside her all the way. When they got into the lift, he threaded his fingers with hers.

'Why did you need to speak with the policeman on your own?' he asked, smiling his you'll-do-anything-for-me-won't-you smile.

If she thought he was being overprotective now, she could imagine what he would be like if she told him that she suspected that the person after her was a would-be rapist. She wouldn't get a moment alone.

And she needed some down time from Dominick Steele. Time to catch her breath, regain her sanity.

'I had a couple of forensic tips for him and I didn't want to embarrass him in front of his colleague.'

'Hmm. And about this whole sex question . . .'

'Dominick—'

He kissed her on the mouth and she tried not to melt. But this time she had the whole memory of what they'd done the night before.

The lift door slid open. A second later Dominick stopped kissing her.

Half a second later, she heard the applause.

Max, Gina, Mad Dog and Pete stood in the lobby, mere feet from the lift door. They all had smiles on their faces, ranging from broad to sardonic, as they clapped. Sophie stepped away from Dominick as quickly as she could, but it was too late.

'About time,' Max said, putting his arms around both of them. 'I was thinking about penning you two in a corral together. Come on, let's get some breakfast.'

Dominick caught Sophie's eye as they walked, and she knew what that look meant. *We're not through*, it said.

To be truthful, she was just as nervous about that as any threats scrawled in ketchup.

D'Licious Nightclub, Leicester

'Here's to us.' Max raised his pint glass, and so did Pete and Mad Dog. The liquid caught the club's flashing lights. Dominick joined the toast with his orange juice. 'The Venusians.'

'The Venusians,' they echoed, clinking glasses, and then Max took a long swallow of bitter and sat back on the leather banquette, smiling broadly and patting his flat stomach.

'There is nothing like a chicken jalfrezi to make you feel that all's right with the world,' he said.

Except maybe having sexual intercourse with a woman you have the hots for, thought Dominick, and then he shook his head. There was no point thinking about Sophie, or rather the fact that he had not yet had sex with her. Max had declared before their gig tonight that things were way too tense following that whacked-out interview and that therefore the band were going to have a good old bonding session over a curry, just the four of them, and then they were going to go to a club and dance their arses off.

Dominick's plans had been distinctly different, but he couldn't refuse Max, especially when Dom felt that a good deal of the tension was his own fault. The four of them had gone straight from the stage to the restaurant, leaving everyone else behind.

The curry had been great, the atmosphere not bad. Pete, sitting beside Dom in the tiny curry house and sharing a massive naan, had downed several pints of Kingfisher and chatted up the pretty but incongruously Polish waitress. Max talked music, Mad Dog happily bashed up poppadums, and for the first time in days with the band Dom hadn't felt as if he had to watch every word he said.

'Your fan club was noisy tonight,' Pete said to him now, in the club, where they occupied a booth between the bar and the dance floor. It was all done out in leather and chrome, obviously to attract upmarket punters, but to Dominick it felt the same as any other club, anywhere else: dark and confined, smelling of alcohol and faintly of damp, laced with a dull electricity of sexual desperation. When the lights went up you would be able to see the stains on the carpets.

'It was a great gig,' Max asserted. 'Packed out.'

'They were yelling your name between every song, mate,' Pete said to Dom.

'I don't know where they came from,' Dominick said cautiously. Pete appeared to be in a good mood, and seemed to be mentioning the squealing girls in the audience to tease him, but after the past few days he wasn't one hundred per cent sure of Pete's motivations. 'By rights they should have all forgotten about me by now.'

'They haven't,' Pete said. 'A dozen girls by the stage door waiting for autographs. I remember those days.'

There'd been twelve of them? Dom couldn't remember. He'd signed some Dirtysweet CDs, the back of a shirt, not because he'd wanted to but because he'd been asked. He hadn't signed much of anything for quite a while except for cheques (some of them bad), and he had felt like a fraud. The whole artist/fan dynamic had its own etiquette and responsibilities, though, which didn't include the artist saying, 'I'm sorry, I can't give you an autograph because I don't think I'm the person you want me to be.'

Mostly he'd been interested in trying to catch Sophie before they went to the restaurant, but she hadn't been there. Between the band's teasing and a fault with his bass amp, which necessitated a long discussion with Owen, he'd had about thirty seconds alone with her that afternoon, and he had to spend that extracting a promise from her that she wouldn't open her hotel room door to anyone while she was alone.

'Listen, mate,' said Pete, 'I know I've been winding you up quite a bit lately, and I wanted to say no hard feelings.'

He held out his hand to Dominick, who took it even though he was pretty sure that as he remembered things, Pete was the one who seemed to be getting wound up by him, largely about things over which Dominick had very little control.

'I'm not sure what happened there,' Dom said, 'but I never meant to annoy you. No hard feelings at all.'

They shook hands and Max applauded. 'Now that's how I like the band to be,' he said. 'One big happy family.'

Pete stood. 'I feel like celebrating,' he said, and went to the bar.

Max leaned forward and clapped Dom on the shoulder. 'We had a long talk, Pete and me. He's a good bloke.'

'I know he is.' Dom wondered how much of Pete's sort-of apology had been down to Max's conversation and the fact that Max was sitting right here, but then he dropped it. He had enough trouble dealing with band tension without inventing it himself.

He was happily involved in a conversation with Mad Dog about whether there had ever been any good songs in the history of music featuring a drum machine, when Pete returned with a tray and the Polish waitress from the restaurant. 'Look who I found,' he said, setting down the tray and slipping into the booth next to the waitress. He immediately put his arm around her shoulders. 'Everyone, this is Anya.'

'I have all of your CD,' Anya told everyone.

'Tequila,' declared Pete, and began unloading the tray of shot glasses, salt, and lemon slices. He put a glass in front of everyone, including Anya and Dom, and then held his own up. 'To making a comeback,' he said.

The rest of the band took a lemon slice and licked the backs of their hands before coating them with salt. Dom picked up his nearly empty orange juice.

'You'll have one shot, mate?' Pete said.

It was Cuervo Gold. He could smell it over the lemons: oily and with a hint of toffee. 'Better not,' he said.

'Just one to celebrate with us. You're allowed to have fun once in a while, aren't you?'

'No,' he said, and it was only when Pete blinked that he realised how sharply he'd spoken. He smiled, then licked and salted his hand. 'I'll ruin my orange juice with salt for you, though. To making a comeback.'

He licked the salt off, downed his juice, and smacked the glass down on the table at the same time the others smacked down theirs.

'Speaking of comebacks,' Max said, wiping lemon juice off his lips, 'you know how we've had a few people yelling for "Sweet Nothings" during our gigs?'

'I'm sorry about that,' Dominick said. 'As far as I'm concerned this tour is about the Venusians. People shouldn't be asking for Dirtysweet songs, it's out of order.'

Max shrugged. 'Makes no odds to me. If the crowd wants something, it's our job to make them happy. I was thinking about maybe doing one of your tunes for an encore one night. What do you think?'

Playing a Dirtysweet song? A bolt of panic went through Dom.

'No,' he said sharply again, and this time he saw Mad Dog and Max blink in surprise too.

'I mean, this tour is about the Venusians, and that's all,' he said. 'I'm not interested in resurrecting Dirtysweet.'

'Fair enough, mate. I only thought it might be fun.' Max finished his pint. 'Who wants another?'

'I'll get it,' Dom said, and went to the bar.

He ordered four shots of Cuervo, two pints of bitter, one of lager, a glass of wine for Anya, and the one orange juice. He hadn't ordered a round of drinks for two years. It still came naturally.

He sat on a high stool as he waited for the barman to get lemons and salt. The drinks were on a tray in front of him and he watched the lights bouncing off them. Maybe buying a round was good for him, another step towards being normal.

Towards *appearing* normal, he amended to himself. He was a long way from being normal. Normal people didn't avoid even touching a tequila shot because of the fear that picking up that glass would trigger a binge. They didn't avoid thinking about their former career because there was a chance the memories might be too bad to cope with. They didn't order pints of bitter for their friends and then stand at the bar watching the pint glasses, longing for frothy swallows and easy beer-scented bonhomie.

Come to think of it, normal people probably didn't have a single satisfying sexual episode with a woman and then skip out during a sound check to buy two dozen condoms. He had them stashed in his bunk, in his hotel room, in the pocket of his jeans, and he'd even slipped a couple into his guitar case. Why the guitar case, he didn't know. It seemed pretty unlikely that he and Sophie would decide to get it on while he was on stage.

What was more likely was that he was obsessed with sex. That his night with Sophie had been a sexual tequila shot, and now all he wanted to do was lick the salt and suck the—

'Hi there.' A voice interrupted his unfortunate metaphor. It belonged to a woman with long dark hair and red lips, who was climbing on to the stool beside him. 'You're Dominick Steele, aren't you?'

'Yes,' he said, and then, because it seemed rude not to, 'And who are you?'

'I'm Mona.' She smiled at him, red lips and white teeth. 'I was at your concert. I loved it.'

'Thank you.' The barman came for his money, and again because it seemed rude not to, Dominick asked, 'Would you like a drink?'

'A Chardonnay,' she said to the barman, and she smiled at Dominick again. This time she crossed her legs on the stool; she was wearing a miniskirt and knee-high high-heeled boots in shiny patent leather. 'I'm a huge fan of yours,' she told him.

'Thank you,' he said again. 'The Venusians are a great band, I'm glad to be on the road with them.'

'I meant I'm a huge fan of *yours*,' she said. She leaned

one elbow on the bar, closer to him, and lowered her eyelids to half-mast. 'Actually,' she murmured, 'I lost my virginity to a Dirtysweet song.'

'Oh.'

Duh. He was way, way out of practice, or he would've spotted from the first hello that Mona hadn't come over here for a Chardonnay and a chat about music.

'I'm glad you found my song so useful,' he said. 'Anyway, I've got to . . .'

She leaned her lithe body closer. It had the effect of pushing her cleavage and her skirt upwards. 'How about you dance with me and I'll tell you about it?'

'I'm sorry, Mona, I don't dance.'

'Just one little dance?' She pouted.

'It's not you, honestly, it's me. If you saw me dancing, you'd know why.'

'How about this, then?' She trailed a lacquered finger-nail through the condensation left by her wine glass. Slow circles, up and down. 'I don't live far from here. Why don't you come home with me and we can get to know each other better?'

Right. This horny, beautiful woman was inviting him home with her for no-strings sex after roughly four minutes of conversation. Pretty much every man's dream come true.

'Can you tell me something?' he asked. 'What's your motivation here? Do you actually want to get to know me, or is it more like a collection thing?'

'Hi,' purred a voice from behind him, and he felt a warm hand on the back of his neck.

When he turned around it was Mona, again. Shiny boots, miniskirt, red lips and half-mast eyes. She dropped her hand from his neck to his thigh.

'This is my twin sister Mina,' said Mona, beside him. 'She's a huge fan of yours too.'

Mina squeezed his thigh and winked at him.

Twins. Holy shit.

'It is great to meet you, Mina and Mona,' he said, 'and I'm sure it would be lots of fun to come home with both of you, but to tell you the truth, I'm on a bonding night out and I've got to get back to the lads with these drinks.'

Pouting in stereo. 'But Dominick . . .'

'Thanks for the offer,' he said, and picked up the tray and backed away from the porn movie towards his band.

He was halfway across the room when he realised what he'd done.

He had a pocketful of condoms. He'd broken the celibacy dam. And within twenty-four hours he'd been offered a threesome with twins. He'd had a lot of things, but he'd never had a threesome with twins.

And he'd turned it down.

He put the drinks down on the table and only barely registered the cheers and thanks from the band. Absently he picked up his orange juice and took a drink.

He hadn't even been tempted by the offer. Because the only person he wanted to have sex with was Sophie.

'Shit,' he said.

'I know, it's crazy, huh?' said Max, and Dominick wondered how Max had read his mind.

'Definitely,' he said. 'I don't think this has ever happened before.'

'Well, not often, I can tell you that. But the thing is, these cheerleader chicks they have on stage? They're completely bald. And not because they shave their heads, either. They *went out and found* cheerleaders who were bald naturally.'

Oh. Max hadn't read his mind, he'd been telling one of his stories and Dom had been too caught up in his own thoughts to notice.

'It's a strange world,' he said.

And getting stranger by the minute.

The Rialto Hotel, Leicester

She'd made a revitalising face mask for Gina; a hand lotion for Mad Dog's wife; a tea tree, eucalyptus and thyme mixture to treat Bob's snoring. She'd mixed patchouli with just about everything she could think of to try to find the perfect scent for Max. She'd checked her stock, made lists of what to order, rung the Nottingham police to follow up on whether they'd found any prints at the hotel and whether they'd tested the drinks. Unfortunately, and unsurprisingly, she couldn't get through to the relevant person. She'd watched *CSI* on television and told herself that there was no way she was going to get a cab to the theatre to watch the gig, because they didn't need her there tonight, and she didn't want to see Dominick tall on stage with a big, long instrument slung in front of his crotch.

She ran herself a bath with enough lavender to sedate a cow, and lay there trying not to think about Dominick coming off stage and wiping a snow-white towel across his forehead and neck to remove the sweat from the lights and from playing.

She really tried not to think about how his sweat would taste.

She topped up the bathwater several times, and when it finally went cold, she dried off and put on pyjamas and a robe. Her skin felt exquisitely sensitive under the cotton, as if it were still responding to Dominick's touch, a day later. The man was some sort of a genius.

Of course, he'd had a lot of sexual experience.

She was trying to think cynically about that. It wasn't really working, which was a measure of how insane she had become.

And then there was this morning, at breakfast, when Dom had sat next to her and flirted openly with her. Touched her fingers handing her the toast. Brushed his knee against hers under the table. Asked the waitress specifically for a pot of honey for her. All the while, Max and Mad Dog and even Pete had been teasing them about tour romances, and in one dizzying moment Sophie had realised that she felt as if she belonged.

She was not going to look for family substitutes in this band. And she was definitely not going to look for the tenderness she'd done without all her life, from Dominick Steele.

She was absolutely fine on her own. Sexually frustrated, of course, but fine.

'God, I wish we'd had a condom so I could have had sex with him before I realised it was a bad idea,' she said. Aloud, the words made very little sense.

Sighing, she got up from the bed and checked her aromatherapy reference manual. Marjoram, it said, was an anaphrodisiac, reputed to dampen sexual desire. She set up a vaporiser with marjoram oil and lit the tea light.

The room was already laced with a dozen scents and overlaid liberally with lavender, but the newer scent of marjoram gave a herby bite to the air. Sophie lay down on the bed, closed her eyes, and breathed in deep.

Dominick, glancing up at her from between her legs, his mouth curled in a little boy's smile. The rasp of his callused fingers and his stubbled chin on her thighs.

'Stop it,' she said aloud.

Her mind quickly changed their positions. *The hot length of his penis moving against her palms, his body shuddering beneath her.*

'Why do people say this works?'

She swung off the bed, blew out the tea light and rinsed out the vaporiser dish. Anaphrodisiac indeed. As if there could possibly be such a thing with Dominick Steele in this world.

Aromatherapy wasn't going to work in this situation. What she needed was a change in attitude. She had to stop being on the back foot, and take control.

She nodded decisively, traded her pyjamas and robe for jeans and T-shirt, slipped on her trainers and found her change purse. Earlier, she had tried to avoid noticing that the women's lavatory downstairs in the public part of the hotel had a condom machine. Now, she used the stairs because she didn't want to wait long enough for the lift.

Sex was only sex, after all. As long as she knew what she was getting into, she could be careful. She could keep control.

It would be fine.

Sophie had three condoms and a lighter change purse when she stepped out of the stairwell on to her floor and saw that Dominick was standing outside her room, pounding on her door.

'Sophie? Soph! Open up, I mean it, it's me.'

She put her hand on his shoulder and he jumped.

'You're okay,' he said, with more relief than she'd ever

heard in his voice before, and he pulled her into his arms and tight against his chest.

This time she knew she could withstand it, so she let him hold her close and breathed him in: Dominick, mixed with lemon and a hint of dry ice. Now that scent, she should market. After a long moment he held her at arm's length and looked into her face.

'Where have you been?' he asked.

'That's a nice question from someone who's been off carousing,' she replied, but she held up her condoms in answer.

She saw and felt the exact moment when his body registered what the little blue packets meant. His eyes dilated, his muscles tensed, his breathing deepened. Then he reached inside his jeans pocket and pulled out a handful of packets. His were red.

Next thing she knew they were kissing and she wasn't sure if she'd initiated it or not, but it didn't really matter because it was what she wanted anyway. The condom packets crinkled between their bodies. Sophie fumbled with her free hand for her key and inserted it into the door by feel and pure desperation. She turned the knob and pulled Dominick inside along with her.

He kicked the door closed behind them and then his nostrils flared. 'What have you been doing in here?'

'Experimenting with some oils.'

'It smells like a pizza in a compost bin.' Then he focused on her again, and Sophie caught her breath because his gaze was so intense. 'A *sexy* pizza in a compost bin,' he amended, and pulled her T-shirt up over her head.

She wasn't wearing a bra, a fact which elicited a groan from Dominick. She tore at his belt and his shirt and pulled him on to the bed with her, half-clothed and panting, kissing so hard that their teeth clicked together when they landed, but she didn't care because he had her jeans off by now and he was touching her while pushing off his own jeans with his other hand. Again by feel she found the condoms scattered on the bed beside them, picked one up and opened it with her teeth. Seconds it took, the longest seconds of her life to roll him over with her on top and to put the condom on him and then sink down on to him, all of him inside her at once in a single long stroke.

'Sophie,' he gasped, and she didn't know how long they stared at each other, registering this barrier broken between them.

Then he grabbed her head in his hands and kissed her, and they began to move. Dominick under her and inside her, holding and guiding her, exactly what she'd wanted for so long. Her climax shook her and made her scream.

He turned them both over, wrapped her legs around him, and this was good too, the weight of his body on hers and his thrusts powerful enough to push them both along the bed. Her fingers dug into his back. His breathing rasped in her ears. When he came he buried his face in her shoulder against her neck and shouted out without words, stiffening for a long shuddery moment against her.

Then he relaxed, his body heavy, his heart beating against her breast. He lifted his head and kissed her on the cheek.

'I thought so,' he said.

'Don't ruin the moment with gloating.' She brushed his damp hair back from his forehead.

'It's not gloating. It's discovery.' Dominick shifted and pulled out of her to take off the condom. He smiled at her small bereft noise.

'Definitely discovery,' he said. He sat up against the headboard and pulled her into his lap. In this position she could feel the semi-hardness of his penis against her bottom and she could see that he was still wearing his socks.

'I'll take them off next time,' he said. He looked down at her. 'What, no argument?'

'No,' she said. 'There's going to be several next times. We can't let these condoms go to waste.'

'That's what I wanted to hear.'

She settled closer to him, feeling his chest rise and fall with his breathing, watching his face. It was beginning not to be strange to have his face close to hers, a fact she didn't want to analyse too much. 'How was your band bonding session?'

'Good, but weird. Very weird.' Dominick frowned. 'Listen, Soph, I'm not sure how to ask this, but is there anyone . . . I mean, I know how you feel about cheating, so I know you wouldn't, but I mean anyone . . .'

He was lost for words, suddenly, in a way she hadn't seen before.

'I'm not even remotely involved with anyone,' she told him. 'No ex-husbands, and I don't see any of my former lovers. I prefer to be alone.'

He nodded quickly, and she wasn't sure if he'd caught her warning.

Not that there was any reason he should have; Dominick Steele wasn't a person to get involved in an actual relationship.

'That's good,' he said. 'I mean . . . yeah. Not to be a hypocrite. But it's good to know, because . . . well, anyway.' He took a deep breath and shook his head. 'Did I say "sexy pizza"?'

'You did.'

'Huh. Lust makes you say strange things.' He hugged her. 'For a minute when you didn't answer your door I thought you'd been hurt. Or that you'd done something stupid and gone off chasing whoever's after you.'

'No. Only a contraception mission.'

His hand curled around her hip, as if he owned it. 'Do you have any idea who they are?'

'Not the slightest,' she said. She felt a momentary twinge of guilt, but then she dismissed it. There was no reason for Dominick to know about Keith Martin, or anyone else on her list of suspects. From past experience, he'd only worry, and most likely get in the way.

She was in control now. To prove it, she kissed his neck, the place underneath his ear where his hair curled, and nibbled gently on his ear lobe. 'Mostly I've been thinking about having sex with you,' she whispered, and traced the whorl of his ear with her tongue. Underneath her, she felt his semi-erection growing.

'That makes two of us,' he said to her. He reached down and pulled his socks off.

29

Behind a Bush in Cambridgeshire

Sophie transferred her binoculars to her left hand and with her right tucked her trouser legs more tightly into her boots. Not that it was going to make a single bit of difference; rainwater still seeped into her socks.

She scanned each of the windows of the pretty flint cottage methodically once again. Fifty-seven minutes ago she'd glimpsed Leonie Steele's flaming red hair through her kitchen window. She'd seen nothing since then except grey pouring rain.

She couldn't blame Leonie for staying snug and tight inside her house; it wasn't exactly a day for frolicking in the garden. And Sophie supposed she had found out what she'd come for, anyway. If Leonie was dry and warm inside her flint cottage, she wasn't following Sophie with deadly intent.

But still she stayed, crouched behind this hawthorn hedge, in the rain.

She wasn't going to get another chance to investigate Leonie. It was only luck that the band was doing an acoustic session on a Cambridge radio station and that therefore Sophie had the afternoon free and away from Dominick's watchful eye.

And from Dominick's bed, of course. The thought that she could be with him there, naked and hot, made her wet toes curl inside her wet boots.

Three days they'd been sleeping together. Three days and most especially three nights. In those three days and three nights she had not mentioned to him that his ex-wife was on her list of stalker suspects.

The glossy green front door of the cottage opened and Leonie emerged, swathed in a raincoat and carrying a large black umbrella. She crossed to her car. Sophie splashed to her own rental car, parked a few metres away in a layby. Leonie drove past as she was starting it up. Sophie waited a few moments and then turned the car around in the narrow lane and followed her.

Leonie was a careful driver, signalling in plenty of time and slowing for oncoming traffic. This made her easy enough to follow, as long as Sophie stayed well back, and especially because now, typically, the rain had stopped. Inside the car, cold droplets ran off the pushed-back hood of Sophie's waterproof coat and trickled down the back of her neck.

Though it was obviously going to extremes, she could sort of see why someone might be driven to assault out of jealousy about Dominick. The man was a genius in bed, and half of that was because he made Sophie feel like a genius in bed too. It had to be difficult to know that your lover was out being a genius with other women, especially the woman who'd been instrumental in dissolving your marriage. Leonie hadn't struck Sophie as the vengeful type, but a lot could change in five years.

For example, Sophie herself, who somewhere in the last three days had started wearing makeup. Not honey-trap slap, but some lipstick and eyeshadow, because it seemed to go with the way she felt when Dominick looked at her.

'Whoops, there we go,' Sophie said as Leonie turned off into the car park of a garden centre. Sophie backed into a parking spot and killed the engine as she watched Leonie get out of her car. She was curious to see Dominick's ex-wife properly, to know if she was as beautiful as ever.

Her hair had the same Pre-Raphaelite tint and luxuriousness and her skin was still so perfect it glowed. But she'd taken off her raincoat and lost the umbrella and Sophie could see her belly, rounded and pregnant. Leonie put a protective hand over it as she crossed the car park towards the garden centre.

Sophie had planned to follow Leonie into the shop. Instead she sat and watched her go inside.

Hormones can make you weird enough to threaten people, she thought with one part of her mind, but the rest of her didn't believe it. The rest of her knew that Leonie Steele had a whole new life and wouldn't care if Sophie and Dominick were having wild sex on the front of every newspaper and magazine in the country. And the rest of her also knew, at that moment, that she hadn't really followed Leonie because she thought she could be the stalker.

She'd been following Leonie Steele because Leonie had once been in love with Dominick.

Her mobile phone vibrated. 'Sophie Tennant,' she said into it without looking away from the door Leonie had gone through.

'Miss Tennant? This is PC Frehley from Nottinghamshire Police. I'm ringing with an update for you on the crime you reported to us on the twenty-fifth of May.'

'Have you caught him?' she asked immediately.

'We've not been so lucky, I'm afraid. We wanted to let

you know, though, because you were the person who suggested it to the SOCO on the scene, that we did find evidence that the bottle of Coca-Cola outside the hotel door had been tampered with.'

'It had Rohypnol in it, didn't it?'

'In a word, yes.'

So there was the answer that she'd supposedly come here to find. She gave PC Frehley Raj's number so they could liaise about Keith Martin. And then she got out of her car and went into the garden centre.

She wasn't poisoning drinks or leaving threatening messages, but if she'd been spying on Leonie because of her own emotional needs, that was only one step up from stalking. So she was finished with lurking around.

She walked through the aisles until she came across Leonie looking at bags of houseplant fertiliser, went straight up to her, and said, 'Excuse me, aren't you Leonie Steele?'

Leonie looked up, her hand instinctively going to her belly again. Sophie saw her taking in her wet hair, dripping waterproof and sodden trousers. 'I'm sorry, do I . . . Wait. Are you . . .'

'Sophie Tennant.' Sophie stuck her hand out. 'You hired me five years ago to look into a problem for you.'

'That's right.' Leonie shook her hand. 'I'm sorry, what they say about pregnancy brain is true, I'm in another world at the moment. What brings you here, Sophie?'

'I'm buying a geranium.'

'Oh.'

'You look like you're doing very well,' Sophie said. 'Congratulations on the baby.'

'Thank you.' Leonie stroked her stomach contemplatively. Sophie saw a slim gold ring with a small diamond on the fourth finger of her left hand. 'It's no offence meant to you, but sometimes I wonder why I hired you in the first place. I had plenty of reason to divorce Dom anyway.'

'I guess sometimes we just want to see things for ourselves, with our own eyes.'

Leonie shook her head. 'I knew already. I was fooling myself. I can see now that Dom isn't capable of love.'

'Um.' Sophie swallowed. 'Well, I'm glad things have worked out so well for you without him. Take care of yourself.'

When she got outside, the sun was shining. She shucked her waterproof into the boot of her rental car, got behind the wheel, and headed for Cambridge, trying not to analyse why she felt so empty when she'd found out exactly what she wanted to know.

30

The Upstairs Bar at the Brooks Theatre, Norwich
Two Days Later

'The Venusians are my life, I have every album on vinyl, and then when they were released on CD I bought them all over again, and now I've got them loaded on my iPod and I just listen to them all the time. Saw them in eighty-one the first time and then I followed them all over the country. I saw them everywhere, London, Peterborough, Aberystwyth. I was at that historic show in Milton Keynes, too, one of the best moments of my life. Could have knocked me over with a feather when I found out they were touring again. My missus Elspeth here couldn't believe it either. Isn't that right, Elspeth?'

Elspeth, one of the few women in the room, was wearing a new Venusians T-shirt over a puffy blouse. 'I'm not really as crazy about the band as Walter is,' she told Sophie, 'but I like how passionate he gets about it.'

Sophie couldn't help glancing at Dominick standing by her side. It was the word 'passion' that did it; it was practically a synonym for his name. He caught her glance and gave her his naughty smile.

Who would've thought it – Mister Brooding Rock Star seemed happy. He'd been acting happy for days. It was incredibly alluring.

Elspeth's husband Walter patted her on the hand. He had on not only a Venusians T-shirt (without the blouse underneath) but a baseball cap and a leather jacket with what looked like a hand-painted Venusians logo on the back.

'Elspeth and me married after the Venusians split up,' he explained. 'So she never got to see the magic herself. But she's a good sport, comes along to all the fan club meetings with me.'

'I make the tea,' Elspeth said, nodding cheerfully.

Well, there was one major good point about being married to a man with an obsession, Sophie mused, sipping her ginger ale and listening to Walter discuss in animated tones with Dominick how wonderful the Venusians were. At least Elspeth would never have to worry about Walter cheating on her. His extramarital energy was one hundred per cent devoted to an all-male eighties rock band.

A few more people joined their group, four men and another woman. The men, like most of the other men at the party, were aged between forty-five and fifty, and wore jeans and Venusians T-shirts. The woman was also middle-aged and was chiefly distinguishable from the men because she wasn't balding. Each of them, as they shook Dominick's hand, had the same gleam in their eyes. They shook Sophie's hand too, which she thought was nice of them.

'Wish Digby could've been on this tour,' one of the men

said. 'I met him in eighty-seven, brilliant guy. No offence to you, of course.'

'None taken,' Dominick said. 'Digby's a great bass-player. I'm honoured to fill his shoes for a little while.'

Earlier, Dominick had confided in Sophie that he was looking forward to the special after-gig party for the Venusians fan club. He hadn't said why, but Sophie knew: this was one place where there was guaranteed to be more attention on Max, Pete and Mad Dog than on him.

And she agreed that it was a genuine pleasure to see the Venusians surrounded by people who adored them. Max stood by the bar, relating a story to an enthralled audience. Mad Dog was signing a stack of LPs, CDs and photographs, each signature requiring an elaborate process of arm-waving. Pete had his guitar and was playing a lick while a group of middle-aged men nodded their heads to the rhythm.

Dominick put his arm around her waist. 'I've thought of something new I want to do with you,' he murmured into her ear, the words so private and so sexy that her body tingled.

'Not here, Dominick,' she whispered back and slipped out of his grip. But the damage had been done; she felt a flush on her cheeks and her nipples were clearly visible beneath her top, broadcasting to nearly one hundred Venusians fan club members precisely what the nature of her relationship was with Dominick Steele.

He wasn't giving up so easily. 'So let's get out of here,' he said, and looped his arm around her waist again. It was as comfortable and as natural as if he owned her.

Here was the problem.

She craved this affection as much as she craved the sex. Every time he put his arm around her she felt a burst of pure happiness, and every time she had to remind herself that this was temporary. Weeks ago, way back at the beginning of the tour, Bob and Owen had told her about the phenomenon of the 'tour fling', how forced proximity could create best friends and lovers who melted away when the tour was done.

The concept made sense to her; she'd often felt a strange intimacy with the subjects she was investigating, or the women she was working for. Or look how she'd become attached to people in her childhood, even though she'd tried her best not to. It all disappeared once the case was over or once she was moved on.

An affair with Dominick Steele was a dream come true, but it was not life-changing. She had the evidence of his ex-wife for that, if she needed it. And there was only one week left until the last show.

Then they'd go back to their normal lives.

Sophie relaxed into Dominick's embrace for a moment, because she was addicted. But she was strong, too, so she broke away from him gently as soon as a Venusians fan started up another conversation with him.

'I'll get us some more drinks,' she said.

Her mobile beeped in her pocket as she went to the bar. She checked her screen and saw it was a text message from a number she didn't recognise.

As always, her stomach flipped, because although her brain knew her mother was never going to find her, her body still hoped. She opened the message.

THINK YOU'RE SO HAPPY?

Her heartbeat accelerated. This person looking for her wasn't her mother.

She pulled out her little notebook and wrote down the number, though she was certain it would turn out to be a pay-and-go phone, either unregistered or, possibly, registered to her.

Keith Martin was a coward. He spiked drinks and he locked doors and he didn't like women getting the better of him.

She hit reply and spelled out a message with her thumb.

I'm going to catch you, you know.

As she sent it, her palms were damp, her heart thrumming with adrenalin.

The reply came within minutes: YOU THINK YOU CAN RUIN PEOPLE'S LIVES AND GET AWAY WITH IT; YOU'RE NOT THAT CLEVER.

Correct semicolon usage in a text message. She'd have to check Keith Martin's old texts to see if he'd used that particular punctuation before. She remembered he hadn't been one for text-speak, instead writing out his words.

Mobile phones, even unregistered ones, were traceable through their signal, but a civilian couldn't do it without permission. Raj might do it for her as an aid to finding Martin. But that would take time, and by the time she talked with Raj, the sending phone might be turned off, its owner anywhere.

She could do better than that. She could goad him.

You're not very brave, hiding behind tinted windscreens and skulking in corridors. Are you afraid to face me and tell me what you think?

She sent it, glancing over her shoulder. Dominick was watching her, so she smiled nonchalantly and continued to the bar.

She was waiting for a reply and for her Coke and ginger ale when Pete joined her. 'Jesus, these people have got to get a life,' he muttered. 'Pint of lager, please.'

'They're a little bit obsessive,' Sophie agreed, 'but it all seems to be quite affectionate and harmless.'

'Sad, more like,' Pete said. 'What happened to all the cool fans? There isn't a single person here under forty-five, and they all look exactly the same, even the women.' He took a long draught of his lager. 'And why are we here? Anybody would've thought a fan club would be based in London, not Norwich.'

'Actually, Wayne was telling me it's in King's Lynn.'

'I was hoping there would at least be . . . Oh, hello.'

Pete perked up as a young girl approached the bar. She was in her early twenties, with an asymmetric hairdo and black eyeshadow. She stood beside Pete and ordered a WKD.

Sophie had no desire to watch Pete pick up women, but she couldn't return to Dominick yet, not when she might still get a reply to her text. She stood so that Dominick wouldn't be able to see she had already got the drinks, and pretended to be smoothing back her hair with the help of the mirror behind the bar.

'I'm Pete. What's your name?'

'Maxine.' The girl took a drink of her WKD and looked Pete up and down.

'It's good to see someone so young and beautiful here,' said Pete. 'Did you enjoy the show?'

She snorted. 'Jesus, no, I don't listen to this stuff. My mum and dad dragged me here. They're crazy about the Plutonians or whatever they are. They even named me after the lead singer. It's like a curse. Why aren't you wearing one of those T-shirts; don't you like the band either?'

Sophie watched Pete going red.

Her mobile beeped and she forgot about Pete. She read her new text.

I'LL SEE YOU AT BLACKBURY FESTIVAL, BITCH.

She had to restrain herself from punching the air. 'Got you,' she said quietly.

Two big, warm hands spanned her waist from behind. 'What are you grinning about?' Dominick asked.

She quickly turned off her mobile. 'Nothing,' she said.

'I thought you were getting some good news on your phone.' She could see him, tall behind her in the mirror, like a dark protecting angel. 'You had that gotcha look, like you're running down a perp or however they say it.'

'No, it was just a service message. Hey, I was wondering, when's the Blackbury Festival gig?'

'It's the last in the tour, a week today.' He removed the clip she'd just replaced in her hair, so it fell over her shoulder. 'I can't get enough of you,' he said. 'Let's go.'

She sidestepped him. 'You go first, it's more discreet. I'll meet you outside in ten minutes.'

'Five.'

'All right.'

He grinned and downed his Coke in one swallow. 'You're very sexy when you go all clandestine.' He kissed her swiftly on the lips and walked away.

She watched his long-legged loose stride. And then how he stopped to talk with fans who weren't his, to make them feel good, to show his loyalty to the band that wasn't his either.

In five minutes, she could touch him. First, she had a job to do. She scrolled to Raj's number to fill him in, but just as she was about to press dial she had second thoughts.

She had a time and a place all arranged with this scumbag. In other words, she was totally in control. She could do this alone.

She sent off a quick text reply: *Are you going to bring your own ketchup this time?*

And then she went off to find Dominick, even though only two minutes had passed. She was addicted, after all.

For the moment.

Outside a Large House in Buckinghamshire Six Days Later

'Yes! Mad Dog United two, DeMilo FC nil!'

Dominick hoisted little Joey on to his shoulders and did a victory lap around the molehill-studded field. When he reached the tree where Mad Dog's wife Sherry was sitting with Sophie and Gina, he collapsed on to the ground, rolling Joey over the grass to his mother's feet.

'I scored a goal, Mama!' yelled Joey, scrambling into Sherry's arms.

'I saw,' she told him.

'Come on, Dommick, let's play some more!' yelled Joey.

'Have pity on your elders,' said Dominick. He rolled over on to his belly and looked at Sophie, who was sitting in a patch of sunlight under the tree, wearing a butter-yellow linen dress and a grey cardigan. He wasn't quite sure how she managed to make such plain clothes sexy, but he liked it. She was also laughing at him, and he liked that too.

Apparently football was an after-lunch tradition in Mad Dog and Sherry's household, and since the band had been invited for Saturday lunch on their day off before travelling to Sunday's Blackbury Festival, Dom felt he should honour the family traditions. He'd never played football with a four-year-old before; it necessitated a lot of dodging the ball and slipping it into the goal when Joey was distracted by a passing bird.

'Come on, mate, get up off your arse and give us the chance to equalise.' Max prodded him with the toe of his cowboy boot. He was surrounded by the rest of his team: Mad Dog's three daughters, Pearl, Daisy and Micky, and his gangly eldest son Rix. Pearl and Micky were holding on to either end of Max's ever-present llama-wool scarf and looking at him as if he were Superman and Elvis all rolled into one. 'Either that, or give me my best player back.' He winked at Joey.

'I wanna play with Daddy and Dominick!' yelled Joey.

'Turncoat.' Max reached down and grabbed Gina's hand. 'Come on, darlin', it's time I taught you the offside rule.'

'Max DeMilo, I've been to more Chelsea games than you've had hot dinners,' Gina said, standing up and brushing grass off her cream trousers. 'And I think you need all the help you can— Oh, sorry, I need to get this.' She pulled her ringing phone from her cream handbag and walked off with it.

'Wimping out, are you, Steele?' said Pete. He wiped sweat from his forehead, took a can of lager from the cooler underneath the tree, and downed a long swallow.

From here, Dom could reach Sophie's ankle if he stretched out a hand. Once at her ankle, he could easily slide his palm up her bare leg, warmed by the sun.

'I think he's got other things on his mind,' Sherry said, and stood up. She was a petite woman, shorter than Mad Dog and pleasantly rounded, with an even wilder mane of hair. 'Come on, I'll join your team, Joey.'

'Zwwwwwwowarrrrgh!' roared Mad Dog and scooped Joey up on to his own shoulders. They scampered off into the field and the other children and Venusians followed them. Within seconds the air filled with shouts and cheers.

'Five kids,' said Dominick, pulling himself over to sit next to Sophie.

'I know. Sherry said they were only planning on three.' She sipped her lemonade, and handed him the glass for a drink. 'And every one of them is a drummer.'

'Makes you wonder . . .'

He stopped. He'd been about to say *what ours would be like.*

'. . . how often they have to replace the furniture,' he finished.

Where had that come from? He never thought about kids. All he should be thinking about right now was where he was going to find a chemist in this godforsaken part of Buckinghamshire, because Sophie and he appeared to have used up more than two dozen condoms in less than two weeks.

It was the atmosphere. Mad Dog's house was huge, Elizabethan, and warmly ramshackle in the way only hundreds of years and five kids could produce. Sherry had cooked enough food to feed the starving millions, and by the end of a whirlwind hour it had all been gone. A full belly, sunshine, and a pick-up football game were probably clinically proven to prompt thoughts about family. Like how Max's cousin's wedding had prompted thoughts about his own marriage.

Stimulus, response. Like Pavlov's dog. Or something.

'They're a nice family,' said Sophie. There was a stiffness in her voice, something he detected there every now and then.

'Mad Dog invited you specifically,' he told her.

'Because he and everybody else on the tour knows we're sleeping together. But that's okay. I'm enjoying it.'

'Sleeping with me? Or being here?'

'Both.' She smiled at him and snagged the bottle of lemonade from the cooler to refill the glass.

He leaned back against the tree. A full belly, a little sunshine, a rowdy game of football in the distance and a beautiful woman he was going to have sex with later. He'd never quite understood the meaning of the word 'contented', but he might nearly be there. Aside from the rogue child-related thought.

'I hope the weather holds for the festival tomorrow,' he said. 'It's been a long time since I've been at one and I was generally too wasted to notice what they were like. I don't even think I have any memories of mud.'

'How much mud would you say there would be? Just a little slippery, or would it definitely impede progress?'

He glanced at her. She had this way of asking the most mundane questions as if she were trying to figure out every little detail of the answer.

'It varies,' he said. 'If it's like today, it probably won't be that messy. The toilets, on the other hand . . .'

'Even I've heard about festival toilets.'

Rix intercepted Mad Dog's pass and kicked the ball into the homemade goal from halfway down the field. Max's whoops of triumph sounded not unlike the beginning of 'Infamous'. Mad Dog bolted to his son and tackled him to the ground. His daughters and Joey piled on top of them. Sherry, laughing, grabbed Mad Dog's ankles and tried to pull him out of the heaving mass of children.

'All of this makes me . . .' said Sophie. He saw her bite her thumbnail, gazing at the family mock-wrestling match.

'What?' asked Dom.

'It makes me wonder. I mean, Mad Dog would be on tour a lot, wouldn't he? What if Sherry thought he was up to something, and she hired someone like me to find out?'

Mad Dog rolled out from beneath his kids and grabbed Sherry by the ankles. She tumbled down on top of him.

'He wouldn't be up to something,' Dominick said.

'No, he wouldn't,' Sophie said. 'But you can get suspicions. Especially if you're left at home a lot, it would be normal to wonder, wouldn't it? And there are groupies and things like that, aren't there?'

'There are,' he said, remembering Mona and Mina. 'But that's not always what you want.'

'I was just thinking,' she said, and bit her nail. Then she put her hand down, decisively, still watching Mad Dog and his wife and children. 'What if I'd honey-trapped someone like him, someone with a family like this? I always thought that if a man was good, he wouldn't take the bait, and if he did, he was a scumbag. But it's . . . there's more to it than that.'

'I was a scumbag, Sophie. What I did was wrong.'

She did glance at him at that. 'It was wrong. But one action doesn't make a whole life. Even a series of actions. People are too complicated to be judged like that. And a honey trap isn't exactly fair.'

He didn't say anything.

'This must be worth preserving, no matter what,' she said. 'A family.'

He remembered what she'd told him about her past: abandoned by her mother, raised in foster homes. She said she never thought about it. He thought she was probably lying.

'I wonder how many of them I broke up,' she said.

He took her hand and moved her over so that she was sitting between his legs. A ray of sun hit her hair and highlighted a faint trace of gold in the brown.

'It might sound self-serving to say this, Sophie Dean,' he said, 'but sometimes I think you have to forget about the past.'

She sighed and leaned back against him. He wrapped his arms around her, enjoying the way her head fitted under his chin and how her hair was warmed by the sun. It was surprising: the pleasure of a simple touch.

A riot of cheers erupted from the field as the ball bounced off Joey's knee and dribbled into the goal.

'I'm sorry for honey-trapping you,' she said. 'It was between you and your wife. I shouldn't have got involved.'

Dom opened his mouth to tell Sophie that he'd deserved it, and besides, at least he'd got to see her in a miniskirt, but then her phone beeped in her pocket.

She sat up and turned herself around to read her text message. The screen was facing away from Dom, so he couldn't see what the message was, but he did see a small pursed smile appear on her mouth.

She tucked the phone back into her pocket. To his disappointment, she didn't settle back into his arms, but instead curled up her knees and put her arms around them. 'Tell me more about Blackbury Festival,' she said.

'It's a small festival, only one stage, and we're on in the afternoon. We don't have to be anywhere afterwards, so maybe we'll get to see a band or two.' He grinned suddenly. 'I haven't seen a band in ages. You should come with me and I'll educate you in modern music.'

'Great, just what I need, more wailing guitars and singers moaning about how miserable life is.'

'Ouch. Fifty years of popular music demolished in one fell swoop.'

They were interrupted by both football teams piling back under the tree for half-time drinks. Max flung himself down on the ground beside them. 'That woman of mine always has her phone to her ear. It's not right.'

'It's her job,' Sophie said.

'And it's all for my continuing fortune and fame, bless her heart. We're going on holiday after this, though. Somewhere without bloody mobile reception.'

Pearl, Micky and Daisy, who had been squabbling about who was going to do it, collectively brought Max a paper cup of lemonade, and he accepted it with grave thanks that had all three girls giggling.

'Anyway, last day of the tour tomorrow,' he said when they had skipped off. 'Got any big plans for afterwards, Dom?'

Dominick had been trying not to think about it. Touring again hadn't been unalloyed pleasure, but the days did have a structure and a purpose that he'd been totally without for the past two years. Especially the last fortnight. Wake up, make love with Sophie, go down to breakfast, travel to venue, try to sneak a quickie with Sophie before the sound check, do the sound check, hang around playing guitar and thinking about sex with Sophie, avoid the knots of Dirtysweet fans who seemed to be turning up before their gigs, get ready to go on stage, play the gig, sit in the dressing room watching Sophie work and going crazy with anticipation for later in the night, dodge as many fans as he could after the show, and then find Sophie wherever she was and get down to the serious work of using up those condoms.

The idea of it finishing left him strangely hollow inside. He would be dumped back into formless days.

And then there was Sophie; they hadn't talked about what would happen between them. He glanced at her. She was examining the grass strand by strand as if she planned to add botany to her list of professions.

'I've never been much of a planner,' he said. 'I'll play a lot of guitar, I guess, which is a big improvement over what I was doing before.'

'What were you doing before?' Max asked.

'Mostly feeling sorry for myself,' he said, and he was surprised to find as he said it that it was true, and also that he didn't feel that way any more.

Somewhere, out of the past few weeks, he'd created a new version of Dominick Steele. Not a perfect version, but someone he liked a whole lot better than the old one.

'Great news!'

Gina was striding back to the group, her phone in her hand and her cheeks flushed with pleasure. 'That was George Henshawe from Blackbury Festival. We've moved up the billing for tomorrow.'

'Too fucking right, we were second from bottom,' Pete muttered.

'Well, we're fourth from top now,' Gina told him. 'Monkeyhouse cancelled and I convinced George to put us in their slot. Partly by reading him this.' She dived into her bag and came up with a copy of *Groovin'* magazine. On the cover was the caption *DeMilo, Steele and the Venusians: Infamous Again?*

'Hey, it's out!' Max said, delighted.

'Yesterday,' Gina told him, 'but I wanted to save it until I knew for certain about the festival so I could give you all the good news at once.' She flipped open the pages and read aloud: '"The twenty years since their last hit have been kind to the original Venusians; DeMilo is as good-naturedly obscure as ever, and my mother threatened to kill me if I washed my hand after shaking his. The real surprise, especially to a Dirtysweet fan who remembers his antics on stage and off, is how well the volatile Steele fits in with the group. 'It was one of the best things that could have happened to me,' he says of DeMilo's invitation to join the tour as a session bassist.

'"The chemistry doesn't only work well during the interview. At their gig the following night, the Venusians' old hits – which I mostly remember hearing from the back seat of my mother's car as she sang aloud full volume – are given an edge by Steele. His presence adds a dangerous air of genius about to break loose, as if any moment the chaotic energy of the Venusians' music could erupt into something fantastic and strange. Maybe it's because my mother's not singing along, maybe it's because of Steele, but the set has a freshness and a relevance I didn't expect to find, even in the songs about sheep."'

'Sheep!' cried Max, outraged.

Dom grimaced. 'I'm sorry, Max. I tried to steer her away from Dirtysweet.'

'Don't be ridiculous,' Gina told him. 'Any publicity is good publicity, and this is the best review we've had. This, and the billing at the festival tomorrow, is going to bring Max DeMilo and the Venusians to an entirely new audience.'

Max nodded. 'It's exactly what we were hoping would happen when we brought Dominick on board.'

'What?' said Dom and Pete at the same time.

Gina smiled at Dom. 'Eighties comeback band reforms with a new young superstar member. It's a great media angle.'

'You didn't tell me you were thinking of this,' Dominick said.

'Well, mostly I asked you because your name begins with D,' said Max. 'But a bit of business can't hurt, as Gina says.'

Dom shook his head. 'I had no idea how devious you were, Max.'

Max threw back his head and laughed. 'Learned it from my girlfriend, mate. Anyway it can't be all that bad, can it? At least I introduced you to a top bird.' He winked at Sophie.

'I wonder what else is going on that I don't know about,' Dominick said.

'More lemonade, anybody?' Sophie asked.

The Tour Bus, on the Way to Wiltshire

She didn't normally do it. But this morning it was no good. Sophie shut her laptop, pulled back the curtain on her bunk, and climbed the ladder to Dominick's bunk above hers.

He was lying reading a book about Dylan. 'Hey,' he said, pleased. She clambered on to his bunk and lay down beside him. Perforce her entire body pressed against his, but he helped it along by wrapping his arm around her.

'What do I owe this to?' he asked.

'It's our last journey on the tour bus,' she said. 'I figured we might as well make the most of it.'

'The last one?'

'The festival is only about twenty miles from Stoneguard, so I'll get a train there afterwards,' she told him. 'It makes more sense than going all the way to London and then back.'

He nodded, slowly. 'Right. So you're definitely going back to Stoneguard after.'

If she didn't mess up and get killed.

'Yes,' she said.

'Okay.'

She waited for him to say something else. Like, 'How about I come back with you?' Or 'Why don't you come to London with me?' Or 'Screw it, let's both head off to Bermuda and have wild sex all over the pink beaches.'

But she didn't know why she was waiting for it. He wouldn't say anything like that, and she didn't want him to anyway.

It was probably the stress of knowing that in the next few hours she was going to face someone who had been sending her threatening text and email messages. Things like that made you think wistfully about going off to pink beaches and other unlikely events.

He didn't say anything. She settled her head on his chest and they listened to the bus.

33

Blackbury Festival, Wiltshire

The sun beamed down on ten thousand smiling people and Sophie, who stood with her back to a Chinese food stall and her front to a group of teenagers smoking pot.

She breathed in the smells of MSG and marijuana and scanned the crowd. It was between sets, and when she glanced up at the stage across the sea of people she could see Owen and Dempsey changing over the equipment to prepare for the Venusians. Festival-goers strolled around, sat on the ground, lolled in the sun, drank beer, laughed and ate and smoked.

Mostly, they were everywhere, in crowds that blocked her view of everything except for the square metre directly in front of her, or the far-off stage.

And Keith Martin, damn him, was short.

The Chinese food stall wasn't a good vantage point. She began to thread her way through the clumps of people, wishing she'd paid more attention to photographs of crowds when she'd researched the festival. She had the timetable of the day by heart, she had the plans of the entire site memorised, she knew the best quick escape routes from every point, she knew the isolated places where a killer would be likely to drag a potential victim.

But she hadn't noticed what people would be wearing. For example, hats: there were more silly hats here than she'd ever seen in one place in her life. Viking hats, cowboy hats, tall stripy Cat-in-the-Hat hats. Although so many people seemed concerned to protect their heads against the sun, that didn't extend to the rest of their bodies: bare-chested men and bikini-topped women sweated and glowed bright red.

Sophie brushed past a man (she thought) dressed as SpongeBob SquarePants. Her supposedly inconspicuous outfit of jeans and a white vest top must stick out like a sore thumb. All Keith Martin would have to do would be to paint himself blue or something and she'd never notice him.

A familiar explosion of drums and guitar on stage told her that the Venusians' set had begun. Her back was exposed but she couldn't help glancing up to the stage. Her eyes went straight to Dominick, standing off to the right looking at his bass guitar as he played, seeming not to hear the cheers of the sunburnt crowd.

She knew that intensity he brought to music, because he brought it to her, too.

Now, however, was not the time to think about that. Now was the time to concentrate on the hunt and the chase, which was a good thing, because even with all her faults as a detective, she was much better at investigation than relationships. She scanned the crowd again, again failing to spot Keith Martin. She did see somebody peeing into a plastic cider bottle.

'Dominick!' screamed a group of five bikini-topped girls next to her, and again her attention was drawn to the stage. Or rather, to the large screens either side of the stage, where Dominick was magnified dozens of times bigger than reality, and breathtakingly beautiful.

'Oh my God, he's so sexy,' squealed one of the girls, clutching her friends.

You should see him naked, Sophie thought, gazing at the screen.

Pathetic. She wasn't much different from these fans. She might as well get used to it, because most likely in a few days the only place she'd be seeing Dominick Steele would be, once again, on the television.

Meanwhile, she was leaving herself wide open to attack. She craned her neck to check over her shoulder.

It was impossible to see anything here. She turned to walk away from the girls towards the back of the arena where it might be less crowded, but found the tide had turned against her. People pressed forward, closer to the stage, and she had to struggle to make any progress the other way.

The first song ended and the crowd cheered. 'Hey, thanks there,' Max's amplified voice said, sounding so hugely pleased that Sophie smiled. They were getting a good audience for their last show.

Maybe it was so good that they'd do another tour and ask her along again. If that happened, she might be tempted to make a habit out of sneaking into Dominick's bunk, of seeing his sudden smile when he spotted her, of hearing those tangled tunes on his guitar.

Tennant, wake up, you're in a crowd with a dangerous criminal who has tried to rape you and run you down.

She pushed through a knot of people and emerged into a clearing of sorts, between the crowd watching the band and the crowd around the beer tent. She could see a bit of slightly higher ground, below one of the speaker towers. If she stood there, she could be seen, from this angle at least, and could also, hopefully, see anyone who approached her.

Once again she pushed through the crowd, past two men in wedding dresses and another gang of girl fans craning their necks to see Dominick. She bumped into bodies and stepped on toes.

Too close, too many. Her skin crawled and her lungs filled with hot sweat and smoke. The hand could come from anywhere, behind her, beside her, and she wouldn't see. Martin had strong hands.

The ground dipped and she stumbled against someone. Her bare arm slid over moist bare flesh and she jerked away. On the stage, Pete's guitar screamed.

She nearly cried out, but swallowed it in time as she found her feet again. The crowd erupted in cheers around her. She hugged her arms close to her body and shouldered through people, more people, till she felt the ground inclining slightly upward beneath her feet and then found herself at the base of the speaker tower, surrounded by a metal fence.

Sophie stationed herself with her back to the fence. Dominick was on the screen again. His hair fell over his eyes and he flicked it back with a toss of his head. Up there, he wasn't quite the man she'd made love with, argued with, helped and asked for reassurance. The stage and the cameras made him into his public self, the celebrity that everyone knew. It was probably a good reminder of how distant from each other they really were.

And watching him could get her killed. She forced herself to look away, to scan the crowd yet again. And again.

*

'Whaaaa-hoooooo!' Max whooped, and Dominick couldn't help laughing.

Maybe it was the crowd, maybe it was the weather, maybe it was the fact that it was the last gig, the last chance of the last chance. But the stage snapped with energy, the music seemed louder and truer. When it was good, the crowd fed off the music and the musicians fed off the crowd and the feeling spiralled up and up. Dom remembered it from the early days. It was like being happy drunk, everything dizzy and significant. He'd spent a lot of drinking time trying to recapture that feeling.

The cheering swelled and Mad Dog drummed them into their final number. Dom's fingers moved over the familiar chords. After the next five minutes or so, it was going to be all improvisation for the foreseeable future. Maybe for his entire life.

For the hundredth time he searched the crowd for Sophie. He knew she was out there, but there were too many people to see anyone in particular. After the gig he'd have to speak with her about what they were going to do. He'd been trying to figure this out, both the words and precisely what he wanted, since they'd been at Mad Dog's yesterday. He'd planned about as far as 'Uh, Soph . . .'

The chord changed and he focused again on the music, and the feeling that the four of them on stage had fused together into something special. He watched Max, felt Mad Dog's rhythm in his chest, knew his fingers were moving in tandem with Pete's, and found himself counting down. Through the middle eight, to the last verse. One more chorus and it was over. Two more lines, eight more beats. And then Max grinned and jumped in the air and the crowd yelled and the four of them bowed and came off the stage to the sound of thousands of people who'd just been given exactly what they needed.

'Yes!' Max hugged Mad Dog, then Pete, then Dom. 'That was pure magic, my friends.' He grabbed Gina, who'd been watching as usual from the wings, and kissed her.

She broke off for air. 'Max, there's some news,' she said, nodding at Nigel the stage manager, who hovered next to them, two-way radio in hand.

'Next band got caught in customs,' Nigel told them. 'They've just arrived but could do with a few extra minutes. Would be much obliged if you could do an encore for us, take up some time.'

'With this audience? You just watch. We'll do—'

'I know what we can do,' said Pete. He swigged from a can of lager, then strode back on to the stage and plucked his guitar off the stand.

Max shrugged and followed, along with Mad Dog and Dom. Dom hoped it wasn't a Venusians song he hadn't played before, though he could pick it up as they went along. He might as well get some practice at improvising.

The crowd's noise swelled again as they came on stage. Somewhere between the last song and their re-entry, the day had turned from afternoon to early evening; the sun blazed orange above the heads of the audience, hesitating before it set.

One more song before the rest of his life. Dom picked up his bass, still warm from his body, and waited for Pete's cue.

Pete began with a clash, dissonant and loud that melted right away into a G minor seventh and the start of a melody that Dominick knew as well as his own face in the mirror.

It was 'Sweet Nothings'. He'd heard it a million times,

with Carver on guitar. Drunken and happy, drunken and mad, with the audience cheering and the tune and words so familiar and strange that sometimes Dominick wondered if he really had written it himself.

He looked over at Pete, who was watching him, and heard Mad Dog joining in with the rhythm. Less than a split second later, Max followed with the rhythm guitar.

The crowd roared. They screamed and waved their shirts and their hats. They moved as a body and threw their expectations up into the air and straight at Dominick.

And Dom's hands moved on his instrument, as they had a million times before, to his own stranger's song.

Sophie had been almost disappointed when she didn't spot Keith Martin before the Venusians finished their set. Attacking her while the band played seemed fitting, somehow, and something that would appeal to Martin's warped sensibilities.

Then the band came on again. And then they started playing a Dirtysweet song.

She strained to see Dominick across the distance and the people, but the giant screens had been shut off. It was 'Sweet Nothings', the song that had catapulted him into stardom, a blessing and a damnation all rolled into one.

He was a blur in the distance. He was playing along, now walking up to the mic to sing with that voice she recognised from the radio and from late at night in darkened rooms. It was rough and dark and rich. It held passion and pain.

The crowd around her screamed and whooped and applauded hard enough so that her ears hurt. All Sophie could think about was Dominick pacing his hotel room, sweating with thirst.

She had no idea why the Venusians were performing this song, but she knew that Dom hated even thinking about Dirtysweet. And he'd told her he only had one way of dealing with stress.

Sophie grabbed her Access All Areas laminate with both hands and began to struggle through the wall of people.

Backstage at the Blackbury Festival

He took the hugs and the handshakes. His head was full of music and memory and he barely heard the conversation, the laughter of the rest of the band, as he let himself walk along with them to the dressing room trailer.

'Absolutely brilliant song,' Max was saying. 'I don't know how you do it. You need to come up to the farm and hang with the llamas for some inspiration, man.'

Dom was halfway through the door and his gaze went immediately to the rider, arranged in the corner. There were three litres of water for him but he didn't see them: he saw the bottles of beer, the half-litre of Jack Daniel's, and he didn't just see them, he tasted them and felt them in his hands.

'And how sneaky were you, Pete? Did you sort that out with Dom beforehand?'

Pete was watching Dom. 'Oh, I was just inspired,' he said.

His gaze was a challenge.

Dom turned around. 'I need something from the bus,' he said, and strode away, his ears ringing with 'Sweet Nothings'.

Even his footsteps were in the rhythm of the song. He'd written it late one night alone, and couldn't sleep afterwards because he couldn't wait to play it for Carver and Tick. He'd sung it on *Top of the Pops* warm from rum and Coke and buzzing with the dream come true; he'd sung it in Paris, in Berlin, in Los Angeles, in New York, in front of so many audiences the same. He'd played it just before he'd hit Carver, he'd played it just after Leonie had left, he'd played it off his mind with his body performing it like an automaton. In Tokyo he'd forgotten the words and he'd stopped and realised the crowd was singing it for him. Strange voices mouthed his lyrics about oblivion and silence.

He reached the tour bus and climbed aboard. The bus muted the sound of the festival. He sat on the bench seat and put his head on the cool table. He knew Bob had a bottle of red wine in his bunk. He didn't go and get it.

He had to feel this. It wasn't thirst. It was pain and happiness and pride and shame and emotions he didn't have names for, every one the opposite of nothing. He closed his eyes and stopped running away.

The bus door hissed open. 'Sophie?' he said, raising his head, but it was Pete who came up the steps.

'You all right, mate?' he asked.

'Wouldn't mind being alone, to tell the truth,' said Dom warily.

'Well, I'm not as pretty as Sophie, I'll give you that.' Pete came closer and leant on the kitchenette cabinet, across from Dom. He had the half-litre bottle of Jack Daniel's in his hand and he took a swig straight from it. 'You looked a bit knocked back on stage; thought maybe this could help.' He held out the bottle to Dom.

Out of the whirl of emotions in his body, anger leapt out

strongest. He stood up so he could look Pete straight in the eye.

'I don't drink, Pete, you know that. You also know exactly why I was knocked back on stage. Why'd you play a Dirtysweet song?'

Pete's eyes opened wide in surprise.

'Mate, that was a tribute to you. I thought you'd love it.'

Dom wasn't fooled. He wasn't willing to sidestep this any more either.

'You were there when I told Max I didn't want to play my own music. You're not making mistakes here. You played it deliberately to get to me, and then you come here trying to get me to drink. Why are you sabotaging me, Pete?'

'I think you're getting paranoid, mate,' said Pete, and took another long swig. 'You wanna have a drink and calm down.'

That was it. Dom exploded.

'Why the hell are you bothered by me?' he shouted. 'I have nothing. No band, no contract, no money, nothing. I'm a no-career alcoholic who's about a year behind on his mortgage payments. There's nothing to envy here, Pete. Nothing to sabotage.'

Pete lowered the bottle from his mouth. His eyes had narrowed to pale slits.

'Yeah, your life is so difficult, isn't it? Girls falling over you, everybody shouting your name, and you're going around like the misunderstood genius, like you don't care. You've got everything.' Pete spat the words along with the odour of alcohol. He raised his voice to a falsetto. '"When are you going to start writing again, Dom?" "Give us some exclusive quotes, Dom." "Wanna fuck me and my twin sister, Dom, or would you rather have the aromatherapist?"'

He downed more bourbon, stepping away from the cabinet towards Dom, close enough to strike. Dom could see his eyes were bloodshot and his mouth was loose and his hands had a tremor.

'Do you know what I've been doing for the past seven years?' Pete yelled. 'Playing in a pub. Every Wednesday night, regular as clockwork, playing covers of AC/DC and Nirvana. Every now and then somebody says, "Man, you look a little familiar" and I pretend I don't know what they mean because I can't deal with explaining to them where the money went, why my wife left, why I'm not touring. And then Max picks me up with his band of misfits and I think there's a second chance. Until I saw you, golden boy.'

'There is a second chance,' Dominick said.

'No, you got that, too. Or didn't you notice that it was you the crowd was going crazy for?'

'They weren't going crazy for me. They don't know me. If you think that fame and booze and girls are what you want, you don't have any reason to be jealous of me, because you're heading exactly where I've been.'

He reached out and took the bottle of Jack Daniel's from Pete's hand. He could smell it, sweet and smoky.

'And this will get you there quicker,' he said. He upended the bottle and poured the bourbon down the sink.

'You bastard.' Pete swung his fist at him. Dom stepped backwards, dropping the bottle on the floor, and the punch missed.

'I've liked playing with you, Pete,' Dom said. 'And thanks for letting me use your guitar. I owe you for that.' Then he walked out of the bus and into the warm evening air.

Once outside, he hesitated. He should probably go

back to the dressing room trailer, but Pete would most likely go there too and he didn't feel like continuing their argument in front of the rest of the band. Instead he skirted the dressing room area and headed for general backstage hospitality. Usually this area was filled with journalists, record company hangers-on and various other blaggers; he might get recognised, but that was the least of his worries right now.

He made his way across the open area to the tent holding the bar and stood in the chaotic queue. He'd have a Coke, give Pete time enough to cool down, and then go back to the dressing room. Sophie was bound to be there by now. Once he saw her . . . he'd improvise.

'Hello, Dominick,' said an unfamiliar voice at his shoulder.

By the time Sophie reached the entrance to the backstage area, she was sweating and swearing and the Venusians had long since gone off stage. Her one consolation was that Martin wouldn't find it any easier to move around than she did. She flashed her AAA laminate at the large men guarding the entrance and headed straight for the band's trailer.

'Sophie!' Max greeted her, jumping up from his chair and giving her a bear hug. 'Were you out in the arena? Did you feel that energy?'

'I certainly did,' she said, not adding *And I've got the bruises to prove it*. She looked around. 'Where's Dominick?'

'He said he had to get something from the bus,' Max told her.

'He's in a right mood,' added Pete, sprawled in a corner chair with a can of lager.

She frowned, alarm chewing at her. 'Do you guys mind if I go and find him – I'll be back in a few minutes to . . .'

Max waved his hands at her. 'No worries, Soph, we can wait for nirvana until you've seen the man.'

'Thanks.' She flew out the door and ran between the tour buses until she reached the Venusians' crew bus. When she opened the door, the smell hit her in the face.

Alcohol.

'Dominick?' she called. She scrambled on to the bus.

He wasn't here; her voice fell dead in the space. The crew would all still be working, and the band were in their dressing room. Sophie went down the aisle anyway to check.

The bottle of Jack Daniel's lay in the centre of the carpet, its cap off. A swallow or two of amber liquid pooled in its side. The smell was overwhelming and sickly.

'Shit.' She squatted to examine it, and then stood. 'Dominick!'

He wasn't in his bunk or in the rear lounge. If he was drinking, he wouldn't stop.

She ran off the bus and followed her memorised routes to the nearest bar.

Dominick turned to the person who'd greeted him.

'Hi,' he said. He didn't think he knew her, but his memory was rotten, and at something like this you could never quite tell. She could be a fan, or someone from his past. For all he knew she was his old record company exec, though record execs usually dressed more stylishly than khakis and a plain pink T-shirt.

'I'm Cathy,' she said, and held out her hand. He shook it and she smiled at him. 'Can I buy you a drink?'

'Thanks, Cathy, that's very kind of you, but I don't—'

'Please,' she interrupted smoothly. 'I owe you one for the pleasure you've given me.' She slipped her thin body between the two people standing before them at the bar, and looked back at him over her shoulder. 'Besides, I can get to the bar more easily. What can I get you?'

'Just a Coke, thanks,' he capitulated. Fresh from dealing with Pete, he listened to her giving her order at the bar. He was half-suspicious she'd ask for a shot of rum in his drink, but she ordered a half a pint of lager for herself and a Coke for him.

He glanced around, in case Sophie had come back here before going to the dressing room. A slight cough by his side told him that Cathy was waiting to give him his drink.

'Here's to you,' she said, and clicked her plastic glass against his.

'Thanks.' He took a swallow. Cathy stood there beaming at him. 'Forgive me for being rude, Cathy, but do I know you?'

'Not yet.'

Her hand on her lager was almost skeletal; there were hollows in her cheeks. Dom drank most of his Coke in one gulp, suddenly eager to be away. He'd finish his drink, thank her and make his excuses and leave.

'Are you enjoying the festival?' he asked her.

'Very much. I gather you've had a very successful tour.'

'It's been good, thank you.'

'I've seen some of your shows,' Cathy said. 'I was impressed. You're a man of many talents.'

She kept on talking, but he didn't really hear her. He scanned the bar area again for Sophie or Max or Pete. None of them were around. Just dozens and dozens of strangers, a collection of bright colours and shadows. He blinked to clear his vision.

The tent was hot and the noise of the people around him slushy. From very far away, he could hear the bass from the band on the stage.

'This is only a Coke, right?' He held up his drink.

'Of course, that's what you asked for.'

'Only . . .' He shook his head. No. He hadn't had any booze. It was the heat in this tent, probably the argument and the song and everything he'd been feeling. And Sophie. Beautiful Sophie, precious Sophie, tough and tender Sophie who he might never see again after today.

His mouth was dry. He sipped his Coke and heard buzzing in his ears.

'I think I need some air,' he said. He stepped backwards and his knees buckled.

'Careful,' said Cathy, grabbing his arm with her thin hands.

'It's nothing,' he said. 'Sweet nothings. Not for me, any more.'

Sophie walked into the tent. He saw her and everything became clear. Pure water and crystal.

'I need to talk to her,' he told Cathy, and pulled away from her spidery grip.

Dominick was already walking towards her when she spotted him and with a sinking heart she saw him stagger.

'Sophie Dean,' he slurred. He reached her and pulled her into his arms, so tight.

'You've been drinking,' she said against his chest.

'No.' He kissed the top of her head and then he loosened his grip enough so she could look up at his face. 'Listen, I have to tell you something. It's important.'

'I know,' she said. His eyes were unfocused, his cheeks flushed. She felt sick with disappointment for him. 'It's okay, Dominick. It's just a setback, you can get through this. It's important that you don't drink any more, though.'

'You're right, I won't, but listen, though. I figured something out, I know why everything feels different.'

He was wavering on his feet; she held on to his waist. 'Dom, you need to sit down. I'll get you a glass of water.'

'Don't need water. Listen, Soph, this is important. I never said this before ever to anyone. You listening?'

'Yes,' she said, hooking a plastic chair with her foot and pulling it over to them. 'Sit down.'

'No. Listen. Sophie, I love you.'

A punch to her gut, sucking her breath away. Dominick was looking straight in her eyes, so close she could feel his breath kissing her face, and she swallowed her feelings down to deal with later, when she could afford the time for pain.

'You don't mean it,' she said. 'You're drunk.'

'No. I love you.'

'Dominick, sit down and I'll get you some water.' She pressed down on his shoulders and he slumped into the chair.

'Didn't think I could,' he said. 'All new.'

'Okay. Stay there, I'll be right back.'

She pushed through the people around the bar, ignoring protests. 'Can I have a glass of water, please, urgently,' she said to the girl behind it.

Damn him. Damn him to hell.

Those words were cheap to him. Words to throw away drunk.

'You wouldn't throw them away if nobody had ever said them to you,' she muttered fiercely, and the bartender, handing over her water, said, 'What?'

'Nothing,' Sophie said. She turned away from the bar

and shouldered her way back through the crowd towards Dominick.

Except Dominick wasn't there any more.

'Come with me.'

He opened his eyes, which seemed to have shut by themselves. A pink blur, and then it was that woman, the record company exec or whatever.

'I don't feel good,' he told her.

'I'm a nurse. Come on, we'll get you better.'

He felt arms lifting him up and was vaguely surprised at how strong they were, but then it took all his concentration to put one foot in front of the other.

'Put your arm around me, there's a good man. Just over here. Only a little ways to walk and you won't feel so bad.'

Colours around him, shadows and noises and a big white thing looming. There was something very wrong. He couldn't speak and dropped his head to whisper, 'Soph . . .'

'Don't worry about Sophie, she'll get what she deserves.'

35

Backstage at the Blackbury Festival

She spotted them leaving the tent. Dominick had his arm around a woman, his head bent down to murmur in her ear. She was brunette, slender, wearing a ponytail and a pink T-shirt.

'Damn him!' She threw the plastic glass of water on the ground, where it failed to break.

Drunk and up to his old tricks. Sex and drink were connected, he'd said. They were evidently so connected that it didn't particularly matter who the sex was with.

She stormed out the opposite exit of the tent. She didn't care where she was going, just as long as she didn't have to see Dominick. The sun had set, though the sky still glowed orange, and the backstage area was lit with pools of artificial light.

Five minutes, she thought, bumping into people, not apologising. That's how long it had taken him to forget what he'd said to her. Not that she should care; he was going to forget it anyway, but the worst thing was that there had been a split second when she'd clutched what he'd said to her heart. Just a fraction of a moment, while her breath had been stolen, before her body hit shock and went straight through it into anger.

She'd *wanted* him to love her.

'Damn,' she whispered, blinking back catastrophic tears, and ran full tilt into something warm and soft. Her head snapped back, her teeth biting the end of her tongue.

'Hey, watch it, love.' A beefy hand closed on her arm, belonging to the large bare-chested man whose belly she'd just bounced off. She winced at the stink of beer on his breath.

'Sorry,' she said, and he moved off. But she stayed where she was, her hand touching the place on her cheek, where she had felt Dominick standing so close his breath kissed her face.

The bus had smelt of Jack Daniel's. The bar had smelt of beer. But Dominick had smelt of Dominick. Not alcohol at all.

She turned around and dodged through people in the direction she'd seen him going off in. With a woman in a pink shirt, couldn't see her face, a very thin woman . . .

Oh, shit.

She could only run in bursts, swerving through the crowd, looking wildly for Dominick in the dusk, not seeing him. From here there were three choices: the arena, the exit to outside the festival grounds, or the backstage area proper, with the dressing rooms and the buses. The arena was too crowded. She sprinted to the exit.

'Have you seen Dominick Steele?' she gasped to the bouncer there. 'Tall, dark-haired, would've looked drunk? With a woman in a pink shirt?'

The bouncer shrugged and Sophie ran off. If he was being noncommittal she might be making a mistake, but there was no time, because those threats that she'd be sorry hadn't been death threats against her after all.

'Come on come on come on,' she panted, pushing through a group of colt-legged girls with cameras, holding up her AAA laminate and running past the bouncer at the backstage entrance, no time to check, although how could Catherine Birkbeck have got through this entrance unless she was with Dominick?

The bus park was the most likely spot. At least a dozen buses were there along with trailers and some caravans, making shelter and shadows. Catherine would want an isolated spot because she wanted to hurt him. A stitch stabbed Sophie's chest but she kept on running.

Back here, the music on stage pounded both loud and muffled, as if it were broadcast through cotton. To her left, the edifice of the stage nearly vibrated with the noise.

So loud nobody could hear a single scream. She saw a flap in the canvas and realised her schematic of the festival, shown from the top, had left one area out.

Sophie ducked through the canvas. She had no time to be wrong but she knew she was right, even before her eyes had had a chance to adjust to the darkness underneath the stage.

It was laced with scaffolding poles and lit with occasional beams of watery light from holes in the canvas. The bass drum above her beat a little bit more slowly than her own heart.

Three steps in, five, around a pole, and then she saw them. Of Dominick, she could only see his face and hands, pale against the dark ground where he lay. Catherine Birkbeck was a brittle shadow above him, straddling his body in a parody of a sexual position, holding something glinting in her hand.

'Catherine!' Sophie screamed, and burst towards them,

fear in her chest. She'd felt fear before but not like this, not since she was a little girl alone, and she wrestled the emotion back and grabbed Catherine by the shoulders and wrenched her off Dominick's body.

They fell together on the dirt. The back of Sophie's head glanced against a scaffolding pole and pain shot through her, but she clambered to her knees. *Where was the knife, away from the knife.* Catherine kicked at Sophie and Sophie scuttled backwards, out of reach.

Catherine was still closer to Dominick than Sophie was.

'You don't want him,' Sophie said to her. Her voice sounded faint under the throbbing music. 'You want me. I'm the one who took Keith away from you.'

'You made him do it,' Catherine said. 'You trapped him. And now he's got someone else.'

'He's not worth it, Catherine. You can walk away from this.'

'I loved him.' Her face was smeared with dirt, her eyes wide. Sophie didn't dare take her own eyes away from her to check Dominick, but she didn't see any blood on her hands or the knife. Catherine could have wiped them, though. He could be bleeding into the dirt.

'Odds were Keith was cheating on you before I ever got near him,' Sophie said. Her head spun, punched with noise and pain.

'I. Loved. Him.' Catherine enunciated each word clearly, as if she were speaking to a child. She crept forward, her knife in her right hand. It was a flick knife, about six inches long. 'You won't understand until I take someone away from you.' She reached Dominick's side and touched his hair.

'You love him, don't you?' Catherine asked. 'Anyone would. Look at him, he's so beautiful.' She stroked his hair back from his forehead tenderly. His eyes were closed. He was pale, so pale. Sophie tensed herself. The knife was too close to his face.

'I saw you in that magazine together,' Catherine continued. 'At first I wanted to hurt you, but then I heard you in his room and I realised it was better this way. You're going to be so sad when he's gone.'

She raised the knife.

Sophie leapt. Her left hand struck Catherine's right wrist, should send the knife flying but she had no time to check. It was her weight against Catherine's and her elbow at Catherine's throat, pinning her down. She was thin, light like a bird beneath her.

Sophie had a split second to be grateful she hadn't forgotten all her self-defence training before Catherine's free hand struck her on the side of the face, clawing at her eyes. Her arms and legs flailed and yes, she was thin, but she was strong. Sophie lost her grip, sliding in the loose dirt, and Catherine struggled free.

'It's all your fault,' Catherine said. She was on her hands and knees, like Sophie, in the dirt. Her skin was stretched taut and white over her skull.

The knife could be anywhere. Sophie looked for it, for the gleam of it between them and Dominick's dark body, and saw it there, next to his shoulder, not half a metre away.

Catherine lunged for it, and that one moment of inattention was all Sophie needed. She tackled Catherine, pushed her face in the dirt and twisted her arms behind her.

'You're wrong,' she told her. With her knees, she held Catherine's arms down and she reached over and touched Dominick's neck. He was warm, his pulse strong, and just as Sophie hadn't had time for the fear, she didn't have time for the relief.

Gripping Catherine's arms again, securely this time and in just the right way to cause her pain, she hauled her up off the ground and marched her to the hole in the canvas. 'Hey!' she hollered to a big man in a black bouncer's shirt who was passing, and only then did she notice that her own hand was bleeding from a gash.

'I need security, police, and medical help right now,' she told the bouncer. 'There's a man back there who's been drugged.'

It was only later, in the back of the police car following the ambulance, that Sophie allowed herself to close her eyes and acknowledge that Catherine Birkbeck had been right after all.

Blackbury Hospital, Wiltshire

Dom opened his eyes and immediately closed them again. The walls were white, the sheets were white, it was all too blinding.

He counted to forty. At least he thought it was forty. And opened them again, slowly.

Sun streamed through the window. The walls weren't actually white, they were pale yellow, which was, if possible, worse. There was a basket of flowers on a table with a Mylar balloon hovering above them, and Sophie sat in a chair next to his bed, gnawing at one of her fingernails. Her other hand was bandaged.

'Hi,' he said, and winced.

She started and sat up in her chair. 'You're awake.'

'I wish I wasn't.' He rubbed his forehead, which didn't help at all with the pulsing pain. 'Any chance of some water and a couple of aspirin?'

She poured him water from the jug beside the bed. He took it and gulped it and then held the glass out to her again.

'I'll ask the nurse to get some aspirin,' she said, refilling it and then going out to the corridor. A moment later she returned. 'How do you feel?'

'I've had worse hangovers, I think, but with them I got to drink beforehand.'

She laid her hand on his forehead. Her touch was warm but somehow detached, as if she were treating him rather than caressing him. He tried to meet her gaze but she was focusing somewhere on his chest.

'You were drugged,' she said. 'You tested positive for Rohypnol. It . . . has an alcohol-like effect.'

'That explains it,' he said.

'Well. Some of it.' She took her hand from his forehead and began worrying at her nail again.

He wished she would look at him.

'Who are the flowers from?' he asked.

'The band. They're in the waiting room. The nurses wouldn't let more than one visitor in at a time while you were asleep.'

He squinted at the balloon. 'It's not my birthday.'

'I think it was all Mad Dog could get at short notice.'

'Is Pete out there?'

'Yes. I don't know what happened between you guys, but he keeps on saying he feels terrible.'

He nodded. It hurt, but a little less.

The nurse came in with two aspirin in a paper cup, which he swallowed. When she left, Sophie pulled the chair closer to his bed and sat down in it.

'Do you know what happened?' she asked.

'When?'

'After you were drugged. Don't worry if you can't remember; Rohypnol can cause anterograde amnesia. That means that you might not remember certain things that happened after the drug was administered.'

'That woman slipped it in my Coke, didn't she?'

'Yes.'

'And then I told you that I loved you. And you told me I was drunk.'

Sophie shifted in her chair. She put down her hand, and then lifted it to her mouth, and then put it down again. 'Yes.'

'I wasn't drunk.'

'I know that now. Though again, Rohypnol can cause slurring and staggering and a certain lowering of inhibitions. In many cases.'

'I don't drink any more, Sophie.'

She swallowed. 'Yes. But you have to admit that appearances—'

'I remember that the woman who drugged me knew who you were,' he said. God, his head was pounding.

Sophie's forehead furrowed with anxiety. In other circumstances, he would feel sorry for her.

'Her name is Catherine Birkbeck,' she told him. 'She was the former fiancée of a man I honey-trapped just over eighteen months ago. She's been charged with two counts of assault.'

'Two counts.'

'She's admitted to trying to run me down in Liverpool.'

Dominick tried to make sense of this, but his brain wasn't working so well. 'So she wasn't after me, she was after you.'

'That's what I thought. But she was after you because she said I needed to know what it was like to lose someone that I . . .' She swallowed again. 'To lose someone.'

He let this sink in for a minute.

'I'm sorry, Dominick,' she said. 'It was my fault. I wasn't looking for her, I was looking for her ex-fiancé out in the arena and I should have been with you. I should have been watching out for you.'

She touched his hand. 'I'm so glad you're all right,' she said, and she did meet his gaze. Her face was tired and worried and he thought she'd probably been sitting here beside him all night.

Then she averted her eyes and removed her hand.

'What else do you remember?' she asked.

'The last thing I remember was her leading me away. Did she try to kill me?'

'She had a knife. That was how . . . I didn't know how I felt until I thought you might die.'

'And how do you feel?'

Sophie got up from her chair. She plucked a lily from the flower arrangement and stuck it back in another place.

'I know you probably didn't mean what you said to me,' she said. 'You weren't drunk, I know that now, but you were under the influence of a drug. And it was an emotional time; you and I were sleeping together and then I'd been getting these threats . . .'

He sat up. It made his stomach roll, but he ignored it.

'You'd been getting more threats?'

She flushed. 'Emails and texts saying she'd see me at Blackbury Festival. Though as I said, I thought it was Keith Martin, because—'

'You were getting threats the whole time we were sleeping together and you didn't tell me?'

'Yes, and I'm sorry I didn't because it almost got you killed. But I thought I could catch him.'

Dominick folded his arms across his chest. He noticed he was wearing a patterned hospital gown.

'You haven't answered my question. How do you feel about me, Sophie?'

Sophie chewed on her lip. She took a deep breath and let it out. 'I . . .'

He waited.

'I didn't want to lose you.'

'Why?'

'You don't deserve to die for something that I did.'

'And that's it?'

She didn't say anything. Dominick's head throbbed.

'You thought I was drunk,' he said. 'And you were as close to me as you could possibly have been and you were still keeping secrets from me.'

She waited a long time, her eyes averted. Finally she said, quietly, 'Yes.'

He'd promised himself he was going to feel things. He didn't think he'd have to feel so sad so soon.

'I don't need much, Sophie. But I need to have changed. I need to be a person you can trust.'

Sophie looked at him, in that way she had as if she were trying to see underneath his mere face. Then she nodded, her lips pressed together, her grey eyes wide.

She looked afraid. But that was wrong, because Sophie Tennant had no fear, not even after being nearly killed.

'I'll go,' she said. She turned around and left the room.

Dom slumped back down in the bed. He rolled over on his side, closed his eyes, and wondered when he'd feel better.

37

*Stoneguard, Wiltshire
Sixteen Days Later*

SOPHIE TENNANT: PRIVATE INVESTIGATOR AND AROMATHERAPIST
Missing persons, corporate investigations
Massage, holistic health treatments
ABSOLUTELY NO INFIDELITY CASES OR HONEY TRAPS

Sophie sighed and rubbed her temples. Maybe she should have two separate newspaper ads; this one was going to attract the whackos for sure.

Then again, people with problems that needed investigation were stressed, right? She was a one-stop solution.

Or something like that.

She got up from her desk and unnecessarily checked the candle underneath the diffuser. She'd been burning the same mixture so often for the past two weeks that she didn't really smell it any more, but maybe that meant that it had well and truly entered her circulation and it would start to work any minute now.

The bell on the top of the door jingled and Barbara Raymond stepped tentatively in.

'Smells good in here,' said Barbara.

'It's supposed to make you happy.'

'That could come in handy.' Barbara smoothed back her blow-dried, straightened, glossy hair. 'Is it working?'

'Time will tell.'

'I like your top,' Barbara said. 'Emerald green suits you.'

Sophie ran her fingers over the silk. 'Thanks. I've had it hanging in my wardrobe for ages. How have you been?'

'Not bad, actually. How was the tour with the rock band?'

'It was interesting. I think I've had half of Stoneguard in here making appointments, itching for gossip about it.'

'I heard you haven't said much.'

'Rock stars are pretty much like normal people, I guess. That was one holding you back from Sally Hershey the last time you were in here.'

Barbara blushed. 'Sophie, I'm sorry I haven't come in before. But I've been embarrassed about what I did. I'm not the kind of person to attack bimbos in public.'

Sophie shrugged. 'You shouldn't be embarrassed. I don't have any universal objection to attacking bimbos.' She gestured to one of the reception chairs and Barbara took it. Sophie sat beside her. 'You looked like you've got a good right hook, too. Have you ever studied martial arts?'

'No,' Barbara said.

'You should. I find it can be quite therapeutic to hit someone who deserves it really hard. Only if they've drawn a weapon on you, though, otherwise you can get in trouble with the law.'

'I've left Charlie,' Barbara told her. 'Best thing I ever did. I've taken up painting.'

'Pictures or houses?'

'Pictures. Mostly the standing stones. I'm showing some of them in the Stoneguard Gallery; maybe you'd like to come and look at them. Your walls could do with a little decoration to break up that yellow.'

'Yes, I suspected they could. Maybe you could give me some advice about that.'

Barbara nodded and gazed at the walls for a few moments. 'It gets lonely, though. Especially once the children are in bed.'

Lonely. Now that was a word Sophie would never have identified with three months ago. *Alone*, fine. *Self-sufficient*, perfect. Not *lonely*, which was a weak word. But lonely was exactly how she felt in the evenings here in Stoneguard, about the time the Venusians would have been going on stage. In the afternoons, when she'd be on the bus with Bob and Owen and Dempsey and Griffin, trading insults and complaints about snoring.

And especially late at night, when she would have been in Dominick's arms.

'I had an affair with one of the rock stars,' she told Barbara.

Barbara put a hand on Sophie's shoulder. 'Oh, hon, I'm sorry.'

Sophie smiled a little at how Barbara immediately knew it wasn't a happy story, as if any romance with a rock star were inherently doomed.

'That's why you look like you haven't had a square meal in weeks,' Barbara said. 'I know, why don't you come over tomorrow night for dinner? I'll feed you up and we can have some wine and watch a movie or something.'

'I'd like that,' Sophie replied, and then she took a deep breath of the scented air. 'Do you mind if I ask you a personal question?'

Barbara looked surprised, but not displeased. 'Go ahead.'

'Do you think being rejected is the worst thing that can happen to you? Or would it be worse to never trust anybody at all?'

It felt good to ask. Sort of like a distant echo of the comfort she felt in Dominick's arms.

'You're asking this question of a bitter soon-to-be ex-wife?' Barbara said.

'You seem the best qualified to answer.'

Barbara thought about it. 'I think you have to trust people, especially if you love them. Otherwise it isn't worth it. Remind me, though, that the next person I love and trust isn't going to prefer blondes.'

'I will.' Sophie got up. 'Barbara, can we postpone our dinner for a few days? I have to investigate something.'

38

The Malt Shovel, Yorkshire

Dominick Steele sat at the bar, his chin propped on both his hands, staring at the glass of orange juice in front of him.

Sophie stood just inside the door, watching him.

Beyond a casual nod, none of the other pub-goers seemed to be paying much attention to Dominick. They talked quietly among themselves in broad Yorkshire, drinking bitter from handled pint jugs, with the air of people who had been doing the same thing every Saturday evening in this pub for years, like their ancestors before them. They wore corduroy and cotton and thick scarred boots.

Dominick wore a red shirt and leather trousers. He should have looked totally out of place. To Sophie, he looked like the best thing in the universe.

She made her way across the pub, smelling damp cotton and malt, hearing muted conversations about tourist drivers and silage-cutting. Silently she slipped on to the bar stool beside Dominick.

'Hi,' she said.

She couldn't help relishing the brief moment of

surprise when he registered who she was. It was professional pride at having confirmation that she'd watched and followed undetected by her subject.

And then, of course, she was relieved that he didn't get up and leave right away.

'How'd you . . .' he began, but then he shook his head. 'Never mind, I can figure it out.'

Just having him look at her was a pleasure. It was as if she'd been slowly starving for the past two weeks, and now she wanted to gorge herself on his attention, his touch, his kiss, everything.

She held herself back. She actually had to sit on her hands. 'Nice trousers,' she said.

'Max gave them to me. I've been breaking them in.'

To Sophie they looked perfect already. 'So what have you been doing at Max's farm?'

'In the evenings, keeping out of Max and Gina's way. In the daytime I've been writing music.'

'You haven't ended up writing a bunch of songs about llamas, have you?'

'No,' he said. 'Actually, most of the songs have ended up being about you.'

Her heart jolted at that, though she wasn't precisely sure why. It wasn't as if Dominick Steele was known for happy love songs. Quite the opposite.

'What can I get you?' asked the barman.

'I'll have the same as he's having, thanks.'

'Another, Dom?' asked the barman, and Dominick nodded.

'Nice bloke,' said Dominick as the barman poured their juice. Sophie set her hands free long enough to pay.

'How are the rest of the band?' she asked.

'Max is great. I haven't seen Mad Dog but I'm sure he's

happy. Pete spent a few days with us last week, but then he went back to Manchester. He's getting back together with his wife.'

'I'm glad.'

Dom nodded. He took a drink of his juice, and then asked, 'Why did you follow me, Sophie?'

'I owe you an apology. For one thing, I was wrong not to tell you about the threats. I'm sorry.'

He turned to her, leant back against the bar and crossed his arms on his chest, his head tilted. It was a music video pose if there ever was one, except it wasn't. It was him protecting himself, and if he needed to protect himself, maybe she had a bit of hope.

'Is this apology because you put me in danger? Or because you should have trusted me?'

'Yes.'

'Yes which?'

'Yes both.'

'You saved my life,' he said. 'That makes up for the danger. And about the trust ... well, I've been thinking about that. Trust needs to be earned. I've never done a very good job at earning it.'

'No,' she said. 'You have changed. You're not the person you were five years ago, Dominick, and I know that. I wanted an excuse not to trust you because I don't want to trust anyone. I've set my whole life up so I don't have to.'

'Like not being noticed?'

'Like trying my best not to get hurt if I'm not wanted.'

Dominick uncrossed his arms. 'I thought you were fearless,' he said.

'Are you kidding? I've been terrified since I met you. I'd rather face a psycho with a knife than have this conversation any day.'

'But you still followed me.'

'Well, it wasn't hard. You don't exactly blend in.'

She'd expected him to laugh at that. Instead he looked at her steadily and seriously with his dark eyes, his face so famous and familiar.

'Sophie Dean—'

'I love you,' she said, as fast as she could before she could think any more about how afraid she was. 'I followed you to say that.'

Dimly she registered that the people around them had stopped talking about silage. In fact they weren't talking about anything.

'And that's all I need to do,' she continued, hearing her voice loud in the silence. 'I've never said it to anyone else before and I need to tell you. I'll understand if you didn't mean it when you said it to me. One of the effects of Rohypnol is to reduce inhib—'

'It doesn't make you lie, Sophie. It might have made me say it a few hours before I would have otherwise. But that's it. I meant what I said to you. I do love you.'

She looked at him. He looked at her.

He was the only person in the world who she could call her own. Which, she guessed, meant that they owned each other.

'What are we doing in this pub, then?' she said.

'I have no idea.' He stood and took her hand. 'Let's get out of here.'

It was June, and a warm night. The moon was waxing towards the full. It lit the sparsely spaced houses, the fields, the stone bridge over the glittering river. The air smelled like the beginning of sweet summer.

Pick up a *little black dress* – it's a girl thing.

IT MUST BE LOVE
Rachel Gibson
PB £4.99

Gabriel Breedlove is the sexiest suspect that undercover cop Joe Shanahan has ever had the pleasure of tailing. But when he's assigned to pose as her boyfriend things start to get complicated.

She thinks he's stalking her. He thinks she's a crook. Surely, it must be love?

978 0 7553 3746 0

ONE NIGHT STAND
Julie Cohen
PB £4.99

When popular novelist Estelle Connor finds herself pregnant after an uncharacteristic one-night stand, she enlists the help of sexy neighbour Hugh to help look for the father. But will she find what she really needs?

One of the freshest and funniest voices in romantic fiction

978 0 7553 3483 4

Pick up a *little black dress* – it's a girl thing.

978 0 7553 3959 4

TANGLED UP IN YOU
Rachel Gibson
PB £4.99

Sex, lies and tequila slammers

When Maddie Dupree arrives at Hennessy's bar looking for the truth about her past she doesn't want to be distracted by head-turning, heart-stopping owner Mick Hennessy. Especially as he doesn't know why she's really in town . . .

SPIRIT WILLING, FLESH WEAK
Julie Cohen
PB £4.99

Welcome to the world of Julie Cohen, one of the freshest, funniest voices in romantic fiction!

When fake psychic Rosie meets a gorgeous investigative journalist, she thinks she can trust him not to blow her cover – but is she right?

978 0 7553 3481 0

You can buy any of these other
Little Black Dress titles from your
bookshop or *direct from the publisher*.

FREE P&P AND UK DELIVERY
(Overseas and Ireland £3.50 per book)

TO ORDER SIMPLY CALL THIS NUMBER

01235 400 414

or visit our website: www.headline.co.uk

Prices and availability subject to change without notice.